THE DREAM OF THE CELT

Mario Vargas Llosa was born in Peru in 1936. He is the author of some of the last half-century's most important novels, including *The War of the End of the World*, *The Feast of the Goat*, *Aunt Julia and the Scriptwriter* and *The Conversation in the Cathedral*. In 2010 he was awarded the Nobel Prize in Literature.

by the same author

The Cubs and Other Stories
The Time of the Hero
The Green House
Captain Pantoja and the Special Service
Conversation in the Cathedral
Aunt Julia and the Scriptwriter
The War of the End of the World
The Real Life of Alejandron Mayta
The Perpetual Orgy
Who Killed Palomino Molero?
The Storyteller
In Praise of the Stepmother
A Fish in the Water
Death in the Andes
Making Waves
The Notebooks of Don Rigoberto

The Dream of the Celt

MARIO VARGAS LLOSA

Translated by Edith Grossman

faber and faber

First published in this edition in 2012
by Faber and Faber Limited
Bloomsbury House,
74–77 Great Russell Street,
London WC1B 3DA

This open market paperback edition published in 2012

Typeset by Faber and Faber Ltd

Printed in the UK by CPI Group (UK) Ltd, Croydon CR0 4YY

A CIP record for this book
is available from the British Library

ISBN 978–0–571–27574–8

4 6 8 10 9 7 5 3

For Alvaro, Gonzalo, and Morgana
And for Josefina, Leandro,
Ariadna, Aitana, Isabella, and Anaís

Each one of us is, successively, not one but many. And these successive personalities that emerge one from the other tend to present the strangest, most astonishing contrasts among themselves.

José Enrique Rodó, *Motives of Proteus*

The Congo

I

When they opened the door to his cell, the street noise that the stone walls had muffled came in along with the stream of light and a blast of wind, and Roger woke in alarm. Blinking, still confused, struggling to calm down, he saw the shape of the sheriff leaning in the doorway. His flabby face, with its blond mustache and reproachful little eyes, contemplated him with a dislike he had never tried to hide. This was someone who would suffer if the English government granted his request for clemency.

"Visitor," muttered the sheriff, not taking his eyes off him.

He stood, rubbing his arms. How long had he slept? Not knowing the time was one of the torments of Pentonville Prison. In Brixton Prison and the Tower of London he had heard the bells that marked the half-hour and the hour; here, thick walls kept the clamor of the church bells along Caledonian Road and the noise of the Islington market from reaching the prison interior, and the guards posted at the door strictly obeyed the order not to speak to him. The sheriff put handcuffs on him and indicated that he should follow him. Was his lawyer bringing him good news? Had the cabinet met and reached a decision? Perhaps the sheriff's gaze was more filled than ever with the anger he inspired in him because his sentence had been commuted. He walked down the long passageway of red brick blackened by grime, past the metal doors of the cells and the discolored walls where every twenty or twenty-five paces a high barred window allowed him to glimpse a small piece of gray sky. Why was he so cold? It was July, the heart of summer, there was no reason for the icy cold that gave him goose-bumps.

When he entered the narrow visitors' room, his heart sank. Waiting for him was not his attorney, Maître George Gavan Duffy, but one of his assistants, a blond, sickly-looking young man with prominent cheekbones who dressed like a fop and whom he had seen during the four days of his trial, carrying and fetching papers for the defense lawyers. Why, instead of coming in person, had Maître Gavan Duffy sent one of his clerks?

The young man looked at him coldly. Anger and disgust were in his eyes. What was wrong with this imbecile? *He looks at me as if I were vermin*, thought Roger.

"Any news?"

The young man shook his head. He inhaled before speaking: "Regarding the petition for pardon, not yet," he murmured drily, making a face that made him look even sicklier. "It's necessary to wait for the Council of Ministers to meet."

The presence of the sheriff and another guard in the small room irritated Roger. Though they remained silent and motionless, he knew they were listening to everything. The idea oppressed his chest and made it difficult for him to breathe.

"But considering recent events," the blond young man added, blinking for the first time and opening and closing his mouth in an exaggerated way, "everything is more difficult now."

"Outside news doesn't reach Pentonville. What happened?"

What if the German admiralty had finally decided to attack Great Britain from the Irish coast? What if the dreamed-of invasion had taken place and the Kaiser's cannon were avenging at this very moment the Irish patriots shot by the English in the Easter Rising? If the war had taken that direction, his plans would be realized in spite of everything.

"Now it has become difficult, perhaps impossible, to succeed," the clerk repeated. He was pale, containing his indignation, and Roger detected his skull beneath the whitish skin of his complexion. He sensed that behind him the sheriff was smiling.

"What are you talking about? Mr. Gavan Duffy was optimistic about the petition. What happened to make him change his mind?"

"Your diaries," the young man hissed, making another disgusted face. He had lowered his voice and it was difficult for Roger to hear him. "Scotland Yard found them in your house on Ebury Street."

He paused for a long time, waiting for Roger to say something. But since he had fallen mute, the clerk gave free rein to his indignation and twisted his mouth: "My good man, how could you be so stupid?" He spoke slowly, making his rage more obvious. "How could you, my good man, put such things on paper? And if you did, how could you not take the basic precaution of destroying those diaries before embarking on a conspiracy against the British Empire?"

It's an insult for this fellow to call me "my good man," Roger thought. Ill-mannered because Roger was at least twice the age of this affected boy.

"Portions of those diaries are circulating everywhere now," the clerk added, calmer, though his disgust was constant, not looking at him now. "In the Admiralty, the minister's spokesman, Reginald Hall himself, has given copies to dozens of reporters. They're all over London. In parliament, the House of Lords, Liberal and Conservative clubs, editorial offices, churches. It's the only topic of conversation in the city."

Roger did not say anything. He did not move. Once again he had the strange sensation that had taken hold of him many times in recent months, ever since that gray, rainy April morning in 1916 when, numb with cold, he was arrested in the ruins of McKenna's Fort, in the south of Ireland: this did not have to do with him, they were talking about someone else, these things were happening to someone else.

"I know your private life is not my business, or Mr. Gavan Duffy's, or anyone's," added the young clerk, making an effort to lower the fury that saturated his voice. "This is a strictly professional matter. Mr. Gavan Duffy wanted to bring you up to date regarding the situation. And prepare you. The request for clemency may be compromised. This morning there are already protests in some newspapers, confidences betrayed, rumors regarding the content of your diaries. The favorable public response to the petition might be affected. Merely a supposition, of course. Mr. Gavan Duffy will keep you informed. Do you wish me to give him a message?"

With an almost imperceptible movement of his head, the prisoner refused. He turned immediately afterward, facing the door of the visitors' room. With his chubby face the sheriff signaled the guard, who unbolted the door and opened it. The return to his cell seemed interminable. During his passage down the long hall with the rocklike walls of blackened red brick, he had the feeling that at any moment he might trip and fall face down on those damp stones and not get up again. When he reached the metal door of his cell, he remembered: on the day they brought him to Pentonville Prison, the sheriff had told him that, without exception, all the prisoners who occupied this cell had ended up on the gallows.

"Could I take a bath today?" he asked before he went in.

The fat jailer shook his head, looking into his eyes with the same repugnance Roger had detected in the clerk's gaze.

"You cannot bathe until the day of your execution," said the sheriff, relishing each word. "And, on that day, only if it's your final wish. Others, instead of a bath, prefer a good meal. A bad business for Mr. Ellis, because then, when they feel the noose, they shit themselves. And leave the place like a pigsty. Mr. Ellis is the hangman, in case you didn't know."

When he heard the door close behind him, he lay face down on the narrow cot and closed his eyes. It would have been good to feel the cold water from that spout invigorating him and turning his skin blue. In Pentonville Prison the convicts, except for those condemned to death, could bathe with soap once a week in that stream of cold water. And the conditions in the cells were passable. On the other hand, he recalled with a shudder the filth in Brixton Prison, where he had been covered with lice and fleas that swarmed in the mattress on his cot and covered his back, legs, and arms with bites. He attempted to think about that, but over and over he kept remembering the disgusted face and hateful voice of the blond clerk decked out like a dandy whom Maître Gavan Duffy had sent instead of coming in person to give him the bad news.

2

Regarding his birth on September 1, 1864, in Doyle's Cottage, Lawson Terrace, in Sandycove, a Dublin suburb, he remembered nothing, of course. Even though he always knew he had seen the light of day in the capital of Ireland, for much of his life he took for granted what his father, Captain Roger Casement, who had served for eight years with distinction in the Third Regiment of Light Dragoons in India, had inculcated in him: his true birthplace was County Antrim, in the heart of Ulster, the Protestant and pro-British Ireland where the Casement line had been established since the eighteenth century.

Roger was brought up and educated as an Anglican in the Church of Ireland, like his sister and brothers, Agnes, whom the family called Nina, Charles, and Tom—all three older than he—but since earliest childhood he had intuited that in matters of religion not everything in his family was as harmonious as in other areas. Even for a very young child it was impossible not to notice that his mother, when she was with her sisters and Scots cousins, behaved in a way that seemed to hide something. He would discover what it was when he was an adolescent: even though Anne Jephson had apparently converted to Protestantism in order to marry his father, behind her husband's back she continued to be a Catholic ("Papist," Captain Casement would have said), going to confession, hearing Mass, and taking communion, and in the most jealously guarded of secrets, he himself had been baptized a Catholic at the age of four, during a vacation trip he and his siblings took with their mother to Rhyl, in the north of Wales, to visit their maternal aunts and uncles.

During those years in Dublin, or the times they spent in London and Jersey, Roger had absolutely no interest in religion, though during the Sunday ceremony he would pray, sing, and follow the service with respect in order not to displease his father. His mother had given him piano lessons, and he had a clear, tuneful voice for which he was applauded at family gatherings when he sang old Irish ballads. What really interested him at that time were the stories Captain Casement, when he was in a good humor, recounted to him and his brothers and sister. Stories about India and Afghanistan, especially his battles with Afghans and Sikhs. Those exotic names and landscapes, those travels crossing forests and mountains that concealed treasures, wild beasts, predatory animals, ancient peoples with strange customs and savage gods, fired his imagination. At times the other children were bored by the stories, but young Roger could have spent hours, even days, listening to his father's adventures along the remote frontiers of the Empire.

When he learned to read, he liked to become involved in the stories of great navigators, the Vikings, Portuguese, Englishmen, and Spaniards who had plowed the world's seas, vaporizing myths claiming that once you reached a certain point, the ocean water began to boil, chasms opened, and monsters appeared with gullets that could swallow entire ships. Yet if he had to choose between adventures listened to or read, Roger always preferred to hear them from his father's mouth. Captain Casement had a warm voice and animatedly described in a rich vocabulary the jungles of India or the crags and boulders of the Khyber Pass in Afghanistan, where his company of light dragoons was once ambushed by a mass of turbaned fanatics whom the brave English soldiers confronted first with bullets, then with bayonets, and finally with fists and bare hands until they had obliged their attackers to withdraw in defeat. But it wasn't feats of arms that most dazzled young Roger's imagination, it was the journeys, the opening of paths through landscapes where white men had never walked, the physical prowess of enduring and conquering the obstacles of nature. His father was entertaining but very severe and did not hesitate to whip his children when they misbehaved, even Nina, the little girl, for this was how mistakes were punished in the army, and he had confirmed that only this form of punishment was effective.

Though he admired his father, the parent Roger really loved was his mother, a slender woman who seemed to float instead of walk, who had light eyes and hair, whose extremely soft hands when they tousled his curls or caressed his body at bath time filled him with happiness. One of the first things he would learn—at the age of five or six—was that he could run into his mother's arms only when the captain was not near by. His father, true to the Puritan tradition of his family, did not believe in coddling children, since this made them soft in the struggle to survive. In his father's presence, Roger kept his distance from the pale, delicate Anne Jephson. But when the captain went out to meet friends at his club or take a walk, the boy would run to her and she would cover him with kisses and caresses. At times Charles, Nina, and Tom protested: "You love Roger more than us." Their mother assured them she did not, she loved them all the same, except Roger was very little and needed more attention and affection than the older ones.

When his mother died, in 1873, Roger was nine years old. He had learned to swim and won all the races with children his age and even older ones. Unlike Nina, Charles, and Tom, who shed many tears during the wake and burial of Anne Jephson, Roger did not cry even once. During those gloomy days, the Casement household was transformed into a funeral chapel filled with people dressed in mourning who spoke in low voices and embraced Captain Casement and the four children with contrite faces, pronouncing words of condolence. For many days he couldn't say a word, as if he had fallen mute. He responded to questions with movements of his head, or gestures, and remained serious, his head lowered and his gaze lost, even at night in the darkened room, unable to sleep. From then on and for the rest of his life, from time to time in dreams the figure of Anne Jephson would come to visit him with that inviting smile, opening her arms where he would huddle, feeling protected and happy with those slim fingers on his head, his back, his cheeks, a sensation that seemed to defend him against the evils of the world.

His brothers and sister were soon comforted. And Roger too, apparently. Because even though he had recovered his speech, it was something he never mentioned. When a relative spoke to him about his mother, he fell silent and remained enclosed in his muteness until the other person changed the subject. In his sleeplessness, he would sense the face of the unfortunate Anne Jephson in the dark, looking at him sadly.

The one who was not comforted and never became himself again was Captain Roger Casement. Since he wasn't effusive and Roger and the other children had never seen him showering his mother with gallantries, the four of them were surprised at the cataclysm his wife's disappearance meant for their father. Always so meticulous, he dressed carelessly now, let his beard grow, scowled, his eyes filled with resentment as if his children were to blame for his being a widower. Shortly after Anne's death, he decided to leave Dublin and sent the four children to Ulster, to Magherintemple House, the family estate, where from then on their paternal great-uncle, John Casement, and his wife, Charlotte, would take charge of their upbringing. Their father, as if wanting to have nothing to do with them, went to live forty kilometers away, at the Adair Arms Hotel in Ballymena where, as Great-uncle John let slip occasionally, Captain Casement, "half mad with grief and loneliness," dedicated his days and his nights to spiritualism, attempting to communicate with the dead woman through mediums, cards, and crystal balls.

From then on Roger rarely saw his father and never again heard him tell those stories about India and Afghanistan. Captain Roger Casement died of tuberculosis in 1876, three years after his wife. Roger had just turned twelve. In Ballymena Diocesan School, where he spent three years, he was a distracted student who received mediocre grades except in Latin, French, and ancient history, classes in which he was outstanding. He wrote poetry, always seemed lost in thought, and devoured books of travels through Africa and the Far East. He engaged in sports, swimming in particular. On weekends he went to the Young family's Galgorm Castle, invited by a classmate. But Roger neglected him and spent more time with Rose Maud Young, beautiful, well educated, and a writer, who traveled the fishing and farm villages of Antrim collecting poems, legends, and songs in Gaelic. From her mouth he heard for the first time the epic battles of Irish mythology. The castle of black stone, with its fortified towers, coats of arms, chimneys, and cathedral-like facade, had been built in the seventeenth century by Alexander Colville, a theologian with an ill-favored face—according to his portrait in the foyer—who, they said in Ballymena, had made a pact with the devil, and whose ghost walked the castle. On certain moonlit nights, a trembling Roger dared to search for him in passageways and empty rooms but never found him.

Only many years later would he learn to feel comfortable in Magherintemple House, the Casement family's ancestral home that had once been called Churchfield and had been a rectory of the Anglican parish of Culfeightrin. Because for the six years he lived there, between the ages of nine and fifteen, with his great-uncle John and great-aunt Charlotte and the rest of his paternal relatives, he always felt something of a foreigner in the imposing mansion of gray stone with its three stories, high ceilings, ivy-covered walls, false Gothic roofs, and hangings that seemed to hide ghosts. The vast rooms, long hallways, and staircases with worn wooden banisters and creaking steps increased his solitude. On the other hand, he enjoyed the outdoors, the robust elms, sycamores, and beech trees that resisted the hurricane-force wind, the gentle hills with cows and sheep where one could see the town of Ballycastle, the ocean, the breakers crashing into Rathlin Island, and on clear days, the blurred silhouette of Scotland. He frequently went to the nearby villages of Cushendun and Cushendall that seemed to be the setting for ancient Irish legends, and the nine glens of Northern Ireland, those narrow valleys surrounded by hills and rocky slopes at whose peaks eagles traced circles, a sight that made him feel valiant and exalted. His favorite diversions were excursions through that harsh land, with its peasants who seemed as old as the landscape, some speaking the ancient Irish among themselves, about which Great-uncle John and his friends sometimes made cruel jokes. Charles and Tom did not share his enthusiasm for life in the open air and did not enjoy cross-country hikes or climbing the rugged hills of Antrim, but Nina did, and for that reason, in spite of her being eight years older, she was his favorite sibling, the one he got along with best. He made several excursions with her to the Bay of Murlough, bristling with black rocks, and its stony little beach at the bottom of Glenshesk, which would stay in his memory his whole life and to which he would always refer, in letters to his family, as "that corner of Paradise."

But even more than walks through the countryside, Roger liked summer vacations. He spent them in Liverpool with his aunt Grace, his mother's sister, in whose house he felt loved and welcomed, by Aunt Grace, of course, but also by her husband, Uncle Edward Bannister, who had traveled much of the world and made business trips to

Africa. He worked for the shipping company the Elder Dempster Line, which transported cargo and passengers between Great Britain and West Africa. Aunt Grace's and Uncle Edward's children, his cousins, were better playmates to Roger than his own siblings, especially his cousin Gertrude Bannister, Gee, with whom, from the time he was very young, he had an intimacy never dimmed by any quarrel. They were so close that Nina once joked with them: "You'll end up marrying each other." Gee laughed but Roger blushed to the roots of his hair. He didn't dare look up and stammered, "No, no, why are you talking nonsense?"

When he was in Liverpool with his cousins, Roger sometimes conquered his timidity and asked Uncle Edward about Africa, a continent whose mere mention filled his head with jungles, wild animals, adventures, and intrepid men. Thanks to Uncle Edward Bannister he heard for the first time of Dr. David Livingstone, the Scots physician and evangelist who had explored Africa for years, traveling rivers like the Zambezi and the Shire, naming mountains and unknown places, and bringing Christianity to tribes of savages. He had been the first European to cross Africa coast to coast, the first to traverse the Kalahari Desert, and he had become the most popular hero in the British Empire. Roger dreamed about him, read the pamphlets that described his exploits, and longed to be part of his expeditions, facing dangers at his side, helping to bring the Christian faith to pagans who had not left the Stone Age. When Dr. Livingstone, looking for the sources of the Nile, disappeared, swallowed up by the African jungles, Roger was two years old. When, in 1872, another legendary adventurer and explorer, Henry Morton Stanley, a reporter of Welsh background employed by a New York newspaper, emerged from the jungle and announced to the world that he had found Dr. Livingstone alive, he was almost eight. The boy followed the novelesque story with astonishment and envy. And when, a year later, he learned that Dr. Livingstone, who never wanted to leave African soil or return to England, had died, Roger felt he had lost a beloved friend. When he grew up, he too would be an explorer like those titans, Livingstone and Stanley, who were expanding the frontiers of the West and living such extraordinary lives.

When Roger turned fifteen, Great-uncle John Casement advised him to abandon his studies and look for work, since he and his brothers and sister had no income to live on. He happily accepted the advice. By mutual agreement they decided Roger would go to Liverpool where there were more possibilities for work than in Northern Ireland. In fact, shortly after he arrived at the Bannisters', Uncle Edward obtained a position for him in the same company where he had worked for so many years. He began as an apprentice in the shipping company soon after his fifteenth birthday. He looked older. He was very tall and slim, with deep gray eyes, curly black hair, very light skin, even teeth, and he was temperate, discreet, neat, amiable, and obliging. He spoke English with an Irish accent, the cause of jokes among his cousins.

He was a serious boy, tenacious and laconic, not very well prepared intellectually but hard-working. He took his duties in the company very seriously, determined to learn. He was placed in the Department of Administration and

Accounting. At first, his tasks were those of a messenger. He fetched and carried documents from one office to another and went to the port to take care of formalities regarding ships, customs, and warehouses. His superiors treated him with consideration. In the four years he worked at the Elder Dempster Line, he did not become intimate with anyone due to his retiring manner and austere habits: opposed to carousing, he practically did not drink and was never seen frequenting the bars and brothels in the port. He did become an inveterate smoker. His passion for Africa and his commitment to doing well in the company led him to read carefully, and fill with notes, the pamphlets and publications dealing with maritime trade between the British Empire and West Africa that made the rounds of the offices. Then he would repeat with conviction the ideas that permeated those texts. Bringing European products to Africa and importing the raw materials that African soil produced was, more than a commercial operation, an enterprise in favor of the progress of peoples caught in prehistory, sunk in cannibalism and the slave trade. Commerce brought religion, morality, law, the values of a modern, educated, free, and democratic Europe, progress that would eventually transform tribal unfortunates into men and women of our time. In this enterprise, the British Empire was in the vanguard of Europe, and one had to feel proud of being part of it and the work accomplished at the Elder Dempster Line. His office colleagues exchanged mocking looks and wondered whether young Roger Casement was a fool or a smart alec, whether he believed that nonsense or declaimed it in order to look good to his superiors.

For the four years he worked in Liverpool, Roger continued to live with his Aunt Grace and Uncle Edward, to whom he gave part of his salary and who treated him as a son. He got on well with his cousins, especially Gertrude, with whom on Sundays and holidays he would go boating and fishing if the weather was good, or stay home reading aloud in front of the fire if it rained. Their relationship was fraternal, without a hint of guile or flirtatiousness. Gertrude was the first person to whom he showed the poems he wrote in secret. Roger came to know the company's activities thoroughly, and without ever having set foot in African ports spoke about them as if he had spent his whole life among their offices, businesses, procedures, customs, and the people who inhabited them.

He made three trips to West Africa on the SS *Bounny*, and the experience filled him with so much enthusiasm that after the third voyage he gave up his job and announced to his siblings, aunt, uncle, and cousins that he had decided to go to Africa. He did this in an exalted way, and as his uncle Edward said to him, "like those crusaders in the Middle Ages who left for the East to liberate Jerusalem." The family went to the port to see him off, and Gee and Nina shed some tears. Roger had just turned twenty.

3

When the sheriff opened the door to the cell and diminished him with his gaze, Roger was thinking in shame that he had always been in favor of the death penalty. He had made it public a few years earlier in his *Report on Putumayo* for the Foreign Office, demanding exemplary punishment for the Peruvian Julio César Arana, the rubber king of Putumayo: "If we could at least achieve his being hanged for those atrocious crimes, it would be the beginning of the end of the interminable martyrdom and infernal persecution of the unfortunate indigenous population." He would not write those same words now. And, before that, he recalled the discomfort he would feel when he entered a house and saw a birdcage. Imprisoned canaries, goldfinches, or parrots had always seemed to him the victims of useless cruelty.

"Visitor," muttered the sheriff, looking at him with contempt in his eyes and voice. While Roger stood and dusted off his prisoner's uniform with his hands, he added sarcastically: "You're in the papers again today, Mr. Casement. Not for being a traitor to your country . . ."

"My country is Ireland," Roger interrupted.

". . . but because of your perversions." The sheriff made a noise with his tongue as if he were going to spit. "A traitor and pervert at the same time. What garbage! It will be a pleasure to see you dancing at the end of a rope, ex-Sir Roger."

"The cabinet turned down the petition for clemency?"

"Not yet," the sheriff hesitated before answering. "But it will. And so will His Majesty the King, of course."

"I won't petition him for clemency. He's your king, not mine."

"Ireland is British," muttered the sheriff. "Now more than ever after crushing that cowardly Easter Rising in Dublin. A stab in the back of a country at war. I wouldn't have shot your leaders, I would've hanged them."

He fell silent because they had reached the visitors' room.

It wasn't Father Carey, the Catholic chaplain at Pentonville Prison, who had come to see him but Gertrude, Gee, his cousin. She embraced him tightly and Roger felt her trembling in his arms. He thought of a little bird numb with cold. How Gee had aged since his imprisonment and trial. He recalled the mischievous, lively girl in Liverpool, the attractive woman in love with the life of London, whom her friends affectionately called Hoppy because of her damaged leg. Now she was a shrunken, sickly old lady, not the healthy, strong, self-confident woman of a few years earlier. The clear light of her eyes had gone out, and there were wrinkles on her face, neck, and hands. She dressed in dark, worn clothing.

"I must stink like all the rubbish in the world," Roger joked, pointing at his coarse blue uniform. "They took away my right to bathe. They'll give it back only once, if I'm executed."

"You won't be, the Council of Ministers will grant clemency," Gertrude asserted, nodding to give more force to her words. "President Wilson will intercede with the British government on your behalf, Roger. He's promised to send a telegram. They'll grant it, there won't be an execution, believe me."

The way she said this was so strained, her voice broke so much, that Roger felt sorry for her, for all his friends who, like Gee, suffered these days from the same anguish and uncertainty. He wanted to ask about the attacks in the papers the jailer had mentioned but controlled himself. The president of the United States would intercede for him? This must be an initiative of John Devoy and other friends from the Clan na Gael. If he did, his action would have an effect. There was still a possibility the cabinet would commute his sentence.

There was no place to sit and Roger and Gertrude remained standing, very close together, their backs to the sheriff and the guard. The four presences transformed the small visitors' room into a claustrophobic place.

"Gavan Duffy told me they had dismissed you from Queen Anne's Academy," Roger said apologetically. "I know it was on account of me. A thousand pardons, my dear Gee. Causing you harm is the last thing I would have wanted."

"They didn't dismiss me, they asked me to accept the cancelation of my contract. And gave me compensation of forty pounds. I don't care. I've had more time to help Alice Stopford Green in the measures she's taken to save your life. That's the most important thing now."

She took her cousin's hand and squeezed it tenderly. Gee had taught for many years in the school of Queen Anne's Hospital, in Caversham, where she had become assistant director. She always liked her job and told amusing anecdotes about it in her letters to Roger. And now, because of her kinship to an outcast, she would be unemployed. Did she have enough to live on, or who would help her?

"No one believes the vile things they're publishing about you," said Gertrude, lowering her voice a great deal, as if the two men standing there might not hear her. "Every decent person is indignant that the government is using this kind of slander to weaken the manifesto so many important people have signed in your favor, Roger."

Her voice broke, as if she were going to sob. Roger embraced her again.

"I've loved you so much, Gee, dearest Gee," he whispered in her ear. "And now more than ever. I will always be grateful for how loyal you've been in good times and bad. That's why your opinion is one of the few that matters to me. You know that everything I've done has been for Ireland, don't you? For a noble, generous cause, like the Irish cause. Isn't that true, Gee?"

She had started to sob, very quietly, her face pressed against his chest.

"You had ten minutes and five have passed," the sheriff reminded them without turning around to look at them. "You have five left."

"Now, with so much time to think," said Roger in his cousin's ear, "I think a great deal about those years in Liverpool, when we were so young and life smiled on us, Gee."

"Everybody thought we were in love and would marry one day," murmured Gee. "I too remember that time with nostalgia, Roger."

"We were more than lovers, Gee. Brother and sister, accomplices. The two sides of a coin. That close. You were many things to me. The mother I lost when I was nine. The friends I never had. I always felt better with you than with my own siblings. You gave me confidence, security in life, joy. Later, during all my years in Africa, your letters were my only bridge to the rest of the world. You don't know how happy I was to receive your letters and how I read them over and over, dear Gee."

He fell silent. He didn't want his cousin to know he was about to cry too. No doubt because of his Puritan upbringing, since childhood he had despised public displays of sentiment, but in recent months he had sometimes indulged certain weaknesses that had once annoyed him so much in others. Gee said nothing. She still embraced him and Roger felt her agitated respiration raising and lowering her chest.

"You were the only person I showed my poems to. Do you remember?"

"I remember they were dreadful," said Gertrude. "But I loved you so much I told you they were wonderful. I even memorized one or two."

"I knew very well you didn't like them, Gee. It was lucky I never published them. I almost did, you know."

They looked at each other and began to laugh.

"We're doing everything, everything to help you, Roger," said Gee, becoming very serious again. Her voice had aged too; firm and pleasant once, now it was hesitant and cracked. "We who love you, and there are many of us. Alice the first, naturally. Moving heaven and earth. Writing letters, visiting politicians, officials, diplomats. Explaining, pleading. Knocking at every door. She's doing what she can to see you. It's difficult. Only kin are permitted. But Alice is well known, she has influence. She'll obtain permission and will come, you'll see. Did you know that when the Dublin Rising broke out, Scotland Yard searched her house from top to bottom? They took a good number of papers. She loves and admires you so much, Roger."

I know, Roger thought. He too loved and admired Alice Stopford Green. The Irish historian, like Casement from an Anglican family, whose house was one of the most crowded intellectual salons in London, the center for discussions and meetings of all the nationalists and Home Rulers from Ireland, she had been more than a friend and adviser to him in political matters. She had educated him and obliged him to discover and love Ireland's past, its long history and flourishing culture before it was absorbed by a powerful neighbor. Alice had recommended books, enlightened him in impassioned conversations, urged him to continue his lessons in the Irish language that, unfortunately, he never succeeded in mastering. *I'll die not speaking Gaelic*, he thought. And later, when he became a radical nationalist, Alice was the first person in London who began calling him by the nickname Herbert Ward had given him that pleased him so much: the Celt.

"Ten minutes," decreed the sheriff. "Time to say goodbye."

He felt his cousin embrace him, her mouth trying unsuccessfully to reach his ear, since he was much taller. She spoke, thinning her voice so much it was almost inaudible: "All those horrible things the papers are saying are slanders, wretched lies. Aren't they, Roger?"

The question was so unexpected he hesitated a few seconds before answering.

"I don't know what the press is saying about me, dear Gee. We don't get papers here. But," and he searched carefully for his words, "I'm sure they are. I want you to keep just one thing in mind, Gee. And believe what I say. Of course I've made many mistakes. But I have nothing to be ashamed of. You and my friends, none of you have to be ashamed of me. You believe me, don't you, Gee?"

"Of course I believe you." His cousin sobbed, covering her mouth with both hands.

On his way back to his cell, Roger felt his eyes filling with tears. He made a great effort to keep the sheriff from noticing. He rarely felt like crying. As far as he could recall, he hadn't cried in all these months since his capture. Not during questioning at Scotland Yard, or during hearings at his trial, or listening to the sentence that condemned him to be hanged. Why now? Because of Gertrude. Because of Gee. Seeing her suffer in that way, doubt in that way, meant at the very least that for her, his person and life were precious. He was not, after all, as alone as he felt.

4

The journey of the British consul, Roger Casement, up the Congo River, which began on June 5, 1903, and would change his life forever, had been scheduled to begin the previous year. He had been suggesting this expedition to the Foreign Office since 1900 when, after serving in Old Calabar, Lourenço Marques, and São Paulo de Luanda, he officially took up residence as consul of Great Britain in Boma—a misbegotten village—claiming that the best way to prepare a report on the situation of the natives in the Congo Free State was to leave this remote capital for the forests and tribes of the Middle and Upper Congo. That was where the exploitation was occurring that he had been reporting to the Foreign Office since his arrival in these territories. Finally, after weighing those reasons of state that never failed to turn the consul's stomach, even though he understood them—Great Britain was an ally of Belgium and did not want to push her into Germany's arms—the Foreign Office authorized him to undertake the journey to the villages, stations, missions, posts, encampments, and factories where the extraction of rubber took place, the black gold avidly coveted now all over the world for tires and bumpers on trucks and cars and a thousand other industrial and household uses. He had to verify on the ground how much truth there was in the denunciations of atrocities committed against natives in the Congo of His Majesty Leopold II, King of the Belgians, made by the Aborigines' Protection Society in London, and some Baptist churches and Catholic missions in Europe and the United States.

He prepared the journey with his customary meticulousness and an enthusiasm he hid from Belgian functionaries and the colonists and merchants of Boma. Now, with a thorough knowledge of the subject, he would be able to argue to his superiors that the Empire, faithful to its tradition of justice and fair play, should lead an international campaign to put an end to this ignominy. But then, in the middle of 1902, he had his third attack of malaria, one even worse than the previous two; he had suffered from the disease ever since he decided in 1884, in an outburst of idealism and a dream of adventure, to leave Europe and come to Africa to work, by means of commerce, for Christianity, western social and political institutions, and the emancipation of Africans from backwardness, disease, and ignorance.

They weren't merely words. He had a profound belief in them when, at the age of twenty, he reached the Dark Continent. The first attacks of malaria came some time later. He had just realized his life's desire: to be part of an expedition headed by the most famous adventurer on African soil, Henry Morton Stanley. To serve at the pleasure of the explorer who in a legendary trek of close to three years between 1874 and 1877 had crossed Africa from east to west, following the course of the Congo River from its source to its mouth in the Atlantic! To accompany the hero who found the missing Dr. Livingstone! Then, as if the gods wanted to extinguish his exaltation, he suffered his first attack of malaria. Nothing, compared to the second three years later—1887—and above all this third attack, in 1902, when for the first time he thought he would die. The symptoms were the same that dawn in the middle of 1902 when, his traveling bag already packed with maps, compass, pencils, and notebooks, he felt himself trembling with cold as he opened his eyes in the bedroom on the top floor of his house in Boma, in the colonists' district, a few steps from Government House, which served as the consul's residence and office. He moved aside the mosquito netting and saw through the windows, without glass or curtains but with metal screens to keep out insects and riddled now by a downpour, the muddy waters of the great river and the outline of islands covered with vegetation. He couldn't stand. His legs collapsed under him, as if they were made of rags. John, his bulldog, was frightened and began to jump and bark. He let himself fall back into bed. His body was burning and the cold penetrated his bones. He shouted for Charlie and Mawuku, the Congolese steward and cook who slept on the lower floor, but no one answered. They must have gone out and, caught by the storm, run to take shelter under a baobab tree until it abated. Malaria again? The consul cursed. Just on the eve of the expedition? He would have diarrhea, hemorrhages and weakness would oblige him to stay in bed for days, weeks, dazed and shivering.

Charlie was the first of the servants to return, dripping water. "Go for Dr. Salabert," Roger ordered, not in French but in Lingala. Dr. Salabert was one of two physicians in Boma, the old slave-trade port—it was called Mboma then—where, in the sixteenth century, Portuguese traffickers from the island of Santo Tomé came to buy slaves from the tribal chiefs of the vanished kingdom of the Kongo, transformed now by the Belgians into the capital of the Congo Free State. In Boma there was no hospital, only a dispensary staffed by two Flemish nuns for emergency cases. The doctor arrived half an hour later, shuffling his feet and leaning on a cane. He was younger than he seemed, but the harsh climate, and especially alcohol, had aged him. He looked like an old man and dressed like a vagabond. His high shoes had no laces and his vest was unbuttoned. Even though the day was just beginning, his eyes were bloodshot.

"Yes, my friend, malaria, what else would it be. What a fever. You know the treatment: quinine, abundant fluids, a diet of broth and biscuits, and lots of blankets to sweat out the infections. Don't even dream of getting up before two weeks. And certainly not of going on a trip, not even to the corner. Tertian fevers demolish the organism, as you know all too well."

It wasn't for two but three weeks that he was devastated by fevers and fits of shivering. He lost eight kilos and on the first day he could stand, he took a few steps and fell to the floor exhausted, in a state of weakness he did not recall having felt before. Dr. Salabert, staring into his eyes, warned him in a cavernous voice and with acid humor: "In your condition it would be suicide to go on that expedition. Your body is in ruins and would not survive even a crossing of the Crystal Mountains, much less several weeks of living outdoors. You wouldn't even reach Mbanza-Ngungu. There are faster ways to kill yourself, Consul: a bullet in the mouth or an injection of strychnine. If you need them, you can count on me. I've helped several people undertake the great journey."

Roger telegraphed the Foreign Office that the state of his health obliged him to postpone the expedition. And since the rains made the forests and river impassable then, the expedition to the interior of the Congo Free State had to wait a few more months that would turn into a year. Another year, recovering very slowly from the fevers and trying to regain the weight he had lost, picking up the tennis racket again, swimming, playing bridge or chess to pass the long nights in Boma, while he resumed his tedious consular tasks: making note of the ships that arrived and departed, the goods the merchant ships of Antwerp unloaded—rifles, munitions, *chicote* whips, wine, holy pictures, crucifixes, colored glass beads—and the ones they carried to Europe, the immense stacks of rubber, ivory, and animal skins. This was the exchange that in his youthful imagination was going to save the Congolese from cannibalism and from the Arabs of Zanzibar who controlled the slave trade, and open the doors of civilization to them!

For three weeks he was laid low by malarial fevers, at times delirious, taking drops of quinine dissolved in herbal infusions that Charlie and Mawuku prepared for him three times a day—his stomach tolerated only broth and pieces of boiled fish or chicken—and playing with John, his bulldog and most loyal companion. He did not even have the energy to concentrate on reading.

During this forced inactivity, Roger often thought about the expedition of 1884 under the leadership of his hero, Henry Morton Stanley. He had lived in the forests, visited countless indigenous villages, made camp in clearings surrounded by stockades of trees where monkeys screeched and wild beasts roared. He was tense and happy in spite of the bites of mosquitoes and other insects, for which rubbing with camphorated alcohol was useless. He swam in lagoons and rivers of dazzling beauty with no fear of crocodiles, still convinced that by doing what they were doing, he, the four hundred African porters, guides, and assistants, the twenty whites—English, German, Flemish, Walloon, French—who made up the expedition and, of course, Stanley himself, constituted the tip of the lance of progress in this world where the Stone Age that Europe had left behind many centuries earlier was only just beginning to be visible.

Years later, in the visionary half-sleep of fever, he blushed to think how blind he had been. He had not even been aware, at first, of the reason for the expedition led by Stanley and financed by the King of the Belgians, then considered—by Europe, the West, the world—to be a great humanitarian monarch bent on exterminating the social degradations of slavery and cannibalism and freeing the tribes from the paganism and servitude that kept them in a feral state.

It would be another year before the great western powers at the Berlin Conference of 1885 granted Leopold II the Congo Free State, more than two and a half million square kilometers—eighty-five times the size of Belgium—but the King of the Belgians had already begun to administer the territory they were going to give him so he could put his redemptive principles into practice with the estimated twenty million Congolese believed to inhabit it. The monarch with the combed beard had contracted the great Stanley to that end, guessing, with his prodigious aptitude for detecting human weaknesses, that the explorer was capable equally of great deeds and formidable villainies if the prize was on a level with his appetites.

The apparent reason for the 1884 expedition in which Roger served his apprenticeship as an explorer was to prepare the communities scattered along the banks of the Upper, Middle, and Lower Congo, in thousands of kilometers of dense jungles, gorges, waterfalls, and mountains thick with vegetation, for the arrival of the European merchants and administrators that the International Congo Society, presided over by Leopold II, would bring in once the western powers granted him the concession. Stanley and his companions had to explain to the half-naked chieftains, tattooed and feathered, sometimes with thorns in their faces and arms, sometimes with reed funnels on their penises, the benevolent intentions of the Europeans: they would come to help them improve their living conditions, rid them of deadly plagues like sleeping sickness, educate them, and open their eyes to the truths of this world and the next, thanks to which their children and grandchildren would attain a life that was decent, just, and free.

I wasn't aware because I didn't want to be aware, he thought. Charlie had covered him with all the blankets in the house. In spite of that and the blazing sun outside, the consul, curled up and freezing, trembled beneath the mosquito net like a sheet of paper. But worse than being a willing blind man was finding explanations for what any impartial observer would have called a swindle. Because in all the villages reached by the expedition of 1884, after distributing beads and trinkets, and then the aforementioned explanations made by interpreters (many of whom could not make themselves understood by the natives), Stanley had the chiefs and witch doctors sign contracts, written in French, pledging to provide manual labor, lodging, guides, and food to the officials, agents, and employees of the International Congo Society in the work they would undertake to achieve the goals that inspired the society. They signed with Xs, lines, blots, drawings, without a word and without knowing what they were signing or what signing was, amused by the necklaces, bracelets, and adornments of colored glass they received and the little swallows of liquor with which Stanley invited them to toast their agreement.

They don't know what they're doing, but we know it's for their good and that justifies the deceit, the young Roger Casement thought. What other way was there to do it? How could they give legitimacy to future colonization with people who could not understand a word of those "treaties" in which their future and the future of their descendants was placed under obligation? It was necessary to give some legal form to the enterprise the Belgian monarch wanted to realize by means of persuasion and dialogue, unlike others carried out with blood and fire, invasions, assassinations, and plunder. Wasn't this peaceable and civil?

As the years passed—eighteen had gone by since the expedition carried out under Stanley's leadership in 1884—Roger reached the conclusion that the hero of his childhood and youth was one of the most unscrupulous villains the West had excreted onto the continent of Africa. In spite of that, like everyone who had worked under his command, he could not fail to acknowledge his charisma, his affability, his magic, that mixture of temerity and cold calculation with which the adventurer accumulated great feats. He came and went through Africa, on one hand sowing desolation and death—burning and looting villages, shooting natives, flaying the backs of his porters with the *chicotes* made of strips of hippopotamus hide that had left thousands of scars on ebony bodies throughout Africa—and on the other opening routes to commerce and evangelization in immense territories filled with wild beasts, predatory insects, and epidemics, which seemed to respect him like one of those titans of Homeric legends and Biblical histories.

"Don't you sometimes feel remorse, have a bad conscience because of what we're doing?"

The question burst from the young man's lips in an unpremeditated way. And he could not take it back. The flames from the bonfire in the center of the camp crackled as small branches and imprudent insects burned there.

"Remorse? A bad conscience?" The head of the expedition wrinkled his nose and the expression on his freckled, sunburned face soured, as if he never had heard those words and was trying to guess what they meant. "For what?"

"For the contracts we have them sign," said young Roger, overcoming his embarrassment. "They place their lives, their villages, everything they have, in the hands of the International Congo Society. And not one of them knows what he's signing because none of them speaks French."

"If they knew French, they still wouldn't understand those contracts." The explorer laughed his frank, open laugh, one of his most amiable attributes. "I don't even understand what they mean."

He was a strong, very short man, almost a midget, still

young, with an athletic appearance, flashing gray eyes, thick mustache, and an irresistible personality. He always wore high boots, a pistol at his waist, and a light jacket with a good number of pockets. He laughed again, and the overseers of the expedition, who with Stanley and Roger drank coffee and smoked around the fire, laughed too, adulating their leader. But Roger did not laugh.

"I do, though it's true the rigmarole they're written in seems intentional, so they won't be understood," he said, respectfully. "It comes down to something very simple. They give their lands to the International Congo Society in exchange for promises of social assistance. They pledge to support the construction projects: roads, bridges, docks, factories. To supply the labor needed for the camps and public order and feed the officials and workers for as long as the work continues. The society offers nothing in return. No salaries, no compensation. I always believed we were here for the good of the Africans, Mr. Stanley. I'd like you, whom I've admired since I was a boy, to give me reasons to go on believing it's true. That these contracts are, in fact, for their good."

There was a long silence, broken by the crackling of the fire and occasional growls of night animals out hunting for food. It had stopped raining a while ago but the atmosphere was still humid and heavy, and it seemed that all around them everything was germinating, growing, becoming dense. Eighteen years later, in the disordered images the fever sent whirling around his head, Roger recalled the look, inquisitive, surprised, mocking at moments, with which Henry Morton Stanley inspected him.

"Africa wasn't made for the weak," he said at last, as if

talking to himself. "The things that worry you are signs of weakness. In the world we're in, I mean. This isn't the United States or England, as you must realize. In Africa the weak don't survive. They're finished off by bites, fevers, poisoned arrows, or the tsetse fly."

He was Welsh but must have lived a long time in the United States because his English had North American tonalities, expressions, and turns of phrase.

"All of this is for their good, of course it is," Stanley added with a movement of his head toward the circle of conical huts in the hamlet on whose outskirts their camp was located. "Missionaries will come to lead them out of paganism and teach them that a Christian shouldn't eat his neighbor. Physicians will vaccinate them against epidemics and cure them better than their witch doctors. Companies will give them work. Schools will teach them civilized languages. They'll be taught how to dress, how to pray to the true God, how to speak like a Christian and not use those monkey dialects. Little by little their barbaric customs will be replaced by those of modern, educated people. If they knew what we're doing for them, they'd kiss our feet. But mentally they are closer to the crocodile and the hippopotamus than to you or me. That's why we decide what is good for them and have them sign those contracts. Their children and grandchildren will thank us. And it wouldn't surprise me if in a little while they begin to worship Leopold II the way they worship their fetishes and hideous objects."

Where on the great river was that camp? He thought vaguely it was between Bolobo and Chumbiri and the tribe belonged to the Bateke. But he wasn't sure. That data appeared in his diaries, if you could give that name to the hodgepodge of notes scattered in notebooks and on loose sheets of paper over the course of so many years. In any event, he remembered that conversation clearly, as well as his uneasiness when he lay down on his cot after the exchange with Henry Morton Stanley. Was that the night his personal holy trinity of the three Cs began to fall apart? Until then he had believed they justified colonialism: Christianity, civilization, and commerce. From the time he was a modest assistant accountant at the Elder Dempster Line in Liverpool, he had assumed there was a price to pay. It was inevitable that abuses would be committed. Among the colonizers there would be not only altruists like Dr. Livingstone but abusive scoundrels as well, but in the final analysis, the benefits would far outweigh the harm. Life in Africa was showing him that things were not as clear as they had been in theory.

In the year he worked in the explorer's service, still admiring the audacity and ability to command with which Henry Morton Stanley led his expedition through the largely unknown territory bordering the Congo River and its myriad tributaries, Roger also learned that the explorer was a walking mystery. The things said about him were always contradictory, so it was impossible to know which were true and which false and how much exaggeration and fantasy were in the true statements. He was one of those men incapable of differentiating reality from fiction.

The only thing clear was that the idea of a great benefactor to the natives did not correspond to the truth. He learned this listening to the overseers who had accompanied Stanley on his journey of 1871–2 in search of Dr. Livingstone, an expedition, they said, much less peaceable than this one on which, no doubt following the instructions of Leopold II, he proved to be more careful in his dealings with the tribes whose chieftains—450 in all—he had sign the allocation of their lands and work force. The things those rough men, dehumanized by the jungle, recounted of the expedition of 1871–2 made his hair stand on end. Villages decimated, chiefs decapitated, their women and children shot if they refused to feed the members of the expedition or provide them with porters, guides, and men to cut trails through the jungle. These old associates of Stanley feared him and accepted his reprimands in silence and with their eyes lowered. But they had blind confidence in his decisions and spoke with religious reverence of his famous 999-day journey, between 1874 and 1877, when all the other whites and a good number of the Africans had died.

When, in February 1885, at the Berlin Conference that not a single Congolese attended, the fourteen participating powers, headed by Great Britain, the United States, France, and Germany, graciously ceded to Leopold II—at whose side Henry Morton Stanley was a constant presence—the two and a half million square kilometers of the Congo and its twenty million inhabitants so that he "would open the territory to commerce, abolish slavery, and civilize and Christianize the pagans," Roger, who had just turned twenty-one and had lived for a year in Africa, celebrated the event. So did all the employees of the International Congo Society who, anticipating this concession, had already spent time in the territory, establishing the foundations of the project the monarch was ready to carry out. Roger was strong, very tall, slim, with intensely black hair and beard, deep gray eyes, and little propensity for jokes, a laconic boy who seemed a mature man. His preoccupations disconcerted his associates. Who among them took seriously the story about the "civilizing mission of Europe in Africa" that obsessed the young Irishman? But they appreciated him because he was hard-working and always prepared to lend a hand and take over a shift or an assignment for anyone who asked. Except for smoking, he seemed free of vices. He drank almost no alcohol and when, in the camps, tongues were loosened by drink and the talk turned to women, he was clearly uncomfortable and wanted to leave. He was a tireless explorer of the jungle and an imprudent swimmer in rivers and lagoons, energetically moving his arms in front of somnolent hippopotamuses. He had a passion for dogs, and his companions recalled the day during the expedition of 1884 when a wild boar buried its tusks in his fox terrier, named Spindler, and he suffered a crisis of nerves when he saw the small animal bleeding to death, its flank torn open. Unlike the other Europeans on the expedition, money did not matter to him. He had not come to Africa dreaming of becoming rich but moved instead by incomprehensible ideas like bringing progress to the savages. He spent his salary of £80 a year treating his associates. He lived frugally. He did, however, care for his person, dressing carefully, washing himself and combing his hair at mealtimes as if instead of camping in a clearing or on a river beach he were in London, Liverpool, or Dublin. He had a facility for languages, had learned French and Portuguese, and managed to speak a few words of their African dialect after spending a few days near a tribe. He was always making notes in student copybooks of what he saw. Someone found out he wrote poetry. They made a joke about it and embarrassment barely permitted him to stammer a denial. He once confessed that when he was a boy, his father would beat him with a strap, and for that reason he was angered by the overseers when they whipped the natives if they dropped a load or failed to carry out an order. He had the gaze of a dreamer.

When Roger thought of Stanley he was hampered by contradictory feelings. He continued to recuperate slowly from malaria. The Welsh adventurer had seen in Africa only a pretext for dramatic exploits and personal plunder. But how could he deny he was one of those mythical, legendary beings who by means of daring, scorn for death, and ambition, seem to have shattered the limits of the human? He had seen him carry in his arms children whose faces and bodies were eaten by smallpox, offer water from his own canteen to natives dying of cholera or sleeping sickness, as if no one could infect him. Who had this champion of the British Empire and the ambitions of Leopold II actually been? Roger was certain the mystery would never be revealed and his life would always remain hidden behind a spider's web of inventions. What was his real name? He had taken the name of Henry Morton Stanley from a New Orleans merchant who, in the dark years of his youth, was generous to him and perhaps adopted him. It was said his real name was John Rowlands, but he never confirmed that to anyone. Or that he had been born in Wales and spent his childhood in one of those orphanages where children were sent who had been picked up on the street by health officials. Apparently, when he was very young, he left for the United States as a stowaway on a freighter, and there, during the Civil War, fought first in the Confederate ranks as a soldier, and then on the Yankee side. Afterward, it was thought, he had become a reporter and written articles about the advance of the pioneers into the west and their battles with the Indians. When the *New York Herald* sent him to Africa in search of David Livingstone, Stanley had no experience at all as an explorer. How did he survive the trek through virgin forests, like someone searching for a needle in a haystack, and succeed in finding in Ujiji, on November 10, 1871, the man he stupefied, according to his boastful confession, with his greeting: "Dr. Livingstone, I presume?"

Of all Stanley's accomplishments, the one Roger Casement had admired most in his youth, even more than his expedition from the sources of the Congo River to its outlet into the Atlantic, was the construction of the caravan trail between 1879 and 1881. The caravan route opened a way for European commerce from the mouth of the great river to the pool, an enormous fluvial lagoon that, as years passed, would be named for the explorer: the Stanley Pool. Afterward, Roger discovered this was another of the farsighted operations of the King of the Belgians to create the infrastructure that would permit the territory to be exploited following the Berlin Conference of 1885. Stanley was the audacious executor of that design.

"And I," Roger would often tell his friend Herbert Ward during his African years, as he was becoming aware of what the Congo Free State meant, "was one of his foot soldiers from the beginning." Though not exactly, since when he reached Africa, Stanley had already spent five years opening the caravan trail, whose first section, from

Vivi to Isanguila, eighty-three kilometers up the Congo River, was completed at the beginning of 1880 and consisted of tangled, fever-ridden jungle filled with deep ravines, worm-infested trees, and putrid swamps where the tops of the trees blocked the sunlight. From there to Muyanga, some 120 turbulent kilometers, the Congo was navigable for pilots familiar with those waters, able to avoid whirlpools and, when it rained and the water rose, to take shelter in shallows or caves and not be thrown against the rocks and destroyed in the rapids that appeared and disappeared endlessly. When Roger began to work for the International Congo Society, which was transformed into the Congo Free State after 1885, Stanley had already founded, between Kinshasa and Ndolo, the station he called Leopoldville. It was December 1881, three years before Roger reached the jungle and four before the Congo Free State would be legally born. By then this colonial possession, the largest in Africa, created by a monarch who would never set foot in it, was a commercial reality to which European businessmen had access from the Atlantic, overcoming the obstacle of a Lower Congo made impassable by rapids, cataracts, and the twists and bends of the Livingstone Falls, thanks to the route Stanley opened over almost five hundred kilometers between Boma and Vivi to Leopoldville and the pool. When Roger came to Africa, bold merchants, the advance guard of Leopold II, were beginning to go deep into Congolese territory and take out the first ivory, skins, and baskets of rubber from a region filled with trees that oozed black latex, within reach of anyone who wanted to gather it.

During his early years in Africa, Roger traveled the

caravan route upriver several times, from Boma and Vivi to Leopoldville, or downriver, from Leopoldville to the river's mouth in the Atlantic, where the dense green waters became salty and where, in 1482, the caravel of the Portuguese Diego Cão entered Congolese territory for the first time. Roger came to know the Lower Congo better than any other European residing in Boma or Matadi, the two points from which Belgian colonization advanced toward the interior of the continent.

For the rest of his life, Roger lamented—he said it again now, in 1902, in his fever—dedicating his first eight years in Africa to working, like a pawn in a game of chess, on the building of the Congo Free State, investing his time, health, effort, and idealism, and believing that in this way he was contributing to a philanthropic plan.

At times, searching for justifications, he asked himself: *How could I have realized what was going on in those two and a half million square kilometers?* Working as an overseer or crew leader in Stanley's expedition of 1884 and in the North American Henry Shelton Sanford's expedition between 1886 and 1888, in stations and factories recently established along the caravan route, he was only a tiny piece of the gigantic apparatus that had begun to take form, and no one except its astute creator and a close group of collaborators knew what it would consist of.

Still, on the two occasions he had spoken with the King of the Belgians in 1900, when he had recently been named consul in Boma by the Foreign Office, Roger felt a deep mistrust of that large, robust man covered in decorations, with his long combed beard, formidable nose, and a prophet's eyes who, knowing he was in Brussels on his way to the Congo, invited him to supper. The magnificence of the palace with its deep, soft carpets, crystal chandeliers, engraved mirrors, and Asian statuettes made him dizzy. There were a dozen guests in addition to Queen Marie Henriette, the king's daughter Princess Clémentine, and Prince Victor Napoleon of France. The monarch monopolized the conversation the entire night. He spoke like an inspired preacher, and when he described the cruelties of the Arab slave traders who left Zanzibar to make their "runs," his strong voice attained mystic intonations. Christian Europe had an obligation to put a stop to that traffic in human flesh. He had proposed this and it would be the offering of little Belgium to civilization: liberating a suffering humanity from such horror. The elegant ladies yawned, Prince Napoleon murmured gallantries to the lady next to him, and no one listened to the orchestra playing a Haydn concerto.

The following morning Leopold II summoned the English consul for a private conversation. He received him in his private reception room. There were many porcelain objects and figurines of jade and ivory. The monarch smelled of cologne and had shiny nails. As on the previous evening, Roger could scarcely say a word. The King of the Belgians spoke of his quixotic quest and how misunderstood it was by journalists and resentful politicians. Errors were committed and there were excesses, no doubt. The reason? It was not easy to contract honorable, capable people willing to risk working in the distant Congo. He asked the consul to inform him personally if, in his new post, he observed anything that needed correction. Roger had the impression that the King of the Belgians was a pompous narcissist.

Now, two years later, in 1902, he told himself the king undoubtedly was that, but also a statesman of cold, Machiavellian intelligence. As soon as the Congo Free State had been established, Leopold II, by means of a decree in 1886, reserved as *Domaine de la Couronne* some 250,000 square kilometers between the Kasai and Ruki Rivers, which his explorers—principally Stanley—had indicated were rich in rubber trees. This expanse lay outside all the concessions to private enterprises and was intended for exploitation by the sovereign. The International Congo Society was replaced as a legal entity by l'Etat Indépendant du Congo, the Congo Free State, whose only president and trustee was Leopold II.

Explaining to international public opinion that the only effective way to suppress the slave trade was with a "security force," the king sent two thousand soldiers from the regular Belgian army to the Congo, to be supplemented by a militia of ten thousand natives, whose maintenance would be assumed by the Congolese population. Even though most of this army was under the command of Belgian officers, its ranks, and above all the leadership positions in the militia, were permeated by individuals of the worst kind, scoundrels, ex-convicts, adventurers hungry for a fortune, who had come from the low districts of vice dens and brothels in half of Europe. The Force Publique became embedded, like a parasite in a living organism, in the tangle of villages scattered over a region the size of Europe measured from Spain to the borders of Russia, to be maintained by an African community that did not understand what was happening to it, except that the invasion that overtook it was a plague more devastating than slave hunters, locusts, red ants, and incantations that brought the sleep of death. Because the soldiers and militiamen of the Force Publique were greedy, brutal, and insatiable when it came to food, drink, women, animals, skins, ivory, in short, everything that could be stolen, eaten, drunk, sold, or fornicated with.

At the same time the exploitation of the Congolese began in this way, the humanitarian monarch, following another of the mandates he had received, started to grant concessions to businesses in order to "open by means of commerce the road to civilization for the natives of Africa." Some traders died, overcome by malaria, bitten by snakes, or devoured by wild beasts due to their ignorance of the jungles, and another few fell to the poisoned arrows and spears of natives who dared rebel against these outsiders with weapons that exploded like thunder or burned like lightning, colonists who explained to them that according to contracts signed by their chiefs, they had to abandon their planting, fishing, hunting, rituals, and routines to become guides, porters, hunters, or harvesters of rubber without any salary at all. A good number of concessionaires, friends and favorites of the Belgian monarch, himself above all, made great fortunes in a very short time.

By means of the system of concessions, companies spread through the Congo Free State in concentric waves, penetrating deeper and deeper into the immense region bathed by the Middle and Upper Congo and its spider's web of tributaries. In their respective domains, they enjoyed sovereignty. In addition to being protected by the Force Publique, they counted on their own militias, always headed by some ex-soldier, ex-jailer, ex-convict, or fugitive, some of whom would become famous throughout all of Africa for their savagery. In a few years the Congo became the leading producer of the rubber the civilized world demanded in larger and larger quantities to turn the wheels of carriages, automobiles, and trains, in addition to all kinds of systems of transport, apparel, decoration, and irrigation.

Roger Casement was not fully conscious of any of this in the eight years—1884 to 1892—when, working very hard, suffering from malaria, turning dark in the African sun, becoming covered with scars from the bites, scratches, and gashes of plants and insects, he labored tenaciously to support the commercial and political creation of Leopold II. What he did know about was the appearance and domination in those infinite domains of the symbol of colonization: the *chicote* whip.

Who invented that delicate, manageable, and efficacious instrument for rousing, frightening, and punishing indolence, clumsiness, or stupidity in those ebony-colored bipeds who never managed to do things in the way the colonists expected, whether it was working in camp, handing over the manioc (*kwango*), antelope or wild boar meat, and other foodstuffs assigned to each village or family, or the taxes to pay for the public works the government was building? It was said the inventor had been a captain in the Force Publique named M. Chicot, a Belgian in the first wave, a man apparently both practical and imaginative and endowed with sharp powers of observation, for he noticed before anyone else that the extremely tough hide of the hippopotamus could be fashioned into a whip more durable and damaging than those made of equine and feline intestines, a vinelike cord able to produce more burning, blood, scars, and pain than any other scourge, and at the same time light and functional, for curled into a small wooden haft, overseers, orderlies, guards, jailers, and foremen could wrap it around their waist or hang it over their shoulder almost without realizing they were carrying it because it weighed so little. Its mere presence among the members of the Force Publique had an intimidating effect: the eyes of black men, women, and children grew large when they saw it, the whites of their eyes gleamed with terror in their deep-black or blue-black faces imagining that after any mistake, slip, or failing, the *chicote* would rip through the air with its unmistakable whistle and fall on their legs, buttocks, and backs, making them shriek.

One of the first concessionaires in the Congo Free State was the North American Henry Shelton Sanford. He had been Leopold II's agent and lobbyist to the United States government and a key player in the monarch's strategy for having the great powers cede him the Congo. In June 1886 he formed the Sanford Exploring Expedition (SEE) to trade in ivory, chewing gum, rubber, palm oil, and copper throughout the Upper Congo. Foreigners who worked for the International Congo Society, like Roger, were transferred to the SEE and their old jobs taken over by Belgians. Roger worked for the Sanford Exploring Expedition for £150 a year.

He began in September 1886 as an agent in charge of stores and transport in Matadi, a word that means stone in Kikongo. When Roger moved there, the station built along the caravan route was barely a jungle clearing opened with machetes on the banks of the great river. Four centuries earlier the caravel of Diego Cão sailed that far, and the Portuguese navigator had carved his name on a rock, still legible today. A firm of German architects and engineers began to build the first house out of pine imported from Europe—importing wood to Africa!—and docks and depositories, work that one morning—Roger clearly recalled the mishap—was interrupted by a sound like an earthquake and the eruption into the clearing of a herd of elephants that almost made the new settlement disappear. Roger spent six, eight, fifteen, eighteen years seeing the tiny village that he began building with his own hands to serve as a depository for the merchandise of the SEE keep expanding, climbing the gentle hills nearby, enlarging the colonists' squared, two-story wooden houses with long terraces, conical roofs, small gardens, windows protected by metal screens, and becoming filled with streets, corners, and people. In addition to the first small Catholic church in Kinkanda, now in 1902 there was another more important one, the Church of Notre Dame Médiatrice, and a Baptist mission, a pharmacy, a hospital with two physicians and several nuns who were nurses, a post office, a beautiful railroad station, a commissary, a court, several customs depots, a solid wharf, and shops selling clothing, food, canned goods, hats, shoes, and farming implements. Around the colonists' city a variegated district of Bakongo huts of reeds and mud had arisen. Here in Matadi, Roger told himself at times, the Europe of civilization, modernity, and the Christian religion was much more present than in Boma, the capital. Matadi already had a small cemetery on Tunduwa Hill, next to the mission. From that height it overlooked both banks and a long stretch of the river.

Europeans were buried there. Only natives who worked as servants or porters and had an identification pass circulated in the city and along the wharf. Any others who violated those limits were expelled from Matadi forever, after paying a fine and receiving some lashes with a *chicote*. In 1902, the governor general still could boast that in Boma and Matadi not a single robbery, homicide, or rape had been recorded.

Roger would always remember two events from the two years he worked for the Sanford Exploring Expedition, between the ages of twenty-two and twenty-four: the months-long transport of the *Florida* along the caravan route from Banana, the tiny port at the mouth of the Congo River in the Atlantic, to Stanley Pool, and the incident with Lieutenant Francqui: for once breaking the serenity of his even temper, joked about by Herbert Ward, he almost threw him into the whirlpools of the Congo River and escaped being shot by the lieutenant only by a miracle.

The *Florida* was an imposing ship the SEE brought to Boma to serve as a merchant vessel in the Middle and Upper Congo, that is, on the other side of the Crystal Mountains. Livingstone Falls, the chain of waterfalls that separated Boma and Matadi from Leopoldville, ended in a cluster of whirlpools that earned the name Devil's Cauldron. Starting there and going east, the river was navigable for thousands of kilometers. But to the west it lost a thousand feet in height as it descended to the ocean, making the river impassable for great distances. In order to be carried by land to Stanley Pool, the *Florida* was disassembled into hundreds of pieces that, classified and packed, traveled on the shoulders of native porters for the 478 kilometers of the caravan route. Roger was entrusted with the largest, heaviest piece: the ship's hull. He did everything, from supervising the construction of the enormous wagon onto which it was hoisted to recruiting the hundred or so porters and trail cutters who hauled the immense load across the peaks and ravines of the Crystal Mountains, widening the trail with machetes. And constructing embankments and defenses, building camps, treating the sick and those hurt in accidents, suppressing disputes among members of different ethnic groups, and organizing shifts of guard duty, the distribution of food, and hunting and fishing when supplies ran short. It was three months of risk and worry, but also of enthusiasm and the awareness of doing something that signified progress, a successful battle against a hostile nature. And, Roger would often repeat in years to come, without using the *chicote* or permitting its abuse by those overseers nicknamed Zanzibarians, either because they came from Zanzibar, capital of the slave trade, or behaved with the cruelty of traffickers.

When, in the great fluvial lagoon of Stanley Pool, the *Florida* was reassembled and ready to sail, Roger traveled in the ship along the Middle and Upper Congo, securing depositories and transport for the goods of the Sanford Exploring Expedition in localities that, years later, he would visit again during his journey to hell in 1903: Bolobo, Lukolela, the region of Irebu, and, finally, the Equator Station renamed Coquilhatville.

The incident with Lieutenant Francqui, who, unlike Roger, felt no repugnance at all toward the *chicote* and used it freely, occurred on his return from a trip to the line of the Equator some fifty kilometers upriver from Boma, in a wretched, nameless village. Lieutenant Francqui, in command of eight soldiers of the Force Publique, all of them natives, had carried out a punitive expedition on account of the eternal problem of laborers. More were always needed to carry goods for the expeditions that came and went between Boma–Matadi and Leopoldville–Stanley Pool. Since the tribes resisted handing over their people for that exhausting work, from time to time the Force Publique or private concessionaires undertook incursions into refractory villages where, in addition to taking away the able-bodied men tied together in lines, huts were burned, hides, ivory, and animals confiscated, and the chiefs whipped soundly so that in the future they would live up to their contractual obligations.

When Roger and his small company of five porters and a Zanzibarian entered the hamlet, the three or four huts were already ashes and the residents had fled. The exception was a boy, almost a child, lying on the ground, his hands and feet tied to stakes, on whose back Lieutenant Francqui was easing his frustration with lashes from his *chicote*. Whippings were generally administered not by officers but by soldiers. But the lieutenant undoubtedly felt offended by the flight of the entire village and wanted revenge. Red with fury, sweating profusely, he gave a small snort with each lash. His expression did not change when he saw Roger and his group appear. He simply responded to his greeting with a nod, not interrupting the punishment. The boy must have lost consciousness some time earlier. His back and legs were a bloody mass, and Roger remembered a detail: a column of ants marching close to his body.

"You have no right to do that, Lieutenant Francqui," he said in French. "That's enough!"

The officer, a short man, lowered the *chicote* and turned to look at Roger's long silhouette, bearded, unarmed, carrying a staff to test the ground and move aside debris during the march. A little dog scampered between his legs. Surprise made the lieutenant's round face, with its trimmed mustache and small blinking eyes, pass from bright red to ashen and back to red again.

"What did you say?" he roared. Roger saw him let go of the *chicote*, move his right hand to his waist, and fumble with the cartridge belt where the butt of his revolver protruded. In a second he realized that in a fit of temper the officer might shoot him. He reacted quickly. Before the lieutenant could take out his weapon, he had him by the back of the neck and at the same time seized the revolver he had just grasped. Lieutenant Francqui tried to loosen the fingers at the nape of his neck. His eyes bulged like a toad's.

The eight soldiers from the Force Publique, who had been watching the punishment as they smoked, had not moved, but Roger supposed that, disconcerted by what had happened, they had their hands on their rifles and were waiting for an order from their leader to take action.

"My name is Roger Casement, I work for the SEE, and you know me very well, Lieutenant Francqui, because we've played poker in Matadi," he said, letting him go, bending down to pick up the revolver, and returning it to him with an amiable expression. "The way you're whipping this young boy is a crime, no matter what offense he committed. As an officer of the Force Publique, you know that better than I, because you undoubtedly know the laws of the Congo Free State. If the boy dies because of this lashing, the crime will weigh on your conscience."

"When I came to the Congo I took the precaution of leaving my conscience behind in my own country," the officer said. Now he wore a mocking expression and seemed to be wondering whether Casement was a fool or a madman. His hysteria had dissipated. "Just as well you moved quickly, I was about to put a bullet in you. I would have found myself involved in a nice diplomatic dispute if I had killed an Englishman. In any case, I advise you not to interfere, as you've just done, with my colleagues in the Force Publique. They're bad characters and things could go worse for you with them than with me."

His anger had passed and now he seemed depressed. He purred that someone had warned them about his coming. Now he would have to go back to Matadi empty-handed. He said nothing when Roger ordered the troops to untie the boy and put him in a hammock, and having tied this between two sticks, he left with him for Boma. When they arrived two days later, in spite of his wounds and the blood he had lost, the boy was still alive. Roger left him at the dispensary. He went to court to register a complaint against Lieutenant Francqui for abuse of authority. In the following weeks he was called twice to make a deposition, and during the judge's long, stupid interrogations, he realized his accusation would be filed away and the officer not even admonished.

By the time the judge finally ruled, throwing out the

complaint for lack of evidence and because the victim refused to offer corroboration, Roger had resigned his post on the Sanford Exploring Expedition and was working once more for Henry Morton Stanley—whom the Kikongos of the region had now nicknamed Bula Matadi (Breaker of Rocks)—on the railroad being constructed parallel to the caravan route, from Boma and Matadi to Leopoldville–Stanley Pool. The boy who had been mistreated remained to work with Roger and from then on was his servant, assistant, and traveling companion through Africa. Since he never could say what his name was, Casement baptized him Charlie. He had been with him sixteen years.

Roger's resignation from the Sanford expedition was due to an incident with one of the company directors. He didn't regret it, for working with Stanley on the railroad, though it demanded an enormous physical effort, gave him back the illusion he'd had when he came to Africa. Opening the jungle and dynamiting mountains to lay down track for the railroad was the pioneering work he had dreamed of. The hours he spent outdoors, burning in the sun or drenched by downpours, directing the laborers and trail cutters, giving orders to the Zanzibarians, making certain the crews did their work well, packing down, leveling, reinforcing the ground where the crossties would be laid and clearing away dense branches, meant hours of concentration and the sense he was doing work that would be of equal benefit to Europeans and Africans, the colonizers and the colonized. Herbert Ward said to him one day: "When I met you, I thought you were only an adventurer. Now I know you're a mystic."

What Roger liked less was leaving the countryside for

the villages to negotiate the assignment of porters and trail cutters to the railroad. The lack of laborers had become the primary problem as the Congo Free State grew. In spite of having signed the "treaties," the chiefs, now that they understood what was involved, were reluctant to allow their people to leave to open roads, build stations and depositories, or harvest rubber. When Roger worked for the SEE, he succeeded in overcoming this resistance by having the company pay the workers a small salary, generally in kind, though it had no legal obligation to do so. Other companies began to follow suit, but even so it was not easy to hire laborers. The chiefs alleged they could not send away men who were indispensable for tending their crops and hunting and fishing for the food they ate. Often, when the recruiters approached, the able-bodied men hid in the underbrush. That was when the punitive expeditions began, the forced recruitments and the practice of locking women into so-called *maisons d'otages* (hostage houses) to make certain their husbands did not escape.

Both in Stanley's expedition and in Henry Shelton Sanford's, Roger was often responsible for negotiating with the indigenous communities for the surrender of native workers. Thanks to his facility in languages, he could make himself understood in Kikongo and Lingala—and later in Swahili as well—though always with the help of interpreters. Hearing him attempting to speak their language eased the mistrust of the natives. His gentle manner, patience, and respectful attitude facilitated dialogues, as did the gifts he brought: clothing, knives and other domestic objects, as well as the glass beads they liked so much. He usually returned to camp with a handful of men to clear the countryside and work as porters. He became famous as "a friend of the blacks," a name that some of his colleagues judged with commiseration while others, especially some officers in the Force Publique, reacted to with contempt.

These visits to the tribes caused a disquiet in Roger that would increase with the years. At first he made them willingly, for they satisfied his curiosity to know something of the customs, languages, apparel, habits, foods, dances, songs, and religious practices of peoples who seemed mired in the depths of time, in whom a primitive innocence, healthy and direct, mixed with cruel customs, like sacrificing twins in certain tribes, or killing a number of servants—almost always slaves—to bury along with the chiefs, and the practice of cannibalism in some groups who, as a consequence, were feared and hated by other communities. He would leave negotiations with an ill-defined uneasiness, the sensation of playing dirty with those men from another time who, no matter how much he tried, would never be able to understand him fully, and consequently, in spite of the precautions he took to attenuate the abusiveness of the agreements, he felt guilty of having acted against his convictions, morality, and that "first principle," as he called God.

Therefore, at the end of December 1888, before he had completed a year on Stanley's *chemin de fer*, he resigned and went to work at the Baptist mission of Ngombe Lutete with the Bentleys, the married missionaries who ran it. He made the decision abruptly after a conversation that began at twilight and ended at the first light of dawn, in a house in the colonists' district in Matadi, with an individual who was passing through. Theodore Horte was a former officer in the British navy, which he had left to become a Baptist missionary in the Congo. The Baptists had been there since David Livingstone began to explore the African continent and preach evangelism. They had opened missions in Palabala, Banza Manteke, Ngombe Lutete, and had just inaugurated another one, Arlhington, in the vicinity of Stanley Pool. Theodore Horte, an inspector of these missions, spent his time traveling from one to another, giving help to the pastors and looking into opening new centers. That conversation produced in Roger an impression he would remember the rest of his life; during the days of convalescence from his third attack of malaria, in the middle of 1902, he could have reproduced it in minute detail.

No one imagined, hearing him speak, that Theodore Horte had been a career officer and, as a sailor, had participated in important military operations of the British navy. He didn't speak about his past or his private life. He was a distinguished-looking, very well-mannered man of about fifty. On that tranquil night in Matadi, with no rain or clouds, a sky studded with stars that were reflected in the river, and the calm sound of the warm breeze ruffling their hair, Casement and Horte, lying in two hammocks hung side by side, began an after-dinner conversation that Roger thought, at first, would last only for the few minutes before sleep after a meal and would be another conventional, forgettable exchange. But shortly after their chat began, something made his heart beat faster than usual. He felt lulled by the sensitivity and warmth of Pastor Horte's voice, inspired to speak about subjects he never shared with his colleagues at work—except, occasionally,

Herbert Ward—and certainly not with his superiors. Preoccupations, anxieties, doubts that he hid as if they were something ominous. Did all of it make sense? Was the European adventure in Africa by any chance what was said, written, believed? Was it bringing civilization, progress, modernity by means of free trade and evangelization? Could those animals in the Force Publique be called civilizers when they stole everything they could on their punitive expeditions? How many of the colonizers—businessmen, soldiers, functionaries, adventurers—had a minimum of respect for the natives and considered them brothers or, at least, human beings? Five per cent? One in a hundred? The truth, the truth was that in the years he had spent here he could count on one hand the number of Europeans who did not treat the blacks like soulless beasts whom they could deceive, exploit, whip, even kill, without the slightest remorse.

Theodore Horte listened in silence to the explosion of bitterness from young Roger. When he spoke, he did not seem surprised by what he had heard. On the contrary, he acknowledged that for years he too had been assailed by terrible doubts. Still, at least in theory, that business about "civilization" had a good deal of truth in it. Weren't the natives' living conditions atrocious? Didn't their levels of hygiene, their superstitions, their ignorance of the most basic notions of health mean they died like flies? Wasn't their life of mere survival tragic? Europe had a great deal to offer to bring them out of primitivism. So they would end certain barbaric customs, the sacrifice of children and the sick in so many communities, for example, the wars in which they killed one another, slavery, and cannibalism, still practiced in some places. And besides, wasn't it good for them to know the true God and replace the idols they worshiped with the Christian God, the God of mercy, love, and justice? True, many evil people, perhaps the worst of Europe, had ended up here. Wasn't there a solution? It was imperative that the good things from the Old Continent come here too. Not the greed of merchants with dirty souls, but science, law, education, inherent human rights, Christian ethics. It was too late to take a step backward, wasn't it? It was pointless to ask whether colonization was good or bad, whether, if left to their fate, the Congolese would have been better off without Europeans. When things could not be turned back, it wasn't worth wasting time wondering whether it would have been better if those things had not occurred. It was better to try to redirect them along the right path. It was always possible to straighten what had become twisted. Wasn't that the greatest teaching of Christ?

When, at dawn, Roger asked him whether it was possible for a layman like him, who had never been very religious, to work in one of the missions that the Baptist Church had in the region of the Lower and Middle Congo, Theodore Horte gave a little laugh: "It must be one of God's jokes," he exclaimed. "The Bentleys, at the Ngombe Lutete mission, need a lay assistant to give them a hand with bookkeeping. And now, you ask me that question. Isn't this something more than mere coincidence? One of those jokes God plays on us sometimes to remind us He's always there and we should never despair?"

Roger's work from January to March of 1889, at the Ngombe Lutete mission, though short-lived, was intense, and it allowed him to leave behind the uncertainty in which he had lived for some time. He earned only ten pounds a month and with that he had to pay his room and board, but seeing Mr. William Holman Bentley and his wife work from morning to night with so much energy and conviction, and sharing with them life in the mission that was not only a religious center but a dispensary, a site for vaccinations, a school, a store for merchandise, and a place of recreation, counseling, and advice, made the colonial adventure seem less harsh, more reasonable, even civilizing. This feeling was encouraged by seeing how around this couple a small African community had arisen of converts to the reformed church who, in their attire and the songs the choir rehearsed every day for Sunday services, as well as in classes in literacy and Christian doctrine, seemed to be leaving tribal life behind and beginning a modern, Christian life.

His work was not limited to keeping the books of income and expenses for the mission. That took him little time. He did everything, from removing excess foliage and weeding the small cleared space around the mission—it was a daily struggle against vegetation determined to recover the clearing that had been snatched away—to going out to hunt down a leopard that was eating the fowl in the yard. He took care of transport by trail or by river in a small boat, fetching and carrying the sick, tools, and workers, and he watched over the operations of the mission store, where natives in the vicinity could sell and acquire goods. This was done principally by barter, but Belgian francs and pounds sterling also circulated. The Bentleys laughed at his ineptitude in business and his vocation for prodigality, for Roger thought all the prices were high and wanted to lower them, even though that would deprive the mission of the small profit margin that allowed it to supplement its meager budget.

In spite of the affection he came to feel for the Bentleys and the clear conscience he had working at their side, Roger knew from the beginning that his stay at the Ngombe Lutete mission would be temporary. The work was honorable and altruistic but made sense only if accompanied by the faith that animated Theodore Horte and the Bentleys and that he lacked, though he might mimic its gestures and manifestations, attending the commented readings of the Bible, the classes on doctrine, and the Sunday service. He wasn't an atheist or an agnostic but something more uncertain, an indifferent man who did not deny the existence of God—the "first principle"—but was incapable of feeling comfortable in the bosom of a church, in common cause and joined with other believers, part of a common denominator. He tried to explain this to Theodore Horte during their long conversation in Matadi and felt clumsy and confused. The former naval officer calmed him: "I understand perfectly, Roger. God has His ways. He makes us uneasy, disturbs us, urges us to search. Until one day everything is illuminated and there He is. It will happen to you, you'll see."

In those three months, at least, it hadn't happened to him. Now, in 1902, thirteen years later, he still felt religious uncertainty. The fevers had passed, he had lost a good deal of weight, and though at times his weakness made him dizzy, he had resumed his duties as consul in Boma. He went to visit the governor general and other authorities.

He returned to the games of chess and bridge. The rainy season was at its height and would last for many more months.

At the end of March 1889, when he finished his contract with Reverend William Holman Bentley and after five years away, he returned to England for the first time.

5

"Coming here has been one of the most difficult things I've done in my life," said Alice by way of greeting, pressing his hand. "I thought I'd never manage it. But here I am at last."

Alice Stopford Green maintained the appearance of a cold, rational person, far removed from sentimentality, but Roger knew her well enough to realize she was moved to the marrow of her bones. He noticed the very slight tremor in her voice she could not hide and the rapid quivering of her nose that appeared whenever something worried her. She was close to seventy but still had her youthful figure. Wrinkles had not erased the freshness of her freckled face or the luminosity of her bright, steely eyes. In them the light of intelligence always shone. With her usual sober elegance, she wore a light suit, thin blouse, and boots with high heels.

"What a pleasure, my dear Alice, what a pleasure," Roger repeated, taking both her hands. "I thought I'd never see you again."

"I brought you books, sweets, and some clothes but the constables at the entrance took everything away." Her expression showed impotence. "I'm sorry. Are you all right?"

"Yes, yes," Roger said eagerly. "You've done so much for me all this time. Is there no news yet?"

"The cabinet meets on Thursday," she said. "I know

from a good source that this matter is at the top of the agenda. We're doing everything possible and even the impossible, Roger. The petition has close to fifty signatures, all of them important people. Scientists, artists, writers, politicians. John Devoy assures us that any time now the telegram from the president of the United States ought to reach the English government. All our friends have mobilized to stop, well, I mean, to counteract the vile campaign in the press. You know about it, don't you?"

"Vaguely," said Roger with a look of displeasure. "We don't get news from outside and the jailers have orders not to say a word to me. The sheriff does, but only to insult me. Do you think there's still a possibility, Alice?"

"Of course I do," she affirmed forcefully, but Roger thought it was a compassionate lie. "All my friends assure me the cabinet decides this unanimously. If a single minister opposes the execution, you're saved. And it seems your former superior at the Foreign Office, Sir Edward Grey, is against it. Don't lose hope, Roger."

This time the sheriff of Pentonville Prison was not in the visitors' room. Only a very young, discreet guard who turned his back on them and looked at the corridor through the grating in the door, pretending disinterest in Roger's conversation with the historian. *If all the jailers at Pentonville were this considerate, life here would be much more bearable*, he thought, and realized he still hadn't asked Alice about events in Dublin.

"I know that when the Easter Week Rising broke out, Scotland Yard went to search your house on Grosvenor Road," he said. "Poor Alice, did they make things hard for you?"

"Not too bad, Roger. They took a good number of papers. Personal letters, manuscripts. I hope they return them, I don't think they'll do them any good," she said with a sigh, distressed. "Compared to what they've suffered in Ireland, what happened to me was nothing."

Would the harsh repression continue? Roger made an effort not to think about the shootings, the dead, the aftermath of that tragic week. But Alice must have read in his eyes his curiosity to know about it.

"The executions have stopped, apparently," she murmured, looking quickly at the guard's back. "We estimate there are 3,500 prisoners. Most have been brought here and are distributed in prisons all across England. We've found eighty women among them. Several associations are helping us. Many English lawyers have offered to take their cases, free of charge."

Questions pounded in Roger's head. How many of his friends among the dead, the wounded, the imprisoned? But he controlled himself. Why find out things he could do nothing about that would only increase his bitterness?

"Do you know something, Alice? One of the reasons I'd like them to commute my sentence is because if they don't, I'll die without having learned Irish. If they do commute it, I'll delve deep into it and I promise that in this very visitors' room you and I will talk one day in Gaelic."

She nodded with a little smile that was only half there.

"Gaelic is a difficult language," she said, patting his arm. "You need a good deal of time and patience to learn it. You've had a very agitated life, my dear. But take comfort, few Irishmen have done as much for Ireland as you."

"Thanks to you, my dear Alice. I owe you so much.

Your friendship, hospitality, intelligence, and culture, those Tuesday get-togethers on Grosvenor Road, the extraordinary people, the pleasant atmosphere, are the best memories of my life. Now I can tell you this and thank you, dear friend. You taught me to love the past and the culture of Ireland. You were a generous teacher, who enriched my life so much."

He said what he had always felt and kept silent about because of shyness. Ever since he met her he had admired and loved the historian and writer Alice Stopford Green, whose books and studies about the historical past and legends and myths of Ireland, and on Gaelic, had contributed more than anything else to giving Roger the "Celtic pride" he boasted of so vigorously that at times it unleashed the ridicule even of his nationalist friends. He had met Alice eleven or twelve years earlier, when he asked for her help in the Congo Reform Association that he had founded with Edmund D. Morel. The public struggle of these new friends against Leopold II and his Machiavellian creation, the Congo Free State, had begun. The enthusiasm with which Alice Stopford Green devoted herself to their campaign to denounce the horrors in the Congo was decisive in having the many writers and politicians who were her friends join as well. Alice became Roger's intellectual tutor and guide, and he, whenever he was in London, attended her weekly salon. These gatherings were attended by professors, journalists, poets, painters, musicians, and politicians who generally, like her, were critics of imperialism and colonialism and supporters of Home Rule for Ireland, and even radical nationalists who demanded total independence. In the elegant, book-lined rooms of the house on Grosvenor Road, where Alice preserved the library of her late husband, the historian John Richard Green, Roger met W. B. Yeats, Sir Arthur Conan Doyle, George Bernard Shaw, G. K. Chesterton, John Galsworthy, Robert Cunninghame Graham, and many other modern writers.

"I have a question I almost asked Gee yesterday but didn't have the courage. Did Conrad sign the petition? My lawyer and Gee haven't mentioned his name."

Alice shook her head.

"I wrote to him myself, asking for his signature," she added with annoyance. "His reasons were confused. He's always been slippery in political matters. Perhaps, as an assimilated British citizen, he doesn't feel very secure. On the other hand, as a Pole, he hates Germany as much as Russia, both of which made his country disappear for so many centuries. In short, I don't know. All your friends regret this very much. One can be a great writer and a coward in political matters. You know that better than anyone, Roger."

Roger agreed. He regretted having asked the question. It would have been better not to know. The absence of that signature would torment him now just as it had tormented him to learn from his lawyer Gavan Duffy that Edmund D. Morel had not wanted to sign the petition for a commutation of his sentence either. His friend, his brother Bulldog! His companion in the struggle to assist the natives of the Congo also refused, claiming reasons of patriotic loyalty in wartime.

"Conrad's not having signed won't change things very much," said the historian. "His political influence with the Asquith government is nil."

"No, of course not," Roger agreed.

Perhaps it had no importance in the success or failure of the petition, but for him, in his heart of hearts, it did. It would have done him good to recall, in the fits of despair that assailed him in his cell, that a person of Conrad's prestige, admired by so many people—himself included—had helped him at this critical moment and sent him, with his signature, a message of comprehension and friendship.

"You met him a long time ago, didn't you?" Alice asked, as if reading his thoughts.

"Twenty-six years ago exactly. In June 1890, in the Congo," Roger specified. "He wasn't a writer yet. Though, if I remember correctly, he told me he had begun a novel. No doubt it was *Almayer's Folly*, the first one he published. He sent it to me, with a dedication. I still have the book somewhere. He hadn't published anything yet. He was a sailor. You could barely understand his English, his Polish accent was so thick."

"You still can't understand him," Alice said with a smile. "He still speaks English with that awful accent. As if he were 'chewing pebbles,' as Bernard Shaw says. But he writes it like an angel, whether we like him or not."

Roger recalled the day in June 1890 when, perspiring in the humid heat of summer that was just beginning and bothered by the bites of mosquitoes gorging on his foreigner's skin, the young captain in the British merchant fleet arrived in Matadi. About thirty, with a high forehead, deep black beard, robust body, and deep-set eyes, his name was Konrad Korzeniowski, a Pole who had become an English citizen a few years earlier. Contracted by the Société Anonyme pour le Commerce du Haut-Congo, he came to serve as captain of one of the small steamboats that carried goods and merchants back and forth between Leopoldville–Kinshasa and the distant cataracts of Stanley Falls in Kisangani. It was his first position as a ship's captain, and he was filled with hopes and projects. He arrived in the Congo imbued with all the fantasies and myths used by Leopold II to create his figure as a great humanitarian, a monarch determined to civilize Africa and free the Congolese from slavery, paganism, and other barbarities. In spite of his long experience sailing the seas of Asia and the Americas, his gift for languages, and his readings, there was something innocent and childlike in the Pole that charmed Roger immediately. The feeling was mutual, for from the day they met until three weeks later, when Korzeniowski left in the company of thirty porters on the caravan route to Leopoldville–Kinshasa, where he would take command of his ship *Le roi des Belges*, they saw each other morning, noon, and night.

They went for excursions in the environs of Matadi, as far as the now non-existent Vivi, the first, transitory capital of the colony of which not even the rubble remained, and the mouth of the Mpozo River where, according to legend, the first rapids and falls of Livingstone Falls and the Devil's Cauldron had stopped the Portuguese Diego Cão four centuries earlier. On the Lafundi plain, Roger showed the young Pole the place where the explorer Henry Morton Stanley built his first house, which disappeared years later in a fire. But, above all, they talked a good deal about a great number of things, though principally about what was going on in the new Congo Free State where Konrad had just set foot and Roger had already spent six years. After a few days of their friendship, the Polish mariner had formed an idea of the place where he had come to work that was very different from the one he had brought with him. And, as he told Roger when they said goodbye at dawn on Saturday, June 28, 1890, en route to the Crystal Mountains, he had been "deflowered." That is how he said it, in his gravelly, stony, sonorous accent: "You've deflowered me, Casement. About Leopold II, about the Congo Free State. Perhaps even about life." And he repeated, dramatically: "Deflowered."

They saw each other again several times, on Roger's trips to London, and exchanged a few letters. Thirteen years after that first meeting, in June 1903, Roger, who was in England, received an invitation from Joseph Conrad (that was his name now, and he was already a prestigious writer) to spend a weekend at Pent Farm, his small country house in Hythe, Kent. The novelist led a frugal, solitary life there with his wife and son. Roger had a warm memory of those few days with the writer. Now he had silver in his hair and a thick beard, he had put on weight and acquired a certain intellectual arrogance in the way he expressed himself. But with him he was exceptionally effusive. When Roger congratulated him on his Congolese novel, *Heart of Darkness*, which he had just read and which had stirred him deeply because it was the most extraordinary description of the horrors people were living through in the Congo, Conrad cut him short with his hands.

"You should have appeared as co-author of that book, Casement," he declared, patting him on the shoulder. "I never would have written it without your help. You removed the scales from my eyes. About Africa, about the

Congo Free State. And about the human beast."

Alone after dinner—the discreet Mrs. Conrad, a woman of very humble background, and the child had gone to bed—the writer, following the second glass of port, told Roger that for what he was doing to help the indigenous Congolese, he deserved to be called "the British Bartolomé de las Casas." Roger blushed to the roots of his hair at such praise. How was it possible that someone who had so high an opinion of him, who had helped him and Edmund D. Morel so much in their campaign against Leopold II, had refused to sign a petition that asked only for his death sentence to be commuted? How could that compromise him with the government?

He recalled other occasional meetings with Conrad on his visits to London. They saw each other once at his club, the Wellington Club on Grosvenor Place, when he was with colleagues from the Foreign Office. The writer insisted that Roger stay to have a cognac with him after his companions had left. They recalled the sailor's disastrous state of mind six months after he had passed through Matadi, when he returned. Roger was still working there, in charge of stores and transport. Konrad Korzeniowski was not even a shadow of the enthusiastic young man full of hope Roger had met half a year earlier. He looked years older, his nerves were frayed, and he had stomach problems because of parasites. Constant diarrhea caused him to lose many kilos. Embittered and pessimistic, he dreamed only of returning to London as soon as possible to put himself in the hands of real doctors.

"I can see the jungle has not been kind to you, Konrad. Don't be alarmed. Malaria is like that, it takes time to leave even when the fever has disappeared."

They talked after supper on the terrace of the small house that was Roger's home and office. There was no moon or stars on this night in Matadi, but it wasn't raining and the drone of the insects lulled them as they smoked and sipped from the glasses in their hands.

"The worst thing wasn't the jungle, this unhealthy climate, the fevers that kept me semi-conscious for close to two weeks," the Pole complained. "Not even the ghastly dysentery that kept me shitting blood for five days in a row. The worst, the worst thing, Casement, was witnessing the horrible things that happen every day in this damn country. The things the black devils and the white devils do wherever you look."

Konrad had made a voyage in the company's steamboat he was to command, *Le roi des Belges*, back and forth between Leopoldville–Kinshasa and the Stanley Falls. Everything had gone wrong on that trip to Kisangani. He almost drowned when the canoe overturned and its inexpert rowers were trapped in a whirlpool near Kinshasa. Malaria kept him in bed in his small cabin with attacks of fever, without the strength to stand. There he learned that the previous captain of *Le roi des Belges* had been shot dead by arrows in a dispute with the natives of a village. Another official of the Société Anonyme pour le Commerce du Haut-Congo, whom Konrad had gone to pick up in a remote settlement where he was harvesting ivory and rubber, died of an unknown disease in the course of the voyage. But the physical misfortunes that had plagued him were not what had so disturbed the Pole.

"It's the moral corruption, the corruption of the soul that

invades everything in this country," he repeated in a hollow, gloomy voice, as if horrified by an apocalyptic vision.

"I tried to prepare you when we first met," Roger reminded him. "I'm sorry I wasn't more explicit about what you were going to find on the Upper Congo."

What had affected him so deeply? Discovering that very primitive practices like cannibalism were still current in some communities? That among the tribes and in commercial posts, slaves were still circulating who changed masters for a few francs? That the supposed liberators subjected the Congolese to even crueler forms of oppression and servitude? Had he been overwhelmed by the sight of the natives' backs cut by the lash of the *chicote*? Did he see for the first time in his life a white flog a black until his body had been transformed into a crossword puzzle of wounds? He didn't ask for details, but the captain of *Le roi des Belges* had undoubtedly been witness to terrible things when he waived his three-year contract in order to return as soon as possible to England. Further, he told Roger that in Leopoldville–Kinshasa, on his return from Stanley Falls, he'd had a violent argument with the director of the Société Anonyme pour le Commerce du Haut-Congo, Camille Delcommune, whom he called a "savage in a vest and hat." Now he wanted to return to civilization, which for him meant England.

"Have you read *Heart of Darkness?*" Roger asked Alice. "Do you think that vision of human beings is fair?"

"I assume it isn't," replied the historian. "We discussed it a great deal one Tuesday, after it came out. That novel is a parable according to which Africa turns the civilized Europeans who go there into barbarians. Your *Congo Report* showed the opposite. That we Europeans were the ones who brought the worst barbarities there. Besides, you were in Africa for twenty years without becoming a savage. In fact, you came back more civilized than when you left here believing in the virtues of colonialism and the Empire."

"Conrad said that in the Congo, the moral corruption of human beings rose to the surface, in whites as well as blacks. *Heart of Darkness* often kept me awake. I don't think it describes the Congo, or reality, or history, but hell. The Congo is a pretext for expressing the awful vision that certain Catholics have of absolute evil."

"I'm sorry to interrupt," said the guard, turning toward them. "It's been fifteen minutes and the visitor's permit was for ten. You'll have to say goodbye."

Roger extended his hand to Alice, but to his surprise, she opened her arms. She gave him a warm embrace. "We'll keep doing everything, everything, to save your life, Roger," she whispered in his ear. He thought: *For Alice to permit herself this much effusiveness, she must be convinced the petition will be rejected.*

As he returned to his cell, he felt sad. Would he see Alice Stopford Green again? She represented so much to him! No one embodied as much as she did his passion for Ireland, the last of his passions, the most intense, the most recalcitrant, a passion that had consumed him and probably would send him to his death. "I don't regret it," he repeated to himself. The many centuries of oppression had caused so much pain in Ireland, so much injustice, that it was worth having sacrificed himself to this noble cause. No doubt he had failed. The plan so carefully structured to accelerate the emancipation of Ireland by associating her struggle with Germany did not work out as he had foreseen. And he wasn't able to stop the rebellion. And now Sean McDermott, Patrick Pearse, Éamonn Ceannt, Tom Clarke, Joseph Plunkett and so many others had been shot. Hundreds of comrades would rot in prison, God only knew for how many years. At least his example remained, as a weakened Joseph Plunkett said with fierce determination in Berlin. An example of devotion, of love, of sacrifice for a cause similar to the one that made him fight against Leopold II in the Congo, against Julio C. Arana and the Putumayo rubber planters in Amazonia. The cause of justice, of the helpless against the abuses of the powerful and the despotic. Would the campaign calling him a degenerate and a traitor succeed in erasing all the rest? In the end, what difference did it make? The important things were being decided on high, the God who at last, after so much time, was beginning to commiserate with him, had the final word.

As he lay on the cot on his back, his eyes closed, Joseph Conrad came to mind again. Would he have felt better if the former sailor had signed the petition? Maybe yes, maybe no. What had he meant that night, in his house in Kent, when he declared: "Before I went to the Congo, I was nothing more than a poor animal?" The phrase had made an impression on Roger, though he didn't understand it entirely. What did it mean? Perhaps that what he did, failed to do, saw, and heard in those six months on the Middle and Upper Congo had wakened more profound and transcendent concerns regarding the human condition, original sin, evil, and history. Roger could understand that very well. The Congo had humanized him as well, if being human meant knowing the extremes that could be reached by greed, avarice, prejudice, and cruelty. That's what moral corruption was: something that did not exist in animals but belonged exclusively to humans. The Congo had revealed to him that those things were part of life. It had opened his eyes, "deflowered" him as well as the Pole. Then he thought that he had arrived in Africa, at the age of twenty, still a virgin. Wasn't it unjust that the press, as the sheriff of Pentonville Prison had told him, accused only him, among the vast human species, of being scum?

To combat the demoralization that was overwhelming him, he tried to imagine the pleasure it would be to take a long bath in a tub, with a great deal of water and soap, holding another naked body against his.

6

He left Matadi on June 5, 1903, on the railroad constructed by Stanley and on which he had worked as a young man. For the two days of the slow journey to Leopoldville, he thought obsessively about an athletic feat of his youth: having been the first white to swim in the largest river along the caravan route between Manyanga and Stanley Pool: the Nkissi. He had already done it, with total unawareness, in smaller rivers along the Lower and Middle Congo, the Kwilo, the Lukungu, the Mpozo, and the Lunzadi, where there were also crocodiles, and nothing had happened to him. But the Nkissi was larger and more torrential, some one hundred meters wide, and filled with whirlpools due to the proximity of the great waterfall. The natives warned him it was imprudent, he could be swept away and smashed against the rocks. In fact, after a few strokes, Roger felt pulled by the legs and forced toward the middle of the river by contrary currents he could not get clear of in spite of energetic kicks and arm strokes. When he was losing his strength—he had already swallowed water—he managed to approach the bank by letting a wave knock him down. There he clutched at some rocks the best he could. When he climbed the slope he was covered with scrapes. His heart was pounding.

The trip he finally undertook lasted three months and ten days. Roger would think afterward that during this time his very being changed and he became another man, more lucid and realistic than he had been before, about the Congo, Africa, human beings, colonialism, Ireland, and life. But that experience also made him a man more given to unhappiness. For the rest of his life he would often say to himself, in moments of discouragement, that it would have been preferable not to have made the journey to the Middle and Upper Congo to verify how much truth lay in the accusations of abuses against the indigenous population in the rubber zones, made in London by certain churches and the journalist, Edmund D. Morel, who seemed to have devoted his life to criticizing Leopold II and the Congo Free State.

On the first section of the trip between Matadi and Leopoldville he was surprised at how empty the countryside was, that villages like Tumba, where he spent the night, and the ones scattered along the valleys of Nsele and Ndolo, which once teemed with people, were semi-deserted, with spectral old people shuffling their feet through clouds of dust or squatting against tree trunks, their eyes closed, as if dead or sleeping.

In those three months and ten days the impression of depopulation and the disappearance of people, the vanished villages and settlements where he had been, spent the night, done business fifteen or sixteen years earlier was repeated over and over again, like a nightmare, in all the regions along the Congo River and its tributaries, or in the interior, in the stops Roger made to collect the testimony of missionaries, functionaries, officers and soldiers of the Force Publique, and of natives whom he could question in Lingala, Kikongo, and Swahili, or in their languages making use of interpreters. Where were the people? Memory was not deceiving him. In his mind was the human effervescence, the flocks of children, women, tattooed men, with their filed incisors, necklaces of teeth, at times spears and masks, who had once surrounded him, examining and touching him. How was it possible that they had ceased to exist in so short a time? Some villages had been wiped out, in others the population had been reduced by half, by two-thirds, even by ninety per cent. In some places he could confirm precise numbers. Lukolela, for example, in 1884, when Roger visited that populous community for the first time, had more than five thousand inhabitants. Now there were just 352, most in a ruinous state because of age or disease, so that after his inspection, Roger concluded that only eighty-two survivors were still able to work. How had more than four thousand inhabitants of Lukolela gone up in smoke?

The explanations of the government agents, the employees of the companies harvesting rubber, the officers of the Force Publique were always the same: the blacks died like flies because of sleeping sickness, smallpox, typhus, colds, pneumonia, malarial fevers, and other plagues that, because of poor nutrition, decimated those organisms unprepared to resist disease. It was true, those epidemics were devastating. Sleeping sickness especially, carried by the tsetse fly, as had been discovered a few years earlier, which attacked the blood and brain and produced in its victims a paralysis of the limbs and a lethargy from which they never emerged. But at this point in his journey, Roger continued asking the reason for the depopulation of the Congo, not searching for an answer but to confirm that the lies he heard were slogans everyone repeated. He knew the answer very well. The plague that had vaporized a good part of the Congolese from the Middle and Upper Congo was greed, cruelty, rubber, an inhumane system, and the implacable exploitation of Africans by European colonists.

In Leopoldville he decided that to preserve his independence and not find himself coerced by the authorities, he would not use any form of official transport. With the authorization of the Foreign Office, he rented the *Henry Reed* and its crew from the American Baptist Missionary Union. The negotiation was slow, as was the gathering of wood and provisions for the journey. His stay in Leopoldville–Kinshasa had to be extended from June 6 to July 2, when they set sail upriver. The delay was a good idea. The freedom it gave him to travel in his own boat, to drop anchor where he wished, allowed him to verify things he never would have discovered if he had been subject to colonial institutions. And he never could have had so many dialogues with the Africans themselves, who dared approach him only when they determined he was not accompanied by any Belgian military or civil authority.

Leopoldville had grown a great deal since the last time Roger was there six or seven years earlier. It was filled with houses, warehouses, missions, offices, courts, customs offices, inspectors, judges, accountants, officers and soldiers, shops, and markets. There were priests and ministers everywhere. Something in the growing city displeased him from the very beginning. He was not received badly. From the governor to the police chief, including the judges and inspectors whom he went to greet, and the Protestant ministers and Catholic missionaries he visited, everyone met him with cordiality. They all were willing to give him the information he asked for, even though it might be, as he would confirm in the following weeks, evasive or shamelessly false. He felt that something hostile and oppressive filled the air and the profile the city was acquiring. On the other hand, Brazzaville, the neighboring capital of the French Congo that stood on the opposite bank of the river, which he visited a few times, made a much less oppressive, even a pleasant, impression on him, perhaps because of its open, well designed streets and the good humor of its people. In it he did not detect the secretly ominous atmosphere of Leopoldville. In the almost four weeks he spent there, negotiating the rental of the *Henry Reed*, he obtained a good many facts but always with the feeling that no one was getting to the bottom of things, that even people with the best intentions were hiding something from him and from themselves, fearful of confronting a terrible, accusatory truth.

Herbert Ward would tell him afterward that it was all pure prejudice, that the things he saw and heard in subsequent weeks retroactively muddied his memory of Leopoldville. If not for this, his memory would retain more than negative images of his stay in the city founded by Henry Morton Stanley in 1881. One morning, following a long walk to take advantage of the cool part of the day, Roger went as far as the wharf. There, suddenly, his attention focused on two dark, half-naked boys unloading some launches and singing. They looked very young. They wore light loincloths not long enough to hide the shape of their buttocks. Both were slim, supple, and with the rhythmic movements they made unloading the bundles, they gave an impression of health, harmony, and beauty. He watched them for a long time. He regretted not having his camera with him. He would have liked to take their picture in order to recall afterward that not everything was ugly and sordid in the emerging city of Leopoldville.

When, on July 2, 1903, the *Henry Reed* weighed anchor and crossed the smooth, enormous, fluvial lagoon of Stanley Pool, Roger was moved: on the French shore, on a clear morning, the sand escarpments were visible, which reminded him of the white cliffs of Dover. Ibises with huge wings flew over the lagoon, elegant and proud, brilliant in the sun. The beauty of the landscape remained invariable for a good part of the day. From time to time the interpreters, porters, and trail cutters pointed excitedly at the tracks in the mud of elephants, hippopotamuses, buffaloes, and antelope. John, his bulldog, happy on the journey, ran back and forth along the wharf, suddenly barking noisily. But when he reached Chumbiri, where they docked to pick up wood, John's mood changed abruptly, the dog became enraged, and in a few seconds he managed to bite a pig, a goat, and the watchman of the garden the ministers of the Baptist Missionary Society had next to their small mission. Roger had to indemnify them with gifts.

After the second day, they began to pass small steamboats and launches loaded with baskets filled with rubber being carried down the Congo River to Leopoldville. This sight would accompany them for the rest of the excursion, as would, from time to time, glimpses through the branches along the banks of telegraph poles under construction and the roofs of villages from which the inhabitants fled into the jungle when they saw them approaching. From then on, when Roger wanted to question the natives in some settlement, he chose to send an interpreter first to explain to the residents that the British consul had come alone, with no Belgian official, to find out about the problems and needs they were facing.

On the third day, in Bolobo, where there was also a mission of the Baptist Missionary Society, he had the first foretaste of what was waiting for him. In the group of Baptist missionaries, the one who impressed him most for her energy, intelligence, and likability was Dr. Lily de Hailes. Tall, tireless, ascetic, talkative, she had been in the Congo for fourteen years, spoke several indigenous languages, and directed the hospital for natives with as much dedication as efficiency. The site was crowded. As they walked past the hammocks, cots, and mats where the patients were lying, Roger asked intentionally why there were so many victims of wounds on the buttocks, legs, and back. Dr. de Hailes looked at him indulgently.

"They're victims of a plague called *chicote*, Mr. Consul. A beast more bloodthirsty than the lion and the cobra. Aren't there *chicotes* in Boma and Matadi?"

"They're not applied as liberally as here."

As a young woman, Dr. de Hailes must have had a great head of red hair, but as the years passed it had turned gray, and she had left only a few flaming locks that escaped the kerchief she used to cover her head. The sun had darkened her bony face, her neck and arms, but her greenish eyes were still young and lively, with an indomitable faith sparkling in them.

"And if you want to know why there are so many

Congolese with bandages on their hands and private parts, I can explain that to you as well," Lily de Hailes added defiantly. "Because the soldiers of the Force Publique cut their hands and penises or crushed them with machetes. Don't forget to put that in your report. They're things that aren't usually said in Europe when they talk about the Congo."

That afternoon, after spending several hours talking through interpreters with the wounded and sick in the Bolobo hospital, Roger could not eat supper. He felt guilty toward the ministers in the mission, among them Dr. de Hailes, who had roasted a chicken in his honor. He excused himself, saying he didn't feel well. He was certain that if he tasted even a single mouthful, he would vomit on his hosts.

"If what you have seen has upset you, perhaps it isn't prudent for you to interview Captain Massard," advised the head of the mission. "Listening to him is a good experience, I would say, for strong stomachs."

"That's why I've come to the Middle Congo, my friends."

Captain Pierre Massard, of the Force Publique, was not stationed in Bolobo but in Mbongo, where there was a garrison and training camp for the Africans who would be soldiers in the force charged with maintaining order and security. He was on an inspection tour and had set up a small campaign tent near the mission. The ministers invited him to speak with the consul, warning Roger that the officer was famous for his irascible character. The natives had nicknamed him Malu Malu, and one of the sinister deeds attributed to him was having killed three intractable Africans, whom he had placed in a row, with a single shot.

It wasn't prudent to provoke him because he was capable of anything.

He was a powerful, rather short man, with a square face, hair cut very close, nicotine-stained teeth, and an icy little smile. He had small, somewhat slanted eyes, and a high-pitched, almost feminine voice. The ministers had prepared a table with cassava pastries and mango juice. They didn't drink alcohol but had no objection to Casement bringing a bottle of brandy and another of claret from the *Henry Reed.* The captain ceremoniously shook hands with everyone and greeted Roger by making a baroque bow, calling him "*son excellence, Monsieur le Consul.*" They toasted, drank, and lit cigarettes.

"If you'll permit me, Captain Massard, I'd like to ask you a question," said Roger.

"How well you speak French, *Monsieur le Consul.* Where did you learn it?"

"I began to study it when I was young, in England. But above all here, in the Congo, where I've been for many years. I imagine I speak it with a Belgian accent."

"Ask me all the questions you wish," said Massard, taking another drink. "Your brandy is excellent, by the way."

The four Baptist ministers were there, still and silent, as if petrified. They were North Americans, two young men and two old. Dr. de Hailes had gone to the hospital. Night began to fall and the buzz of nocturnal insects could already be heard. To chase away mosquitoes, they had lit a fire that crackled gently and smoked at times.

"I'm going to tell you with utter frankness, Captain Massard," said Roger, not raising his voice, very slowly. "I think the crushed hands and cut-off penises that I've seen in the Bolobo hospital are unacceptable savagery."

"They are, of course they are," the officer admitted immediately, with an expression of disgust. "And something worse than that, *Monsieur le Consul*: a waste. Those mutilated men won't be able to work any more, or they'll do it badly, and their yield will be minimal. With the lack of labor we have here, it's a real crime. Bring me the soldiers who cut off those hands and penises and I'll thrash their backs until there's no blood left in their veins."

He sighed, overwhelmed by the degrees of imbecility the world suffered from. He took another sip of brandy and inhaled his cigarette deeply.

"Do the laws or regulations permit the mutilation of indigenous people?" asked Roger.

Captain Massard guffawed, and when he laughed his square face rounded and comic dimples appeared.

"They prohibit it categorically," he declared, waving away something in the air. "Make those two-legged animals understand what laws and regulations are. Don't you know them? If you've spent so many years in the Congo, you must. It's easier to make a hyena or a tick understand things than a Congolese."

He laughed again, but then immediately became enraged. Now his expression was hard and his slanted little eyes had almost disappeared beneath swollen lids.

"I'm going to explain to you what happens, and then you'll understand," he added, sighing, fatigued in advance at having to explain things as obvious as the world being round. "Everything stems from a very simple concern," he said, waving away his winged enemy with greater fury. "The Force Publique cannot waste munitions. We cannot permit the soldiers to squander the bullets we distribute killing monkeys, snakes, and other revolting animals they like to stick in their bellies, sometimes raw. During training they are taught that munitions can only be used in self-defense, when officers order them to. But it's hard for these blacks to follow orders, no matter how many *chicote* lashes they receive. That's why the decree was issued. Do you understand, *Monsieur le Consul*?"

"No, I don't understand, Captain," said Roger. "What decree is that?"

"That each time they fire they cut off the hand or penis of the man they shot," the captain explained. "To confirm that bullets are not being wasted on hunting. A sensible way to avoid wasting ammunition, isn't that so?"

He sighed again and took another drink of brandy. He spat into the emptiness.

"But no, that isn't what happened." The captain complained immediately, enraged again. "Because these shits found a way to get around the decree. Can you guess how?"

"I have no idea," said Roger.

"Very simple. By cutting off the hands and penises of the living to make us think they've fired at people when they've shot monkeys, snakes, and the other filth they eat. Do you understand now why all those poor devils are there in the hospital without hands and pricks?"

He fell silent for a long while and drank the rest of the brandy in his glass. He seemed to become sad and even pouted.

"We do what we can, *Monsieur le Consul*," Captain Massard added sorrowfully. "It's not at all easy, I assure you.

Because in addition to being stupid, the savages are born falsifiers. They lie, deceive, lack feelings and principles. Not even fear opens their minds. I assure you that the punishments in the Force Publique for those who cut off the hands and pricks of the living to deceive and continue to hunt with ammunition given to them by the state are very severe. Visit our posts and see for yourself, *Monsieur le Consul*."

The conversation with Captain Massard lasted as long as the fire throwing off sparks at their feet, two hours at least. When they said goodbye, the four Baptist ministers had gone to bed some time earlier. The officer and the consul had drunk the brandy and the claret. They were somewhat tipsy, but Roger was still lucid. Months or years later he could have recounted in detail the brusque remarks and confessions he heard and the way Captain Pierre Massard's square face became congested with alcohol. In the following weeks he would have many other conversations with officers of the Force Publique, Belgian, Italian, French, and German, and would hear terrible things from their mouths, but what would always stand out in his memory as the most thought-provoking, a symbol of Congolese reality, was the chat at night in Bolobo with Captain Massard. After a certain point the officer became sentimental. He confessed to Roger how much he missed his wife. He hadn't seen her for two years and received few letters from her. Perhaps she had stopped loving him. Perhaps she had taken a lover. It wasn't surprising. It happened to many officers and functionaries who, to serve Belgium and His Majesty the King, buried themselves in this hell, to contract diseases, be bitten by snakes, live without the most basic comforts. And for what? To earn miserable salaries that barely allowed them to save. And afterward, in Belgium, would anyone thank them for their sacrifice? On the contrary, in the mother country there was an unyielding prejudice against "colonials." The officers and functionaries who returned from the colony were discriminated against, kept at a distance, as if, after spending so much time with savages, they had become savages too.

When Captain Pierre Massard drifted to the topic of sex, Roger felt an anticipatory disgust and tried to say good night. But by now the officer was drunk, and in order not to offend him or have an altercation with him, he had to stay. In the meantime, enduring his nausea, he listened to him, telling himself he wasn't in Bolobo to dispense justice but to investigate and accumulate information. The more exact and complete his report, the more effective his contribution to the struggle against the institutionalized evil the Congo had become. Captain Massard felt compassion for those young lieutenants or non-commissioned officers from the Belgian army who came filled with illusions to teach these poor devils to be soldiers. And what about their sex lives? They had to leave behind in Europe their fiancées, wives, and mistresses. And what about here? Not even prostitutes worthy of the name in these godforsaken wastelands. Only some disgusting black women covered with insects, and you had to be very drunk to fuck them, running the risk of catching crabs, the clap, or a chancre. It was hard for him, for example. He couldn't perform, *nom de Dieu*! It had never happened to him in Europe. Him, Pierre Massard, impotent in bed!

It wasn't even a good idea to have a blowjob, because with those teeth so many black women were in the habit of filing down, they could give you a sudden bite and castrate you.

He grabbed his fly and began to laugh, making an obscene face. Taking advantage of the fact that Massard was still having a good time, Roger stood.

"I have to go, Captain. I have to leave very early tomorrow and I'd like to rest a little."

The captain shook his hand in a mechanical way but continued speaking, not getting up from his seat, his voice faint and his eyes glassy. When Roger walked away, he heard him at his back, muttering that choosing a military career had been the great mistake of his life, and for the rest of his life he would keep paying for it.

He set sail the next morning in the *Henry Reed* on his way to Lukolela. He spent three days there, speaking day and night with all kinds of people: functionaries, colonists, overseers, natives. Then he advanced to Ikoko, where he entered Lake Mantumba. Near it he found that enormous extension of land called the *Domaine de la Couronne*. Around it the principal private rubber companies operated, the Lulonga Company, the ABIR Company, and the Société Anversoise du Commerce au Congo, which had vast concessions throughout the region. He visited dozens of villages, some on the shores of the immense lake and others in the interior. To reach these it was necessary to shift to small canoes powered by oars or poles and walk for hours in dense undergrowth that was dark and damp, through which the natives cut a path with machetes and where he was often obliged to wade in water up to his waist over flooded terrain and pestilential quagmires amid clouds of mosquitoes and the silent shapes of bats. For all these weeks he resisted fatigue, natural difficulties, and inclement weather without flagging, in a feverish spiritual state, as if bewitched, because each day, each hour, he seemed to be sinking into deeper layers of suffering and evil. Would the hell Dante described in his *Divina Commedia* be like this? He hadn't read the book, and during this time he swore he would as soon as he could get his hands on a copy.

The indigenous people, who at the beginning of the trip ran away as soon as they saw the *Henry Reed* approach, believing the steamboat carried soldiers, soon began to come out to meet it and send emissaries so that he would visit their villages. Word had spread among the natives that the British consul was traveling the region to listen to their complaints and requests, and then they went to him with testimonies and stories, each one worse than the other. They believed he had the power to straighten everything that was crooked in the Congo. He explained the situation to them in vain. He had no power at all. He would report on these injustices and crimes and Great Britain and her allies would demand that the Belgian government put an end to the abuses and punish the torturers and criminals. That was all he could do. Did they understand? He wasn't even sure they were listening. They felt so pressed to speak, to recount the things that had happened to them, that they paid him no attention. They spoke in a rush, choking with despair and rage. The interpreters had to interrupt them, pleading with them to speak more slowly so they could do their job.

Roger listened, taking notes. Then, for nights on end he wrote on his cards and in his notebooks what he had heard so none of it would be lost. He barely ate. He was so tormented by the fear that all those papers he had scrawled on might be lost, that he didn't know where to hide them or what precautions to take. He chose to carry them with him, on the shoulders of a porter who had been ordered never to leave his side.

He barely slept, and when fatigue overwhelmed him, nightmares attacked, moving him from fear to stunned bewilderment, from satanic visions to a state of desolation and sadness in which everything lost its meaning and reason for being: his family, friends, ideas, country, feelings, and work. At those moments he longed more than ever for his friend Herbert Ward and his infectious enthusiasm for all of life's manifestations, an optimistic joy that nothing and no one could crush.

Afterward, when the journey ended and he wrote his report and left the Congo, and his twenty years in Africa were only a memory, Roger often said to himself that if there was a single word at the root of all the horrible things happening here, that word was greed. Greed for the black gold found in abundance in the Congolese jungles, to the misfortune of their people. That wealth was the curse that had befallen those unfortunate people, and if things continued in the same way, it would cause them to disappear from the face of the earth. He reached this conclusion during those three months and ten days: if the rubber was not consumed first, the Congolese would be the ones consumed by a system that was annihilating them by the hundreds of thousands.

During those weeks, after he entered the waters of Lake Mantumba, memories would be mixed like shuffled cards. If he had not kept a detailed record of dates, places, testimonies, and observations in his notebooks, all of it would be scrambled and out of order in his memory. He would close his eyes and in a dizzying whirlwind those ebony bodies would appear and reappear with reddish scars like snakes slicing across their backs, buttocks, and legs, the stumps of children and old people whose arms had been cut off, the emaciated, cadaverous faces that seemed to have had the life, fat, and muscles drained from them, leaving only the skin, the skull, and the fixed stare or grimace expressing, more than pain, an infinite stupefaction at everything they were suffering. And it was always the same, the same acts repeated over and over again in all the villages and settlements where Roger set foot with his notebooks, pencils, and camera.

The point of departure was simple and clear. Certain precise obligations had been fixed for each village: delivering weekly or semi-monthly quotas of food—cassava, fowl, antelope meat, wild pigs, goats, or ducks—to feed the garrison of the Force Publique and the laborers who opened roads, installed telegraph poles, and constructed piers and storehouses. Moreover, the village had to deliver a fixed quantity of rubber harvested in baskets woven of vines by the natives themselves. The punishments for not fulfilling these obligations varied. For delivering less than the established quantities of foodstuffs or rubber, the penalty was lashing with the *chicote*, never less than twenty strokes and sometimes as many as fifty or one hundred. Many of those punished bled to death. The indigenous people who fled—very few of them—sacrificed their families because in those cases, their wives were kept as hostages in the *maisons d'otages* that the Force Publique had in all its garrisons. There, the wives of fugitives were whipped, condemned to the torments of hunger and thirst, and at times subjected to tortures as evil-minded as being forced to eat their own or their guards' excrement.

Not even the orders issued by the colonial power—both private companies and the king's holdings—were respected. Everywhere the system was violated and made worse by the soldiers and officers charged with making it function, because in each village the military men and government agents increased the quotas in order to keep for themselves a part of the food and some baskets of rubber, reselling them in small transactions.

In all the villages Roger visited, the complaints of the chiefs were identical: if all the men dedicated themselves to harvesting rubber, how could they go out to hunt and cultivate cassava and other foods to feed the authorities, the bosses, the guards, and the laborers? Besides, the rubber trees were giving out, which obliged the harvesters to go deeper and deeper into unknown, inhospitable regions where many had been attacked by leopards, lions, and snakes. It wasn't possible to satisfy all these demands no matter how they tried.

On September 1, 1903, Roger turned thirty-nine years old. They were navigating the Lopori River. The night before they had left the settlement of Isi Isulo in the hills surrounding Bongandanga Mountain. This birthday would remain permanently etched in his memory, as if on that day God or perhaps the devil wanted to prove there were no limits in matters of human cruelty, that it was always possible to go further in devising ways to inflict torment on another human being.

The day dawned cloudy with the threat of a storm, but the rain didn't come and all morning the atmosphere was charged with electricity. Roger was about to have breakfast when Father Hutot, a Trappist monk from the mission the order had in the area of Coquilhatville, came to the improvised dock where the *Henry Reed* was anchored. He was tall and thin, like an El Greco figure, with a long gray beard and eyes where something stirred that could have been anger, fright, astonishment, or all three at once.

"I know what you're doing in these lands, Consul," he said, extending a skeletal hand to Roger. He spoke French rushed by an imperative urgency. "I beg you to accompany me to the village of Walla. It's only an hour or an hour and a half from here. You have to see it with your own eyes."

He spoke as if he had the fever and tremors of malaria.

"Fine, *mon père*," Roger agreed. "But first sit down, let's have coffee and something to eat."

While they ate, Father Hutot explained to the consul that the Trappists at the mission in Coquilhatville had permission from the order to break the strict cloistered regime that rules elsewhere in order to give aid to the natives, "who need it so much in this land where Beelzebub seems to be winning the struggle with the Lord."

Not only the monk's voice trembled but also his eyes, his hands, his spirit. He blinked unceasingly, wore a coarse tunic that was stained and wet, and on his feet, covered with mud and scratches, were strapped sandals. Father Hutot had been in the Congo for some ten years. For the past eight he had traveled periodically to the villages in the region, climbed to the top of Bongandanga, and seen at close range a leopard that, instead of jumping him, moved off the path, waving its tail. He spoke indigenous languages and had gained the confidence of the natives, especially those from Walla, "those martyrs."

They started out on a narrow trail between the branches of tall trees, intercepted from time to time by narrow streams. The song of invisible birds could be heard, and at times a flock of parrots flew screeching over their heads. Roger noticed that the monk walked through the jungle with assurance, not tripping, as if he had long experience of these treks through the undergrowth. Father Hutot explained to him what had happened in Walla. Since the village, already very reduced, could not deliver in full the last quota of food, rubber, and wood, or give over the number of laborers the authorities demanded, a detachment of thirty soldiers from the Force Publique, under the command of Lieutenant Tanville, came from the garrison at Coquilhatville. When they saw them approach, the entire village fled to the forest. But the interpreters followed and assured them they could return. Nothing would happen to them, Lieutenant Tanville wanted only to explain the new directives and negotiate with the village. The chief ordered them to return. As soon as they did, the soldiers fell on them. Men and women were tied to the trees and whipped. A pregnant woman who tried to move away to urinate was shot to death by a soldier, who believed she was fleeing. Another ten women were taken to the *maison d'otages* in Coquilhatville as hostages. Lieutenant Tanville gave Walla a week to fulfill their quota or those ten women would be shot and the village burned.

When Father Hutot arrived in Walla a few days later, he encountered a hideous sight. In order to fulfill the quotas they owed, the families in the village had sold their sons and daughters, and two of the men their wives, to traveling merchants who practiced the slave trade behind the backs of the authorities. The Trappist believed the children and women sold numbered at least eight, but perhaps there were more. The natives were terrified. They had gone to buy rubber and food to satisfy the debt, but it wasn't certain the money from the sale would be enough.

"Can you believe things like that happen in this world, Consul?"

"Yes, *mon père.* Now I believe everything evil and terrible that people tell me. If I've learned anything in the Congo it's that there's no bloodthirsty animal worse than the human being."

I didn't see anyone cry in Walla, Roger would think afterward. And he didn't hear anyone complain. The village seemed inhabited by automata, ghostly beings who walked back and forth among the thirty or so huts made of wooden sticks with conical roofs of palm leaves, disoriented, not knowing where to go, having forgotten who they were, where they were, as if a curse had fallen on the village, transforming its inhabitants into phantoms. But phantoms with backs and buttocks covered in fresh scars, some with traces of blood as if the wounds were still open.

With the help of Father Hutot, who spoke the tribe's language fluently, Roger carried out his work. He questioned each and every one of the villagers, listening to them repeat what he had already heard and would often hear afterward. Here too, in Walla, he was surprised that none of those poor creatures complained about the main thing: with what right the foreigners had come to invade, exploit, and mistreat them. They took into consideration only the immediate problem: the quotas. They were excessive, there was no human force that could gather so much rubber, so much food, give up so many laborers. They didn't even complain about the beatings and the hostages. They asked only that their quotas be lowered a little so they could fulfill them and in this way keep the authorities happy with the people of Walla.

Roger spent the night in the village. The following day, his notebooks filled with notes and testimonies, he said goodbye to Father Hutot. He had decided to change his planned trajectory. He returned to Lake Mantumba, boarded the *Henry Reed*, and headed for Coquilhatville. It was a large village, with irregular dirt streets, dwellings scattered among groves of palm trees, and small cultivated fields. As soon as he disembarked, he went to the garrison of the Force Publique, a vast space of rough buildings and a stockade of yellow slats.

Lieutenant Tanville had gone out on an assignment, but Roger was received by Captain Marcel Junieux, the head of the garrison and the man responsible for all the stations and posts of the Force Publique in the region. He was in his forties, tall, slim, muscular, his skin bronzed by the sun and his hair, already gray, cut close to the scalp. He had a little medal of the Virgin hanging around his neck and the tattoo of a small animal on his forearm. He led him to a crude office that had some banners and a photograph of Leopold II in parade uniform on the walls. He offered him a cup of coffee and had him sit at a small worktable covered with notebooks, regulations, maps, and pencils, on a very fragile chair that seemed about to collapse at each movement Roger made. The captain had spent his childhood in England, where his father had a business, and spoke good English. He was a career officer who had volunteered to come to the Congo five years earlier "to serve my country, Consul." He said this with acid irony.

He was about to be promoted and return to the mother country. He listened to Roger without once interrupting him, very serious and, it seemed, deeply focused on what he was hearing. His grave, impenetrable expression did not alter at any detail. Roger was precise and meticulous. He made very clear what he had been told and what he had seen with his own eyes: the scarred backs and buttocks, the testimonies of those who had sold their children to fulfill the quotas they hadn't been able to satisfy. He explained that His Majesty's government would be informed of these horrors, but he also believed it was his duty, in the name of the government he represented, to lodge his protest against the Force Publique that was responsible for abuses as outrageous as those committed in Walla. He was an eye witness to the fact that the village had been turned into a small hell. When he finished speaking, Captain Junieux's face did not change. He waited some time, in silence. Finally, moving his head slightly, he said quietly, "As you no doubt know, Consul, we, I mean the Force Publique, do not issue the laws. We simply see that they are carried out."

His gaze was clear and direct, with no trace of discomfort or irritation.

"I know the laws and regulations that govern the Congo Free State, Captain. Nothing in them authorizes you to mutilate the natives, to whip them until they bleed to death, to keep the women hostage so their husbands don't run away, to extort the villages to the extreme that mothers have to sell their children to deliver the quotas of food and rubber you demand of them."

"We?" Captain Junieux exaggerated his surprise. He shook his head and as he moved, the little tattooed animal moved. "We demand nothing of anyone. We receive orders and carry them out, that's all. The Force Publique does not set the quotas, Mr. Casement. The political authorities and the directors of the concessionaire companies set them. We are the executors of a policy in which we have not intervened in the slightest. No one ever asked for our opinion. If they had, perhaps things would go better."

He stopped speaking and seemed distracted for a moment. Through the large windows with metal screens, Roger saw a rectangular treeless clearing where a formation of African soldiers were marching, wearing drill trousers, theirs torsos and feet bare. They changed direction at the command of a sergeant major wearing boots, a uniform shirt, and a kepi.

"I'll investigate. If Lieutenant Tanville has committed or facilitated extortion, he will be punished," said the captain. "The soldiers too, of course, if they were excessive in the use of the *chicote*. This is all I can promise you. The rest is beyond my authority; it is a legal question. Changing this system is not the task of the military but of judges and politicians. Of the Supreme Government. You know that too, I imagine."

Suddenly a slight inflection of discouragement had appeared in his voice.

"There's nothing I'd like better than for the system to change. I'm disgusted too by what happens here. What we're obliged to do offends my principles," and he touched the medal around his neck. "My faith. I'm a very Catholic man. Over there, in Europe, I always tried to act according to my beliefs. That isn't possible here in the Congo, Consul. That's the sad truth. That's why I'm very happy to return to Belgium. I won't be the one to set foot in Africa again, I assure you."

Captain Junieux got up from his table and walked to one of the windows. Turning his back on the consul, he was silent for a long time, observing the recruits who never learned the rhythm of the march, who tripped, whose lines in their formation were crooked.

"If that's the case, you could do something to put an end to these crimes," Roger murmured. "This isn't why we Europeans came to Africa."

"Ah, isn't it?" Captain Junieux turned to look at him and the consul saw that the officer had paled somewhat. "What have we come for, then? I know: to bring civilization, Christianity, and free commerce. Do you still believe that, Mr. Casement?"

"Not any more," Roger replied immediately. "Though I did believe it before. With all my heart. I believed it for many years, with all the ingenuousness of the idealistic boy I once was. That Europe came to Africa to save lives and souls, to civilize the savages. Now I know I was wrong."

Captain Junieux's expression changed, and it seemed to

Roger that suddenly the officer's face had traded the hieratic mask for a more human one that even looked at him with the pitying sympathy idiots deserve.

"I'm trying to redeem that sin of my youth, Captain. That's why I've come to Coquilhatville. That's why I'm documenting, as fully as I can, the abuses committed here in the name of so-called civilization."

"I wish you success, Consul." Captain Junieux mocked him with a smile. "But if you'll allow me to speak frankly, I'm afraid you won't have any. There's no human power that can change this system. It's too late for that."

"If you don't mind, I'd like to visit the jail and the *maison d'otages* where you have the women brought here from Walla," said Roger, abruptly changing the topic.

"You can visit anything you like," the officer agreed. "Make yourself at home. But permit me to remind you again of what I said. We aren't the ones who invented the Congo Free State. We only make it function. That is, we're victims too."

The jail was a hut of wood and brick, with no windows and a single entrance, guarded by two native soldiers with shotguns. There were a dozen half-naked men, some very old, lying on the ground. What he found most shocking wasn't the abject or inexpressive faces of those silent skeletons whose eyes followed him back and forth as he walked around the hut, but the reek of urine and excrement.

"We've tried to teach them to take care of their business in those buckets." He read the captain's mind as he pointed at a receptacle. "But they're not used to that. They prefer the ground. They don't care about the stink. It's their problem. Maybe they don't smell it."

The *maison d'otages* was smaller but the spectacle was more dramatic because it was so crowded Roger could barely circulate among those packed-together, half-naked bodies. The space was so tight that many women could not sit or lie down but had to remain standing.

"This is exceptional," said Captain Junieux, gesturing. "There are never so many. Tonight, so they can sleep, we'll move half of them to one of the soldiers' barracks."

Here too the stink of urine and excrement was compelling. Some women were very young, almost girls. They all had the same gaze—lost, somnambulistic, beyond life—which Roger would see in so many Congolese women during this journey. One of the hostages had a newborn in her arms, so still it seemed dead.

"What criterion do you follow for letting them go?" the consul asked.

"I don't decide that, sir, a magistrate does. There are three in Coquilhatville. There is only one criterion: when the husbands turn in the quotas they're supposed to, they can take their wives away."

"And if they don't?"

The captain shrugged.

"Some manage to escape," he said, not looking at him and lowering his voice. "The soldiers take others and make them their wives. Those are the luckiest. Some go mad and kill themselves. Others die of sorrow, rage, and hunger. As you've seen, they have almost nothing to eat. That isn't our fault either. I don't receive enough supplies to feed the soldiers. Even less for the prisoners. Sometimes we take up small collections among the officers to improve the rations. That's how things are. I'm the first to regret it isn't different. If you succeed in improving this, the Force Publique will thank you."

Roger went to visit the three Belgian magistrates in Coquilhatville, but only one received him. The other two invented pretexts for avoiding him. Maître Duval, on the other hand, a plump, self-satisfied man in his fifties who, in spite of the tropical heat, wore a vest, false shirt cuffs, and a frock coat with a watch chain, led him to his stripped-down office, and offered him a cup of tea. He listened politely, sweating profusely. He wiped his face from time to time with a handkerchief that was already wet. At times he made disapproving movements of his head and wore an afflicted expression because of what the consul was saying. When Roger finished, he asked him to detail everything in writing. In that way he would be able to file with the court of which he formed part a requisitory to open a formal investigation into these lamentable episodes. Though perhaps, Maître Duval rectified, with a reflective finger on his chin, it would be preferable if the consul would file that report with the Superior Court, established now in Leopoldville. Because it was a higher, more influential court, it could act more efficiently throughout the colony. Not only remedying this state of things, but at the same time indemnifying with economic compensation the families of the victims and the victims themselves. Roger told him he would. He said goodbye, convinced that Maître Duval would not lift a finger and neither would the Superior Court in Leopoldville. But even so, he would file the brief.

At dusk, when he was about to leave, a native came to tell him the monks at the Trappist mission wanted to see him. There he saw Father Hutot again. The monks—there were half a dozen—wanted to ask him to secretly carry away on his steamboat a handful of fugitives they had been hiding in the monastery for some days. They were all from the village of Bonginda, up the Congo River, where, on account of not fulfilling their quotas of rubber, the Force Publique had carried out a punishing action as severe as the one in Walla.

The Trappist mission in Coquilhatville was a large two-story house of clay, stones, and wood, which looked like a small fort from the outside. The windows were closed up. The abbot, Dom Jesualdo, of Portuguese origin, was very old, as were another two monks, emaciated and almost lost in their white tunics, with black scapulars and crude leather belts. Only the oldest were monks, the others were lay brothers. All of them, like Father Hutot, displayed the semi-skeletal thinness that was like the emblem of the Trappists here. Inside, the building was bright, for only the chapel, the refectory, and the monks' dormitory had roofs. There was a garden, an orchard, a yard with fowl, a cemetery, and a kitchen with a large stove.

"What crime have these people committed that you ask me to take them away in secret from the authorities?"

"Being poor, Consul," said Dom Jesualdo, sorrowfully. "You know that very well. You've just seen in Walla what it means to be poor, humble, and Congolese."

Roger agreed. Surely it was an act of mercy to give the help the Trappists had requested. But he hesitated. As a diplomat, secretly spiriting away fugitives from justice, even if persecuted for unjust reasons, was risky. It could compromise Great Britain and completely taint the informative mission he was carrying out for the Foreign Office.

"May I see and speak to them?"

Dom Jesualdo agreed. Father Hutot withdrew and returned with the group almost immediately. There were seven, all male, including three boys. They all had their left hands cut off or maimed by blows from a rifle butt, and traces of lashes from a *chicote* on their chests and backs. The head of the group was named Mansunda and wore a crest of feathers and necklaces of animal teeth; his face displayed old scars from the initiation rites of his tribe. Father Hutot acted as interpreter. Twice in a row the village of Bonginda had not fulfilled its deliveries of rubber—the trees in the area had run out of latex—to the emissaries of the Lulonga Company, the concessionary in the region. Then the African guards brought to the village by the Force Publique began to whip them and cut off hands and feet. There was an outburst of rage and the village rebelled and killed a guard while the others managed to run away. A few days later the village of Bonginda was occupied by a column of the Force Publique that set fire to all the houses, killed a good number of the residents, men and women, burning some inside their huts and taking the rest to the jail in Coquilhatville and the *maison d'otages*. Chief Mansunda believed they were the only ones who had escaped, thanks to the Trappists. If the Force Publique captured them they would be victims of extreme punishment, like all the rest, because throughout the Congo rebellion by the natives was always punished by the extermination of the entire community.

"Fine, *mon père*," said Roger. "I'll take them with me on

the *Henry Reed* until they're away from here. But only to the closest French shore."

"God will reward you, Consul," said Father Hutot.

"I don't know, *mon père*," replied the consul. "In this case you and I are breaking the law."

"Man's law," the Trappist corrected him. "We are violating it, and rightly so, in order to be faithful to God's law."

Roger shared the monks' frugal vegetarian supper. He spoke with them for a long time. Dom Jesualdo joked that in his honor the Trappists were violating the rule of silence that governed the order. Monks and lay brothers seemed oppressed and defeated by this country, just as he was. How could it have come to this, he reflected aloud with them. And he told them that nineteen years earlier he had come to Africa filled with enthusiasm, convinced the colonial enterprise was going to bring a decent life to the Africans. How was it possible that colonization had become this horrible plundering, this dizzying cruelty, with people who called themselves Christians torturing, mutilating, killing defenseless creatures and subjecting them, even children and the old, to atrocious cruelties? Hadn't we Europeans come here to put an end to the slave trade and bring the religion of charity and justice? Because what occurred here was even worse than the slave trade, wasn't it?

The monks let him unburden himself, not saying a word. Was it because, in spite of what the abbot said, they didn't want to break the rule of silence? No: they were as confused and wounded by the Congo as he was.

"God's ways are inscrutable to poor sinners like us, Consul," Dom Jesualdo said with a sigh. "The important thing is not to fall into despair. Not to lose faith. That there are men here like you encourages us, returns hope to us. We wish you success in your mission. We will pray that God permits you to do something for these unfortunate people."

The seven fugitives boarded the *Henry Reed* at dawn the next day, at a bend in the river, when the steamboat was already some distance from Coquilhatville. For the three days they were with him, Roger was tense and anxious. He had given the crew a vague explanation to justify the presence of the seven mutilated natives and thought the men distrusted and looked with suspicion at the group, with whom they had no communication. At Irebu, the *Henry Reed* approached the French side of the Congo River and that night, while the crew slept, seven silent silhouettes slipped away and disappeared into the undergrowth on the bank. Afterward no one asked the consul what had become of them.

At this point in his journey, Roger began to feel ill. Not only morally and psychologically, but his body too was showing the effects of lack of sleep, insect bites, excessive physical effort, and perhaps, above all, his state of mind as rage alternated with demoralization, the desire to complete his work with the premonition that his report would do no good because in London the bureaucrats in the Foreign Office and the politicians in His Majesty's service would decide it was imprudent to antagonize an ally like Leopold II, that publishing a report with such serious accusations would have detrimental consequences for Great Britain, since it would be equivalent to pushing Belgium into the arms of Germany. Weren't the interests of the Empire more important than the plaintive laments of some half-naked savages who worshiped felines and serpents and were cannibals?

Making superhuman efforts to control the squalls of depression, the headaches and nausea, the deterioration of his body—he felt he was losing weight because he had to make new holes in his belt—he continued visiting villages, posts, stations, questioning villagers, functionaries, employees, guards, rubber harvesters, doing his best to overcome the daily spectacle of bodies martyrized by whippings, hands chopped off, and nightmarish accounts of murders, imprisonments, extortions, and disappearances. He began to think the generalized suffering of the Congolese had saturated the air, the river, the vegetation around him with a particular odor, a stench that not only was physical but also spiritual, metaphysical.

"I believe I'm losing my mind, dear Gee," he wrote to his cousin Gertrude from the station at Bongandanga on the day he decided to turn around halfway and return to Leopoldville. "Today I've begun my return to Boma. According to my plans, I should have continued on the Upper Congo for a few more weeks. But the truth is I already have more than enough material to show the things that occur here in my report. I'm afraid if I continue to scrutinize the extremes to which human evil and ignorance can go, I won't even be able to write it. I'm on the verge of madness. A normal human being cannot submerge himself for so many months in this hell without losing his sanity, without succumbing to some mental disturbance. Some nights, in my sleeplessness, I feel it happening to me. Something is disintegrating in my mind. I live with constant anguish. If I continue so close to what occurs here I too will eventually give whippings with a *chicote*, lop off hands, and murder Congolese between lunch and dinner without feeling the slightest pang of conscience or losing my appetite. Because that is what happens to Europeans in this damned country."

Yet that very long letter did not deal primarily with the Congo, but with Ireland. "This is why, dear Gee, it may seem like another symptom of madness to you, but this journey into the depths of the Congo has been useful in helping me discover my own country and understand her situation, her destiny, her reality. In these jungles I've found not only the true face of Leopold II. I've also found my true self: the incorrigible Irishman. When we see each other again you'll have a surprise, Gee. It will be difficult for you to recognize your cousin Roger. I have the impression I've shed the skin, like certain ophidians, of my mind and perhaps my soul."

It was true. During all the days it took the *Henry Reed* to sail down the Congo River to Leopoldville–Kinshasa, where it finally docked at dusk on September 15, 1903, the consul barely said a word to the crew. He had remained in his narrow cabin, or if the weather permitted, lay on his hammock in the stern, the faithful John settled at his feet, still and attentive, as if the sorrow in which he saw his master submerged had infected him too.

Simply thinking about the country of his childhood and youth, for which he had suddenly felt profound nostalgia during this entire journey, pushed out of his mind the images of Congolese horror bent on destroying him morally and perturbing his psychic equilibrium. He recalled his early years in Dublin, spoiled and protected by his mother, his school years in Galgorm, his outings with his sister

Nina in the countryside north of Antrim (so tame compared to Africa!) and the happiness afforded him by those excursions to the peaks guarding Glenshesk, his favorite of the nine glens of the county, summits raked by the winds where he could sometimes see the flight of eagles, their great wings spread and crests erect, defying the sky.

Wasn't Ireland a colony too, like the Congo? Though for so many years he had insisted on not accepting a truth that his father and so many Ulster Irishmen like him rejected with blind indignation. Why would what was bad for the Congo be good for Ireland? Hadn't the English invaded Ireland? Hadn't they incorporated it into the Empire by force, not consulting those who had been invaded and occupied, just as the Belgians did with the Congolese? Over time the violence had eased, but Ireland was still a colony whose sovereignty disappeared because of a stronger neighbor. It was a reality that many Irish refused to see. How would his father react if he had heard him saying such things? Would he pull out his small *chicote*? And his mother? Would Anne Jephson be scandalized if she knew that in the desolation of the Congo her son was becoming, if not in deed at least in thought, a nationalist? On those solitary afternoons, surrounded by the brown waters of the Congo River filled with leaves, branches, and tree trunks, Roger made a decision: as soon as he returned to Europe, he would obtain a good collection of books dedicated to Irish history and culture, which he hardly knew.

He spent barely three days in Leopoldville, not seeking anyone out. In his current state he didn't have the heart to visit authorities and acquaintances and speak to them—lying, of course—about his voyage along the

Middle and Upper Congo and what he had seen during those months. He sent a telegram in code to the Foreign Office saying he had enough material to confirm the accusations of mistreatment of indigenous people. He requested authorization to move to the neighboring Portuguese possession to write his report with more serenity than he would have subject to the pressures of consular service in Boma. And he wrote a long denunciation that was also a formal protest to the Prosecutor's Office of the Supreme Court of Leopoldville–Kinshasa regarding the events in Walla, requesting an investigation and sanctions for those responsible. He carried his document personally to the Prosecutor's Office. A circumspect functionary promised to inform the prosecutor, Maître Leverville, of everything as soon as he returned from an elephant hunt with the head of the city's Office of Commercial Records, M. Clothard.

Roger took the train to Matadi, where he stayed only one night. From there he went down to Boma in a cargo steamer. In the consular office he found a pile of correspondence and a telegram from his superiors authorizing him to travel to Luanda to write his report. It was urgent that he write it, and in the greatest detail possible. In England, the campaign of accusations against the Congo Free State had reached a frenzy and the principal daily papers were taking part, confirming or denying the "atrocities." For some time, in addition to the denunciations of the Baptist Church, there were those of Edmund D. Morel, the British journalist of French origin and Roger's secret friend and accomplice. His publications were causing a great deal of agitation in both the House of Commons and public opinion. There had already been a debate in parliament on the subject. The Foreign Office and Lord Chancellor Lansdowne himself were impatiently awaiting Roger's testimony.

In Boma, as in Leopoldville–Kinshasa, Roger avoided government people as much as he could, even breaking protocol, something he had never done in all his years in the consular service. Instead of visiting the governor general he sent him a letter, apologizing for not going in person to pay his respects and claiming problems with his health. He didn't play a single game of tennis, billiards, or cards and didn't give or accept invitations to lunches or dinners. He didn't even go to swim early in the morning in the backwaters of the river, something he usually did almost every day, even in bad weather. He didn't want to see people or have any social life. Above all, he didn't want to be asked about his journey and find himself obliged to lie. He was sure he could never describe sincerely to his friends and acquaintances in Boma what he thought about everything he had seen, heard, and experienced on the Middle and Upper Congo in the past fourteen weeks.

He devoted all his time to resolving the most urgent consular matters and preparing his trip to Cabinda and Luanda. He hoped that by leaving the Congo, even though he went to another colonial possession, he would feel less oppressed and freer. Several times he tried to begin a rough draft of the report but couldn't. Not only his dejection stopped him; his right hand contracted in a muscle spasm as soon as he began to move pen on paper. His hemorrhoids returned. He barely ate and his two servants, Charlie and Mawuku, concerned at seeing him in such bad health, told him to call the doctor. But even though he too was uneasy about his insomnia, lack of appetite, and physical ailments, he didn't because seeing Dr. Salabert would mean speaking, remembering, recounting everything that for the moment he wanted only to forget.

On September 28 he left by boat for Banana and there, the following day, another small steamboat transported him and Charlie to Cabinda. John the bulldog stayed behind with Mawuku. But not even the four days he spent there, where he had acquaintances with whom he had dinner and who, since they knew nothing about his trip to the Upper Congo, did not oblige him to speak about what he wished to keep silent, made him feel calmer and more sure of himself. Only in Luanda, where he arrived on October 3, did he begin to feel better. The English consul, Mr. Briskley, a discreet, obliging person, furnished him with a small room in his suite of offices. There he began at last to work morning and evening, sketching the large contours of his report.

But he felt he was beginning to be really well, to be the man he had been before, only three or four days after arriving in Luanda, one afternoon as he sat at a table in the old Café Paris, where he went to eat after working all morning. He was glancing at an old newspaper from Lisbon when he noticed, on the street outside, several half-naked natives unloading a large wagon filled with bales of some agricultural product, perhaps cotton. One of them, the youngest, was very beautiful. He had a long, athletic body, muscles that appeared on his back, legs, and arms with the effort he was making. His dark skin, gleaming with sweat, had a blue tinge. With the movements he made as he carried the load on his shoulder from the wagon to the interior of the storehouse, the light piece of cloth he wore around his hips opened and offered a glimpse of his sex, reddish and hanging and larger than normal. Roger felt a warm surge and urgent desires to photograph the handsome porter. It hadn't happened to him for months. A thought animated him: *I'm myself again*. In the small diary he always carried with him, he wrote: "Very beautiful and enormous. I followed him and persuaded him. We kissed hidden by the giant ferns in a clearing. He was mine, I was his. I howled." He breathed deeply, in a fever.

That same afternoon, Mr. Briskley handed him a telegram from the Foreign Office. The chancellor himself, Lord Lansdowne, ordered him to return to England immediately to write his *Report on the Congo* in London. Roger had recovered his appetite and dined well that night.

Before boarding the *Zaire*, which left Luanda for England with a stop in Lisbon, on November 6, he wrote a long letter to Edmund D. Morel. They had been corresponding secretly for six months but had never met. He first learned of his existence in a letter from Herbert Ward, who admired the journalist, and then in Boma, listening to Belgian functionaries and other random people commenting on the extremely harsh articles loaded with criticisms of the Congo Free State that Morel, who lived in Liverpool, was publishing, denouncing the abuses that victimized the natives of the African colony. Discreetly, through his cousin Gertrude, he obtained some pamphlets edited by Morel. Impressed by the seriousness of his accusations, in a bold gesture Roger wrote to him, sending the letter through Gee. He told him he had been in Africa for many years and could give him first-hand information for his righteous campaign, which he supported. He couldn't do this openly because of his position as a British diplomat, and therefore it was necessary to take precautions with their correspondence in order to keep his informant in Boma from being identified. In the letter he wrote to Morel from Luanda, Roger summarized his most recent experience and said that as soon as he reached Europe, he would get in touch with him. Nothing made him more hopeful than a personal meeting with the only European who seemed fully conscious of the Old Continent's responsibility for the transformation of the Congo into a hell.

On the trip to London, Roger recovered energy, enthusiasm, and hope. Once again he was certain his report would be useful in putting an end to those horrors. The impatience with which the Foreign Office awaited his report demonstrated this. The facts were of such magnitude that the British government would have to act, demand radical changes, convince its allies, revoke the senseless personal concession to Leopold II of an immense Congo. In spite of the storms that shook the *Zaire* between Santo Tomé and Lisbon and caused half the crew to be seasick, Roger managed to continue writing his report. As disciplined as he had once been, and devoted with apostolic zeal to the task, he tried to write with the greatest precision and sobriety without recourse to sentimentality or subjective considerations, describing objectively only what he had been able to confirm. The more exact and concise the report, the more persuasive and effective it would be.

He arrived in London on an icy December 1. He barely had time to look at the rainy, cold, and spectral city, because once he left his luggage in his Philbeach Gardens apartment, in Earls Court, and glanced at the accumulated correspondence, he had to hurry to the Foreign Office. For three days there were meetings and interviews. He was very impressed. No doubt about it, the Congo was at the center of the news since the debate in parliament. The denunciations of the Baptist Church and Edmund D. Morel's campaign had had an effect. Everyone was demanding a statement from the government, which was counting on his report before making one. Roger discovered that without desiring or knowing it, circumstances had made him an important man. In two presentations, an hour each, before functionaries of the ministry—the director for African affairs and the vice-minister attended one of them—he could see the impact his words had on the audience. The initial incredulous looks turned into expressions of repugnance and horror when he responded to questions with new details.

They gave him an office in a quiet spot in Kensington, far from the Foreign Office, and a young, efficient typist, Mr. Joe Pardo. He began dictating his report on Friday, December 4. News had spread that the British consul in the Congo had arrived in London with an exhaustive document on the colony, and the Reuters Agency, the *Spectator*, *The Times,* and several correspondents for papers in the United States tried to interview him. But he, by agreement with his superiors, said he would speak with the press only after the government had made a statement on the subject.

In the days following he did nothing but work on the report morning and evening, adding, cutting, and rewriting the text, reading over and over again his copybooks with travel notes he already knew by heart. At midday he ate a sandwich, and every night he had dinner early at his club, the Wellington. Sometimes Herbert Ward joined him. It did him good to talk with his old friend, who dragged him one day to his studio, at 53 Chester Square, and distracted him by showing him his strong sculptures inspired by Africa. On another day, to make him forget his obsessive preoccupation for a few hours, Herbert obliged him to go out and buy a stylish jacket of checked cloth, a French-style cap, and shoes with white spats. Then he took him for lunch to the favorite spot of London intellectuals and artists, the Eiffel Tower restaurant. During this time, these were his only diversions.

Since his arrival he had asked the Foreign Office for authorization to have an interview with Morel. He gave as a pretext his desire to check some of his data with the journalist. He received their authorization on December 9. And the next day, Roger Casement and Edmund D. Morel saw each other's faces for the first time. Instead of shaking hands, they embraced. They talked, had dinner together at the Comedy, went to Roger's apartment in Philbeach Gardens where they spent the rest of the night drinking cognac, chatting, smoking, and debating until they saw through the blinds that it was the next day. They had spent twelve hours in uninterrupted dialogue. Afterward they both would say this meeting had been the most important of their lives.

They couldn't have been more different. Roger was tall and very thin, and Morel was rather short and husky, with a tendency to put on weight. Every time he saw him, Roger had the impression that his friend's suits were too tight. Roger was thirty-nine, but in spite of the physical effects of the African climate and malaria, he looked, perhaps because of how carefully he dressed, younger than Morel, who was only thirty-two; Morel had been good-looking when younger but now had aged, with badly cut hair that was already gray, like his handlebar mustache, and burning, somewhat bulging eyes. It was enough to see each other to get along and—they would not have thought the word exaggerated—love each other.

What did they talk about for those twelve uninterrupted hours? A great deal about Africa, of course, but also about their families, their childhoods, their adolescent dreams, ideals, and longings, and about how, without their intending it, the Congo had established itself at the center of their lives and transformed them completely. Roger was amazed that someone who had never been there knew the country so well: its geography, history, people, and problems. He listened in fascination to how, many years ago now, Morel, an obscure employee of the Elder Dempster Line (the same company Roger had worked for as a young man in Liverpool), responsible in the port of Antwerp for inspecting the ships and making an audit of their cargos, began to be suspicious when he noticed that the free trade His Majesty Leopold II had supposedly opened between Europe and the Congo Free State was not merely asymmetrical but a farce. What kind of free trade was it when the ships that came from the Congo to the great Flemish port unloaded tons of rubber and quantities of ivory, palm oil, minerals, and skins, and to go there carried only rifles, *chicotes*, and cases of colored glass?

This was how Morel began to be interested in the Congo, to investigate, to question those who went there or returned to Europe, merchants, functionaries, travelers, pastors, priests, adventurers, soldiers, police officers, and to read everything he could lay his hands on about that immense country whose misfortunes he came to know thoroughly, as if he had undertaken dozens of inspection tours like the ones Roger had made to the Middle and Upper Congo. Then, without giving up his position in the company yet, he began to write letters and articles in magazines and newspapers in Belgium and England, at first under a pseudonym and later using his own name, denouncing what he had discovered and disproving with facts and testimonies the idyllic image of the Congo that hacks in the service of Leopold II offered to the world. He had been doing this for many years, publishing articles, pamphlets, and books, speaking in churches, cultural centers, and political organizations. His campaign had caught fire. Many people now supported him. *This is Europe too*, Roger often thought, *not only the colonists, police, and criminals we send to Africa. Europe is also this clear, exemplary spirit: Edmund D. Morel.*

From then on they saw each other often and continued the dialogues that excited both of them. They began to call each other by affectionate pseudonyms: Roger was Tiger and Edmund Bulldog. During one of these conversations the idea emerged of creating a foundation, the Congo Reform Association. Both were surprised by the vast support they received in their efforts to obtain sponsors and adherents. The truth is that very few of the politicians, journalists, writers, clergy, and well-known figures they asked to help the association refused. This was how Roger met Alice Stopford Green. Herbert Ward introduced them. Alice was one of the first to give money, her name, and her time to the association. Joseph Conrad did as well, and many intellectuals and artists followed his lead. They gathered funds and respectable names and very soon began their public activities in churches and cultural and humanitarian centers, presenting testimonies, promoting debates and publications to open the public's eyes to the true situation in the Congo. Even though Roger, as a diplomat, could not appear officially on the association's board of directors, he dedicated all his free time to it once he had finally turned in his report to the Foreign Office. He donated a portion of his savings and salary to the association and wrote letters, visited many people, and succeeded in persuading a good number of diplomats and politicians to become promoters of the cause Morel and he defended.

Many years later, when Roger thought about those feverish weeks at the end of 1903 and the beginning of 1904, he would tell himself that most important for him had not been the popularity he achieved even before His Majesty's government published his *Report*, or much later, when agents in the service of Leopold II began to attack him in the press as an enemy and slanderer of Belgium, but, thanks to Morel, the association, and Herbert, his meeting Alice Stopford Green, whose intimate friend and, as he boasted, disciple he would be from that time on. From the first moment there sprang up between them an understanding and affection that time would only make more profound.

The second or third time they were alone, Roger opened his heart to his new friend, as a believer would have done with his confessor. He dared tell her, like him from an Irish

Protestant family, what he hadn't told anyone yet: there in the Congo, living with injustice and violence, he had discovered the great lie of colonialism and begun to feel "Irish," that is, like the citizen of a country occupied and exploited by the Empire that had bled and weakened Ireland. He was ashamed of so many things he had said and believed, repeating his father's teachings. And he vowed to make amends. Now that he had discovered Ireland, thanks to the Congo, he wanted to be a real Irishman, know his country, take possession of her tradition, history, and culture.

Affectionate, somewhat maternal, Alice—who was nineteen years older—reprimanded him at times for having childish bouts of enthusiasm when he was a man of forty, but helped him with advice, books, talks that were for him masterclasses, while they had tea with biscuits or scones with cream and marmalade. In those early months of 1904, Alice Stopford Green was his friend, his teacher, the woman who introduced him to an ancient past where history, myth, and legend—reality, religion, and fiction—blended together to create the tradition of a people who continued to maintain, in spite of the denationalizing drive of the Empire, their language, their way of being, their customs, something about which any Irish man or woman, Protestant or Catholic, believer or doubter, liberal or conservative, had to feel proud and obliged to defend. Nothing helped so much to calm Roger's spirit, cure him of the moral wounds caused by his trip to the Upper Congo, as having established a friendship with Morel and with Alice. One day as she was saying goodbye to Roger who, having requested a three-month leave from the Foreign

Office, was about to leave for Dublin, the historian said: "Do you realize you've become a celebrity, Roger? Everybody is talking about you here, in London."

It wasn't something that pleased him since he had never been vain. But Alice was telling him the truth. The publication of his *Report* by the British government had enormous repercussions in the press, parliament, the political class, and public opinion. The attacks aimed at him in Belgium in official publications, and by English gossip columnists who were propagandists for Leopold II, served only to strengthen his image as a great humanitarian fighter for justice. He was interviewed in the press, invited to speak at public meetings and at private clubs, showered with invitations from liberal and anti-colonialist salons, and leaflets and articles appeared praising to the skies his *Report* and his commitment to the cause of justice and freedom. The Congo campaign took on a new impetus. The press, the churches, the most advanced sectors of English society, horrified at the revelations in the *Report*, demanded that Great Britain ask her allies to revoke the decision by the western countries to hand the Congo to the King of the Belgians.

Overwhelmed by this sudden fame—people recognized him in theaters and restaurants and pointed him out with interest on the street—Roger left for Ireland. He spent a few days in Dublin but soon continued on to Ulster, North Antrim, and Magherintemple House, the family home of his childhood and adolescence. His uncle and namesake Roger, the son of his great-uncle John, who had died in 1902, had inherited it. Aunt Charlotte was still alive. She received him with great affection, as did his other family members, cousins and nieces and nephews. But he felt that an invisible distance had grown up between him and his paternal family, who were still committed Anglophiles. Yet the Magherintemple countryside, the big old house of gray stone, surrounded by sycamores resistant to salt and wind, many of them smothered in ivy, the poplars, elms, and beech trees dominating the meadows where sheep lay, and beyond that the sea, the view of the island of Rathlin and the small town of Ballycastle with its snow-white cottages, moved him deeply. Walking through the stables, the orchard at the back of the house, the large rooms with deer antlers on the walls, or the ancient villages of Cushendun and Cushendall, where several generations of ancestors were buried, brought back memories of his childhood and filled him with nostalgia. But new ideas and feelings about his country meant that this visit, of several months' duration, would become another great adventure for him. An adventure, unlike his journey to the Upper Congo, that was pleasant and stimulating and which would also give him the sensation as he lived it that he was shedding his skin.

He had brought a pile of books, grammars, and essays, recommended by Alice, and he spent many hours reading about Irish traditions and legends. He tried to learn Gaelic, first on his own and, when he realized he never would, with the help of a teacher from whom he took lessons several times a week.

But, above all, he began to spend time with new people from County Antrim who were Protestant like him but were not unionists. On the contrary, they wanted to preserve the personality of ancient Ireland, fought against the

Anglicization of the country, defended the return to old Irish, traditional songs and customs, and opposed the recruitment of Irishmen into the British army. They dreamed of a separate Ireland, safe from destructive modern industrialism, living a bucolic, rural life, liberated from the British Empire. This was how Roger became connected to the Gaelic League, which promoted Irish and the culture of Ireland. When it was founded in Dublin, in 1893, its president, Douglas Hyde, reminded the audience in his speech that until then, "only six books had been published in Gaelic." Roger met Hyde's successor, Eoin MacNeill, professor of ancient and medieval Irish history at University College, and they became friends. He began to attend readings, lectures, recitals, marches, academic assemblies, and the raising of monuments to nationalist heroes, sponsored by Sinn Fein, whose name meant "Ourselves alone." And he began to write political articles defending Irish culture in its publications under the pseudonym Shan van Vocht ("The poor old woman"), taken from an old Irish ballad he was in the habit of humming. At the same time he grew very close to a group of women, among them the chatelaine of Galgorm, Rose Maud Young, Ada McNeill, and Margaret Dobbs, who traveled the villages of Antrim collecting old legends from Irish folklore. Thanks to them he heard a *seanchaí* or traveling storyteller at a popular fair, though he barely could understand more than a word or two of what he said.

During an argument in Magherintemple House with his uncle one night, Roger declared excitedly, "Like the Irishman I am, I hate the British Empire."

The next day he received a letter from the Duke of

Argyll informing him that His Majesty's government had decided to honor him with the decoration Companion of St. Michael and St. George for his excellent service in the Congo. Roger excused himself from attending the investiture ceremony by claiming that a knee problem would not allow him to kneel before the king.

7

"You hate me and can't hide it," Roger Casement said. The sheriff, after a moment's surprise, agreed with a grimace that for an instant transformed his bloated face.

"I have no reason to hide it," he murmured. "But you're wrong. I don't feel hatred for you. I feel contempt. That's all traitors deserve."

They were walking along the corridor of soot-stained bricks toward the visitors' room, where the Catholic chaplain, Father Carey, was waiting for the prisoner. Through the narrow barred windows, Roger could see large patches of dark, swollen clouds. Was it raining there, outside, on Caledonian Road and the Roman Way where centuries ago the first Roman legionnaires marched through forests filled with bears? He imagined the stalls and stands at the nearby market, in the middle of Islington's large park, soaked and shaken by the storm. He felt a sting of envy thinking about the people who were buying and selling, protected by raincoats and umbrellas.

"You had everything," the sheriff grumbled behind him. "Diplomatic posts. Decorations. The king knighted you. And you went and sold yourself to the Germans. How vile. How ungrateful."

He fell silent and Roger thought the sheriff was sighing.

"Whenever I think about my poor son killed over there

in the trenches, I tell myself you're one of his killers, Mr. Casement."

"I'm very sorry you lost a son," Roger replied, not turning around. "I know you won't believe me, but I haven't killed anyone yet."

"You won't have time left to do that now," was the sheriff's judgment. "Thank God."

They had reached the door of the visitors' room. The sheriff stayed outside, next to the jailer on guard. Only visits from chaplains were private. In all the others the sheriff or a guard always remained, and sometimes both. Roger was happy to see the stylized silhouette of the cleric. Father Carey came forward to meet him and took his hand.

"I made inquiries and have the reply," he announced, smiling. "Your memory was exact. In effect, you were baptized as a child in the parish of Rhyl, in Wales. Your name is in the register. Your mother and two of your maternal aunts were present. You don't need to be received again into the Catholic Church. You've always been in it."

Roger agreed. The very distant impression that had accompanied him his whole life was, in fact, correct. His mother had baptized him, hiding it from his father, on one of their trips to Wales. He was glad because of the complicity the secret established between him and Anne Jephson. And because in this way he felt more in tune with himself, his mother, and Ireland. As if his approach to Catholicism were a natural consequence of everything he had done and attempted in these last few years, including his mistakes and failures.

"I've been reading Thomas à Kempis, Father Carey," he said. "Before, I could barely manage to concentrate on reading. But recently I've been able to. Several hours a day. *The Imitation of Christ* is a very beautiful book."

"When I was in the seminary we read a good deal of Thomas à Kempis," the priest agreed. "Especially *The Imitation of Christ.*"

"I feel calmer when I can manage to become involved in those pages," said Roger. "As if I had cut free from this world and entered another one with no preoccupations, a purely spiritual reality. Father Crotty was right to recommend it to me so often in Germany. He never imagined under what circumstances I'd read the Thomas à Kempis he admired so much."

Not long before a small bench had been installed in the visitors' room. They sat on it, their knees touching. Father Carey had been a chaplain in London prisons for more than twenty years and accompanied many men condemned to death on their last journey. His constant dealings with prison populations had not hardened his character. He was considerate and attentive, and Roger liked him from their first encounter. He did not recall ever having heard him say anything that might wound him; on the contrary, when it was time to ask questions or talk to him he showed extreme delicacy. He always felt good with him. Father Carey was tall, bony, almost skeletal, with very white skin and a graying, pointed beard that covered part of his chin. His eyes were always damp, as if he had just cried, even though he was laughing.

"What was Father Crotty like?" he asked. "I can see you two got along very well in Germany."

"If it hadn't been for Father Crotty I would have gone mad during those months in the Limburg camp," Roger agreed. "He was very different from you, physically. Shorter, more robust, and instead of your pallor he had a red face that grew even redder with the first glass of beer. But from another point of view, he did resemble you. In his generosity, I mean."

Father Crotty was an Irish Dominican sent from Rome by the Vatican to the prisoner-of-war camp the Germans had set up in Limburg. His friendship had been a life raft for Roger during those months in 1915 and 1916 when he was trying to recruit volunteers for the Irish Brigade from among the prisoners.

"He was a man immune to discouragement," said Roger. "I went with him to visit the sick, administer the sacraments, pray the rosary with the prisoners at Limburg. A nationalist as well. Though less impassioned than me, Father Carey."

The priest smiled.

"Don't think that Father Crotty tried to bring me closer to Catholicism," Roger added. "He was very careful in our conversations so I wouldn't feel he wanted to convert me. That was happening to me on my own, here inside," he said, touching his breast. "I was never very religious, as I've told you. Ever since my mother died, religion for me had been something mechanical and secondary. Only after 1903, after that trip of three months and ten days into the interior of the Congo that I told you about, did I pray again. When I thought I would lose my mind in the face of so much suffering. That was how I discovered that a human being can't live without believing."

He felt his voice would break and stopped speaking.

"Did he speak to you of Thomas à Kempis?"

"He was very devoted to him," Roger agreed. "He gave me his copy of *The Imitation of Christ*. But I couldn't read it then. I didn't have the head for it with all the concerns I had at the time. I left that copy in Germany, in a suitcase with my clothes. They didn't allow us to carry luggage on the submarine. Just as well you found me another one. I'm afraid I won't have time to finish it."

"The English government hasn't decided anything yet," the priest admonished him. "You mustn't lose hope. There are many people outside who love you and are making enormous efforts to have the petition for clemency heard."

"I know that, Father Carey. In any event, I'd like you to prepare me. I want to be accepted formally by the Church. Receive the sacraments. Make my confession. Take communion."

"That's why I'm here, Roger. I assure you you're already prepared for all of that."

"One doubt distresses me a great deal," said Roger, lowering his voice as if someone else might hear him. "Won't my conversion to Christ seem inspired by fear? The truth is, Father Carey, that I am afraid. Very afraid."

"He is wiser than you and me," the priest declared. "I don't believe Christ sees anything wrong in a man being afraid. He was, I'm sure, on the road to Calvary. It's the most human thing there is, isn't it? We all feel fear, it's part of our condition. Just a little sensitivity is enough for us to sometimes feel powerless and frightened. Your approach to the Church is pure, Roger. I know that."

"I was never afraid of death until now. I saw it at close range many times. In the Congo, on expeditions through inhospitable places filled with wild animals. In Amazonia, in rivers replete with whirlpools and surrounded by outlaws. Just a short while ago, when I left the submarine at Tralee, on Banna Strand, when the rowboat capsized and it seemed we would all drown. I've often felt death very close. And I wasn't afraid. But I am now."

His voice broke and he closed his eyes. For some days now these rushes of terror seemed to freeze his blood, stop his heart. His entire body had begun to tremble. He made an effort to be calm but failed. He felt the chattering of his teeth and to his panic was added embarrassment. When he opened his eyes he saw that Father Carey had his hands together and his eyes closed. He was praying in silence, barely moving his lips.

"It's passed," he mumbled in confusion. "I beg you to forgive me."

"You don't have to feel uncomfortable with me. Being afraid, weeping, is human."

Now he was calm again. There was a great silence in Pentonville Prison, as if the prisoners and the jailers in its three enormous pavilions, those blocks with gable roofs, had died or fallen asleep.

"I thank you for not asking me anything about those loathsome things they apparently are saying about me, Father Carey."

"I haven't read them, Roger. When someone has attempted to talk to me about them, I've made him be quiet. I don't know and don't want to know what that's about."

"I don't know either," Roger said with a smile. "You can't read newspapers here. One of my lawyer's clerks told me they were so scandalous they put the petition for clemency at risk. Degeneracies, terrible vileness, it seems."

Father Carey listened to him with his usual tranquil expression. The first time they had spoken in Pentonville, he told Roger that his paternal grandparents spoke Gaelic to each other but changed to English when they saw their children nearby. The priest hadn't succeeded in learning ancient Irish either.

"I believe it's better not to know what they're accusing me of. Alice Stopford Green thinks it's an operation mounted by the government to counteract the sympathy in many sectors for the petition for clemency."

"Nothing can be excluded in the world of politics," said the priest. "It's not the cleanest of human activities."

There were some discreet knocks at the door, which opened, and the sheriff's plump face appeared: "Five more minutes, Father Carey."

"The director of the prison gave me half an hour. Weren't you told?"

The sheriff's face showed surprise.

"If you say so, I believe you," and he apologized. "Excuse the interruption, then. You still have twenty minutes."

He disappeared and the door closed again.

"Is there more news from Ireland?" Roger asked, somewhat abruptly, as if he suddenly wanted to change the subject.

"It seems the shootings have stopped. Public opinion, not only there but in England too, has been very critical of the summary executions. Now the government has announced that all those arrested in the Easter Rising will pass through the courts."

Roger became distracted. He looked at the window in the wall, also barred. He saw only a tiny square of gray sky and thought about the great paradox: he had been tried and sentenced for carrying arms for an attempt at violent secession by Ireland, and in fact he had undertaken that dangerous, perhaps absurd trip from Germany to the coast of Kerry to try to stop the uprising he was sure would fail from the moment he learned it was being prepared. Was all of history like that? The history learned at school? The one written by historians? A more or less idyllic fabrication, rational and coherent, about what had been in raw, harsh reality a chaotic and arbitrary jumble of plans, accidents, intrigues, fortuitous events, coincidences, multiple interests that had provoked changes, upheavals, advances, and retreats, always unexpected and surprising with respect to what was anticipated or experienced by the protagonists.

"It's likely I'll go down in history as one of those responsible for the Easter Rising," he said with irony. "You and I know I came here risking my life to try to stop that rebellion."

"Well, you and I and someone else," Father Carey said with a laugh, pointing up with a finger.

"Now I feel better, finally." Roger laughed as well. "The panic has passed. In Africa I often saw blacks as well as whites fall suddenly into a crisis of despair. In the middle of the undergrowth, when we lost our way. When we entered a territory the African porters considered hostile. In the middle of the river, when a canoe overturned. Or in the villages sometimes, during ceremonies with singing and dancing directed by witch doctors. Now I know what those hallucinatory states brought on by fear are like. Are the trances of the mystics the same, the suspension of oneself and all carnal reflexes produced by the encounter with God?"

"It's not impossible," said Father Carey. "Perhaps the path traveled by the mystics and by all those who experience trance states is the same. Poets, musicians, sorcerers."

They were silent for a long while. At times, out of the corner of his eye, Roger observed the priest and saw him motionless, his eyes closed. *He's praying for me*, he thought. *He's a compassionate man. It must be terrible to spend your life helping people who are going to die on the gallows*. Without ever having been in the Congo or Amazonia, Father Carey must be as well informed as he about the dizzying extremes reached by human cruelty and despair.

"For many years I was indifferent to religion," he said, very slowly, as if talking to himself, "but I never stopped believing in God. In a general principle of life. Though it's true, Father Carey, I often asked myself in horror: 'How can God permit things like this to happen?' 'What kind of God tolerates so many thousands of men, women, and children suffering such horrors?' It's difficult to understand, isn't it? You must have seen so many things in the prisons; don't you sometimes ask the same questions?"

Father Carey had opened his eyes and listened to him with his usual courteous expression, not affirming or denying.

"Those poor people whipped, mutilated, those children with their hands and feet chopped off, dying of hunger and disease," Roger recited. "Those creatures squeezed to extinction and then murdered. Thousands, dozens, hundreds of thousands. By men who received a Christian education. I have seen them go to Mass, pray, take communion, before and after committing those crimes. Many days I thought I'd go mad, Father Carey. Perhaps, during those years in

Africa, in Putumayo, I lost my mind. And everything that has happened to me since has been the work of someone who, though he didn't realize it, was crazy."

The chaplain didn't say anything this time, either. He listened with the same affable expression and the patience for which Roger had always been grateful.

"Curiously, I believe it was in the Congo, when I had those periods of great demoralization and asked myself how God could permit so many crimes, that I began to be interested in religion again," he continued. "Because the only beings who seemed to have maintained their sanity were some Baptist ministers and Catholic missionaries. Not all of them, of course. Many did not want to see what was happening past their own noses. But a few did what they could to stop the injustices. Real heroes."

He fell silent. Recalling the Congo or Putumayo did him harm: it stirred up the mud in his spirit, brought back images that plunged him into anguish.

"Injustices, tortures, crimes," murmured Father Carey. "Didn't Christ suffer these in his own flesh? He can understand your state better than anyone, Roger. Of course the same thing happens to me at times. To all believers, I'm sure. It's difficult to understand certain things, naturally. Our capacity for understanding is limited. We are fallible, imperfect. But I can tell you one thing. You've made many mistakes, like all human beings. But with regard to the Congo, to Amazonia, you cannot reproach yourself for anything. Your labor was generous and brave. You made many people open their eyes, you helped to correct great injustices."

All the good I could have done is being destroyed by this

campaign launched to ruin my reputation, he thought. It was a subject he preferred not to touch, one he pushed out of his mind each time it returned. The good thing about Father Carey's visits was that with the chaplain, he spoke only about what he wanted to. The priest's discretion was absolute, and he seemed to guess everything that might disturb Roger and avoided it. At times they did not say a word for a long while. Even so, the presence of the priest calmed him. When he left, Roger would remain serene and resigned for some hours.

"If the petition is rejected, will you be with me until the end?" he asked, not looking at him.

"Of course," said Father Carey. "You shouldn't think about that. Nothing has been decided yet."

"I know that, Father Carey. I haven't lost hope. But it does me good to know you will be there with me. Your presence will give me courage. I won't make an unfortunate scene, I promise."

"Would you like us to pray together?"

"Let's talk a little more, if you don't mind. This will be the last question I'll ask you about the matter. If I'm executed, can my body be taken to Ireland and buried there?"

He sensed the chaplain hesitating and looked at him. Father Carey had paled slightly. He saw his discomfort as he shook his head.

"No, Roger. If that happens, you'll be buried in the prison cemetery."

"In enemy territory," Roger murmured, trying to make a joke that failed. "In a country I've come to hate as much as I loved and admired it as a young man."

"Hate doesn't serve any purpose," Father Carey said

with a sigh. "The policies of England may be bad. But there are many decent, respectable English people."

"I know that very well, Father. I tell myself that whenever I fill with hatred toward this country. It's stronger than I am. Perhaps it happens because as a boy I believed blindly in the Empire, that England was civilizing the world. You would have laughed if you had known me then."

The priest agreed and Roger suddenly gave a little laugh.

"They say converts are the worst," he added. "My friends have always reproached me. Being too impassioned."

"The incorrigible Irishman of legend," said Father Carey, smiling. "My mother used to say that when I was little and misbehaved. 'Your incorrigible Irishman got out.'"

"If you like, we can pray now, Father."

Father Carey agreed. He closed his eyes, clasped his hands, and began to murmur very quietly an Our Father, and then some Hail Marys. Roger closed his eyes and prayed as well, not letting his voice be heard. For a time he did this mechanically, without concentrating, while various images whirled around his head, until gradually he allowed himself to be absorbed by the prayer. When the sheriff knocked on the door of the visitors' room and came in to warn them they had five minutes left, Roger was focused on the invocation.

Whenever he prayed he thought of his mother, that slim figure dressed in white, a broad-brimmed straw hat with a blue ribbon that danced in the wind, walking under the trees in a field. Were they in Wales, in Ireland, in Antrim, in Jersey? He didn't know where, but the countryside was as beautiful as the smile shining on Anne Jephson's face. How proud the young Roger felt holding the soft, tender hand that brought him so much security and joy. Praying like this was a marvelous balm, it brought back to him a childhood when, thanks to his mother's presence, everything in life was beautiful and happy.

Father Carey asked if he wanted to send a message to anyone, if he could bring him anything on his next visit in the next few days.

"All I want is to see you again, Father. You don't know the good it does me to talk and listen to you."

They parted with a handshake. In the long, damp corridor, without having planned it, Roger said to the sheriff: "I'm very sorry about the death of your son. I haven't had children. I imagine there's no more terrible pain in this life."

The sheriff made a small noise with his throat but did not respond. In his cell, Roger lay on his cot and picked up *The Imitation of Christ*. But he couldn't concentrate on reading. The letters danced before his eyes and in his head images threw out sparks in a mad round. The figure of Anne Jephson appeared more than once.

What would his life have been like if his mother, instead of dying so young, had been alive as he became an adolescent, a man? He probably would not have undertaken the African adventure. He would have remained in Ireland or in Liverpool and had a bureaucratic career and an honorable, obscure, and comfortable life with a wife and children. He smiled: no, that kind of life wasn't for him. The one he had led, with all its misfortunes, was preferable. He had seen the world, his horizons had broadened enormously, he had a better understanding of life, human reality, the innermost core of colonialism, the tragedy of so many peoples caused by that aberration.

If the subtle Anne Jephson had lived he would not have discovered the sad, beautiful history of Ireland, the one they never taught him in Ballymena High School, the history still hidden from the children and adolescents of North Antrim. They were still made to believe that Ireland was a savage country with no past worth remembering, raised to civilization by the occupier, educated and modernized by the Empire that stripped it of its tradition, language, and sovereignty. He had learned all this in Africa, where he never would have spent the best years of his youth and early maturity or ever come to feel so much pride in the country where he was born and so much rage because of what Great Britain had done, if his mother had lived.

Were they justified, the sacrifices of his twenty years in Africa, the seven in South America, the year or so in the heart of the Amazonian jungles, the year and a half of loneliness, sickness, and frustration in Germany? He never had cared about money, but wasn't it absurd that after having worked so hard all his life, he was now a pauper? The last balance in his bank account had been £10. He had never learned to save. He had spent all his income on others—on his three siblings, on humanitarian organizations like the Congo Reform Association, and on Irish nationalist institutions like St. Enda's School and the Gaelic League, to which for some time he had handed over his entire income. In order to spend money on those causes he had lived very austerely; for example, residing for long periods of time in very cheap boarding houses not appropriate to his rank (as his colleagues at the Foreign Office had insinuated). No one would remember the donations, gifts, or assistance now that he had failed. Only his final defeat would be remembered.

But that was not the worst thing. Devil take it, the damn idea was back again. Degeneracies, perversions, vices, all human lewdness. That is what the English government wanted to remain of him. Not the diseases that the rigors of Africa had inflicted on him, jaundice, the malarial fevers that undermined his organism, arthritis, the surgeries for hemorrhoids, the rectal problems that had caused him so much suffering and shame from the first time an anal fissure had to be operated on in 1893.

"You should have come earlier, this operation would have been simple three or four months ago. Now, it's serious."

"I live in Africa, doctor, in Boma, a place where my physician is a confirmed alcoholic whose hands tremble because of delirium tremens. Was I going to be operated on by Dr. Salabert, whose medical science is inferior to that of a Bakongo witch doctor?"

He had suffered from this almost his entire life. A few months earlier, in the German camp at Limburg, he'd had a hemorrhage sutured by a surly, coarse military doctor. When he decided to accept the responsibility of investigating the atrocities committed by the rubber barons in Amazonia, he was already very ill. He knew the effort would take him months and bring him only problems, and still he took it on, thinking he was serving justice. That part of him wouldn't remain either if they executed him.

Could it be true that Father Carey had refused to read the scandalous things attributed to him by the press? The chaplain was a good man who displayed solidarity. If he had to die, having him near would help him maintain his dignity to the last moment.

Demoralization overwhelmed him from head to toe. It turned him into a being as helpless as the Congolese attacked by the tsetse fly, and sleeping sickness prevented them from moving their arms, feet, lips, or even keeping their eyes open. Did it keep them from thinking as well? Unfortunately, these gusts of pessimism sharpened his lucidity, turned his brain into a crackling bonfire. The pages of the diary handed by the Admiralty spokesman to the press, which so horrified the red-faced assistant to Maître Gavan Duffy, were they real or falsified? He thought of the stupidity that formed a central part of human nature, and also, naturally, of Roger Casement. He was very thorough and well known, as a diplomat, for not taking any initiative or the slightest step without foreseeing all possible consequences. And now, here he was, caught in a stupid trap constructed throughout his life by himself, giving his enemies a weapon that would sink him in disrepute.

Startled, he realized he was bellowing with laughter.

Amazonia

8

When, on the last day of August 1910, Roger arrived in Iquitos after a little more than six weeks of an exhausting voyage that transported him and the members of the commission from England to the heart of the Peruvian Amazon, the old infection that irritated his eyes had become worse, as had the attacks of arthritis and the general state of his health. But, faithful to his Stoic character (Herbert Ward called him "Senecan"), at no moment during the journey did he allow his ailments to be evident, making an effort instead to raise the spirits of his companions and help them endure the suffering that troubled them. Colonel R. H. Bertie, a victim of dysentery, had to return to England when the ship docked at Madeira. The one who held up best was Louis Barnes, familiar with African agriculture since he had lived in Mozambique. The botanist Walter Folk, an expert in rubber, suffered in the heat and had neuralgia. Seymour Bell feared dehydration and always had a bottle of water in his hand, sipping from it constantly. Henry Fielgald had been in Amazonia the previous year, sent by Julio C. Arana's company, and gave advice on how to protect against mosquitoes and the "evil temptations" of Iquitos.

There were certainly a good number of those. It seemed incredible in a city so small and unattractive—an immense muddy district with crude constructions of wood and adobe topped with palm leaves, a few buildings of noble materials with galvanized metal roofs, spacious mansions whose facades were decorated with tiles imported from Portugal—that there should be so great a proliferation of bars, taverns, brothels, and gambling houses, and that prostitutes of all races and colors should be on display so shamelessly from the earliest hours of the day on the high sidewalks. The countryside was superb. Iquitos was on the banks of a tributary of the Amazon, the Nanay River, surrounded by luxuriant vegetation, very high trees, a permanent murmur from the groves, and river water that changed color as the sun moved across the sky. But few streets had sidewalks or asphalt, ditches ran along them carrying excrement and garbage, there was a stench that at nightfall thickened to the point of nausea, and music from the bars, brothels, and centers of diversion never stopped, playing twenty-four hours a day. Mr. Stirs, the British consul, who welcomed them at the docks, indicated that Roger would stay in his house. The company had prepared a residence for the members of the commission. That same night, the prefect of Iquitos, Señor Rey Lama, gave a dinner in their honor.

It was a little after midday and Roger, saying that instead of lunch he preferred to rest, withdrew to his bedroom. They had prepared a simple room for him that had indigenous fabrics with geometric drawings hanging on the walls and a small terrace from which a stretch of the river was visible. The street noise diminished here. He lay down without even removing his jacket or shoes and fell asleep immediately. He was filled with a peaceful feeling he hadn't experienced for the month and a half of his journey.

He dreamed not of the four years of consular service he had just completed in Brazil—in Santos, Pará, and Rio de Janeiro—but the year and a half he had spent in Ireland between 1904 and 1905 following the months of heightened excitement and a demented rush of activity while the British government prepared the publication of his report on the Congo, and the scandal that would make of him a hero and a pariah as praise from the liberal press and humanitarian organizations and diatribes from Leopold II's hacks rained down on him at the same time. To escape the publicity while the Foreign Office decided his new assignment—after the *Report* it was unthinkable that "the most hated man in the Belgian Empire" would set foot again in the Congo—Roger left for Ireland in search of anonymity. He did not pass unnoticed, but he was free of the invasive curiosity that in London left him no private life. Those months meant the rediscovery of his country, his immersion in an Ireland he had known about only in conversations, fantasies, and readings, very different from the one where he had lived as a child with his parents, or as an adolescent with his great-aunt and great-uncle and the rest of his paternal family, an Ireland that was not the tail and shadow of the British Empire, that fought to recover its language, traditions, and customs. "Roger, dear: you've become an Irish patriot," his cousin Gee joked in a letter. "I'm making up for lost time," he replied.

During those months he had made a long trek through Donegal and Galway, taking the pulse of the geography of his captive homeland, observing like a lover the austerity of her deserted fields and wild coast, chatting with her fishermen, fatalistic, unyielding men, independent of time, and her frugal, laconic farmers. He had met many Irish people "from the other side," Catholics and some Protestants who, like Douglas Hyde, founder of the National Literary Society, promoted the renaissance of Irish culture, wanted to restore native names to towns and villages, resuscitate the ancient songs of Éireann, the old dances, the traditional spinning and needlework of tweed and linen. When his appointment to the consulate in Lisbon was announced, he delayed his departure repeatedly, inventing pretexts regarding his health, in order to attend the first Feis na nGleann (Festival of the Glens) in Antrim, attended by close to three thousand people. During those days Roger felt his eyes grow wet when he heard the joyous melodies executed by bagpipers and sung in chorus, or listened—not understanding what they were saying—to the storytellers recounting in Gaelic the ballads and legends submerged in the medieval night. Even a hurling match, that centuries-old sport, was held at the festival, where Roger met nationalist politicians and writers like Sir Horace Plunkett, John Bulmer Hobson, Stephen Gwynn, and was reunited with the women friends who, like Alice Stopford Green, had made the struggle for Irish culture their own: Ada McNeill, Margaret Dobbs, Alice Milligan, Agnes O'Farrelly, and Rose Maud Young.

From then on he dedicated part of his savings and income to the associations and schools of the Pearse brothers, which taught Gaelic, and the nationalist journals to which he contributed under a pseudonym. In 1905, when Arthur Griffith founded Sinn Fein, Roger communicated with him, offered to collaborate, and subscribed to all his publications. This journalist's ideas coincided with those of

Bulmer Hobson, with whom Roger had become friends. It was necessary to create, along with colonial institutions, an Irish infrastructure (schools, businesses, banks, industries) that gradually would replace the one imposed by England. In this way the Irish would become conscious of their own destiny. It was necessary to boycott British products, refuse to pay taxes, replace English sports like cricket and soccer with national sports, and literature and the theater as well. In this way, peacefully, Ireland would break free of colonial subjugation.

In addition to reading a great deal about the Irish past, under Alice's tutelage, Roger tried again to study Gaelic and hired a teacher, but made little progress. In 1906 the new foreign secretary, Sir Edward Grey of the Liberal Party, offered to send him as consul to Santos, in Brazil. Roger accepted, though not happily, because his pro-Irish patronage had used up his small patrimony, he existed on loans, and he needed to earn a living.

Perhaps the scant enthusiasm with which he returned to his diplomatic career contributed to making his four years in Brazil—1906 to 1910—a frustrating experience. He never really became accustomed to that vast country in spite of its natural beauty and the good friends he acquired in Santos, Pará, and Rio de Janeiro. What depressed him most was that, unlike the Congo where, in spite of the difficulties, he always had the impression he was working for something transcendent that went far beyond the consular framework, in Santos his principal activity had to do with drunken British sailors who got into fights and whom he had to get out of jail, then pay their fines and return them to England. In Pará he heard for the first time about violence in the rubber regions. But the Foreign Office ordered him to concentrate on the inspection of port and commercial activity. His work consisted of recording the movement of ships and facilitating matters for the English who arrived intending to buy and sell. His worst time was in Rio de Janeiro, in 1909. The climate made all his ailments worse and added to them allergies that kept him from sleeping. He had to live eighty kilometers from the capital, in Petrópolis, situated in highlands where the heat and humidity were lower and the nights were cool. But daily travel by train to his office turned into a nightmare.

In his sleep he recalled insistently that in September 1906, before leaving for Santos, he wrote a long epic poem, *The Dream of the Celt*, about the mythic past of Ireland, and a political pamphlet, with Alice Stopford Green and Bulmer Hobson, *The Irish and the English Army*, objecting to the recruitment of Irishmen into the British army.

Biting mosquitoes woke him, taking him from a pleasurable siesta and submerging him in the Amazonian twilight. The sky had turned into a rainbow. He felt better: his eye burned less and the arthritic pain had eased. Showering in Mr. Stirs's house turned out to be a complicated operation: the pipe holding the showerhead came out of a receptacle into which a servant poured buckets of water while Roger soaped and rinsed. The lukewarm temperature of the water made him think of the Congo. When he went down to the first floor, the consul was waiting for him at the door, ready to take him to the house of Prefect Rey Lama.

They had to walk several blocks in a land wind that obliged Roger to keep his eyes half-closed. In the semi-darkness they stumbled over holes, rocks, and garbage in the street. The noise had increased. Each time they passed the door of a bar the music swelled and they could hear toasts, fights, and the shouts of drunks. Stirs, advanced in years, a widower with no children, had spent half a decade in Iquitos and seemed a weary man without illusions.

"What's the attitude in the city toward the commission?" Roger asked.

"Frankly hostile," the consul replied immediately. "I suppose you already know that half of Iquitos lives off Señor Arana. I mean, off the enterprises of Señor Julio C. Arana. People suspect the commission intends harm to the person who gives them work and food."

"Can we expect any help from the authorities?"

"Just the opposite: all the obstacles in the world, Mr. Casement. The authorities in Iquitos also depend on Señor Arana. The prefect, the judges, and the military haven't received their salaries from the government for months. Without Señor Arana they would have starved to death. Bear in mind that Lima is farther from Iquitos than New York and London because of the lack of transportation. In the best of circumstances it's two months of travel."

"This is going to be more complicated than I imagined," remarked Roger.

"You and the gentlemen of the commission must be very prudent," the consul added, hesitating now and lowering his voice. "Not here in Iquitos. There, in Putumayo. Anything can happen in those remote places. It's a savage world, without law or order. No more and no less than the Congo, I suppose."

The Prefecture of Iquitos was on the Plaza de Armas,

a large space without trees or flowers, where, the consul pointed out, indicating a curious iron structure that looked like a partially completed Meccano model, an Eiffel house ("Yes, the same Eiffel as the Tower in Paris") was being assembled. A prosperous rubber-grower had bought it in Europe, brought it back to Iquitos in pieces, and now was reassembling it to be the best social club in the city.

The Prefecture occupied almost half a block. It was a large, faded one-story house, lacking grace or form, with spacious rooms and barred windows, and divided into two wings, one used for offices and the other for the prefect's residence. Señor Rey Lama, a tall, gray-haired man with a large mustache waxed at the ends, wore boots, riding pants, a shirt buttoned to the neck, and a strange bolero jacket with embroidered decorations. He spoke some English and gave Roger an excessively cordial welcome full of bombastic rhetoric. The members of the commission were all there, packed into their evening clothes, perspiring. The prefect introduced Roger to the other guests: magistrates from the Superior Court; Colonel Arnáez, commander of the garrison; Father Urrutia, Father Superior of the Augustinians; Señor Pablo Zumaeta, general manager of the Peruvian Amazon Company; and four or five other people: merchants, the head of the customs office, the editor of *El Oriental*. There was not a single woman in the group. He heard champagne being uncorked. They were offered glasses of a white sparkling wine that, though lukewarm, seemed of good quality, undoubtedly French.

The supper had been prepared in a large courtyard lit by oil lamps. Countless indigenous servant girls, barefoot and wearing aprons, served hors d'oeuvres and brought in platters of food. It was a mild night, and stars twinkled in the sky. Roger was surprised at how easily he understood Loretan speech, a somewhat syncopated and musical Spanish in which he recognized Brazilian expressions. He felt relieved: he'd be able to understand a good deal of what he heard on the journey and this, even though they'd have an interpreter, would support the investigation. Around him at the table, where they had just been served a greasy turtle soup he swallowed with difficulty, several conversations were being held at the same time, in English, Spanish, and Portuguese, with interpreters who interrupted them, creating parentheses of silence. Suddenly the prefect, sitting across from Roger and his eyes already alight with glasses of wine and beer, clapped his hands. Everyone stopped talking. He offered a toast to the new arrivals. He wished them a pleasant stay, a successful mission, and hoped they would enjoy Amazonian hospitality. "Loretan and especially Iquitian," he added.

As soon as he sat down, he spoke to Roger in a voice loud enough to stop the other conversations and start another one, with the participation of the twenty or so guests.

"If you'll permit me a question, my esteemed Consul? What exactly is the purpose of your trip and this commission? What have you come here to find out? Don't take this as impertinent. On the contrary. My desire, and the desire of all the authorities, is to assist you. But we have to know why the British Crown has sent you. A great honor for Amazonia, of course, and we would like to prove ourselves worthy."

Roger had understood almost everything Rey Lama

said, but he waited patiently for the interpreter to translate his words into English.

"As you no doubt know, in England, in Europe, there have been denunciations of atrocities committed against the indigenous people," he explained calmly. "Torture, murder, very serious accusations. The principal rubber company in the region, the one that belongs to Señor Julio C. Arana, the Peruvian Amazon Company, is, and I assume this is well known, an English company, registered on the London stock market. The government and public opinion would not tolerate an English company violating human and divine laws in this way in Great Britain. The reason for our journey is to investigate the truth of those accusations. Señor Julio C. Arana's company has sent the commission. His Majesty's government has sent me."

An icy silence fell over the courtyard when Roger opened his mouth. The noise from the street seemed to diminish. There was a curious immobility, as if all those gentlemen who a moment earlier had been drinking, eating, conversing, moving, gesturing, had become victims of a sudden paralysis. All eyes were on Roger. A climate of distrust and disapproval had replaced the cordial atmosphere.

"The company of Julio C. Arana is prepared to cooperate in defense of its good name," Señor Pablo Zumaeta said, almost shouting. "We have nothing to hide. The ship that will take you to Putumayo is the best in our firm. There you will have every opportunity to confirm with your own eyes the vileness of these slanders."

"We are grateful, Señor," Roger agreed.

And at that very moment, with an excitement unusual

in him, he decided to subject his hosts to a test that, he was sure, would unleash reactions which would be instructive for him and the members of the commission. In the casual voice he would have used to speak of tennis or the rain, he asked: "By the way, Señores. Do you know whether the journalist Benjamín Saldaña Roca, I hope I'm pronouncing his name correctly, happens to be in Iquitos? Would it be possible to speak to him?"

His question had the effect of a bomb. The diners exchanged looks of shock and anger. A long silence followed his words, as if no one dared touch so thorny a subject.

"But is it possible!" the prefect exclaimed at last, theatrically exaggerating his surprise. "The name of that blackmailer has reached even London?"

"That's true, Señor," Roger agreed. "The denunciations of Señor Saldaña Roca and of the engineer Walter Hardenburg made the scandal concerning the Putumayo rubber plantations explode in London. No one has answered my question: Is Señor Saldaña Roca in Iquitos? Might I see him?"

There was another long silence. The discomfort of the guests was manifest. Finally the Father Superior of the Augustinians spoke. "No one knows where he is, Señor Casement," said Father Urrutia in a very pure Spanish clearly different from that of the Loretans. Roger had more difficulty understanding him. "He disappeared from Iquitos some time ago. People say he's in Lima."

"If he hadn't fled, we Iquitians would have lynched him," declared an old man, shaking a choleric fist.

"Iquitos is the land of patriots," exclaimed Pablo Zumaeta. "No one forgives that individual who invented despicable stories to slander Peru and bring down the enterprise that has brought progress to Amazonia."

"He did it because the knavery he had prepared did not succeed," added the prefect. "Were you informed that Saldaña Roca, before publishing those infamies, tried to extort money from Señor Arana's company?"

"We refused, and he published that fairy tale about Putumayo," stated Pablo Zumaeta. "He has been prosecuted for libel, slander, and extortion, and prison is waiting for him. That's why he fled."

"There's nothing like being on the spot to find out about things," Roger remarked.

The private conversations destroyed the general one. The dinner continued with a dish of assorted Amazonian fish, one of which, called the *gamitana*, had a delicate, delicious flesh, Roger thought. But the seasoning made his mouth burn.

When the meal ended, after saying goodbye to the prefect, he spoke briefly with his friends on the commission. According to Seymour Bell, it had been imprudent to bring up so abruptly the subject of the journalist Saldaña Roca, who irritated the prominent people of Iquitos so much. But Louis Barnes congratulated him because, he said, it had allowed them to study the irate response of these people to the journalist.

"It's a shame we can't talk to him," replied Roger. "I would have liked to meet him."

They said good night and Roger and the consul walked back to the diplomat's house along the same route they had taken earlier. The noise, revelry, songs, dances, toasts, and fights had become even louder and Roger was surprised at the number of small boys—ragged, half-naked, barefoot—standing at the doors of the bars and brothels, spying with mischievous faces on what was happening inside. There were also a good number of dogs digging through the garbage.

"Don't waste your time looking for him, because you won't find him," said Stirs. "Saldaña Roca is probably dead."

Roger wasn't surprised. He too suspected, when he saw the verbal violence the mere name of the journalist had provoked, that his disappearance was permanent.

"Did you know him?"

The consul had a round, bald head, and his skull sparkled as if covered with little drops of water. He walked slowly, testing the muddy ground with his stick, fearful perhaps of stepping on a snake or a rat.

"We spoke two or three times," said Stirs. "He was very short and somewhat hunchbacked. What they call a *cholo* here, a *cholito*. That is, a mestizo. The *cholos* tend to be gentle and formal, but not Saldaña Roca. He was brusque, very sure of himself. With the fixed gaze that believers and fanatics have and that always, truth be told, makes me very nervous. My temperament doesn't go in that direction. I don't have much admiration for martyrs, Mr. Casement. Or for heroes. People who sacrifice themselves for truth or justice often do more harm than the thing they want to change."

Roger said nothing: he was trying to imagine the small man with physical deformities and a heart and will like those of Edmund D. Morel. A martyr and a hero, certainly. He imagined him inking with his own hands the metal plates of his weekly publications, *La Felpa* and *La Sanción*. He probably edited them in a small artisanal press that undoubtedly operated in a corner of his house. This modest dwelling also must have been the editorial and administrative offices of his two small papers.

"I hope you didn't take offense at my words," the British consul apologized, suddenly sorry for what he had just said. "Señor Saldaña Roca was very brave to make those accusations, of course. A reckless man, almost a suicide, when he filed a judicial complaint against Casa Arana for torture, kidnapping, flogging, and other crimes on the Putumayo rubber plantations. He was not naïve. He knew very well what would happen to him."

"What happened to him?"

"It was predictable," said Stirs without a shred of emotion. "They burned the press on Calle Morona. You can still see the charred remains. They shot at his house too. The bullet holes are in full view, on Calle Próspero. He had to take his son out of the Augustinian fathers' academy because the other boys made his life impossible. He was obliged to send his family to a secret site, who knows where, because their lives were in danger. He had to shut down his two little publications because no one gave him another advertisement and no press in Iquitos would agree to print them. He was shot at twice in the street as a warning. Twice he was saved by a miracle. One attack left him lame, with a bullet embedded in his calf. The last time he was seen was in February 1909, on the embankment. He was being shoved toward the river. His face was swollen from the beating a gang had given him. They put him in a boat heading for Yurimaguas. He was never heard from again.

It may be that he managed to escape to Lima. I hope so. Or, with his hands and feet tied and bleeding wounds, they might have tossed him in the river for the piranhas to finish off. If that's the case, his bones, which is the only thing those animals don't eat, must be in the Atlantic by now. I suppose I'm not telling you anything you don't already know. In the Congo you must have seen things like this, or worse."

They had reached the consul's house. He lit the lamp in the small hallway at the entrance and offered Roger a glass of port. They sat together on the terrace and lit cigarettes. The moon had disappeared behind some clouds but stars were still in the sky. The distant uproar of the streets mixed with the synchronous sound of insects and the splashing of water against the branches and reeds along the banks.

"What good did so much courage do for poor Benjamín Saldaña Roca?" the consul reflected with a shrug. "None at all. He ruined his family and probably lost his life. And we lost those two little papers, *La Felpa* and *La Sanción*, that were amusing to read every week for their gossip."

"I don't believe his sacrifice was totally useless," Roger corrected him gently. "Without Saldaña Roca, we wouldn't be here. Unless, of course, you think our coming won't do any good either."

"God forbid," exclaimed the consul. "You're right. All the furor in the United States and Europe. Yes, Saldaña Roca began all of it with his accusations. And then, Walter Hardenburg's denunciations. What I said was foolish. I hope your arrival does some good and changes things. Forgive me, Mr. Casement. Living so many years in Amazonia has made me somewhat skeptical about the idea of progress. In Iquitos, you eventually don't believe any of it. Above all, that one day justice will force injustice to retreat. Perhaps it's time for me to go back to England and take a bath in English optimism. I can see that all those years serving the Crown in Brazil have not made you a pessimist. I wish I were like you. I envy you."

When they said good night and went to their rooms, Roger stayed awake for a long while. Had he done the right thing in accepting this assignment? A few months earlier, Sir Edward Grey, the foreign secretary, had called him to his office and said: "The scandal concerning the Putumayo crimes has reached intolerable limits. Public opinion demands that the government do something. No one is as qualified as you to travel there. An investigative commission will go as well, made up of independent people whom the Peruvian Amazon Company itself has decided to send. But even though you travel with them, I want you to prepare a personal report for the government. You have a great deal of prestige because of what you did in the Congo. You're a specialist in atrocities. You can't say no." His first reaction had been to find an excuse and refuse. Then, upon reflection, he told himself that precisely because of his work in the Congo, he had a moral obligation to accept. Had he done the right thing? Stirs's skepticism seemed a bad omen. From time to time Sir Edward Grey's phrase, "a specialist in atrocities," resounded in his mind.

Unlike the consul, he believed that Benjamín Saldaña Roca had performed a great service for Amazonia, his country, and humanity. The journalist's accusations in *La Sanción: Bisemanario Comercial, Político y Literario* constituted the first thing he read about the Putumayo rubber plantations following his conversation with Sir Edward, who had given him four days to decide whether to travel with the investigative commission. The Foreign Office immediately placed in his hands a file of documents; two direct testimonies of persons who had been in the region stood out: the articles by the North American engineer, Walter Hardenburg, in the London weekly *Truth*, and the articles by Benjamín Saldaña Roca, some of which had been translated into English by the Anti-Slavery and Aborigines' Protection Society, a humanitarian institution.

His first reaction was disbelief: the journalist, beginning with real events, had so magnified the abuses that his articles exuded unreality, and even a somewhat sadistic imagination. But Roger immediately recalled the disbelief that had been the reaction of many Englishmen, Europeans, and North Americans when he and Morel made public the iniquities in the Congo Free State. It was how humans defended against everything that demonstrated the indescribable cruelties they were capable of when driven by greed and base instincts in a lawless world. If those horrors had occurred in the Congo, why couldn't they have happened in Amazonia?

Distressed, he got out of bed and went to sit on the terrace. The sky was dark and the stars had disappeared. There were fewer lights in the direction of the city but the uproar still continued. If Saldaña Roca's denunciations were true, it was likely, as the consul believed, that the journalist had in fact been thrown in the river, hands and feet tied, and bleeding to excite the appetite of the piranhas. Stirs's fatalistic, cynical attitude irked him. As if everything that had happened was caused not by cruel people but a fatidic determination, just as the stars move or the tides rise. He had called him a "fanatic." A fanatic for justice? Yes, undoubtedly. A reckless man. A modest man, without money or influence. An Amazonian Morel. A believer, perhaps? He had done it because he believed that the world, society, life could not go on if this shame continued. Roger thought about his youth, when his experience of evil and suffering in Africa flooded him with belligerent emotion, that pugnacious desire to do anything to make the world better. He felt something fraternal toward Saldaña Roca. He would have liked to shake his hand, be his friend, tell him: "You have done something beautiful and noble in your life, sir."

Had he been there, in Putumayo, in the gigantic region where Julio C. Arana's company operated? Had he gone there knowingly to put himself in harm's way? His articles didn't say so but the precision of names, places, and dates indicated that Saldaña Roca had been an eye witness to what he recounted. Roger had read the testimonies of Saldaña Roca and Walter Hardenburg so often that at times it seemed he had been there himself.

He closed his eyes and saw the immense region, divided into stations, the principal ones being La Chorrera and El Encanto, each with its own chief. *That is, its monster*. That and only that was what people like Víctor Macedo and Miguel Loaysa, for example, could be. Both had played a leading role in the most memorable event of 1903, when close to eight hundred Ocaimas came to La Chorrera to turn in their baskets of balls of rubber harvested in the forests. After weighing and storing them, the assistant manager of La Chorrera, Fidel Velarde, pointed out to his superior, Víctor Macedo, there with Miguel Loaysa from El Encanto, the twenty-five Ocaimas separated from the others because they hadn't brought the minimum quota of *jebe*—latex or rubber—they were responsible for. Macedo and Loaysa decided to teach the savages a good lesson. Indicating to the overseers—blacks from Barbados—that they should keep the rest of the Ocaimas at bay with their Mausers, they ordered the "boys" to cover the twenty-five in sacks soaked in gasoline. Then they set fire to them. Shrieking, transformed into human torches, some managed to put out the flames by rolling on the ground but were left with terrible burns. Those who threw themselves into the river like flaming meteors drowned. Macedo, Loaysa, and Velarde finished off the wounded with their revolvers. Each time he evoked the scene, Roger felt dizzy.

According to Saldaña Roca, the managers did that as a warning but also for amusement. They enjoyed it. Making people suffer, competing in cruelties, was a vice they had contracted from engaging so frequently in flagellations, beatings, and tortures. Often, when they were drunk, they looked for pretexts for their blood games. Saldaña Roca cited a letter from the company manager to Miguel Flores, a station chief, admonishing him for "killing Indians just for sport," knowing that laborers were scarce and reminding him that one should have recourse to those excesses only "in cases of necessity." Miguel Flores's reply was worse than the accusation: "I protest because in these past two months only forty Indians died at my station."

Saldaña Roca enumerated the different types of punishment: from floggings, to being put in stocks or on the rack, to cutting off ears, nose, hands, and feet, to killing. Hanged, shot, burned, or drowned in the river. In Matanzas, he affirmed, there were more Indian remains than in any other station. It wasn't possible to calculate but the bones probably corresponded to hundreds, perhaps thousands, of victims. The man responsible for Matanzas was Armando Normand, a young Bolivian-Englishman, barely twenty-two or twenty-three years old. He asserted he had studied in London. His cruelty had been transformed into an "infernal myth" among the Huitotos, whom he had decimated. In Abisinia, the company fined the chief, Abelardo Agüero, and his assistant, Augusto Jiménez, for target shooting at the Indians, knowing that in this way they had irresponsibly sacrificed laborers who were useful to the firm.

In spite of being so far apart, once again Roger thought that the Congo and Amazonia were joined by an umbilical cord. The same horrors were repeated, with minor variations, inspired by greed, the original sin that accompanied human beings from birth, the hidden inspiration of their infinite wickedness. Or was there something else? Had Satan won the eternal struggle?

Tomorrow promised to be a very intense day for him. The consul had located three blacks from Barbados in Iquitos who were British nationals. They had worked for several years on Arana's rubber plantations and agreed to be questioned by the commission if they were repatriated afterward.

Though he slept very little, he woke at first light. He did not feel bad. He washed, dressed, put on a panama hat, picked up his camera, left the house without seeing either the consul or the servants. Outside, the sun had risen in a cloudless sky, and it was growing hot. At midday Iquitos would be an oven. There were people on the streets, and the small, noisy trolley, painted red and blue, was already running. From time to time Indian pedlars with Asian features, yellowish skin, and faces and arms painted with geometric figures offered him fruits, drinks, live animals—monkeys, macaws, and small lizards—or arrows, mallets, and blowguns. Many bars and restaurants were still open but had few patrons. There were drunks sprawled under roofs of palm leaf and dogs digging through the trash. *This city is a vile, stinking hole*, he thought. He took a long walk on the unpaved streets, crossing the Plaza de Armas where he recognized the Prefecture, and found himself on an embankment with stone railings, a pretty walk from which one could see the enormous river with its floating islands and, in the distance, sparkling in the sun, the line of tall trees on the other bank. At the end of the embankment, where it disappeared into a grove of trees and a wooded hillside at the foot of which was a wharf, he saw some boys, barefoot and wearing only short pants, driving in stakes. They had put on paper hats as protection from the sun.

They looked not like Indians but *cholos*. One of them, not yet twenty, had a harmonious torso with muscles that stood out with each hammer blow. After hesitating a moment, Roger walked up to him, showing him his camera.

"Would you allow me to take your photograph?" he asked in Portuguese. "I can pay."

He repeated the question twice in his poor Spanish until the boy smiled. He said something Roger could not understand to the others. And, finally, he turned back and asked, snapping his fingers: "How much?" Roger searched through his pockets and took out a handful of coins. The boy examined them visually, counting them.

He took several photoplates, amid the laughter and jokes of his friends, having him remove the paper hat, raise his arms, show off his muscles, and adopt the posture of a discus thrower. For the last shot he had to touch the boy's arm for a moment. He felt his hands wet with nervousness and the heat. He stopped taking photographs when he realized he was surrounded by ragged little boys observing him as if he were a strange animal. He handed the coins to the boy and hurried back to the consulate.

His friends from the commission, sitting at the table, were having breakfast with the consul. He joined them, explaining that he began every day with a long walk. As they drank watery, very sweet coffee and ate slices of fried yucca, Stirs explained who the Barbadians were. He began by warning them that the three had worked in Putumayo but had ended on bad terms with Arana's company. They felt they had been deceived and cheated by the Peruvian Amazon Company and for that reason their testimony would be filled with resentment. He suggested that the Barbadians not appear before all the commission members at the same time because they would feel intimidated and not say a word. They decided to divide into groups of two or three for their appearance.

Roger was paired with Seymour Bell who, as he had expected, said he didn't feel well a short while after beginning the interview with the first Barbadian, referring to his dehydration problem, and left, leaving him alone with the former overseer for Casa Arana.

His name was Eponim Thomas Campbell and he was not sure of his age, though he thought he was no older than thirty-five. He was black with long kinky hair where some white shone. He wore a faded blouse open down to his navel, and coarse trousers that reached only to his ankles and were held up at his waist with a length of rope. He was barefoot, and his enormous feet, with their long toenails and many scabs, seemed to be made of stone. His English was full of colloquialisms that Roger found difficult to understand. At times Portuguese and Spanish words were mixed in.

Using simple language, Roger assured him his testimony would be confidential and in no case would he find himself compromised by what he might say. He would not even take notes, he would just listen. He asked only for truthful information about what was going on in Putumayo.

They were sitting on the small terrace off Roger's bedroom, and on the table, in front of the bench they shared, was a pitcher with papaya juice and two glasses. Eponim Thomas Campbell had been hired seven years earlier in Bridgetown, the capital of Barbados, with eighteen other Barbadians, by Lizardo Arana, the brother of Don Julio César, to work as an overseer in one of the stations in Putumayo. And right there the deception began because, when they hired him, they never told him he would have to spend a good part of his time on *correrías*.

"Explain to me what *correrías* are," said Roger.

Going out to hunt Indians in their villages to make them come to harvest rubber on the company's lands. Whoever they were: Ocaimas, Muinanes, Nonuyas, Andoques,

Rezígaros, or Boras. Any of the Indians in the region. Because all of them, without exception, were unwilling to collect *jebe*. They had to be forced. *Correrías* required very long expeditions, sometimes with no result. They would arrive and find the villages deserted. The inhabitants had fled. Other times not, happily. They would attack, shooting to frighten them and keep them from defending themselves, but they did, with their blowguns and garrotes. There would be a battle. Then the ones who could walk, men and women, had to be driven back, tied together by the neck. The old people and newborns were left behind so they wouldn't hold up the march. Campbell never committed the gratuitous cruelties of Armando Normand in spite of having worked for him for two years in Matanzas, where Mr. Normand was the manager.

"Gratuitous cruelties?" Roger interrupted. "Give me some examples."

Campbell shifted on the bench, uncomfortable. His large eyes rolled in their sockets.

"Mr. Normand had his eccentricities," he murmured, looking away. "When someone behaved badly. That is, when he didn't behave the way he expected. He would drown his children in the river, for example. Himself. With his own hands, I mean."

He paused and explained that Mr. Normand's eccentricities made him nervous. You could expect anything at all from so strange a man, even that one day he'd feel like emptying his revolver into the person closest to him. That's why he asked to transfer to another station. When they sent him to Último Retiro, whose chief was Mr. Alfredo Montt, Campbell slept easier.

"Did you ever have to kill Indians in the course of your duties?"

Roger saw that the Barbadian's eyes looked at him, moved away, then looked at him again.

"It was part of the job," he admitted, shrugging. "For the overseers and the boys, who are also called rationals. In Putumayo a lot of blood flows. People end up getting used to it. Life there is killing and dying."

"Would you tell me how many people you had to kill, Mr. Campbell?"

"I never kept count," Campbell quickly replied. "I did the job I had to do and tried to turn the page. I did what I had to. That's why I say the company treated me very badly."

He became entangled in a long, confused monologue against his former employers. They accused him of being involved in the sale of some fifty Huitotos to a plantation that belonged to some Colombians, the Señores Iriarte, with whom the company of Señor Arana was always fighting for laborers. It was a lie. Campbell swore and swore again he had nothing to do with the disappearance of those Huitotos from Último Retiro, who, it was learned later, reappeared working for the Colombians. The one who had sold them was the station chief himself, Alfredo Montt. A greedy man and a miser. To hide his guilt he denounced him and Dayton Cranton and Sinbad Douglas. Pure slander. The company believed him and the three overseers had to flee. They suffered terrible hardships to reach Iquitos. The company chiefs in Putumayo had ordered the "rationals", those men on company rations, to kill the three Barbadians on sight. Now Campbell and his two companions lived by begging and doing occasional odd jobs. The company refused to pay their return passage to Barbados. It had denounced them for abandoning their work and the judge in Iquitos ruled in favor of Casa Arana, of course.

Roger promised that the government would take care of repatriating him and his two colleagues, since they were British citizens.

Exhausted, he went to lie down as soon as he had said goodbye to Eponim Thomas Campbell. He was perspiring, his body ached, and he felt a traveling indisposition that was tormenting him little by little, organ by organ, from his head to his feet. The Congo. Amazonia. Was there no limit to the suffering of human beings? The world was infested with these enclaves of savagery that awaited him in Putumayo. How many? Hundreds, thousands, millions? Could the hydra be defeated? Its head was cut off in one place and reappeared in another, bloodier and more horrifying. He fell asleep.

He dreamed about his mother at a lake in Wales. A faint, distant sun shone through the leaves of the tall oaks, and agitated, feeling palpitations, he saw the muscular young man he had photographed this morning on the embankment in Iquitos. What was he doing at that Welsh lake? Or was it an Irish lake in Ulster? The slender silhouette of Anne Jephson disappeared. His uneasiness was due not to the sadness and pity caused in him by an enslaved humanity in Putumayo, but the sensation that although he didn't see her, Anne Jephson was nearby, spying on him from a circular grove of trees. Fear, however, did not weaken his growing excitement while he watched the boy from

Iquitos approach. His torso dripped water as he emerged from the lake like a lacustrian god. At each step his muscles stood out, and on his face was an insolent smile that made Roger shudder and moan in his sleep. When he awoke, he confirmed with disgust that he had ejaculated. He washed and changed his trousers and underwear. He felt ashamed and uncertain.

He found the members of the commission overwhelmed by the testimonies they had just received from the Barbadians Dayton Cranton and Sinbad Douglas. The ex-overseers had been as raw in their statements as Eponim Thomas Campbell had been with Roger. What horrified them most was that Dayton as well as Sinbad seemed obsessed above all with disproving they had "sold" those fifty Huitotos to the Colombian plantation owners.

"They weren't in the least concerned with the floggings, mutilations, or murders," Walter Folk kept repeating, a man who did not seem to suspect the evil that greed could provoke. "Such horrors seem the most natural thing in the world to them."

"I couldn't bear Sinbad's entire statement," Henry Fielgald confessed. "I had to go out to vomit."

"You've read the documentation collected by the Foreign Office," Roger reminded them. "Did you think the accusations of Saldaña Roca and Hardenburg were pure fantasies?"

"Not fantasies," replied Walter Folk, "but certainly exaggerations."

"After this aperitif, I wonder what we're going to find in Putumayo," said Louis Barnes.

"They'll have taken precautions," suggested Folk.

"They'll show us a very cosmetic reality."

The consul interrupted to announce that lunch was served. Except for him, who with appetite ate *sábalo* fish served with a salad of *chonta* fruit and wrapped in corn husks, the commissioners barely tasted a mouthful. They were silent, absorbed in their memories of the recent interviews.

"This journey will be a descent into hell," prophesied Seymour Bell, who had just rejoined the group. He turned to Roger. "You've already gone through this. One survives, then."

"The wounds take time to close," Roger suggested.

"It's not so serious, gentlemen." Mr. Stirs tried to raise their spirits; he had eaten in very good humor. "A good Loretan siesta and you'll feel better. With the authorities and the heads of the Peruvian Amazon Company, things will go better for you than with the blacks, you'll see."

Instead of taking a siesta, Roger sat at the small night table in his room and wrote in his notebook everything he remembered of his conversation with Eponim Thomas Campbell and made summaries of the testimonies the commission members had taken from the other two Barbadians. Then, on a separate paper, he wrote down the questions he would ask that afternoon of the prefect Rey Lama and the manager of the company, Pablo Zumaeta, who, Stirs had told him, was Julio C. Arana's brother-in-law.

The prefect received the commission in his office and offered them glasses of beer, fruit juices, and cups of coffee. He'd had chairs brought in and distributed straw fans for ventilation. He still wore the riding trousers and boots he'd had on the night before, but had changed his embroidered vest for a white linen jacket and a shirt closed to the neck, like a Russian tunic. He had a distinguished air with his snowy temples and elegant manners. He let them know he was a career diplomat. He had served in Europe for several years and accepted this prefecture at the behest of the president of the republic—he indicated the photograph on the wall, a small, elegant man, dressed in tails and a top hat, with a sash across his chest—Augusto B. Leguía.

"Who sends through me his most cordial greetings," he added.

"How good that you speak English and we can do without the interpreter, Prefect," responded Roger.

"My English is very bad," Rey Lama interrupted affectedly. "You'll have to be indulgent."

"The British government regrets that its requests that President Leguía's government initiate an investigation into the accusations in Putumayo have been useless."

"There is a judicial action in progress, Señor Casement," the prefect interrupted. "My government did not need His Majesty to initiate it. That is why it has appointed a special judge who is on his way now to Iquitos. A distinguished magistrate: Judge Carlos A. Valcárcel. You know that the distance between Lima and Iquitos is enormous."

"But in that case, why send a judge from Lima?" Louis Barnes intervened. "Aren't there judges in Iquitos? Yesterday, at the dinner you held for us, you introduced several magistrates."

Roger noted that Rey Lama gave Barnes a pitying look, the kind appropriate for a child who has not reached the age of reason, or an imbecilic adult.

"This talk is confidential, isn't it, gentlemen?" he asked at last.

Every head nodded. The prefect still hesitated before answering.

"My government sending a judge from Lima to investigate demonstrates its good faith," he explained. "The easiest thing would have been to ask a local judge to do it. But then . . ."

He stopped, uncomfortable.

"A word to the wise," he added.

"Do you mean that no judge from Iquitos would dare confront the company of Señor Arana?" Roger asked quietly.

"This is not cultured, prosperous England, gentlemen," the prefect murmured sorrowfully. He had a glass of water in his hand and he drank it all in one swallow. "If a person takes months to come here from Lima, the remuneration for magistrates, authorities, the military, and functionaries takes even longer. Or, quite simply, it never arrives at all. And what can these people live on while they wait for their salaries?"

"The generosity of the Peruvian Amazon Company?" suggested Walter Folk.

"Don't put words I haven't said in my mouth," Rey Lama balked, raising his hand. "Señor Arana's company advances their salaries to functionaries as a loan. These sums are to be paid back, in principle, with minimal interest. They are not a gift. There is no bribery. It is an honorable agreement with the state. But even so, it's natural that magistrates who live thanks to those loans are not absolutely impartial when dealing with Señor Arana's company. You understand, don't you? The government has sent a judge from Lima to carry out an absolutely independent investigation. Isn't this the best proof that it is determined to find out the truth?"

The commission members drank from their glasses of water or beer, confused and demoralized. *How many are already looking for a pretext to return to Europe?* Roger thought. They certainly hadn't foreseen any of this. With the exception perhaps of Louis Barnes, who had lived in Africa, the others did not imagine that in the rest of the world not everything functioned the way it did in the British Empire.

"Are there authorities in the region whom we'll visit?" asked Roger.

"Except for inspectors who pass through when a bishop dies, none," said Rey Lama. "It is a very isolated region. Until a few years ago, virgin forest, populated only by savage tribes. What authority could the government send there? And to what end? For the cannibals to eat? If there's commercial life there now, and work, and a beginning of modernity, it is due to Julio C. Arana and his brothers. You should consider that as well. They have been the first to conquer that Peruvian land for Peru. Without the company, all of Putumayo would already have been occupied by Colombia, which hungers for the region. You cannot leave out that aspect, gentlemen. Putumayo is not England. It is an isolated and remote world of pagans who, when they have twins or children with a physical deformity, drown them in the river. Julio C. Arana has been a pioneer, he has brought in boats, medicines, Catholicism, clothes, Spanish. Abuses must be punished, naturally. But don't forget, we're dealing with a land that awakens greed. Don't you find it strange that in the accusations of Señor Hardenburg, all the Peruvian plantation owners are monsters while the Colombians are archangels filled with compassion for the natives? I've read the articles in the journal *Truth*. Didn't you find that odd? Sheer coincidence that the Colombians, bent on taking over that land, have found a defender like Señor Hardenburg, who saw only violence and abuses among the Peruvians but not a single comparable case among the Colombians. Before he came to Peru he worked on the railroads in Cauca, remember. Couldn't we be dealing with an agent?"

He gasped, fatigued, and decided to drink beer. He looked at them, one by one, with eyes that seemed to say: *A point in my favor, isn't that so?*

"Whippings, mutilations, rapes, murders," murmured Henry Fielgald. "Is that what you call bringing modernity to Putumayo, Prefect? Not only Hardenburg bore witness. So did Saldaña Roca, your compatriot. Three overseers from Barbados, whom we questioned this morning, have confirmed those horrors. They acknowledge having committed them."

"They should be punished then," stated the prefect. "And they would have been if there were judges, or police, or authorities in Putumayo. For now there is nothing but savagery. I defend no one. I excuse no one. Go there. See with your own eyes. Judge for yourselves. My government could have prevented your entering Peru, for we are a sovereign nation and Great Britain has no reason to interfere in our affairs. But we haven't. On the contrary, I have been instructed to facilitate matters for you in any way I can.

President Leguía is a great admirer of England, gentlemen. He would like Peru to be a great country one day, like yours. That is why you are here, free to go anywhere and investigate everything."

It started to pour. The light dimmed and the clatter of water on corrugated metal was so strong it seemed the roof would cave in and streams of water would fall on them. Rey Lama had adopted a melancholy expression.

"I have a wife and four children whom I adore," he said, with a dejected smile. "I haven't seen them for a year and God knows whether I'll ever see them again. But when President Leguía asked me to come to serve my country in this remote corner of the world, I didn't hesitate. I'm not here to defend criminals, gentlemen. Just the opposite. I ask only for you to understand that working, trading, setting up an industry in the heart of Amazonia is not the same as doing it in England. If this jungle one day reaches the living standards of western Europe, it will be thanks to men like Julio C. Arana."

They spent a long time in the prefect's office. They asked many questions and he answered all of them, sometimes evasively and sometimes with bravado. Roger had not yet formulated a clear idea of the man. At times he seemed to be a cynic playing a part, and other times a good man with crushing responsibilities that he tried to carry out as successfully as possible. One thing was certain: Rey Lama knew the atrocities were real and didn't like it, but his position demanded that he minimize them any way he could.

When they took their leave of the prefect, it had stopped raining. On the street, the roofs were still dripping water, there were puddles everywhere with splashing toads, and the air had filled with blowflies and mosquitoes that peppered them with bites. Heads lowered, silent, they walked to the Peruvian Amazon Company, a spacious mansion with a tile roof and glazed tiles on the facade, where the general manager, Pablo Zumaeta, was expecting them for the final interview of the day. They had a few minutes and took a turn around the large cleared space of the Plaza de Armas. Curiously they contemplated the metal house of the engineer Gustave Eiffel exposing its iron vertebrae to the elements like the skeleton of an antediluvian animal. The surrounding bars and restaurants were already open and the music and din deafened the Iquitos twilight.

The Peruvian Amazon Company, on Calle Perú, a few meters from the Plaza de Armas, was the largest, most solid building in Iquitos. Two stories, constructed of cement and metal plates, its external walls were painted light green, and in the small sitting room next to his office, where Pablo Zumaeta received them, a fan with wide wooden blades hung motionless from the ceiling, waiting for electricity. In spite of the intense heat, Señor Zumaeta, who must have been close to fifty, wore a dark suit with a brightly decorated vest, a string tie, and shiny half-boots. He ceremoniously shook hands with each person and asked each of them, in a Spanish marked by the lilting Amazonian accent that Roger had learned to identify, whether their lodgings were satisfactory, Iquitos hospitable, or whether they needed anything. He repeated to each one that he had orders cabled from London by Señor Julio C. Arana himself to offer them every assistance for the success of their mission. When he mentioned Arana, the manager of the Peruvian Amazon Company bowed to the large portrait hanging on one of the walls.

While Indian domestics, barefoot and dressed in white tunics, passed trays with drinks, Roger contemplated the serious, square, dark face with penetrating eyes of the owner of the Peruvian Amazon Company. Arana's head was covered by a French beret, and his suit looked as if it had been cut by one of the good Parisian tailors or, perhaps, in Savile Row in London. Was it true that this all-powerful rubber king, with elegant houses in Biarritz, Geneva, and the gardens of Kensington Road in London, began his career selling straw hats on the streets of Rioja, the godforsaken village in the Amazon jungle where he was born? His gaze revealed a clear conscience and great self-satisfaction.

Pablo Zumaeta, through the interpreter, announced that the company's best ship, the *Liberal*, was ready for them to board. He had provided the most experienced captain and best crew on the Amazonian rivers. Even so, sailing to Putumayo would demand sacrifices of them. It took between eight and ten days, depending on the weather. And before any of the members of the commission had time to ask him a question, he hurried to hand Roger a pile of papers in a folder: "I've prepared this documentation for you, anticipating some of your concerns," he explained. "They are the orders from the company to the managers, chiefs, assistant chiefs, and overseers of stations with regard to the treatment of personnel."

Zumaeta disguised his nervousness by raising his voice and gesticulating. As he displayed the papers filled with inscriptions, stamps, and signatures, he enumerated what they contained with the tone and attitudes of an orator in a small square: "A strict prohibition against imparting physical punishment to the natives, their wives, children, and kin, and offending them in word or deed. They are to be reprimanded and counseled in a severe manner when they have committed a verified misdeed. According to the gravity of the misdeed, they may be fined or, in the case of a very serious misdeed, fired. If the misdeed has criminal connotations, they are to be transferred to the nearest competent authority."

He took a long time to summarize the indications, oriented—he repeated it unceasingly—toward avoiding the commission of "abuses against the natives." He made a parenthesis to explain that "humans being what they are," at times employees violated these orders. When that occurred, the company sanctioned the person responsible.

"The important thing is that we do the possible and the impossible to avoid the commission of abuses on the rubber plantations. If they were committed, it was the exception, the act of some miscreant who did not respect our policy toward the indigenous."

He sat down. He had talked a great deal and with so much energy that his exhaustion was obvious. He wiped the perspiration from his face with a handkerchief that was already soaked.

"In Putumayo will we find the station heads incriminated by Saldaña Roca and Engineer Hardenburg or have they fled?"

"None of our employees has fled," the manager of the Peruvian Amazon Company said indignantly. "Why would they? Because of the slanders of two blackmailers who, since they couldn't get money out of us, invented that filth?"

"Mutilations, murders, floggings," Roger recited. "Of dozens, perhaps hundreds of people. They are accusations that have moved the entire civilized world."

"They would move me too if they had happened," an incensed Pablo Zumaeta protested. "What moves me now is that cultured and intelligent people like you credit such lies without prior investigation."

"We are going to carry one out on site," Roger reminded him. "A very serious one, you can be sure."

"Do you believe that Arana, that I, that the administrators of the Peruvian Amazon Company are suicidal and kill natives? Don't you know that the number one problem for plantation owners is the lack of harvesters? Each worker is precious to us. If those killings were true, there wouldn't be a single Indian left in Putumayo. They all would have left, isn't that so? Nobody wants to live where they're whipped, mutilated, and killed. The accusation is infinitely imbecilic, Señor Casement. If the indigenous people run away we are ruined, and the rubber industry goes under. Our employees there know it. And that's why they make an effort to keep the savages happy."

He looked at the members of the commission, one by one. He was always indignant, but now he was saddened too. He made some faces that looked like pouting.

"It isn't easy to treat them well, to keep them satisfied," he confessed, lowering his voice. "They're very primitive. Do you know what that means? Some tribes are cannibals. We can't permit that, can we? It isn't Christian, it isn't human. We prohibit it and sometimes they get angry and act like what they are: savages. Should we allow them to drown the children born with deformities? A harelip, for example. No, because infanticide isn't Christian either, is it? Well. You'll see with your own eyes. Then you'll understand the injustice England is committing against Señor Julio C. Arana and a company that, at the cost of enormous sacrifices, is transforming this country."

It occurred to Roger that Pablo Zumaeta was going to shed some tears. But he was mistaken. The manager gave them a friendly smile.

"I've spoken a great deal and now it's your turn," he apologized. "Ask me whatever you wish and I'll answer you frankly. We have nothing to hide."

For nearly an hour the members of the commission questioned the general manager of the Peruvian Amazon Company. He answered them with long tirades that at times confused the interpreter, who had him repeat words and phrases. Roger did not take part in the questioning and often was distracted. It was evident that Zumaeta would never tell the truth, would deny everything and repeat the arguments used by Arana's company to respond in London to criticisms in the newspapers. There were, perhaps, occasional excesses committed by intemperate individuals, but it was not the policy of the Peruvian Amazon Company to torture, enslave, and certainly not to kill the indigenous people. The law prohibited it, and it would have been madness to terrorize the laborers who were so scarce in Putumayo. Roger felt himself transported in space and time to the Congo. The same horrors, the same contempt for truth. The difference, Zumaeta spoke Spanish and the Belgian functionaries French. They denied the obvious with the same boldness because all of them believed that harvesting rubber and making money was a Christian ideal that justified the worst atrocities against pagans who, of course, were always cannibals and killers of their own children.

When they left the Peruvian Amazon Company building, Roger accompanied his colleagues to the house where they were staying. Instead of returning directly to the British consul's house, he walked through Iquitos with no particular destination. He had always liked to walk, alone or in the company of a friend, to begin and end the day. He could do it for hours, but on the unpaved streets of Iquitos he often stumbled over holes and puddles where frogs were croaking. The noise was enormous. Bars, restaurants, brothels, dance halls, and gambling dens were filled with people drinking, eating, dancing, or arguing. And in every doorway, clusters of half-naked little boys, spying. He saw the last reddish clouds of twilight disappear on the horizon and took the rest of the walk in the dark, along streets lit at intervals by the lamps in the bars. He realized he had reached that quadrangular lot with the pompous name of Plaza de Armas. He walked around the square and suddenly heard someone, sitting on a bench, greet him in Portuguese: "*Boa noite*, Señor Casement." It was Father Ricardo Urrutia, superior of the Augustinians in Iquitos, whom he had met at the dinner given by the prefect. He sat beside him on the wooden bench.

"When it doesn't rain, it's pleasant to go out and see the stars and breathe a little fresh air," the Augustinian said in Portuguese. "As long as you cover your ears so you don't hear that infernal noise. They must have told you already about this iron house that a half-mad plantation owner bought in Europe and is erecting on that corner. It was shown in Paris, at the Great Exposition of 1889, it seems. They say it will be a social club. Can you imagine what an oven it will be, a metal house in the climate of Iquitos? For now it's a bat cave. Dozens of them sleep there, hanging from a rod."

Roger told him to speak Spanish, that he understood it. But Father Urrutia, who had spent more than ten years of his life with the Augustinians in Ceará, in Brazil, preferred to continue speaking Portuguese. He had been in Peruvian Amazonia less than a year.

"I know you've never been on Señor Arana's rubber plantations. But undoubtedly you know a great deal about what happens there. May I ask your opinion? Can Saldaña Roca's and Walter Hardenburg's accusations be true?"

The priest sighed. "Unfortunately, they can be, Señor Casement," he murmured. "We're very far from Putumayo here. A thousand, twelve hundred kilometers at least. Yes, in spite of being in a city with authorities, a prefect, judges, military men, police, things we know about happen here. What can happen there where there are only the employees of the company?"

He sighed again, this time with anguish.

"The great problem here is the buying and selling of young indigenous girls," he said, his voice sorrowful. "No matter how hard we try to find a solution, we can't."

The Congo, again. The Congo, everywhere, Roger thought.

"You've heard about the famous *correrías*," the Augustinian added. "Those assaults on indigenous villages to capture harvesters. The attackers don't steal only men. They also take little boys and girls. To sell here. Sometimes they take them to Manaus, where, it seems, they can get a better price. In Iquitos, a family buy a little maid for twenty or thirty *soles* at the most. They all have one, two, five little servants. Slaves, really. Working day and night, sleeping with the animals, beaten for any reason, and of course, taking care of the sexual initiation of the family's sons."

He sighed again and breathed with difficulty.

"Can't you do anything with the authorities?"

"We could, in principle, said Father Urrutia. "Slavery was abolished in Peru more than half a century ago. We could have recourse to the police and the judges. But all of them also have bought their little servants. Besides, what would the authorities do with the girls they rescued? Keep them or sell them, of course. And not always to families. Sometimes to brothels for whatever you can imagine."

"Is there no way to return them to their tribes?"

"The tribes around here are almost non-existent by now. The parents were abducted and driven to the rubber plantations. There's no place to take them. Why rescue those poor creatures, and for what? In these circumstances, perhaps it's a lesser evil for them to stay in families. Some people treat them well, are fond of them. Does that seem monstrous to you?"

"Monstrous," Roger repeated.

"It does to me, to us, as well," said Father Urrutia. "We spend hours at the mission, racking our brains. What's the solution? We can't find it. We've taken steps in Rome to see if nuns can come and open a small school here for the girls. At least they'd receive some instruction. But will the families agree to send them to school? Very few, in any case. They consider them animals."

He sighed again. He had spoken with so much bitterness that Roger, infected by the priest's dejection, wanted to return to the British consul's house. He stood.

"You can do something, Señor Casement," said Father Urrutia in farewell, shaking his hand. "What's happened is a kind of miracle. I mean, the denunciations, the scandal in Europe. The coming of this commission to Loreto. If anyone can help these poor people, it is all of you. I'll pray for you to come back from Putumayo safe and sound."

Roger walked back very slowly, not looking at what was going on in the bars and brothels where he could hear voices, singing, strumming guitars. He thought about those children torn away from their tribes, separated from their families, packed into the bilge of a launch, brought to Iquitos, sold for twenty or thirty *soles* to a family where they would spend their lives sweeping, scrubbing, cooking, cleaning toilets, washing dirty clothes, insulted, hit, and at times raped by their owner or the sons of the owner. The same old story. The never-ending story.

9

When the cell door opened and he saw in the doorway the bulky silhouette of the sheriff, Roger thought he had a visitor—Gee or Alice, perhaps—but the jailer, instead of indicating that he should get to his feet and follow him to the visitors' room, stood looking at him in a strange way, not saying anything. *They turned down the petition*, Roger thought. He remained lying on his cot, certain that if he stood the trembling in his legs would make him collapse.

"You always want a shower?" the cold, slow voice of the sheriff asked.

My last wish, he thought. *After the bath, the hangman*.

"This goes against the rules," the sheriff murmured with some emotion. "But today's the first anniversary of the death of my son in France. I want to offer an act of compassion to his memory."

"I thank you," said Roger, standing. What had gotten into the sheriff? When had he ever shown him any kindnesses?

It seemed as if the blood in his veins, frozen when he saw the jailer appear at the door of his cell, began to circulate again through his body. He went out to the long, soot-stained hall and followed the fat jailer to the bathroom, a dark area that had a row of chipped toilets along one wall, a line of showers along the opposite wall, and some unpainted concrete receptacles with rusted spouts that poured out the water. The sheriff remained standing at the entrance, while Roger undressed, hung his blue uniform and convict's cap on a nail in the wall, and went into the shower. The stream of water made him shiver from head to toe and, at the same time, produced a feeling of joy and gratitude. He closed his eyes, and before soaping himself with the cake he had taken from one of the rubber boxes hanging on the wall, while he rubbed his arms and legs, he felt the cold water slide along his body. He was happy and exalted. With the stream of water not only did the dirt that had accumulated on his body for so many days disappear, but preoccupations, distress, and remorse as well. He soaped and rinsed himself for a long while until the sheriff indicated from a distance, with a clap of his hands, that he should hurry. Roger dried with the same clothing he put on. He did not have a comb and smoothed his hair with his hands.

"You have no idea how grateful I am for this wash, Sheriff," he said as they returned to his cell. "It has given me back life and health."

The jailer replied with an unintelligible murmur.

When he lay down on his cot again, Roger attempted to go back to reading Thomas à Kempis's *The Imitation of Christ*, but he couldn't concentrate and put the book back on the floor.

He thought about Captain Robert Monteith, his assistant and friend for the last six months he spent in Germany. A magnificent man! Loyal, efficient, and heroic. His companion in travel and travails on the U-19 German submarine that brought them, along with Sergeant Daniel Julian Bailey, alias Julian Beverly, to the coast near Tralee, where the three almost drowned because they didn't know how to row. Didn't know how to row! That's how things were: foolish little things could become mixed with great events and wreck them. He recalled the gray, rainy dawn, rough sea, and heavy mist on Good Friday, April 21, 1916, and the three of them in the unsteady boat with three oars where the German submarine had left them before disappearing into the fog. "Good luck," Captain Raimund Weisbach shouted by way of farewell. Again he had the awful feeling of impotence, trying to control the boat pitching in the violent waves, and the inability of three makeshift rowers to head it toward the coast whose location none of them knew. The boat spun around, went up and down, leaped, traced circles with a variable radius, and since none of the three managed to maneuver past them, the waves, striking the side of the boat, made it shudder so much that at any moment it might capsize. And in fact, it did capsize. For a few minutes the three men were on the point of drowning. They splashed and swallowed salt water until they succeeded in righting the boat and, helping one another, climbed back in. Roger recalled the valiant Monteith, his hand infected by the accident he'd had in Germany, in the port of Heligoland, trying to learn to drive a motor launch. They moored there to change submarines because the U-2 on which they sailed from Wilhelmshaven had a flaw. The wound had tormented him during the entire week's voyage between Heligoland and Tralee Bay. Roger, who made the crossing suffering atrocious seasickness and vomiting, hardly eating or getting off his narrow bunk, recalled Monteith's stoic patience as his wound swelled. The anti-inflammatories the German sailors on the U-19 gave him did no good. His hand continued suppurating and Captain Weisbach, commander of the U-19, predicted that if it wasn't taken care of as soon as they landed, the wound would develop gangrene.

The last time he saw Captain Robert Monteith was in the ruins of McKenna's Fort at dawn on April 21, when his two companions decided Roger should remain hidden there while they went to ask the Tralee Volunteers for help. They decided this because he was the one who ran the greatest risk of being recognized by the soldiers—the most sought-after prize for the watchdogs of the Empire—and because he could not endure any more. Sick and weakened, he had fallen down twice, exhausted, and the second time was unconscious for several minutes. After shaking his hand, his friends left him in the ruins of Fort McKenna with a revolver and a small bag of clothes. Roger recalled how, when he saw the larks flying around him and heard their song and discovered he was surrounded by wild violets growing out of the sandy ground of Tralee Bay, he thought, *I have reached Ireland at last*. His eyes filled with tears. Captain Monteith, when he left, had given him a military salute. Small, strong, agile, untiring, an Irish patriot to the marrow of his bones: during the six months they had lived together in Germany, Roger didn't hear a single complaint from his adjunct or detect the slightest symptom of weakness in him, in spite of the failures he'd had in Limburg Camp because of the resistance—when it wasn't open hostility—of the prisoners to enrolling in the Irish Brigade Roger wanted to form to fight alongside Germany ("but not under their command") for the independence of Ireland.

Monteith was soaked from head to foot, his swollen, bleeding hand badly wrapped in a rag that was coming loose, and with an expression of great fatigue. Walking with energetic strides in the direction of Tralee, he and Sergeant Bailey, who was limping, were lost in the fog. Had Robert Monteith arrived without being captured by the officers of the Royal Irish Constabulary? Had he managed to make contact in Tralee with people from the IRB (the Irish Republican Brotherhood) or the Volunteers? He never learned how and where Bailey was captured. His name was never mentioned in the long interrogations to which Roger was subjected, first in the Admiralty by the heads of the British intelligence services, and then by Scotland Yard. The sudden appearance of Daniel Bailey at his trial for treason as a witness for the public prosecutor dismayed Roger. In his statement, filled with lies, Monteith was not named once. Was he still free or had they killed him? Roger prayed the captain was safe and sound now, hiding in some corner of Ireland. Or had he taken part in the Easter Rising and perished there like so many anonymous Irish fighting in an adventure as heroic as it was rash? This was most likely. That he had been in the Dublin Post Office, firing, beside Tom Clarke whom he so admired, until an enemy bullet put an end to his exemplary life.

His had been a rash adventure as well. Believing that by coming to Ireland from Germany he would be able, by himself, using pragmatic and rational arguments, to stop the Easter Rising planned so secretly by the Military Council of the Irish Volunteers—Tom Clarke, Sean McDermott, Patrick Pearse, Joseph Plunkett, and one more—that not even the president of the Irish Volunteers, Professor

Eoin MacNeill, had been informed of the Rising. Wasn't it another delirious fantasy? *Reason doesn't convince mystics or martyrs*, he thought. In the bosom of the Irish Volunteers, Roger had been a participant in and witness to long, intense arguments regarding his thesis that the only way an armed action by the Irish nationalists against the British Empire would succeed was if it coincided with a German military offensive that would keep the bulk of British military power immobilized. He and young Plunkett had spent many hours in Berlin arguing about this without coming to an agreement. Was it because the heads of the Military Council never shared his conviction, that the IRB and the Volunteers who prepared the insurrection hid their plans from him until the last moment? When, at last, the information reached him in Berlin, Roger already knew that the German admiralty had rejected a naval offensive against England. When the Germans agreed to send arms to the insurrectionists, he insisted on going in person to Ireland, accompanying the weapons, secretly intending to persuade the leaders that an uprising at this moment would be a useless sacrifice. He had not been wrong about that. According to all the news he had been able to gather here and there since the days of his trial, the Rising was a heroic gesture, but it cost the lives of the most intrepid leaders of the IRB and the Volunteers and the imprisonment of hundreds of revolutionaries. The repression now would be interminable. The independence of Ireland had taken yet another step backward. What a sad, sad history!

He had a bitter taste in his mouth. Another serious mistake: having put too much hope in Germany. He recalled his argument with Herbert Ward in Paris, the last time he saw him. His best friend in Africa from the time they met, both young and eager for adventures, he mistrusted all nationalisms. He was one of the few educated, sensitive Europeans on African soil, and Roger learned a great deal from him. They exchanged books, commented on their readings, talked and argued about music, painting, poetry, and politics. Herbert dreamed of being an artist exclusively some day and stole all the time he could from his job and dedicated it to sculpting human African types in wood and clay. Both had been harsh critics of the abuses and crimes of colonialism, and when Roger became a public figure and the target of attacks for his *Report on the Congo*, Herbert and Sarita, his wife, living in Paris where he had become an acclaimed sculptor who, for the most part, made castings in bronze, always inspired by Africa, were his most enthusiastic defenders. And they were as well when his *Report on Putumayo*, denouncing the crimes committed by the rubber barons in Putumayo against the indigenous people, provoked another scandal around the figure of Roger Casement. Herbert had even shown sympathy at first for Roger's nationalist conversion, though often in letters he joked about the dangers of "patriotic fanaticism" and reminded him of Dr. Johnson's phrase, according to which "patriotism is the last refuge of the scoundrel." Their rapport came to an end on the subject of Germany. Herbert always rejected energetically the positive, beautified vision Roger had of Chancellor Bismarck, unifier of the German states, and of the "Prussian spirit," which he thought rigid, authoritarian, coarse, hostile to imagination and sensitivity, and more akin to barracks and military hierarchies than to democracy and the arts. When, in the middle of the war, he learned from denunciations in the English newspapers that Roger had gone to Berlin to conspire with the enemy, he had a letter sent to him, through his sister Nina, putting an end to their friendship of so many years. In the same letter he let him know that his and Sarita's eldest son, a boy of nineteen, had just died at the front.

How many other friends had he lost, people like Herbert and Sarita Ward, who had appreciated and admired him and now considered him a traitor? Even Alice Stopford Green, his teacher and friend, had objected to his trip to Berlin even though, after he was captured, she never mentioned their disagreement again. How many others were repelled by him because of the vile things the English press attributed to him? A stomach cramp obliged him to curl up on his cot. He remained like that for a long time until the sensation of a stone in his belly crushing his intestines had passed.

During the eighteen months in Germany he often had wondered if he hadn't made a mistake. But no, facts had confirmed all his theses when the German government made public a statement—written for the most part by him—declaring solidarity with the idea of Irish sovereignty and a desire to help the Irish recover the independence seized by the British Empire. But later, after long waits on Unter den Linden to be received by the authorities in Berlin, broken promises, his ailments, and his failures with the Irish Brigade, he had begun to doubt.

He felt his heart pounding, as it did each time he recalled those icy days of whirling snow storms when at last, after so many negotiations, he finally could speak to the 2,200 Irish prisoners in the Limburg camp. He explained, carefully repeating a speech he had rehearsed in his mind over months, that this wasn't a question of "going over to the enemy camp" or anything like that. The Irish Brigade would not be part of the German army. It would be an independent military force with its own officers and would fight for the independence of Ireland from its colonizer and oppressor "alongside, but not inside" the German armed forces. What hurt him most, an acid that corroded his spirit unendingly, was not that of 2,200 prisoners only some fifty had joined the Brigade. It was the hostility his proposal encountered, the shouts and muttering when he clearly heard the words "traitor," "yellow," "sold," "cockroach," used by many prisoners to show him their contempt, and finally, the spittle and attempts at aggression directed at him the third time he attempted to speak to them (attempted, because he could say only a phrase or two before he was silenced by whistles and insults). And the humiliation he felt when he was rescued from a possible attack, perhaps a lynching, by his escort of German soldiers who ran out of the place with him.

He had been deluded and naïve to think the Irish prisoners would enlist in a brigade equipped, dressed—though the uniform had been designed by Roger—fed, and advised by the German army they had just fought, which had gassed them in the Belgian trenches, killed, maimed, and wounded so many of their companions, and had them now behind barbed wire. One had to understand the circumstances, be flexible, remember what the Irish prisoners had suffered and lost, and not feel rancor toward them. But that brutal collision with a reality he had not expected was very difficult for Roger. It had repercussions in his body as well as his spirit, for when he lost almost all hope, the fevers immediately began that kept him in bed for so long.

During those months, the solicitous loyalty and affection of Captain Robert Monteith were a balm without which he probably would not have survived. The difficulties and frustrations found everywhere had no effect—not, at least, a visible one—on his conviction that the Irish Brigade conceived of by Roger would eventually become a reality and recruit into its ranks the majority of Irish prisoners, and Captain Monteith devoted himself enthusiastically to directing the training of the fifty volunteers to whom the German government had granted a small camp in Zossen, near Berlin. He even succeeded in recruiting a few more. All of them wore the Brigade uniform designed by Roger, including Monteith. They lived in field tents, had marches, maneuvers, and firing practice with rifles and pistols, but with blank bullets. Discipline was strict, and in addition to exercises, military drills, and sports, Monteith insisted that Roger continually give talks to members of the Brigade on the history of Ireland, its culture, its singularity, and the perspectives that would open once its independence had been achieved.

What would Captain Robert Monteith have said if he had seen that handful of Irishmen from the Limburg camp—freed thanks to an exchange of prisoners—file in as prosecution witnesses at the trial, among them even Sergeant Daniel Bailey. All of them, responding to questions from the public prosecutor, swore that Roger Casement, surrounded by officers of the German army, had exhorted them to go over to the enemy ranks, dangling as bait the prospect of freedom, a salary, and future earnings. And all of them had corroborated the flagrant lie that the Irish prisoners who gave in to his hounding and joined the Brigade immediately received better rations, more blankets, and a more flexible regime of furloughs. Captain Robert Monteith wouldn't have become indignant with them. He would have said, once again, that those compatriots were blind or, rather, blinded by the poor education, ignorance, and confusion in which the Empire kept Ireland, placing a veil over their eyes regarding their true situation as a people occupied and oppressed for the past three centuries. One mustn't despair, all of that was changing. And perhaps, as he did so often in Limburg and Berlin, he would tell Roger, to raise his spirits, how enthusiastically and generously young Irishmen—farmers, laborers, fishermen, artisans, students—had entered the ranks of the Irish Volunteers since the organization was founded at a great meeting in the Rotunda in Dublin on November 25, 1913, as a response to the militarization of unionists in Ulster, led by Sir Edward Carson, who openly threatened to disobey the law if the British parliament approved Home Rule. Captain Robert Monteith, a former officer in the British army who had fought in the Boer War in South Africa and been wounded in two battles, was one of the first to enlist in the Volunteers. He was put in charge of the military training of recruits. Roger, who attended that emotional meeting in the Rotunda and was one of the treasurers of funds for the purchase of weapons, elected to that position of extreme confidence by the leaders of the Irish Volunteers, did not recall having known Monteith then. But Monteith assured him he had shaken his hand and told him he was proud it was an Irishman who denounced to the entire world the crimes committed against the indigenous of the Congo and Amazonia.

He recalled the long walks he took with Monteith around Limburg Camp or along the streets of Berlin, at times in the pale, cold dawn, at times at dusk in the first shadows of the night, speaking obsessively about Ireland. In spite of the friendship that grew between them, he never succeeded in having Monteith treat him with the informality that exists between friends. The captain always addressed him as his political and military superior, granting him the right of way on paths, opening doors, placing chairs close to him, and saluting him before or after shaking his hand, clicking his heels, and bringing his hand martially up to his kepi.

Captain Monteith heard for the first time about the Irish Brigade Roger was attempting to form in Germany from Tom Clarke, the reserved leader of the IRB and the Irish Volunteers, and immediately offered to go and work with him. Monteith had been confined at the time in Limerick by the British army as punishment after it was discovered that he was giving clandestine military instruction to the Volunteers. Tom Clarke consulted with the other leaders and his proposal was accepted. His journey, which Monteith recounted to Roger in full detail as soon as they saw each other in Germany, had as many mishaps as an adventure novel. Accompanied by his wife in order to disguise the political content of his trip, Monteith left Liverpool for New York in September 1915. There the Irish nationalist leaders placed him in the hands of the Norwegian Eivind Adler Christensen (when he thought of it, Roger felt his stomach turn) who, in the port of Hoboken, secretly brought him aboard a ship that would soon leave for Christiania, the capital of Norway. Monteith's wife remained in New York. Christensen had him travel as a stowaway, frequently changing berths and spending long hours hidden in the bilge where the Norwegian brought him water and food. The ship was stopped by the Royal Navy in mid-crossing. A squad of English sailors boarded and examined the documentation of crew and passengers, searching for spies. For the five days it took the English sailors to search the ship, Monteith jumped from one hiding place to another—at times as uncomfortable as squatting in a closet under piles of clothing and other times sunk in a barrel of tar—without being discovered. At last he disembarked secretly in Christiania. His crossing of the Swedish and Danish borders to enter Germany was no less novelesque and obliged him to use various disguises, one of them as a woman. When he finally reached Berlin, he discovered that the leader he had come to serve, Roger Casement, was ill in Bavaria. Not wasting a moment, he immediately took the train and when he arrived at the Bavarian hotel where Roger was convalescing, clicking his heels and touching his head, he introduced himself with the words: "This is the happiest moment of my life, Sir Roger."

The only time Roger recalled having disagreed with Captain Robert Monteith was one afternoon, in the military camp at Zossen, after he had given a talk to the members of the Irish Brigade. They were having tea in the canteen when Roger, for some reason he didn't remember, mentioned Eivind Adler Christensen. The captain's face transformed into a grimace of disgust.

"I see you don't have a good memory of Christensen,"

he said jokingly. "Are you angry with him for having you travel as a stowaway from New York to Norway?"

Monteith did not smile. He had become very serious.

"No, sir," he muttered. "That's not why."

"Why, then?"

Monteith hesitated, uncomfortable. "Because I've always believed the Norwegian is a spy for British intelligence."

Roger recalled that those words had the effect on him of a punch in the stomach.

"Do you have any proof of such a thing?"

"None, sir. Just a hunch."

Roger reprimanded him and ordered him not to make such conjectures without having proof. The captain stammered an apology. Now Roger would have given anything to see Monteith if only for a few moments to beg his pardon for having reproved him. "You were absolutely right, my good friend. Your intuition was correct. Eivind is something worse than a spy: he's a real demon. And I'm a naïve imbecile for having believed in him."

Eivind, another of his great mistakes in this final stage of his life. Anyone who wasn't the "overgrown boy" that he was, as he had been told by Alice Stopford Green and Herbert Ward, would have detected something suspicious in the way that incarnation of Lucifer had entered his life. Not Roger. He had believed in the accidental meeting, in a connivance of fate.

It happened in July 1914, the same day he arrived in New York to promote the Irish Volunteers among the Irish communities in the United States, obtain support and weapons, and meet with the veteran fighters John Devoy and Joseph McGarrity, the nationalist leaders of the North American branch of the IRB, called Clan na Gael. He had gone out to walk around Manhattan, fleeing the humid, steaming little hotel room burning in the New York summer, when he was approached by a blond young man as handsome as a Viking god, whose amiability, charm, and confidence seduced him immediately. Eivind was tall, athletic, with a feline walk, deep blue eyes, and a smile between archangelic and raffish. He didn't have a cent and let him know it with a comic grimace, showing him the inside of his empty pockets. Roger invited him to have a beer and something to eat. And he believed everything the Norwegian told him: he was twenty-four and had run away from his home in Norway when he was twelve. He had managed to travel as a stowaway to Glasgow. Since then he had worked as a stoker on Scandinavian and English ships on all the seas of the world. Now, stranded in New York, he managed to scrape by.

And Roger had believed him! On his narrow cot he pulled in his legs, in pain with another of those stomach cramps that took his breath away. They attacked in moments of great nervous tension. He controlled his desire to cry. Each time he felt sorry for and ashamed of himself to the point where his eyes filled with tears, he felt depressed and repelled afterward. He had never been a sentimental man given to displaying his feelings, he had always known how to hide behind a mask of perfect serenity the upheavals that shook his emotions. But his character had changed since he arrived in Berlin, accompanied by Eivind Adler Christensen, on the last day of October 1914. Had his being sick, broken, and with his nerves frayed contributed to the change? During his final months in Germany especially, when in spite of the injections of enthusiasm that Captain Robert Monteith wanted to inoculate him with, he realized his project for the Irish Brigade had failed, began to feel that the German government distrusted him (perhaps thinking he was a British spy), and learned that his denunciation of the supposed plot of British Consul Findlay in Norway to kill him did not have the international repercussions he had expected. The final blow was discovering that his comrades in the IRB and the Irish Volunteers in Ireland hid from him until the last moment their plans for the Easter Rising. ("They had to take precautions, for reasons of security," Robert Monteith reassured him.) Furthermore, they insisted that he remain in Germany and forbade him to join them. ("Think of your health, sir," Monteith offered as an excuse.) No, they weren't thinking of his health. They too were distrustful because they knew he opposed armed action if it did not coincide with a German military offensive. He and Monteith took the German submarine, contravening the orders of the nationalist leaders.

But of all his failures, the greatest had been to trust so blindly and stupidly in Eivind/Lucifer, who accompanied him to Philadelphia to visit Joseph McGarrity and was with him in New York, at the meeting organized by John Quinn, where Roger spoke before an audience filled with members of the Ancient Order of Hibernians, and at the parade of more than a thousand Irish Volunteers in Philadelphia, on August 2, whom Roger addressed to thundering applause.

From the very beginning he noticed the distrust

Christensen provoked in the nationalist leaders in the United States. But he was so vigorous in assuring them they should trust the discretion and loyalty of Eivind as they did his own that the leaders of the IRB and its North American branch, the Clan na Gael, eventually accepted the Norwegian's presence at all Roger's public activities (not in private political meetings) in the United States, and agreed to his traveling as Roger's aide to Berlin.

The extraordinary thing was that not even the strange episode in Christiania made Roger suspicious. They had just arrived in the Norwegian capital on their way to Germany, when on the same day they arrived, Eivind, who had gone out alone to take a walk, was—according to his account—accosted by strangers, abducted, and taken by force to the British consulate at 79 Drammensveien. There he was interrogated by the consul himself, Mr. Mansfeldt de Cardonnel Findlay, who offered him money to reveal his companion's identity and intentions in coming to Norway. Eivind swore to Roger he hadn't revealed anything, and they let him go after he promised the consul to find out what they wanted to know concerning that gentleman about whom he was totally ignorant, and whom he accompanied only as a guide in a city—a country—he was unfamiliar with.

And Roger had swallowed that fantastic lie without thinking for a second he was the victim of a trap! He had fallen into it like a stupid child!

Was Eivind Adler Christensen working then for the British services? Admiral Reginald Hall, head of British Naval Intelligence, and Basil Thomson, head of the Criminal Investigation Department of Scotland Yard, his interrogators since he was brought to London under arrest—he'd had very long and cordial exchanges with them—gave him contradictory information about the Scandinavian. But Roger had no illusions about this. Now he was certain it was absolutely false that Eivind had been abducted on the streets of Christiania and taken by force to the consul with the grandiose family name: Mansfeldt de Cardonnel Findlay. The interrogators showed him, no doubt to demoralize him—he had confirmed what fine psychologists they both were—the report of the British consul in the Norwegian capital to his superior in the Foreign Office regarding the inopportune arrival at the consulate at 79 Drammensveien of Eivind Adler Christensen, demanding to speak with the consul in person. And how he revealed, when the diplomat agreed to receive him, that he was accompanying an Irish nationalist leader traveling to Germany with a false passport and the assumed name of James Landy. He asked for money in exchange for this information and the consul gave him twenty-five kroner. Eivind offered to continue giving him private, secret material about the incognito individual as long as the English government compensated him generously.

Moreover, Hall and Thomson let Roger know that all his movements in Germany—talks with high functionaries, military men, and government ministers in the Ministry of Foreign Relations on Wilhelmstrasse as well as his encounters with Irish prisoners in Limburg—had been recorded with great precision by British intelligence. So that Eivind, as he pretended to plot with Roger, preparing a trap for Consul Mansfeldt de Cardonnel Findlay, continued communicating to the English government everything he said, did, wrote, and who he received and who he visited during his German stay. *I've been an imbecile and deserve my fate*, he repeated to himself for the thousandth time.

At this point the cell door opened. They were bringing him lunch. Was it midday already? Lost in memories, the morning had passed without his being aware of it. How wonderful it would be if every day were like this. He barely tasted a few mouthfuls of insipid broth and the cabbage stew with pieces of fish. When the guard came to take away the dishes, Roger asked his permission to go and clean the bucket of excrement and urine. Once a day he was allowed to go to the latrine to empty and rinse it. When he returned to his cell, he lay down again on his cot. The smiling, beautiful naughty boy's face of Eivind/Lucifer came to mind again, and with it, dejection and the sharp pangs of bitterness. He heard Eivind murmur "I love you" in his ear and it seemed he embraced him and pressed him close. He heard himself moan.

He had traveled a great deal, had intense experiences, known all kinds of people, investigated horrible crimes against primitive peoples and indigenous communities on two continents. And was it possible he would be left stupefied by so duplicitous, unscrupulous, and base a personality as that of the Scandinavian Lucifer? He had lied to him, systematically deceived him at the same time he appeared to be cheerful, useful, and affectionate as he accompanied Roger like a faithful dog, served him, took an interest in his health, went to buy him medicines, called the doctor, took his temperature. But he also took all the money from him that he could. And then he invented trips to Norway on the pretext of visiting his mother, his sister, in order to run to the consulate and report on the conspiratorial, political, and military activities of his superior and lover. And there he charged them as well for those accusations. And Roger had thought he was the one managing the thread of the plot! He had instructed Eivind, since the British wanted to kill him—according to the Norwegian, Consul Mansfeldt de Cardonnel Findlay had literally assured him of it—to continue on course until he obtained proof of the criminal intentions of British functionaries toward him. Eivind had also communicated this to the consul, for how many kroner or pounds sterling? And therefore, what Roger believed would be a devastating publicity campaign against the British government—accusing it publicly of planning the murder of its adversaries and violating the sovereignty of third countries—did not have the slightest repercussions. His public letter to Sir Edward Grey, a copy of which he had sent to all the governments represented in Berlin, did not even merit acknowledgement of its receipt at a single embassy.

But the worst—Roger again felt that pressure in his stomach—came later, at the end of his long interrogations in Scotland Yard, when he believed Eivind/Lucifer would not permeate those dialogues again. The final blow! The name of Roger Casement was in all the newspapers of Europe and the world—a British diplomat knighted and decorated by the Crown was going to be tried as a traitor to his country—and news of his imminent trial was announced everywhere. Then, Eivind Adler appeared in the British consulate in Philadelphia, proposing, with the consul as intermediary, to travel to England to testify against

Roger, as long as the English government would cover all his travel and lodging expenses "and he would receive acceptable remuneration." Roger did not doubt for a second the authenticity of the report from the British consul in Philadelphia that Hall and Thomson showed him. Fortunately, the rubicund face of the Scandinavian Satan did not appear in the witnesses' dock during the four days of his trial in the Old Bailey. Because when he saw him perhaps Roger would not have been able to contain his rage and the longing to strangle him.

Was that the face, the mentality, the viperish contortion of original sin? In one of his conversations with Edmund D. Morel, when both were wondering how it was possible for cultured, civilized people who had received a Christian education to perpetrate and take part in the horrifying crimes both men had documented in the Congo, Roger said: "When there are no more historical, sociological, psychological, cultural explanations, there is still a vast field in darkness where you can reach the root of evil in human beings, Bulldog. If you want to understand it, there is a single path: stop reasoning and turn to religion: it is original sin."

"That explanation doesn't explain anything, Tiger."

They argued for a long time without reaching a conclusion. Morel affirmed: "If the ultimate reason for evil is original sin, then there is no solution. If we humans are made for evil and carry it in our souls, why fight to find a remedy for what is irremediable?"

Bulldog was right, one mustn't fall into pessimism. Not all human beings were Eivind Adler Christensen. There were others, noble, idealistic, good, and generous, like Captain Robert Monteith and Morel himself. Roger grew sad. Bulldog had not signed any of the petitions in his favor. No doubt he disapproved of his friend (former friend now, like Herbert Ward?) taking Germany's side. Even though he opposed the war and waged a pacifist campaign and had been tried for it, no doubt Morel did not forgive him for his support of the Kaiser. Perhaps he also considered him a traitor. Like Conrad.

Roger sighed. He had lost many admirable, dear friends, like these two. How many more had turned their backs on him! But in spite of everything, he hadn't changed his way of thinking. No, he had not been wrong. He still believed that in this conflict, if Germany won, Ireland would be closer to independence. And further away from it if victory favored England. He had done what he did not for Germany but for Ireland. Couldn't men as lucid and intelligent as Ward, Conrad, and Morel understand that?

Patriotism blinded lucidity. Alice had affirmed this in a hard-fought debate during one of the evening get-togethers at her house on Grosvenor Road that Roger always recalled with so much nostalgia. What had the historian said exactly? "We should not allow patriotism to do violence to our lucidity, our reason, our intelligence." Something like that. But then he remembered the ironic dart thrown by George Bernard Shaw at all the Irish nationalists present: "They're irreconcilable, Alice. Make no mistake: patriotism is a religion, the enemy of lucidity. It is pure obscurantism, an act of faith." He said this with the mocking irony that always made the people he spoke to uncomfortable, because everyone intuited that beneath what the dramatist said in a genial way there was always a destructive intention. "Act of faith" in the mouth of this skeptic and unbeliever meant "superstition, fraud" or even worse. Still, this man who did not believe in anything and railed against everything was a great writer and had brought more prestige to Irish letters than any other of his generation. How could you construct a great work without being a patriot, without feeling that profound kinship to the land of your forebears, without loving and being moved by the ancient lineage behind you? For that reason, if asked to choose between two great creators, Roger secretly preferred Yeats to Shaw. The first was certainly a patriot who had nourished his poetry and theater with the old Irish and Celtic legends, adapting them, renovating them, demonstrating they were alive and could bear fruit in present-day literature. An instant later he regretted having thought this way. How could he be ungrateful to George Bernard Shaw: among the great intellectual figures in London, in spite of his skepticism and articles against nationalism, no one had acted more explicitly and courageously in defense of Roger Casement than the dramatist. He advised a line of defense to his lawyer that, unfortunately, poor Serjeant A. M. Sullivan, that greedy nonentity, did not accept, and after the sentence, George Bernard Shaw wrote articles and signed manifestos in favor of commuting the death penalty. It was not indispensable to be a patriot and nationalist to be generous and brave.

Having thought for just a moment of Serjeant Sullivan demoralized him, made him relive his trial for high treason in the Old Bailey, those four sinister days at the end of June 1916. It had been in no way easy to find a litigant attorney who would agree to defend him in the High Court. Everyone that Maître George Gavan Duffy, his family, and his friends contacted in Dublin and London refused on a variety of pretexts. No one wanted to defend a traitor to his country in wartime. Finally, the Irishman Sullivan, who had never defended anyone before a London court, agreed, though he did demand an excessive sum of money which his sister Nina and Alice Stopford Green had to collect by means of donations from sympathizers with the Irish cause. Going against Roger's wishes, for he wanted to openly accept responsibility as a rebel and fighter for independence and use the trial as a platform to proclaim Ireland's right to sovereignty, Sullivan imposed a legalistic, formal defense, avoiding the political and maintaining that the statute of Edward III under which Roger was being tried applied only to acts of treason in the territory of the Crown, not abroad. The acts the accused was charged with committing had taken place in Germany, and therefore Casement could not be considered a traitor to the Empire. Roger never believed this defense strategy would succeed. To make matters even worse, on the day he made his statement, Serjeant Sullivan presented a pitiable spectacle. Shortly after beginning his argument he began shaking, convulsing, until overcome by a corpse-like pallor, he exclaimed: "Your Honors! I cannot continue!" and fell to the courtroom floor in a faint. One of his assistants had to conclude his statement. Just as well that Roger, in his final exposition, was able to take over his own defense, declaring himself a rebel, defending the Easter Rising, asking for the independence of his country, and saying he was proud to have served it. That text filled him with pride and, he thought, would justify him to future generations.

What time was it? He couldn't become accustomed to not knowing the time. What thick walls Pentonville Prison had, because no matter how closely he listened, he never could hear sounds from the street: bells, motors, shouts, voices, whistles. The din of Islington Market, did he really hear it or did he invent it? He no longer knew. Nothing. At this moment, a strange sepulchral silence seemed to suspend time and life. The only noises that filtered into his cell came from inside the prison: muffled steps in the corridor outside, metal doors opening and closing, the sheriff's nasal voice giving orders to a jailer. Now no sound reached him, not even from the interior of Pentonville. The silence filled him with distress and kept him from thinking. He tried to resume his reading of Thomas à Kempis's *The Imitation of Christ*, but he couldn't concentrate and put the book back on the floor. He attempted to pray but the prayer seemed so mechanical, he stopped. He was motionless for a long time, tense, uneasy, his mind blank and his gaze fixed on a point in the ceiling that seemed damp, as if there were a leak, until he fell asleep.

He had a quiet dream that took him to the Amazonian jungles on a luminous, sunny morning. The breeze blowing over the bridge of the ship attenuated the devastating heat. There were no mosquitoes and he felt well, without the burning in his eyes that had tormented him recently, an infection seemingly invulnerable to all the drops and washes of the ophthalmologists, without the muscular pains of arthritis, or the fire of hemorrhoids that at times seemed like burning metal in his intestines, or the swelling of his feet. He didn't suffer from any of those discomforts, diseases, and ailments, the aftermath of his twenty years in Africa. He was young again and wanted to do here, in the exceedingly wide Amazon River whose banks he could not even see, one of those mad acts he had done so often in Africa: strip and dive from the railing of the ship into the water green with clumps of grass and splashed with foam. He would feel the impact of the warm, dense water all over his body, a benign, purifying sensation, as he propelled himself up to the surface, emerged, and began to swim, gliding with the ease and elegance of a dolphin to the side of the boat. From the deck the captain and some passengers would make exaggerated gestures for him to get back in the boat, not run the risk of drowning or being devoured by a *yacumama*, one of the river snakes that sometimes were ten meters long and could swallow a man whole.

Was he near Manaus? Tabatinga? Putumayo? Iquitos? Was he sailing up or down the river? It made no difference. The important thing was that he felt better than he had for a long time, and as the boat moved slowly on the green surface, the drone of the motor cradling his thoughts, Roger reviewed once again what his future would be like now that he finally had renounced diplomacy and recovered total freedom. He would give up his London flat on Ebury Street and go to Ireland. He would divide his time between Dublin and Ulster. He would not devote his entire life to politics. He would reserve one hour a day, one day a week, one week a month for study. He would resume learning Irish and one day would surprise Alice by speaking to her in fluent Gaelic. And the hours, days, weeks devoted to politics would concentrate on great politics that had to do with the primary, central plan—the independence of Ireland and the struggle against colonialism—and he would refuse to waste his time on the intrigues, rivalries, competitiveness of hack politicians eager to win small areas of power, in the party, the cell, the brigade, even though to do so, they would have to forget and even sabotage the essential task. He would travel a great deal in Ireland, long excursions through the glens of Antrim and Donegal, through Ulster, Galway, and remote, isolated places like the district of Connemara and Tory Island where the fishermen knew no English and spoke only Gaelic, and he would get along with the peasants, artisans, fishermen who, with their stoicism, hard work, and patience had resisted the crushing presence of the colonizer, preserving their language, their customs, their beliefs. He would listen to them, learn from them, write essays and poems about the silent, heroic, centuries-long saga of those humble people thanks to whom Ireland had not disappeared and was still a nation.

A metallic noise pulled him out of that pleasant dream. He opened his eyes. The jailer had come in and handed him a large bowl with the semolina soup and piece of bread that was every night's supper. He was about to ask the time but refrained because he knew he wouldn't answer. He broke the bread into small pieces, put them in the soup, and ate it in widely spaced spoonfuls. Another day had passed and perhaps tomorrow would be the decisive one.

10

The night before he sailed on the *Liberal* for Putumayo, Roger Casement decided to speak frankly to Consul Stirs. During the thirteen days he spent in Iquitos he'd had many conversations with the English consul but hadn't dared bring up the subject with him. He knew his mission had earned him a good number of enemies, not only in Iquitos but in the entire Amazonian region; it was absurd to also estrange a colleague who could be of great use to him in the days and weeks to come if he found himself in serious difficulty with the rubber barons. Better not to mention this indelicate matter to him.

And yet that night, as he and the consul were drinking their usual glass of port in Stirs's small living room, listening to the clatter of rain on the tin roof and the spouts of water beating on the windows and the railing of the terrace, Roger abandoned his prudence.

"What opinion do you have of Father Ricardo Urrutia, Stirs?"

"The superior of the Augustinians? I don't know him very well. In general, my opinion is good. You've seen a great deal of him recently, haven't you?"

Did the consul guess they were entering shaky ground? In his small bulging eyes there was an uneasy gleam. His bald head shone in the light of the oil lamp sputtering on the little table in the middle of the room.

"Well, Father Urrutia has been here barely a year and hasn't left Iquitos," said Roger. "So he doesn't know a great deal about what occurs on the rubber plantations in Putumayo. On the other hand, he's spoken to me about another human drama in the city."

The consul savored a mouthful of port. He began to fan himself again and Roger had the feeling his round face had reddened slightly. Outside, the storm roared with long, muffled claps of thunder, and at times a flash of lightning lit the darkness of the forest for an instant.

"The one about the little girls and boys stolen from the tribes," Roger continued. "Brought here and sold to families for twenty or thirty *soles*."

Stirs remained silent, observing him. He was fanning himself furiously now.

"According to Father Urrutia, almost all the servants in Iquitos were stolen and sold," Roger added, looking fixedly into the consul's eyes. "Is that the case?"

Stirs heaved a prolonged sigh and moved in his rocking chair, not hiding an expression of annoyance. His face seemed to say: *You don't know how happy I am that you're leaving tomorrow for Putumayo. I really hope we don't see each other again, Mr. Casement.*

"Didn't those things occur in the Congo?" he replied evasively.

"Yes, they did occur, though not in the general way they do here. Forgive my impertinence. The four servants you have, did you hire them or buy them?"

"I inherited them," the British consul said drily. "They came with the house when my predecessor, Consul Cazes, left for England. You can't say I hired them because that's not the custom here in Iquitos. The four of them are illiterate and wouldn't know how to read or sign a contract. They sleep and eat in my house, I clothe them, and give them tips as well, something that isn't frequent in this territory, I assure you. They are free to leave whenever they like. Speak to them and ask them if they'd like to find work elsewhere. You'll see their reaction, Mr. Casement."

Roger nodded and sipped at his glass of port.

"I didn't mean to offend you," he apologized. "I'm trying to understand the country I'm in, the values and customs of Iquitos. I have no desire for you to look on me as an inquisitor."

Now the consul's expression was hostile. He moved the fan slowly and in his gaze was apprehension as well as hatred.

"Not as an inquisitor but as righteous," he corrected him, making another grimace of dislike. "Or, if you prefer, a hero. I've already told you, I don't like heroes. Don't take my frankness in the wrong way. As for the rest, don't have any hopes. You're not going to change what happens here, Mr. Casement. And Father Urrutia won't either. In a certain sense, for these children, what happens to them is a stroke of luck. Being servants, I mean. It would be a thousand times worse if they grew up in the tribes, eating their own lice, dying of fevers or some other epidemic before they're ten, or working like animals on the rubber plantations. They live better here. I know my pragmatism will displease you."

Roger said nothing. He knew now what he wanted to know. And also that from now on the British consul in

Iquitos would probably be another enemy he ought to watch out for.

"I've come here to serve my country on a consular assignment," Stirs added, looking at the fiber mat on the floor. "I carry it out with precision, I assure you. I know the British citizens, who don't number many, and I defend and serve them in every way necessary. I do all I can to encourage trade between Amazonia and the British Empire. I keep my government informed regarding commercial activity, ships that come and go, any border incidents. Combating slavery or the abuses committed by the mestizos and whites of Peru against the Amazonian Indians is not one of my obligations."

"I'm sorry to have offended you, Mr. Stirs. Let's not speak of the matter again."

Roger stood, said good night to the master of the house, and retired to his room. The storm had subsided but it was still raining. The terrace next to the bedroom was soaked. There was a dense odor of plants and wet earth. The night was dark and the sound of insects intense, as if they were not only in the forest but inside the room. With the storm another rain had fallen: the black beetles called *vinchucas*. Tomorrow their corpses would carpet the terrace, and if you stepped on them, they would crack like nuts and stain the floor with dark blood. He undressed, put on his pajamas, and got into bed under the mosquito net.

He had been imprudent, of course. Offending the consul, a poor man, perhaps a good man, who was merely waiting to reach his retirement without becoming involved in problems, return to England, and bury himself in tending the garden of the cottage in Surrey he probably had been paying for gradually with his savings. That's what he should have done, and then he would have fewer ailments in his body and less anguish in his soul.

He recalled his violent argument on the *Huayna*, the ship on which he traveled from Tabatinga, the border between Peru and Brazil, to Iquitos, with the rubber planter Victor Israel, a Maltese Jew, who had lived in Amazonia for many years and with whom he'd had long and very diverting conversations on the terrace of the boat. Victor Israel dressed in an eccentric manner, always seemed to be in disguise, spoke impeccable English, and while they played poker recounted with great charm his adventurous life that seemed to have come from a picaresque novel, drinking glasses of cognac that the planter loved. He had the awful habit of shooting with a huge old-fashioned pistol at the pink herons that flew over the boat, but, happily, rarely hit one. Until, one fine day, Roger did not remember why, Victor Israel defended Julio C. Arana. The man was taking Amazonia out of savagery and integrating it into the modern world. He defended the *correrías*, thanks to which, he said, there were still laborers to harvest the rubber. Because the great problem in the jungle was a lack of workers to collect the precious substance the Maker had wanted to present as a gift to the region and a blessing to the Peruvians. This "manna from heaven" was being squandered because of the laziness and stupidity of the savages who refused to work as harvesters of latex and obliged the planters to go to the tribes and take them by force. Which meant a great loss of time and money for the enterprises.

"Well, that's one way of looking at things," Roger interrupted tersely. "There's also another way."

Victor Israel was a long, very thin man with white streaks in his mane of straight hair that reached to his shoulders. He had several days' growth of beard on his large bony face and dark, triangular, somewhat Mephistophelian eyes that fixed on Roger disconcertedly. He wore a red vest and over that, suspenders as well as a brightly colored scarf.

"What do you mean?"

"I'm referring to the point of view of the people you call savages," Roger explained in a light-hearted tone, as if he were talking about the weather or the mosquitoes. "Put yourself in their place for a moment. There they are, in their villages, where they've lived for years, or centuries. One day some white or mestizo gentlemen come with rifles and revolvers and demand that they abandon their families, their plantings, their houses, to go and harvest rubber dozens or hundreds of kilometers away, for the benefit of strangers whose only reason is the force at their disposal. Would you go willingly to harvest your famous latex, Don Victor?"

"I'm not a savage who lives naked, worships the *yacumama*, and drowns their children if they're born with a harelip," replied the planter with a sardonic guffaw that accentuated his irritation. "Do you put the cannibals of Amazonia on the same plane as the pioneers, entrepreneurs, and merchants who work in heroic conditions and risk our lives to transform these forests into a civilized land?"

"Perhaps you and I have different concepts of what civilization is, my friend," said Roger, always in that comradely tone that seemed to irritate Victor Israel beyond measure.

At the same poker table were Walter Folk and Henry Fielgald, while the other members of the commission had gone to lie in their hammocks and rest. It was a calm, warm night, and a full moon illuminated the water of the Amazon with silvery brilliance.

"I'd like to know what your idea of civilization is," said Victor Israel. His eyes and voice were throwing off sparks. His irritation was so great that Roger wondered if the planter would not suddenly pull out the archaeological revolver he carried in his holster and shoot him.

"It could be summed up by saying that it's an idea of a society where private property and individual liberty are respected," he explained very calmly, all his senses alert in case Victor Israel meant to attack him. "For example, British laws prohibit colonists from occupying indigenous lands in the colonies. And they also prohibit, under pain of imprisonment, employing force against natives who refuse to work in the mines or camps. You don't believe that's civilization, do you? Or am I wrong?"

Victor Israel's thin chest rose and fell, agitating the strange blouse with loose sleeves he wore buttoned to the neck, and the red vest. He had both thumbs caught in his suspenders and his narrow, triangular eyes were as red as if they were bleeding. His open mouth displayed a row of uneven teeth stained with nicotine.

"According to that criterion," he stated, mocking and offensive, "Peruvians would have to allow Amazonia to remain in the Stone Age for the rest of eternity, in order not to offend the pagans or occupy lands they don't know what to do with because they're lazy and don't want to work. Waste a resource that could raise the standard of living for

Peruvians and make Peru a modern country. Is that what the British Crown proposes for this country, Señor Casement?"

"Amazonia is a great emporium of resources, no doubt," Roger agreed, without becoming agitated. "Nothing more just than that Peru should take advantage of it. But not by abusing the natives, or hunting them down like animals, or forcing them to work as slaves. Rather, by incorporating them into civilization by means of schools, hospitals, and churches."

Victor Israel burst into laughter, shaking like a puppet on springs.

"What a world you live in, Consul!" he exclaimed, raising his hands with their long, skeletal fingers in a theatrical way. "It's obvious you've never seen a cannibal in your life. Do you know how many Christians have been eaten here by the natives? How many whites and *cholos* they've killed with their spears and poisoned darts? How many have had their heads shrunk, the way the Shapras do? Let's talk when you have a little more experience of barbarism."

"I lived close to twenty years in Africa and know something about those things, Señor Israel," Roger assured him. "By the way, I met a good number of whites there who thought the way you do."

To keep the disagreement from becoming even more bitter, Walter Folk and Henry Fielgald turned the conversation to less thorny subjects. Tonight, in his wakefulness, after ten days in Iquitos interviewing all kinds of people, of writing down dozens of opinions gathered here and there from authorities, judges, military men, restaurant owners, fishermen, pimps, vagrants, prostitutes and waiters in brothels and bars, Roger told himself that the immense majority of the whites and mestizos in Iquitos, Peruvians and foreigners, thought as Victor Israel did. For them the Amazonian indigenous were not, strictly speaking, human beings, but an inferior, contemptible form of existence, closer to animals than civilized people. That's why it was legitimate to exploit them, whip them, abduct them, take them to the rubber plantations or, if they resisted, kill them like rabid dogs. It was so generalized a view of the Indian that, as Father Ricardo Urrutia said, no one was shocked that the domestic servants in Iquitos were girls and boys stolen and sold to Loretian families for the equivalent of one or two pounds sterling. Anguish obliged him to open his mouth and breathe deeply until air reached his lungs. If he had seen and learned these things in this city, what wouldn't he see in Putumayo?

The members of the commission left Iquitos on September 14, 1910, mid-morning. Roger had hired Frederick Bishop, one of the Barbadians he interviewed, as an interpreter. Bishop spoke Spanish and assured him he could understand and make himself understood in the two most common indigenous languages spoken on the rubber plantations: Bora and Huitoto. The *Liberal*, the largest of the fleet of fifteen ships belonging to the Peruvian Amazon Company, was well maintained. It had small cabins that could accommodate two travelers. There were hammocks in the prow and stern for those who preferred to sleep outdoors. Bishop was afraid to go back to Putumayo and asked Roger for a written guarantee that the commission would protect him during the journey and afterward the British government would repatriate him to Barbados.

The passage from Iquitos to La Chorrera, capital of the enormous territory between the Napo and Caquetá Rivers where Julio C. Arana's Peruvian Amazon Company had its operations, lasted for eight days of heat, clouds of mosquitoes, boredom, and the monotony of the landscape and the noises. The ship sailed down the Amazon, whose width, once they had left Iquitos, grew until its banks became invisible, crossed the Brazilian border in Tabatinga, continued down the Yavarí, and then re-entered Peru along the Igara Paraná. On this stretch of river the banks were closer and at times the vines and branches of extremely tall trees hung over the deck. They heard and saw flocks of parrots zigzagging and screeching in the trees, or solemn pink herons taking the sun on an islet and balancing on one leg, turtle shells whose brown color stood out in somewhat paler water, and, at times, the bristling back of an alligator dozing in the mud of the bank and shot at with rifles or revolvers from the boat.

Roger spent a good part of the crossing arranging his notes and notebooks from Iquitos and outlining a work plan for the months he would spend in the territories of Julio C. Arana. According to the Foreign Office's instructions, he was to interview only the Barbadians who worked at the stations, because they were British citizens, leaving the employees from Peru and other nations alone in order not to wound the susceptibilities of the Peruvian government. But he didn't intend to respect those limits. His investigation would be left one-eyed, maimed, and crippled if he didn't also obtain information from the station chiefs, their boys or rationals—Hispanicized Indians responsible for guarding the works and dispensing punishments—and from the indigenous themselves. Only in this way would he have a complete vision of how Arana's company violated laws and ethics in its relations with the natives.

In Iquitos, Pablo Zumaeta informed the members of the commission that on Arana's instructions, the company had sent ahead to Putumayo one of its principal officers, Señor Juan Tizón, to receive them and facilitate their movements from place to place and their work. The commissioners supposed the real reason for Tizón's trip to Putumayo was to hide evidence of abuses and present a cosmetic image of reality.

They arrived in La Chorrera, or The Rapids, at midday on September 22, 1910. The name of the place was due to the torrents and waterfalls caused by an abrupt narrowing of the riverbed, a tumultuous, magnificent spectacle of foam, noise, wet rocks, and whirlpools that broke the monotonous flow of the Igara Paraná, the tributary on whose banks the general headquarters of the Peruvian Amazon Company were located. To move from the dock to the offices and residences of La Chorrera, it was necessary to climb a steep slope of mud and brambles. The travelers' boots sank into the mud and sometimes, in order not to fall, they had to lean on the Indian porters carrying the luggage. As he greeted those who had come out to receive them, Roger, with a small shudder, confirmed that one out of every three or four of the half-naked Indians carrying their baggage or looking at them curiously from the bank, smacking their arms with open hands to chase the mosquitoes, had on their backs, buttocks, and thighs scars that could have come only from floggings. The Congo, yes, the Congo was everywhere.

Juan Tizón was a tall man, dressed in white, with aristocratic manners, very courteous, who spoke enough English to be understood. He must have been close to fifty and it was obvious from miles away, because of his carefully shaved face, small trimmed mustache, fine hands and clothing, that he was not in his element here in the middle of the jungle, but was a man of offices, salons, the city. He welcomed them in English and in Spanish and introduced his companion, whose mere name produced repugnance in Roger: Víctor Macedo, chief of La Chorrera. He, at least, hadn't fled. The articles of Saldaña Roca and those by Hardenburg in the magazine *Truth* in London singled him out as one of the cruelest of Arana's lieutenants in Putumayo.

As they climbed the slope, Roger observed him. He was a man of indeterminate age, husky, on the short side, a light-skinned *cholo* but with the somewhat Asian features of an Indian, a flat nose, a mouth with very full lips that were always open, revealing two or three gold teeth, the hard expression of someone weathered by the outdoors. Unlike the newcomers, he climbed the steep hill easily. He had a rather oblique gaze, as if he looked sideways to avoid the glare of the sun or because he was afraid to face people. Tizón was unarmed, but Víctor Macedo wore a revolver in his belt.

In the very large clearing, there were wooden buildings on pilings—thick tree trunks or cement columns—with verandas on the second floor, the larger ones with corrugated roofs, the smaller ones with roofs of braided palm leaves. Tizón was talking as he pointed—"There are the offices," "Those are rubber storerooms," "All of you will stay in this house,"—but Roger barely heard him. He was observing the groups of partly or completely naked Indians who looked at them indifferently or avoided looking at them at all: men, women, and sickly children, some with paint on their faces and chests, their legs as skinny as reeds, pale yellowish skin, and sometimes incisions and pendants in their lips and ears that reminded him of the African natives. But there were no blacks here. The few mulatto and dark-skinned men he could see wore trousers and boots and undoubtedly were part of the contingent from Barbados. He counted four. He recognized the "boys" or "rationals" immediately, for though they were Indian and barefoot they had cut their hair and combed it like "Christians," wore trousers and shirts, and had clubs and whips hanging from their belts.

While the other members of the commission had to sleep two in a room, Roger had the privilege of a room to himself. It was small, with a hammock instead of a bed and a piece of furniture that could be both trunk and desk. On a small table were a basin, a pitcher of water, and a mirror. They explained to him that on the first floor, beside the entrance, were a septic tank and a shower. As soon as he had settled in and put away his things, before he sat down to have lunch, Roger told Juan Tizón he wanted to interview all the Barbadians in La Chorrera, beginning that afternoon.

By then the rank, penetrating, oily stench, similar to the smell of rotting plants and leaves, was in his nostrils. It saturated every corner of La Chorrera and would accompany him morning, noon, and night for the three months his stay in Putumayo lasted, a smell he never became accustomed to, that made him vomit and retch, a pestilence that seemed to come from the air, the earth, objects, and human beings, and from then on would become for Roger the symbol of the evil and suffering that greed for the rubber exuded by the trees in Amazonia had exacerbated to dizzying extremes. "It's curious," he remarked to Tizón on the day of his arrival. "In the Congo I was often on rubber plantations and rubber depositories. But I don't recall Congolese latex giving off so strong and unpleasant an odor." "They're different varieties," Tizón explained. "This smells more and is also stronger than African rubber. They sprinkle talc on the bales going to Europe to reduce the stink."

Even though the number of Barbadians in the entire region of Putumayo was 196, there were only six in La Chorrera. Two refused from the outset to talk to Roger, even though he, with the intervention of Bishop, assured them their testimony would be private and in no case would they be indicted for what they told him, and that he personally would take care of returning them to Barbados if they did not wish to continue working for Arana's company.

The four who agreed to give testimony had been in Putumayo close to seven years and had served the Peruvian Amazon Company at different stations as overseers, a position halfway between the chiefs and the boys or rationals. The first one he spoke to, Donal Francis, a tall, strong black who limped and had a clouded eye, was so nervous and distrustful that Roger immediately assumed he wouldn't obtain much from him. He responded in monosyllables and denied every accusation. According to him, in La Chorrera chiefs, employees, and "even the savages" got along very well. There were never problems, much less violence. He had been carefully coached regarding what he had to say and do before the commission.

Roger perspired profusely. He kept sipping water. Would the other interviews with Barbadians in Putumayo be as useless as this one? They weren't. Philip Bertie Lawrence, Seaford Greenwich, and Stanley Sealy, especially the third, after overcoming an initial caution and receiving Roger's promise, in the name of the British government, that they would be repatriated to Barbados, began to talk, to tell everything and incriminate themselves vehemently, at times frantically, as if impatient to unburden their conscience. Stanley Sealy illustrated his testimony with so many details and examples that, in spite of his long experience of human atrocities, Roger at certain moments became dizzy and felt an anguish that barely allowed him to breathe. When the Barbadian finished speaking, night had fallen. The hum of nocturnal insects seemed thunderous, as if thousands were flying around them. They were sitting on a wooden bench on the terrace that led to Roger's bedroom. Between the two of them they had smoked a pack of cigarettes. In the growing darkness, Roger could no longer see the features of Stanley Sealy, a small mulatto, only the outline of his head and muscular arms. He had been in La Chorrera a short time. He had worked for two years at the Abisinia station, the right arm of the chiefs Abelardo Agüero and Augusto Jiménez, and before that at Matanzas, with Armando Normand. They both were silent. Roger felt mosquitoes biting him on the face, neck, and arms but did not have energy to drive them away.

Suddenly he realized that Sealy was crying. He had brought his hands to his face and sobbed slowly, with sighs that filled his chest. Roger saw the gleam of tears in his eyes.

"Do you believe in God?" he asked. "Are you a religious person?"

"I was as a boy, I think," the mulatto moaned, his voice breaking. "My godmother would take me to church on Sunday, back in St. Patrick, the village where I was born. Now, I don't know."

"I ask because it probably will help you to talk to God. I'm not saying to pray, just to talk. Try it. As frankly as you've talked to me. Tell Him what you're feeling, why you're crying. In any case, He can help you more than I can. I don't know how. I feel as upset as you do."

Like Lawrence and Greenwich, Sealy was prepared to repeat his testimony to the members of the commission and even to Señor Tizón, as long as he could stay close to Roger and travel with him to Iquitos and then to Barbados.

Roger went into his room, lit the oil lamps, removed his shirt, and washed his chest, underarms, and face with water from the basin. He would have liked to take a shower but would have had to go downstairs and do it outdoors, and he knew his body would be devoured by the mosquitoes that multiplied in numbers and ferocity at night.

He went down to the ground floor for supper in a dining room lit by oil lamps. Juan Tizón and his travel companions were drinking lukewarm, watery whiskey. They stood and talked, while three or four half-naked indigenous servants carried in fried and baked fish, boiled yucca, sweet potatoes, and cornflour with which they powdered food just as the Brazilians did with *farinha*. Others drove flies away with straw fans.

"How did things go with the Barbadians?" Tizón asked, handing him a glass of whiskey.

"Better than I expected, Señor Tizón. I was afraid they'd be reluctant to talk. But just the opposite. Three of them spoke with total frankness."

"I hope you share with me the complaints you receive," said Tizón, half joking, half serious. "The company wants to correct what it lacks and improve. That has always been Señor Arana's policy. Well, I imagine you must be hungry. To the table, gentlemen!"

They sat and began to help themselves from the various serving dishes. The members of the commission had spent the afternoon looking over the installations in La Chorrera and, with Bishop's help, conversing with the employees in administration and the storehouses. They all seemed tired and not very interested in talking. Could their experiences this first day have been as depressing as his?

Tizón offered them wine but, since he had warned them that with transportation and the climate, French wine arrived here disturbed and at times sour, everyone preferred to continue with whiskey.

Halfway through the meal, Roger remarked, glancing at the Indians serving them: "I've seen that many native men and women in La Chorrera have scars on their backs, buttocks, and thighs. That girl, for example. How many lashes do they receive as a rule when they're whipped?"

A general silence fell in which the sputtering of the oil lamps and the hum of the insects increased. Everyone looked at Juan Tizón very seriously.

"Most of the time they make those scars themselves," he stated, uncomfortably. "In their tribes they have fairly barbaric initiation rites, you know, like making holes in their faces, lips, ears, noses, to insert rings, teeth, and all kinds of pendants. I don't deny some might have been made by overseers who did not respect the company's orders. Our regulations categorically prohibit physical punishment."

"That wasn't the intention of my question, Señor Tizón," Roger apologized. "I meant that even though so many scars are visible, I haven't seen any Indians with the company's brand on their bodies."

"I don't know what you mean," Tizón replied, lowering his fork.

"The Barbadians explained to me that many indigenous are branded with the company initials: CA, that is, Casa Arana. Like cows, horses, and pigs. So they won't escape or be taken by Colombian rubber planters. They themselves had branded many of them. Sometimes with fire, and sometimes with a knife. But I still haven't seen anyone with the brand. What happened to them, Señor?"

Tizón suddenly lost his composure and elegant manners. He had turned red and trembled with indignation.

"I will not allow you to speak to me in that tone," he exclaimed, mixing English and Spanish. "I'm here to facilitate your work, not to suffer your ironic remarks."

Roger agreed, not changing expression. "I beg your pardon, I didn't mean to offend you," he said calmly. "It's just that even though I was witness to unspeakable cruelties in the Congo, I haven't yet seen the branding of human beings with fire or a knife. I'm sure you're not responsible for this atrocity."

"Of course I'm not responsible for any atrocity!" Tizón raised his voice again, gesticulating. He rolled his eyes in their sockets, beside himself. "If atrocities are committed, it's not the fault of the company. Don't you see what kind of place this is, Señor Casement? Here there is no authority, no police, no judges, nothing. Those who work here, as chiefs, overseers, assistants, are not educated people but, in many cases, illiterate adventurers, rough men hardened by the jungle. At times they commit abuses that horrify a civilized man. I know that very well. We do what we can, believe me. Señor Arana agrees with you. Everyone who has committed outrages will be dismissed. I'm not an accomplice to any injustice, Señor Casement. I have a respected name, a family that means something in this country, I'm a Catholic who practices his religion."

Roger thought Tizón probably believed what he was saying. A good man, who in Iquitos, Manaus, Lima, or London would not know or want to know what went on here. He probably cursed the hour it occurred to Julio C. Arana to send him to this godforsaken corner of the world to carry out a thankless assignment and suffer a thousand discomforts and difficulties.

"We ought to work together, collaborate," Tizón repeated, somewhat calmer, moving his hands a great deal. "What is going badly will be corrected. The employees who have committed atrocities will be sanctioned. I give you my word of honor! All I ask is that you see me as a friend, someone who's on your side."

Shortly afterward, Tizón said he wasn't feeling very well and preferred to retire. He said good night and left.

Only the members of the commission remained at the table.

"Branded like animals?" murmured Walter Folk, with

a skeptical air. "Can that be true?"

"Three of the four Barbadians I questioned today assured me of that," Roger asserted. "Stanley Sealy says he did it himself, at the Abisinia station, on the orders of his chief, Abelardo Agüero. But I don't think branding is the worst thing. I heard even more terrible things this afternoon."

They continued talking, not eating a mouthful, until they had finished the two bottles of whiskey on the table. The commissioners were affected deeply by the scars on the backs of the Indians and by the pillory or rack for torture they had discovered in one of the warehouses in La Chorrera where rubber was stored. With Señor Tizón present, who experienced a very difficult time, Bishop explained how that framework of wood and ropes worked, how the Indian was placed in it and forced into a squatting position, unable to move his arms or legs. He was tortured by adjustments of the wooden bars or by being suspended in midair. Bishop explained that the pillory was always in the center of the clearing in every station. They asked one of the rationals at the warehouse when the device had been brought inside. The boy said only on the eve of their arrival.

They decided the commission would listen the next day to Philip Bertie Lawrence, Seaford Greenwich, and Stanley Sealy. Seymour Bell suggested that Juan Tizón be present. There were divergent opinions, especially from Walter Folk, who feared that before the high-level official, the Barbadians would retract what they had said.

That night Roger did not close his eyes. He made notes on his conversations with the Barbadians until the lamp went out because there was no more oil. He lay down on his hammock and remained awake, dozing for a moment and then waking with aching bones and muscles, unable to shake off the uneasiness that afflicted him.

And the Peruvian Amazon Company was a British firm! On its board of directors were individuals highly respected in the world of business and in the City, such as Sir John Lister-Kaye, the Baron de Sousa-Deiro, John Russell Gubbins, and Henry M. Read. What would those partners of Julio C. Arana say when they read in the report he would present to the government that the enterprise they had legitimized with their name and money practiced slavery, obtaining harvesters of rubber and servants by means of *correrías* by armed thugs who captured indigenous men, women, and children and took them to the rubber plantations, where they were exploited iniquitously, hanged from the pillory, branded with fire and knife, and whipped until they bled to death if they didn't bring in the minimum quota of thirty kilos of rubber every three months. Roger had been in the offices of the Peruvian Amazon Company in Salisbury House, E.C., in the financial center of London. A spectacular place, with a Gainsborough landscape on the walls, uniformed secretaries, carpeted offices, leather sofas for visitors, and a multitude of clerks in striped trousers, black frock coats, and shirts with stiff white collars and cravats, keeping accounts, sending and receiving telegrams, selling and collecting remittances for powdered, odoriferous rubber in all the industrial cities of Europe. And, at the other end of the world, in Putumayo, Huitotos, Ocaimas, Muinanes, Nonuyas, Andoques, Rezígaros, and Boras were gradually being exterminated without anyone moving a finger to change that state of affairs.

"Why haven't these indigenous attempted to rebel?" Walter Folk had asked during supper. And he added: "It's true they don't have firearms. But there are so many of them, they could rebel, and though some would die, they would defeat their tormenters by dint of numbers." Roger replied that it wasn't so simple. They didn't rebel for the same reasons the Congolese hadn't in Africa. It was an exceptional occurrence, localized and sporadic suicidal acts by an individual or a small group. Because when the system of exploitation was so extreme, it destroyed spirits even before bodies. The violence that victimized them annihilated the will to resist, the instinct to survive, and transformed the indigenous people into automata paralyzed by confusion and terror. Many did not understand what was happening to them as a consequence of the evil in concrete, specific men, but as a mythic cataclysm, a curse of the gods, a divine punishment from which there was no escape.

Though here, in Putumayo, Roger discovered in the documents he consulted concerning Amazonia that a few years earlier there had been an attempt at rebellion at the Abisinia station, where the Boras were. It was a subject no one wanted to talk about. All the Barbadians had avoided it. One night, a young Bora village chief, named Katenere, supported by a small group from his tribe, stole the rifles of the chiefs and rationals, killed Bartolomé Zumaeta (a relative of Pablo Zumaeta), who had raped Katenere's wife when he was drunk, and disappeared into the jungle. The company put a price on his head. Several expeditions went out looking for him. For almost two years they couldn't lay a hand on him. Finally, a party of hunters, led by an Indian informant, surrounded the hut where Katenere was hiding with his wife. The chief managed to escape, but his wife was captured. The manager, Vásquez, raped her himself, in public, and put her in the pillory without water or food. He kept her like that for several days. From time to time, he had her flogged. Finally, one night, the chief appeared. No doubt he had seen the torture of his wife from the undergrowth. He crossed the clearing, threw down the carbine he was carrying, and went to kneel in a submissive attitude beside the pillory where his wife was dying or already dead. Vásquez shouted at the rationals not to shoot him. He himself took out Katenere's eyes with a wire. Then he had him burned alive, along with his wife, before the natives from the surrounding area who had been placed in a circle. Was this the way things had happened? The story had a melodramatic ending that Roger thought had probably been altered to bring it closer to the appetite for ferocity so prevalent in these hot places. But at least it had the symbol and the example: a native had rebelled, punished a torturer, and died a hero.

At the first light of dawn, he left the house where he was staying and went down the slope to the river. He swam naked after finding a small pool where he could resist the current. The cold water had the effect of a massage. When he dressed he felt refreshed and strengthened. On his return to La Chorrera he turned off to visit the sector where the Huitotos' huts were located. The huts, scattered among plantings of yucca, corn, and plantains, were round, with partitions of tucuma wood held down with lianas and protected by roofs of woven *yarina* leaves that reached down to the ground. He saw skeletal women carrying infants—none of them responded to the gestures of greeting he made to them—but no men. When he returned to his cabin, an indigenous woman was putting the clothing he had given her to wash on the day of his arrival in his bedroom. He asked how much he owed her but the woman—young, with green and blue stripes on her face—looked at him, not understanding. He had Frederick Bishop ask her how much he owed. Bishop asked in Huitoto, but the woman seemed not to understand.

"You don't owe her anything," said Bishop. "Money doesn't circulate here. Besides, she's one of the women of the chief of La Chorrera, Víctor Macedo."

"How many does he have?"

"Five, now," the Barbadian explained. "When I worked here, he had at least seven. He's changed them. That's what everyone does."

He laughed and made a joke: "In this climate, women get used up very fast. You have to replace them all the time, like clothing." But Roger didn't laugh.

He would remember the next two weeks they spent in La Chorrera, until the commission members moved on to the Occidente station, as the busiest, most intense of the journey. His entertainment consisted of swimming in the river, the fords, or the less torrential waterfalls, long walks in the forest, taking a good number of photographs, and, late at night, a game of bridge with his companions. The truth was that most of the day and evening he spent investigating, writing, questioning the local people, or exchanging impressions with his colleagues.

Contrary to their fears, Philip Bertie Lawrence, Seaford

Greenwich, and Stanley Sealy were not intimidated before the full commission or by the presence of Juan Tizón. They confirmed everything they had told Roger and expanded their testimonies, revealing new bloody deeds and abuse. At times, during the questioning, Roger saw one of the commissioners turn pale, as if he were going to faint.

Tizón remained silent, sitting behind them, not opening his mouth. He took notes in small notebooks. The first few days, following the interrogatories, he attempted to tone down and question the testimonies that referred to torture, murder, and mutilation. But after the third or fourth day, a transformation took place in him. He said nothing during meals, barely ate, and responded with monosyllables and murmurs when addressed. On the fifth day, as they were having a drink before dinner, he erupted. With reddened eyes he addressed all those present: "This goes beyond anything I could ever imagine. I swear on the souls of my sainted mother, my wife, my children, what I love most in the world, that all of this is an absolute surprise to me. The horror I feel is as great as yours. I'm sick at the things we've heard. It's possible there are exaggerations in the accusations of these Barbadians, who might want to ingratiate themselves with you. But even so, there is no doubt that intolerable, monstrous crimes have been committed here that should be denounced and punished. I swear to you that . . ."

His voice broke and he looked for a chair. He sat for a long time with his head bowed, holding his glass. He stammered that Señor Arana could not suspect what was going on here and neither could his principal collaborators in Iquitos, Manaus, or London. He would be the first to demand that a remedy be found for all this. Roger, moved by the first part of what he said, thought that Tizón was less spontaneous now. And, human after all, he was thinking about his situation, his family, and his future. In any case, beginning that day, Juan Tizón seemed to stop being a high official in the Peruvian Amazon Company and become one more member of the commission. He collaborated with them zealously and diligently, often bringing them new data. And all the time he demanded that they take precautions. He had become distrustful, and peered around filled with suspicions. Because they knew what was occurring here, all their lives were in danger, principally the general consul's. He lived in a state of constant alarm. He feared the Barbadians would reveal to Víctor Macedo what they had confessed. If they did, one could not discount the fact that this individual, before he was taken to court or handed over to the police, would ambush them and say afterward they had perished at the hands of the savages.

The situation was overturned one dawn when Roger heard someone knocking at the door with his knuckles. It was still dark. He went to open the door and made out a silhouette that belonged not to Frederick Bishop but to Donal Francis, the Barbadian who had insisted that everything was normal here. He spoke in a very low, frightened voice. He had thought about it and now he wanted to tell him the truth. Roger asked him in. They talked, sitting on the floor because Donal was afraid that if they went out to the terrace, they might be overheard.

He assured him he had lied out of fear of Víctor Macedo, who had threatened him: if he told the English what was happening here, he would not set foot in Barbados again, and once they had left, after Macedo had cut off his testicles he would tie him naked to a tree so the ants would eat him. Roger calmed him down. He would be repatriated to Bridgetown, like the other Barbadians. But he did not want to hear this new confession in private. Francis ought to speak before the commissioners and Tizón.

He testified that same day, in the dining room, where they held their working sessions. He displayed a great deal of fear. His eyes spun, he bit his thick lips, and sometimes he didn't find words. He spoke close to three hours. The most dramatic moment of his confession occurred when he said that a couple of months earlier, two Huitotos claimed to be sick to justify the ridiculously small amount of rubber they had harvested, and Víctor Macedo ordered him and a "boy" named Joaquín Piedra to tie their hands and feet, throw them in the river, and hold them under water until they drowned. Then he had the rationals drag the bodies to the forest to be eaten by animals. Donal offered to take them to the spot where some limbs and bones of the two Huitotos could still be found.

On September 28, Roger and the members of the commission left La Chorrera in the Peruvian Amazon Company launch *Veloz*, headed for Occidente. They sailed up the Igara Paraná River for several hours, made stops at the rubber-storing posts of Victoria and Naimenes to eat something, slept in the launch, and the next day, after another three hours of navigating, they anchored at the Occidente wharf. The station chief, Fidel Velarde, received them with his assistants Manuel Torrico, Rodríguez, and Acosta. *They all have the faces and attitudes of thugs and out-*

laws, thought Roger. They were armed with pistols and Winchester carbines. Surely they were following instructions to be deferential to the new arrivals. Juan Tizón once again asked for their prudence. Under no circumstances should they reveal to Velarde and his "boys" the things they had found out.

Occidente was a smaller camp than La Chorrera, surrounded by a stockade of wooden shafts sharpened like spears. Rationals armed with carbines guarded the entrances.

"Why is the station so protected?" Roger asked Tizón. "Are they expecting an attack by Indians?"

"No, not by Indians. Though you never know whether another Katenere will appear one day. No, it's the Colombians, who want these lands."

Fidel Velarde had 530 indigenous at Occidente, most of whom were in the forest now, harvesting rubber. They brought in what they had collected every two weeks. Their wives and children stayed here, in a settlement that extended along the banks of the river outside the stockade. Velarde added that the Indians would offer the "visiting friends" a fiesta that evening.

He took them to the house where they would stay, a quadrangular, two-story construction on pilings, the door and windows covered with screens to keep out mosquitoes. In Occidente the smell of rubber coming out of the depositories and saturating the air was as strong as in La Chorrera. Roger was glad to discover that here he would sleep in a bed instead of a hammock. A cot, rather, with a mattress made of seeds, where he could at least lie flat. The hammock had worsened his muscular aches and his insomnia.

The fiesta took place early in the evening, in a clearing near the Huitoto settlement. A multitude of indigenous people had brought out tables, chairs, pots of food, and drinks for the strangers. They waited for them, in a circle, very serious. The sky was clear and there was no visible threat of rain, but the good weather and the sight of the Igara Paraná cutting through the plain of thick forests and zigzagging around them could not cheer Roger. He knew that what they would see would be sad and depressing. Three or four dozen Indian men and women—the men very old or children, the women generally fairly young—some naked and others draped in the *cushma* or tunic Roger had seen many wearing in Iquitos, danced in a circle to the beat of the sounds of the *manguaré*, drums made of hollowed-out tree trunks that the Huitotos struck with rubber-tipped sticks, drawing out hoarse, prolonged sounds that, it was said, carried messages and allowed them to communicate over great distances. The rows of dancers had rattles filled with seeds on their ankles and arms, which clattered when they made their arrhythmic hops. At the same time they sang some monotonous melodies touched by a bitterness that matched their serious, sullen, fearful, or indifferent faces.

Afterward, Roger asked his companions whether they had noticed the great number of Indians who had scars on their backs, buttocks, and legs. They disagreed among themselves over what percentage of the Huitotos who danced bore the marks of floggings. Roger said eighty per cent, Fielgald and Folk thought no more than sixty. But all of them agreed that what had affected them most deeply was an emaciated little boy, nothing but skin and bone, with burns all over his body and part of his face. They asked Frederick Bishop to find out if those marks were due to an accident or to punishments and torture.

At this station they intended to discover in detail how the system of exploitation operated. They began very early the next morning, after breakfast. As soon as they began to visit the rubber depositories, led by Fidel Velarde himself, they discovered by chance that the scales that weighed the rubber were rigged. It occurred to Seymour Bell to get on one of them because, since he was a hypochondriac, he believed he had lost weight. He was shocked. But how was it possible? He had lost close to ten kilos! Still, he didn't feel it in his body, otherwise his trousers would be falling down and his shirts would be slipping off. Roger weighed himself too and encouraged his colleagues and Juan Tizón to do the same. They were all several kilos under their normal weight. During lunch, Roger asked Tizón if he believed all the scales belonging to the Peruvian Amazon Company in Putumayo had been tampered with like the one at Occidente to make the Indians believe they had collected less rubber than they actually had. Tizón, who had lost all his ability to dissimulate, only shrugged: "I don't know, gentlemen. The only thing I know is that here everything is possible."

Unlike La Chorrera, where they had hidden it in a warehouse, in Occidente the pillory was in the middle of the clearing around which the residences and depositories were located. Roger asked Fidel Velarde's assistants to put him inside that instrument of torture. He wanted to know what a person felt in the narrow cage. Rodríguez and Acosta hesitated, but since Tizón authorized it, they told

Roger to curl up and, pushing him with their hands, wedged him inside the pillory. It was impossible to close the wooden rods that held down legs and arms because his limbs were too stout, so they did no more than bring them together. But they could fasten the handles around his neck, which, without completely choking him, interfered with his breathing. He felt an intense pain in his body and it seemed impossible for a human being to endure that posture for hours, that pressure on back, stomach, chest, legs, neck, and arms. When he came out, before he had recovered the ability to move, he had to lean for a long time on the shoulder of Louis Barnes.

"For what kinds of crimes do you place Indians in the pillory?" he asked the chief of Occidente that night.

Fidel Velarde was a rather plump mestizo, with a walrus mustache and large, prominent eyes. He wore a wide-brimmed hat, high boots, and an ammunition belt.

"When they commit very serious crimes," he explained, lingering over each phrase. "When they kill their children, disfigure their wives when they're drunk, or commit robberies and won't confess where they've hidden what they stole. We don't use the pillory all the time. Just once in a while. In general the Indians here are well behaved."

He said this in a tone somewhere between cheerful and mocking, looking at the commissioners one by one with a fixed, disparaging gaze that seemed to be saying: *I find myself obliged to say these things but please, don't believe them.* His attitude revealed so much arrogance and contempt for the rest of humanity that Roger tried to imagine the paralyzing fear this bully must inspire in the indigenous, with his pistol at his waist, his carbine on his shoulder, his belt filled with bullets. A short while later, one of the five Barbadians from Occidente testified to the commission that on one drunken night he had seen Fidel Velarde and Alfredo Montt, who was then station chief at Último Retiro, wager on who could cut off the ear of a Huitoto being punished in the pillory more quickly and cleanly. Velarde succeeded in cutting off the Indian's ear with a single slash of his machete, but Montt, who was a confirmed drunkard and whose hands trembled, instead of removing the other ear struck the middle of the Indian's skull with his machete. When this session ended, Seymour Bell suffered a crisis. He confessed to his colleagues that he couldn't bear any more. His voice was breaking and his eyes were red and filled with tears. They had already seen and heard enough to know that the most atrocious cruelty prevailed here. It made no sense to continue investigating this world of inhumanity and psychopathic cruelties. He proposed they conclude their trip and return to England immediately.

Roger said he would not oppose the others leaving, but he would remain in Putumayo, in accordance with the original plan, and visit a few more stations. He wanted their report to be extensive and well documented so it would have greater effect. He reminded them that all these crimes were being committed by a British company whose board of directors included highly respected Englishmen, and that the stockholders of the Peruvian Amazon Company were filling their pockets with what went on here. It was necessary to put an end to the offenses and sanction those responsible. To achieve this, their report had to be exhaustive and definitive. His words convinced the others, including the demoralized Seymour Bell.

To shake off the effects that the wager between Fidel Velarde and Alfredo Montt had on all of them, they decided to take a day off. The next morning, instead of continuing with interviews and inquiries, they went to swim in the river. They spent hours hunting butterflies with a net while the botanist, Walter Folk, explored the jungle searching for orchids. There was as great an abundance of butterflies and orchids in the area as mosquitoes and the bats that came at night, in silent flight, to bite the dogs, chickens, and horses on the station, sometimes infecting them with rabies so they had to be killed and burned to avoid an epidemic.

Roger and his companions were amazed at the variety, size, and beauty of the butterflies flying about in the vicinity of the river. They came in all shapes and colors and their graceful fluttering and the splashes of light they gave off when they rested on a leaf or plant seemed to dazzle the air with delicate notes, a compensation for the moral ugliness they discovered at every turn, as if there were no end to wickedness, greed, and pain in this unfortunate land. Walter Folk was surprised at the quantity of orchids hanging from the great trees, their elegant, exquisite colors illuminating everything around them. He did not cut them and did not allow any of his companions to do so either. He spent a long time observing them with a magnifying glass, making notes, and photographing them.

In Occidente Roger came to have a fairly complete idea of the system that made the Peruvian Amazon Company function. Perhaps at the beginning there had been some kind of agreement between the rubber barons and the tribes. But by now that was history, because the indigenous people did not want to go into the jungle to harvest rubber. For that reason, it all began with the *correrías* carried out by the chiefs and their "boys." No wages were paid and the Indians never saw a cent. They received from the company store the tools for harvesting—knives to make incisions in the trees, tin cans for the latex, baskets for collecting strips or balls of rubber—in addition to domestic goods like seeds, clothing, lamps, and some foodstuffs. Prices were determined by the company, so that the native was always in debt and would work the rest of his life to pay off what he owed. Since the chiefs did not receive salaries but commissions on the rubber harvested in each station, their demands to obtain the maximum were implacable. Each harvester went into the jungle for two weeks, leaving his wife and children as hostages. The chiefs and rationals made use of them as they chose, for domestic service or their sexual appetites. All of them had real harems, with many girls who had not reached puberty, and they exchanged them on a whim, even though sometimes, because of jealousy, there was a settling of accounts with bullets and stabbings. Every two weeks the harvesters returned to the station to bring in the rubber. This was weighed on the dishonest scales. If after three months they had not fulfilled thirty kilos, they received punishments that ranged from floggings to the pillory, cutting off ears and noses, or in extreme cases, the torture and killing of the wife, children, and the harvester himself. The corpses were not buried but dragged into the forest to be eaten by animals. Every three months the launches and steamboats of the company came for the rubber which, in the meantime, had been steamed, washed, and powdered. The boats sometimes took their cargo from Putumayo to Iquitos, and others went directly to Manaus for export to Europe and the United States.

Roger confirmed that a large number of rationals did no productive work. They were only jailers, torturers, and exploiters of the indigenous. They spent the entire day lying down, smoking, drinking, amusing themselves, kicking a ball, telling one another jokes, or giving orders. All the work fell on the Indians: building houses, replacing roofs damaged by the rains, repairing the path down to the wharf, washing, cleaning, cooking, carrying things back and forth, and in the little free time they had left, tending to their crops, without which they would have had nothing to eat.

Roger understood his companions' state of mind. If he, who after twenty years in Africa thought he had seen it all, was disturbed by what occurred here, his nerves shattered, experiencing moments of total discouragement, how must it be for those who had spent most of their lives in a civilized world, believing the rest of the earth was the same, composed of societies with laws, churches, police, customs, and a morality that kept human beings from behaving like beasts?

Roger wanted to remain in Putumayo so his report would be as complete as possible, but that was not the only reason. Another was his curiosity to meet the individual who, according to every testimony, was the paradigm of cruelty in this world: Armando Normand, the chief of Matanzas.

Since Iquitos he had heard anecdotes, comments, and allusions to this name, always associated with such wickedness and ignominy that he had obsessed about him to the point of having nightmares, from which he would wake bathed in sweat, his heart racing. He was certain many things he had heard from the Barbadians about Normand were exaggerations inflamed by the heated imagination so frequent in people in these areas. But even so, the fact that this individual had been able to generate this kind of mythology indicated he was someone who, though it seemed impossible, surpassed in savagery villains like Abelardo Agüero, Alfredo Montt, Fidel Velarde, Elías Martinengui, and others of their kind.

No one knew his nationality with any certainty—it was said he was Peruvian, Bolivian, or English—but everyone agreed he was not yet thirty and had studied in England. Juan Tizón had heard he had been certified as an accountant in an institute in London. Apparently he was short, thin, and very ugly. According to the Barbadian Joshua Dyall, from his seemingly insignificant person radiated a "malignant force" that made anyone who approached him tremble, and his gaze, penetrating and icy, was like a snake's. Dyall asserted that not only the Indians but also the "boys" and even the overseers felt insecure near him, because at any moment Armando Normand could order or carry out himself an act of chilling ferocity without any change in his contemptuous indifference toward everything around him. Dyall confessed to Roger and the commission that one day at the Matanzas station, Normand ordered him to kill five Andoques as punishment for not having met their rubber quotas. Dyall shot the first two, but the manager ordered that for the next two he should first crush their testicles with a stone for grinding yucca and then finish them off by garroting them. He had him strangle the last one with his bare hands. During the entire operation Normand sat on a tree trunk, smoking and watching, with no change in the indolent expression on his reddish face.

Seaford Greenwich, who had worked for some months with Armando Normand at Matanzas, recounted that the talk among the rationals at the station was the chief's habit of placing chili peppers, either ground or in their skins, inside the sex of his young concubines to hear them shriek at the burning. According to Greenwich, only in this way could he become aroused and fuck them. At one time, the Barbadian added, instead of placing those being punished in the pillory, Normand would raise them with a chain tied to a tall tree and then release them to see how their heads split open and their bones broke or their teeth severed their tongues when they fell to the ground. Another overseer who had served under Normand assured the commission that even more than him the Andoque Indians feared his dog, a mastiff he had trained to sink its teeth into and tear off the flesh of any Indian he ordered it to attack.

Could all those monstrous acts be true? Roger told himself, sifting through his memory, that among the vast collection of villains he had known in the Congo, whom power and impunity had turned into monsters, none had reached the extremes of this individual. He was rather perversely curious to meet him, hear him speak, see him act, and learn his origins and what he could say about the crimes attributed to him.

From Occidente, Roger and his friends traveled, always in the launch *Veloz*, to the Último Retiro station. It was smaller than the previous ones and also had the look of a fort, with its palisade fence and armed guards around the handful of residences. The Indians seemed more primitive and taciturn than the Huitotos. They were half-naked, with loincloths that barely covered their sex. Here Roger saw for the first time two natives with the company's brand on their buttocks: CA. They looked older than most of the others. He tried to talk to them but they didn't understand Spanish or Portuguese, or Frederick Bishop's Huitoto. Later, walking around Último Retiro, they discovered other branded Indians. From a station employee they learned that at least a third of the Indians living here carried the CA brand on their body. The practice had been suspended some time earlier, when the Peruvian Amazon Company agreed to the commission's visit to Putumayo.

To reach Último Retiro from the river, one had to climb a slope muddied by the rain, one's legs sinking into the mud to the knees. When Roger could remove his shoes and lie down on his cot, all his bones ached. His conjunctivitis had returned. The burning and tearing in one eye were so great that after putting in eye drops, he bandaged it. He spent several days like that, looking like a pirate, with one eye bandaged and protected by a damp cloth. Since these precautions did not put an end to the inflammation and tearing, from then on and until the end of the journey, every moment of the day when he wasn't working—there weren't many—he hurried to lie down in his hammock or cot and remained there, both eyes covered with wet, lukewarm cloths. In this way his discomfort was eased. During these periods of rest and at night—he slept barely four or five hours—he tried to organize mentally the report he would write for the Foreign Office. The general outline was clear. First, a picture of conditions in Putumayo some twenty years earlier when the pioneers came and settled here, invading the tribes' lands, and how, desperate at the lack of labor, they initiated the *correrías* with no fear of sanctions because there were no judges and no police in these places. They were the only authority, sustained by firearms against which slings, spears, and blowguns proved futile.

He had to describe clearly the system of exploitation of rubber based on slave labor and the mistreatment of the indigenous which was inflamed by the greed of the station chiefs, who, since they worked for a percentage of harvested rubber, made use of physical punishment, mutilations, and murders to increase the amount gathered. Impunity and absolute power had developed in these individuals sadistic tendencies that could be manifested freely here against natives deprived of all rights.

Would his report be useful? No doubt, at least the Peruvian Amazon Company would be sanctioned. The British government would ask the Peruvian government to bring those responsible for crimes to trial. Would President Leguía have the courage to do it? Tizón said he would, that just as in London, in Lima a scandal would erupt when people learned what went on here. Public opinion would demand punishment for the guilty. But Roger had his doubts. What could the Peruvian government do in Putumayo, where it didn't have a single representative, where Julio C. Arana's company boasted, and with reason, that with its gangs of killers it was the power that maintained Peruvian sovereignty in these lands? Nothing would go beyond some rhetorical posturing. The martyrdom of the indigenous communities in Amazonia would continue until they were obliterated. This prospect depressed him. But instead of paralyzing him, it incited him to greater efforts, investigating, interviewing, and writing. He already had a pile of notebooks and cards written in his clear, careful hand.

From Último Retiro they went to Entre Ríos, in a journey by river and land that submerged them in thickets for an entire day. The idea delighted Roger: in this physical contact with wild nature he would relive the years of his youth, the long expeditions on the African continent. But even though in those twelve hours of going through the jungle, sinking at times to his waist in mud, slipping in underbrush that hid slopes, traveling certain sections in canoes that, powered by the Indians' poles, slipped through extremely narrow water channels covered by foliage that darkened the light of the sun, he sometimes felt the excitement and joy of long ago, the experience served above all to confirm the passage of time, the wearing away of his body. It was not only the pain in his arms, back, and legs, but also the unconquerable weariness against which he had to struggle, making heroic efforts to hide it from his companions. Louis Barnes and Seymour Bell were so exhausted that after the middle of the journey each of them had to be carried in hammocks by four Indians of the twenty or so who escorted them. Roger observed, impressed, how these natives with such thin legs and skeletal bodies moved easily as they carried on their shoulders baggage and provisions, not eating or drinking for hours. During a rest break, Juan Tizón agreed to Roger's request and ordered the distribution of tins of sardines among the Indians.

As they traveled they saw flocks of parrots and the playful monkeys with lively eyes called *frailecillos*, many kinds of birds, and iguanas with sleepy eyes whose wrinkled skins blended into the branches and trunks where they lay flat. And a *Victoria regia* as well, those enormous circular leaves that floated on lagoons like rafts.

They reached Entre Ríos late in the afternoon. The station was in an upheaval because a jaguar had eaten an Indian who had left the camp to give birth, alone, as native women usually did, on the riverbank. A hunting party led by the station chief had gone out to search for the jaguar, but they returned at nightfall without having found the animal. The chief of Entre Ríos was named Andrés O'Donnell. He was young and good-looking and said his father was Irish, but Roger, after questioning him, detected so much misinformation with respect to his forebears and Ireland that O'Donnell's grandfather or great-grandfather was probably the first Irishman in his family to set foot on Peruvian soil. It pained him that a descendant of Irishmen was one of Arana's lieutenants in Putumayo, though according to testimonies, he seemed less cruel than other chiefs: he had been seen whipping the indigenous and stealing their wives and daughters for his private harem—he had seven women living with him and a multitude of children—but in his record he apparently hadn't killed anyone with his own hands or ordered any murders. But in a prominent place in Entre Ríos the pillory was raised and all the "boys" and Barbadians carried whips at their waist (some used them as belts for their trousers). And a large number of Indian men and women showed scars on their backs, legs, and buttocks.

Even though his official mission required that he interview only British citizens who worked for Arana's company, that is, Barbadians, after Occidente Roger also began to interview the rationals willing to answer his questions. In Entre Ríos this practice extended to the entire commission. On the days they were there, the chief himself and a good number of his "boys" testified, in addition to the three Barbadians who served Andrés O'Donnell as overseers.

The same thing almost always occurred. At first, they were all reticent and evasive and told brazen lies. But a slip, an involuntary imprudence that revealed the world of truths they were hiding was enough for them to suddenly begin to talk and tell more than what they were asked for, implicating themselves as proof of the veracity of what they were recounting. In spite of several attempts, Roger could not gather direct testimony from any Indian.

On October 16, 1910, when he and his colleagues on the commission, accompanied by Juan Tizón, three Barbadians, and some twenty Muinane Indian porters, led by their chief, walked through the forest along a narrow trail from Entre Ríos to the Matanzas station, Roger noted in his diary an idea that had been taking shape in his mind since he disembarked in Iquitos: "I have reached the absolute conviction that the only way the indigenous people of Putumayo can emerge from the miserable condition to which they have been reduced is by rising up in arms against their masters. It is an illusion devoid of all reality to believe, as Tizón does, that this situation will change when the Peruvian state comes here and there are authorities, judges, police to enforce the laws that have prohibited servitude and slavery in Peru since 1854. Will they enforce them as they do in Iquitos, where families buy girls and boys stolen by traffickers for twenty or thirty *soles*? Will those authorities, judges, and police enforce the laws when they receive their salaries from Casa Arana because the state has no money to pay them or because thieves and bureaucrats steal the money on its way to them? In this society the state is an inseparable part of the machinery of exploitation and extermination. The indigenous should not hope for anything from such institutions. If they want to be free they have to conquer their freedom with their arms and their courage. Like the Bora chief Katenere. But without sacrificing themselves for sentimental reasons, as he did. Fighting until the end." Meanwhile, absorbed by these words he had etched in his diary, he walked at a good pace, cutting his way with a machete through lianas, thickets, trunks and branches that obstructed the path. In the afternoon it occurred to him to think: "We Irish are like the Huitotos, the Boras, the Andoques, and the Muinanes of Putumayo. Colonized, exploited, and condemned to be that way forever if we continue trusting in the laws, institutions, and governments of England to attain our freedom. They will never give it to us. Why would the Empire that colonized us do that unless it feels an irresistible pressure that obliges it to do so? That pressure can come only from weapons." This idea that in future days, weeks, months, and years he would keep polishing and reinforcing—that Ireland, like the Indians of Putumayo, if it wanted to be free, would have to fight to achieve it—so absorbed him during the eight hours the trek took that he even forgot to think that very shortly he would meet the chief of Matanzas: Armando Normand.

To reach the Matanzas station, situated on the bank of the Cahuinari River, a tributary of the Caquetá, one had to climb a steep slope which a heavy rain a little before their arrival had transformed into a gully of mud. Only the Muinanes could climb it without falling. The rest slipped, rolled, got up covered with mud and bruises. In the clearing, also protected by a stockade of reeds, some Indian women poured pails of water on the travelers to remove the mud.

The chief was not there. He was leading a *correría* against five fugitive Indians who apparently had succeeded in crossing the Colombian border, which was very close. There were five Barbadians in Matanzas and all five treated "Mr. Consul" with great respect, having been informed of his arrival and mission. They led the commissioners to the houses where they would stay. They put Roger, Louis Barnes, and Juan Tizón in a large plank house with a *yarina* roof and screened windows that they said was used by Normand and his wives when they were in Matanzas. But his usual residence was in La China, a small camp a few kilometers upriver, where Indians were forbidden to go. The chief lived there surrounded by his armed rationals, for he feared being the victim of an assassination attempt by the Colombians, who accused him of not respecting the border and crossing it on his *correrías* to abduct porters or capture deserters. The Barbadians explained that Armando Normand always took the girls in his harem with him because he was very jealous.

In Matanzas there were Boras, Andoques, and Muinanes, but no Huitotos. Almost all the indigenous people had whipping scars and at least a dozen of them had the

Casa Arana brand on their buttocks. The pillory was in the center of the clearing, beneath the tree called the *lupuna*, covered with furuncles and parasitic plants, for which all the tribes in the region professed a reverence suffused with fear.

In his room, which undoubtedly was Normand's, Roger saw yellowing photographs where his childish face appeared, a 1903 diploma from the London School of Bookkeepers, and another earlier one from a senior school. It was true, then: he had studied in England and held an accounting diploma.

Armando Normand entered Matanzas as night was falling. Through the small screened window, Roger saw him pass by in the light from the lanterns and go into the neighboring house, looking almost as slight as an Indian, followed by "boys" with the faces of hangmen and armed with Winchesters and revolvers, and by eight or ten women dressed in the *cushma* or Amazonian tunic.

During the night Roger woke several times, in anguish, thinking about Ireland. He felt nostalgia for his country. He had lived there so little and yet felt increasing solidarity with its fate and suffering. Since he had seen first-hand the *via crucis* of other colonized peoples, Ireland's situation pained him more than ever. He felt an urgency to finish with all this, to complete the report on Putumayo, turn it in to the Foreign Office, and return to Ireland to work, now without distractions, with his idealistic compatriots devoted to the cause of emancipation. He would make up for lost time, become more involved in the nationalist movement, study, take action, write, and by all the means at his disposal try to persuade the Irish that if they wanted freedom, they would have to win it with boldness and sacrifice.

The next morning, when he went downstairs for breakfast, Armando Normand was there, sitting at a table with fruit, pieces of yucca in place of bread, and cups of coffee. He was short and skinny, with the face of a prematurely aged boy and a gaze that was blue, fixed, and hard, and appeared and disappeared because of his constant blinking. He wore boots, blue jeans, a white shirt, and over that a leather vest with a pencil holder and a small notebook visible in one of the pockets. He carried a revolver at his waist.

Normand greeted him with an almost imperceptible nod, not saying a word. He was very close-mouthed, almost monosyllabic, in responding to questions about his life in London or specific information about his nationality—"let's say I'm Peruvian." He spoke perfect English, with a strange accent whose origin Roger could not identify, and he replied with a certain arrogance when Roger told him that he and the members of the commission had been affected by seeing that in the territories of a British company the indigenous were mistreated in an inhuman way.

"If all of you lived here, you would think differently," he remarked, drily, not at all intimidated. And after a brief pause, he added: "You can't treat animals like human beings. A *yacumama* river snake, a jaguar, a puma don't understand words. Neither do the savages. Well, I already know that outsiders passing through here cannot be convinced."

"I lived for twenty years in Africa and I didn't turn into a monster," said Roger. "Which is what you have become, Mr. Normand. Your reputation has traveled with us throughout the entire journey. The horrors told about you in Putumayo go beyond anything imaginable. Did you know that?"

Armando Normand was not troubled in the least. Looking at him constantly with that blank, inexpressive gaze, he only shrugged and spat on the floor.

"Can I ask how many men and women you've killed?" Roger fired at him point-blank.

"All those who have committed a crime," replied the chief of Matanzas, not changing his tone and standing up. "Excuse me. I have work to do."

The distaste Roger felt for this little man was so great he decided not to interview him personally and to leave the task to the commission members. That murderer would tell them only an avalanche of lies. He devoted himself to listening to the Barbadians and rationals who agreed to testify. He did this in the morning and afternoon, dedicating the rest of the day to developing the notes he had taken during the interviews. In the mornings he went down to swim in the river, took some photographs, and then didn't stop working until it grew dark. He would fall, exhausted, on his cot. His sleep was intermittent and feverish. He noticed he was losing weight day by day.

He was exhausted and sick of it. As had happened at a certain moment in the Congo, he began to be afraid that the maddening succession of crimes, violent acts, and horrors of every kind he uncovered on a daily basis would affect his mental balance. Would the health of his spirit resist this quotidian horror? It demoralized him to think that in civilized England few people would believe that the whites and mestizos in Putumayo could reach these extremes of savagery. Once again he would be accused of exaggeration and prejudice, of magnifying abuses to make his report more dramatic. Not only the iniquitous mistreatment of the indigenous had him in this state, but knowing that after seeing, hearing, and witnessing what went on here, he would never again have the optimistic view of life he'd had in his youth.

When he learned that an expedition of porters was going to leave Matanzas carrying the rubber harvested in the last three months to the Entre Ríos Station and from there to Puerto Peruano to be shipped abroad, he told his companions he would go with them. The commission could remain here until it finished its inspection and the interviews. His friends were as exhausted and discouraged as he was. They told him that Armando Normand's insolent manner had changed suddenly when they let him know that "Mr. Consul" had been assigned the mission to investigate the atrocities in Putumayo by Sir Edward Grey himself, the minister of foreign affairs for the British Empire, and that the killers and torturers, since they worked for an English company, could be brought to trial in England – above all if they had English nationality or were attempting to acquire it, as might be true in his case. Or they could be turned over to the Peruvian or Colombian governments to be tried here. When he heard this, Normand adopted a submissive, servile attitude toward the commission. He denied his crimes and assured them that from now on the errors of the past would not be repeated: the Indians would be well fed, healed when they fell ill, paid for their work, and treated like human beings. He had ordered a handbill saying these things to be placed in the middle of the clearing. It was ridiculous, since the indigenous, all illiterate, could not read it and neither could the majority of the rationals. It was exclusively for the commissioners to read.

The journey on foot through the jungle, from Matanzas to Entre Ríos, accompanying the eighty Indians—Boras, Andoques, and Muinanes—who were carrying on their shoulders the rubber harvested by Armando Normand's people, would be one of the most horrifying memories of Roger's first trip to Peru. Normand wasn't leading the expedition but Negretti, one of his lieutenants, an Asian-looking mestizo with gold teeth who was always digging in his mouth with a toothpick and whose stentorian voice made the army of wounded, branded, and scarred skeletons in the expedition, among them many women and children, some very young, tremble, jump, hurry, their faces distorted by fear. Negretti carried a rifle on his shoulder, a revolver in a holster, and a whip at his waist. On the day they left, Roger asked his permission to photograph him and Negretti agreed, laughing. But his smile vanished when Roger warned him, pointing at the whip: "If I see you use that on the Indians, I'll personally turn you over to the Iquitos police."

Negretti's expression was one of total confusion. After a moment he murmured: "Do you have any authority in the company?"

"I have the authority granted me by the English government to investigate the abuses committed in Putumayo. You know that the Peruvian Amazon Company you work for is British, don't you?"

Disconcerted, the man moved away. And Roger never saw him flog the porters; he only yelled at them so they would move faster or harassed them with curses and other insults when they dropped the "sausages" of rubber they carried on their shoulders and heads because their strength failed or they tripped.

Roger had brought three Barbadians with him: Bishop, Sealy, and Lane. The other nine remained with the commission. Roger recommended to his friends that they never get far away from these witnesses, for they ran the risk of being intimidated or bribed by Normand and his henchmen to retract their testimonies, or even murdered by them.

The most difficult part of the expedition was not the large buzzing blowflies that hounded them day and night with their stings, or the rainstorms that sometimes fell, soaking them and turning the ground into slippery streams of water, mud, leaves, and dead trees, or the discomfort of the camps they set up at night to sleep the poor sleep God sent them after eating a can of sardines or soup and taking a few swallows of whiskey or tea from a flask. The terrible thing, a torture that filled him with remorse and gave him a bad conscience, was seeing these naked Indians bent over by the weight of the sausages of rubber, whom Negretti and his "boys" pushed forward with shouts, always hurrying them, with very widely spaced rests and without giving them a mouthful of food. When he asked Negretti why the rations weren't also distributed to the indigenous workers, the overseer looked at him as if he didn't understand. When Bishop explained the question to him, Negretti stated, with total shamelessness: "They don't like what we Christians eat. They have their own food."

But they had none, because you couldn't call the little

handfuls of yucca flour they sometimes put in their mouths food, or the stems and leaves of plants they rolled up very carefully before swallowing them. What Roger found incomprehensible was how children of ten or twelve could carry for hours and hours those sausages that weighed—he had tried carrying them—never less than twenty kilos and sometimes thirty or more. On the first day of the trek a Bora boy suddenly fell on his face, crushed by his load. He moaned weakly when Roger tried to revive him by having him drink a can of soup. The boy's eyes showed an animal panic. Two or three times he attempted to get up, without succeeding. Bishop explained: "He's so afraid because if you weren't here, Negretti would finish him off with a bullet as a warning so no other pagan would decide to faint." The boy was in no condition to stand, so they abandoned him in the forest. Roger left him two cans of food and his umbrella. Now he understood why these feeble creatures could carry so much weight: they feared being killed if they dared to faint. Terror increased their strength.

On the second day, an old woman suddenly fell down dead when she tried to climb a slope with thirty kilos of rubber on her back. Negretti, after confirming she was lifeless, quickly distributed the dead woman's two sausages among the other natives with a grimace of annoyance and a hoarse voice.

In Entre Ríos, as soon as he had bathed and rested a while, Roger hurried to write in his notebooks the vicissitudes of the trip and his reflections. An idea came to mind over and over again, an idea that in the following days, weeks, and months would return obsessively and begin to shape his conduct: *We should not permit colonization to castrate the spirit of the Irish as it has castrated the spirit of the Amazonian Indians. We must act now, once and for all, before it is too late and we turn into automata.*

He wasted no time while he waited for the arrival of the commission. He had some interviews, but above all he reviewed the payrolls, store account books, and administrative records. He wanted to establish how much the company increased the prices of foodstuffs, medicines, articles of clothing, weapons, and tools it advanced to the Indians as well as to the overseers and "boys." The percentages varied from product to product, but the constant was that for everything it sold, the store doubled, tripled, and at times quintupled prices. He bought two shirts, a pair of trousers, a hat, a pair of hiking boots, and could have acquired everything in London for a third of the price. Not only the indigenous were swindled but also those poor wretches, vagabonds, and thugs who were in Putumayo to carry out the station chiefs' orders. It was not strange that all of them were always in debt to the Peruvian Amazon Company and were tied to it until they died or the firm considered them useless.

Roger found it more difficult to form an approximate idea of how many indigenous people were in Putumayo in 1893, when the first rubber plantations were established in the region and the *correrías* began, and how many remained in this year of 1910. There were no serious statistics: what had been written on the subject was vague, and the figures differed a good deal. The person who seemed to have made the most trustworthy calculation was the unfortunate French explorer and ethnologist Eugène Robuchon (who disappeared mysteriously in the Putumayo region in

1905 when he was mapping the entire territory of Julio C. Arana), according to whom the seven tribes in the area—Huitotos, Ocaimas, Muinanes, Nonuyas, Andoques, Rezígaros, and Boras—must have amounted to one hundred thousand before rubber drew "civilized" men to Putumayo. Juan Tizón considered the figure highly exaggerated. He, through different analyses and comparisons, maintained that forty thousand was closer to the truth. In any case, now no more than ten thousand survivors remained. In this way, the system imposed by the rubber barons had already annihilated three-fourths of the indigenous population. Many undoubtedly had been victims of smallpox, malaria, beriberi, and other epidemics. But the immense majority disappeared because of exploitation, hunger, mutilations, the pillory, and murder. At this rate what had happened to the Iquarasi, who had been totally exterminated, would happen to all the tribes.

Two days later his colleagues from the commission arrived in Entre Ríos. Roger was surprised to see Armando Normand with them, followed by his harem of young girls. Folk and Barnes informed him that even though the reason the Matanzas chief gave for coming with them was that he had to oversee personally the loading of the rubber in Puerto Peruano, he had done so because of how frightened he was with respect to his future. As soon as he learned of the accusations the Barbadians had made against him, he set in motion a campaign of bribes and threats to force them to retract what they had said. And he had been successful with some, like Levine, who sent a letter to the commission (no doubt written by Normand himself) saying they denied all their statements, which they had been "tricked" into making, and they wanted to make it clear, in writing, that the Peruvian Amazon Company had never mistreated the indigenous and that employees and porters worked in friendship for the greatness of Peru. Folk and Barnes thought Normand would try to bribe or intimidate Bishop, Sealy, and Lane, and perhaps Casement himself.

Very early the next morning, Armando Normand came to knock on Roger's door and propose "a frank, friendly conversation." The manager of Matanzas had lost his confidence and the arrogance with which he had previously addressed Roger. He seemed nervous and rubbed his hands and bit his lower lip as he spoke. They went to the rubber depository, in a clearing among brambles that the previous night's storm had filled with puddles and frogs. A stench of latex came from the depository and the idea passed through Roger's mind that the smell didn't come from the rubber sausages stored in the large shed but from the small red-faced man who looked like a midget beside him.

Normand had prepared his speech carefully. The seven years he had spent in the jungle demanded huge privations for someone who had been educated in London. He didn't want his life cut short by legal entanglements that would keep him from satisfying his longing to return to England. He swore on his honor he had no blood on his hands or his conscience. He was severe but just and was prepared to apply all the measures the commission and "Mr. Consul" might suggest to improve the operation of the enterprise.

"Put an end to *correrías* and the abduction of Indians," Roger enumerated slowly, counting on his fingers, "get rid of the pillory and whips, don't have the Indians work free of charge any more, don't allow the chiefs, overseers, and "boys" to rape or steal the wives and daughters of the Indians, get rid of physical punishments, and pay reparations to the families of those who have been murdered, burned alive, or had their ears, noses, hands, and feet chopped off. Stop stealing from the porters with dishonest scales and inflated prices at the store to keep them forever in debt to the company." All of that was just a beginning, because many more reforms would be needed for the Peruvian Amazon Company to deserve to be a British company.

Armando Normand was livid and looked at him with incomprehension.

"Do you want the Peruvian Amazon Company to disappear, Mr. Casement?" he finally stammered.

"Exactly. And for all its killers and torturers, beginning with Señor Julio C. Arana and ending with you, to go on trial for your crimes and end your days in prison."

He increased his pace and left the Matanzas chief with his face contorted, motionless where he stood, not knowing what to say. Roger immediately regretted having given in to the contempt this individual deserved. He had gained a mortal enemy who now might very well feel the temptation to kill him. He had warned him, and Normand, neither stupid nor lazy, would act accordingly. He had made a very serious mistake.

A few days later, Juan Tizón let them know that the Matanzas chief had asked the company for the money owed him, in cash, not in Peruvian *soles* but in pounds sterling. He would travel back to Iquitos in the *Liberal* along with the commission. What he was attempting was obvious: to weaken, with the help of friends and accomplices, the charges and accusations against him and to assure himself of an escape to another country—undoubtedly Brazil—where he would have a good amount of money waiting for him. The chances of his going to prison had been reduced. Tizón informed them that for the past five years, Normand had received twenty per cent of the rubber harvested at Matanzas and a bonus of two hundred pounds sterling a year if the yield was higher than that of the previous year.

The subsequent days and weeks followed a suffocating routine. The interviews with Barbadians and rationals continued to reveal an impressive catalogue of atrocities. Roger felt his strength leaving him. Since he had begun to run a fever in the evenings, he was afraid it was malaria again and increased his dose of quinine when he went to bed. The fear that Armando Normand or any other station chief might destroy his notebooks with the transcriptions of the testimonies meant that in all the stations—Entre Ríos, Atenas, Sur, and La Chorrera—he carried those papers with him and would not allow anyone else to touch them. At night he placed them under the cot or hammock where he slept, a loaded revolver always within reach.

In La Chorrera, as they were packing their suitcases for the return to Iquitos, Roger saw about twenty Indians from the village of Naimenes come into camp. They were carrying rubber. The porters were young or adult men, except for a very skinny boy of nine or ten, who carried on his head a rubber sausage bigger than he was. Roger went with them to the scale where Víctor Macedo was accepting delivery. The little boy's weighed twenty-four kilos and he, Omarino, only twenty-five. How could he walk all those kilometers through the jungle with that weight on his head? In spite of the scars on his back, he had lively, joyful eyes and smiled frequently. Roger had him take a tin of soup and another of sardines that he bought at the store. From that time on, Omarino did not leave his side. He accompanied him everywhere and was always ready to do any errand. One day Víctor Macedo said to him, pointing at the little boy: "I see he's become fond of you, Señor Casement. Why don't you take him with you? He's an orphan. I'll give him to you."

Afterward, Roger would think the phrase, "I'll give him to you," with which Víctor Macedo had wanted to ingratiate himself, said more than any other testimony: the station chief could "give" any Indian in his territory, since porters and harvesters belonged to him just like the trees, the houses, the rifles, and the rubber sausages. He asked Juan Tizón if there would be any problem with his taking Omarino to London—the Anti-Slavery Society would place him under its protection and be responsible for his education—and Tizón offered no objection.

Arédomi, an adolescent who belonged to the Andoque tribe, would join Omarino a few days later. He had come to La Chorrera from the Sur station, and the next day, in the river, as he swam, Roger saw him naked, splashing in the water with other Indians. He was a beautiful boy, with a well-proportioned, agile body, who moved with natural elegance. Roger thought Herbert Ward could make a beautiful sculpture of this adolescent, the symbol of Amazonian man stripped of his land, his body, and his beauty by the rubber barons. He distributed tins of food to the Andoques who were swimming. Arédomi kissed his hand in gratitude. He was displeased and, at the same time, moved. The boy followed him to his house, talking and gesturing energetically, but Roger didn't understand him. He called Frederick Bishop who translated: "He wants you to take him with you, wherever you're going. He'll serve you well."

"Tell him I can't, that I'm already taking Omarino with me."

But Arédomi was obstinate. He stood motionless outside the cabin where Roger slept or followed him wherever he went, a few steps behind, a silent plea in his eyes. He decided to consult with the commission and Juan Tizón. Did they think it was all right if he took Arédomi to London along with Omarino? Perhaps the two boys would give greater persuasive strength to his report: both had flogging scars. Then too, they were young enough to be educated and incorporated into a way of life that was not slavery.

On the eve of the departure of the *Liberal*, Carlos Miranda, chief of the Sur station, arrived in La Chorrera. He brought with him about one hundred natives with the rubber harvested in that region in the past three months. He was fat, in his forties, and very white. From his way of speaking and behaving, he seemed to have been better educated than other station chiefs. No doubt he came from a middle-class family. But his record was as bloodthirsty as those of his colleagues. Roger and the other members of the commission had heard several testimonies about the episode of the old Bora woman who, a few months earlier, in Sur, in an attack of despair or madness, suddenly began to shout, exhorting the Boras to fight and not allow themselves to be humiliated any more or treated as slaves. Her shouting paralyzed the indigenous around her with terror. Infuriated, Carlos Miranda attacked her with the machete he snatched from one of his "boys" and decapitated her. Brandishing her head, which drenched him in blood, he told the Indians this would happen to all of them if they didn't do their work or imitated the old woman. The decapitator was a genial, cheerful man, talkative and easygoing, who tried to win over Roger and his colleagues by telling jokes and recounting anecdotes about the bizarre, picturesque individuals he had known in Putumayo.

On Wednesday, November 16, 1910, when he boarded the *Liberal* at the La Chorrera wharf to begin the return to Iquitos, Roger opened his mouth and breathed deeply. He had an extraordinary feeling of relief. He thought this departure would cleanse his body and spirit of an oppressive anguish he hadn't felt before, not even in the most difficult moments of his life in the Congo. In addition to Omarino and Arédomi, the *Liberal* carried eighteen Barbadians, five indigenous women who were their wives, and the children of John Brown, Allan Davis, James Mapp, Joshua Dyall, and Philip Bertie Lawrence.

The Barbadians being on the ship was the result of a difficult negotiation, filled with intrigues, concessions, and rectifications, with Juan Tizón, Víctor Macedo, the other members of the commission, and the Barbadians themselves. All of them, before testifying, had asked for guarantees, for they knew very well they were exposing themselves to reprisals from the chiefs their testimony could send to prison. Roger had pledged he would be responsible for taking them out of Putumayo alive.

But in the days before the *Liberal* arrived in La Chorrera, the company initiated a cordial offensive to retain the overseers from Barbados, assuring them they would not be victims of reprisals and promising them pay raises and better conditions if they would not leave their jobs. Víctor Macedo announced that whatever their decision, the Peruvian Amazon Company had decided to reduce by twenty-five per cent what they owed the store for the purchase of medicine, clothing, household utensils, and food. All of them accepted the offer. And in less than twenty-four hours, the Barbadians announced to Roger that they wouldn't leave with him but would continue to work at the stations. Roger knew what that meant: pressure and bribery would make them retract their confessions as soon as he left and accuse him of having invented the testimonies or coerced them with threats. He spoke to Juan Tizón, who reminded him that even though he was as affected as Roger by the things that were occurring and determined to correct them, he was still one of the directors of the Peruvian Amazon Company and could not and should not influence the Barbadians to leave if they wanted to stay. One of the commissioners, Henry Fielgald, supported Tizón with the same arguments: he too worked in London with Mr. Julio C. Arana, and even though he would demand deep reforms in the methods of working in Amazonia, he could not become the liquidator of the firm that employed him. Roger had the feeling the world was falling down around him.

But as in one of those rocambolesque changes of circumstance in French serials, that entire panorama changed radically when the *Liberal* arrived in La Chorrera at dusk on November 12. It brought correspondence and newspapers from Iquitos and Lima. The daily *El Comercio*, from the Peruvian capital, in a long article two months old, announced that the government of President Augusto B. Leguía, mindful of requests from Great Britain and the United States regarding alleged atrocities committed on the rubber plantations of Putumayo, had sent a leading magistrate of the Peruvian judiciary, Dr. Carlos A. Valcárcel, to Amazonia with special powers. His mission was to investigate and immediately initiate the proper judicial actions, taking police and military forces to Putumayo if he considered it necessary, so that those responsible for crimes would not escape justice.

This information exploded like a bomb among the employees of Casa Arana. Juan Tizón told Roger that Víctor Macedo, in great alarm, had summoned all the station chiefs, including the most distant ones, to a meeting in La Chorrera. Tizón gave the impression of a man torn by an insoluble contradiction. He was happy, for the honor of his country and because of an innate sense of justice, that the Peruvian government had finally decided to act. On the other hand, he did not hide the fact that this scandal could mean the ruin of the Peruvian Amazon Company and, consequently, of himself. One night, while drinking lukewarm whiskey, Tizón confessed to Roger that his entire inheritance, except for a house in Lima, was invested in company stocks.

The rumors, gossip, and fear generated by the news from Lima meant that once again the Barbadians changed their minds. Now they wanted to leave. They were afraid the Peruvian chiefs would try to avoid their responsibility for the torture and murder of Indians by blaming them, the "black foreigners," and they wanted to leave Peru as soon as possible and return to Barbados. They were plagued by uncertainty and apprehension.

Roger, without saying anything about it to anyone, thought that if the eighteen Barbadians came to Iquitos with him, anything could happen. For example, the company would make them responsible for all the crimes and send them to prison, or try to bribe them to rectify their confessions and accuse Roger of having falsified them. The solution was for the Barbadians to disembark before reaching Iquitos at one of the ports of call in Brazilian territory and wait there for Roger to pick them up in the ship *Atahualpa*, on which he would sail from Iquitos to Europe, with a stop in Barbados. He confided his plan to Frederick Bishop, who agreed with it but told Roger the best thing would be not to communicate it to the Barbadians until the last minute.

There was a strange atmosphere on the La Chorrera wharf when the *Liberal* left. None of the station chiefs came to say goodbye. It was said that several of them had decided to leave, heading for Brazil or Colombia. Juan Tizón, who would stay another month in Putumayo, embraced Roger and wished him luck. The commission members, who would also stay another week in Putumayo to do technical and administrative studies, said goodbye at the foot of the stairs. They agreed to meet in London to read Roger's report before he presented it to the Foreign Office.

On the first night of travel on the river, a full, reddish moon lit the sky. It was reflected in the dark water with a spatter of stars that looked like small luminous fish. Everything was warm, beautiful, and serene, except for the smell of rubber that was still there, as if it had entered one's nostrils forever. Roger leaned on the rail for a long time at the stern, contemplating the spectacle, and suddenly realized his face was wet with tears. *What miraculous peace, my God.*

For the first days of the voyage, fatigue and anxiety kept him from reviewing his cards and notebooks and outlining his report. He slept little and had nightmares. He often got up at night and went out to the bridge if it was clear to look at the moon and stars. A Brazilian customs administrator was traveling on the boat. Roger asked him if the Barbadians could disembark at a Brazilian port and then travel to Manaus to wait for him so they could continue on together to Barbados. The official assured him there was absolutely no problem. Even so, Roger was still concerned. He was afraid something would happen that would save the Peruvian Amazon Company from all sanctions. After having seen so directly the fate of the Amazonian indigenous peoples, it was urgent for the entire world to know about it and do something to remedy the situation.

Another reason for his distress was Ireland. Ever since he had become convinced that only resolute action, an uprising, could save his country from "losing its soul" because of colonization, as had happened to the Huitotos, the Boras, and the other unfortunate peoples of Putumayo, he burned with impatience to throw himself body and soul into preparing the insurrection that would put an end to so many centuries of servitude in his country.

The day the *Liberal* crossed the Peruvian border—by now it was sailing on the Yavarí—and entered Brazil, the feeling of distrust and danger that had hounded him disappeared. But then they would return to the Amazon and sail up to Peruvian territory where, he was certain, he would again feel the anxiety that an unforeseen catastrophe would frustrate his mission and render the months spent in Putumayo useless.

On November 21, 1910, in the Brazilian port of La Esperanza on the Yavarí River, Roger had fourteen Barbadians, the wives of four of them, and four children disembark. The night before he had gathered them together to explain the risk they would run if they accompanied him to Iquitos. The company, in collusion with the judges and the police, would arrest them and hold them responsible for all the crimes, making them the object of pressures, insults, and extortion so they would retract the confessions that incriminated Casa Arana.

Fourteen Barbadians accepted his plan to get off in La Esperanza and take the first boat for Manaus where, protected by the British consulate, they would wait for Roger to pick them up in the *Atahualpa*, of the Booth Line, which sailed the route Iquitos–Manaus–Pará. From this last city another ship would take them home. Roger said goodbye and left them with abundant provisions he had bought for them, certification that their passage to Manaus would be guaranteed by the British government, and a letter of introduction for the British consul in that city.

Continuing with him to Iquitos, in addition to Arédomi and Omarino, were Frederick Bishop, John Brown with his wife and son, Larry Clarke, and Philip Bertie Lawrence, also with two small children. These Barbadians had things to pick up and company checks to cash in the city.

Roger spent the four days it took to reach Iquitos working on his papers and preparing a memorandum for the Peruvian authorities.

On November 25 they landed in Iquitos. The British consul, Mr. Stirs, once again insisted that Roger stay in his house. And he accompanied him to a nearby rooming house where they found lodging for the Barbadians, Arédomi, and Omarino. Stirs was uneasy. All of Iquitos was very agitated at the news that Judge Valcárcel would arrive soon to investigate the accusations of England and the United States against the company of Julio C. Arana. Not only the employees of the Peruvian Amazon Company were afraid but Iquitians in general, for everyone knew the life of the city depended on the company. There was great hostility toward Roger, and the consul advised him not to go out alone, since he could not discount the possibility of an attempt on his life.

When, after supper and the customary glass of port, Roger summarized for him what he had seen and heard in Putumayo, Stirs, who listened very seriously and silently, had only one question to ask: "As terrible, then, as the Congo of Leopold II?"

"I'm afraid so, and perhaps worse," Roger replied. "Though it seems obscene to establish hierarchies among crimes of this magnitude."

In his absence, a new prefect had been appointed in Iquitos, a gentleman from Lima named Esteban Zapata. Unlike the previous one, he was not an employee of Julio C. Arana. From the time of his arrival he had maintained a certain distance from Pablo Zumaeta and the other company directors. He knew Roger was about to arrive and awaited him impatiently.

The interview with the prefect took place the next morning and lasted more than two hours. Esteban Zapata was young, very swarthy, and well mannered. In spite of the heat—he perspired constantly and wiped his face with a large purple handkerchief—he did not remove his woolen frock coat. He listened very attentively to Roger, showing astonishment at times, interrupting occasionally to ask for details, exclaiming frequently with indignation. ("How terrible! How awful!") From time to time he offered him small glasses of cool water. Roger told him everything, in great detail, names, numbers, places, concentrating on facts and avoiding commentaries except at the end, when he concluded his account with these words: "In short, Prefect, the accusations of the journalist Saldaña Roca and of Mr. Hardenburg were not exaggerated. On the contrary, everything the journal *Truth* has published in London, though it may seem false, is still not the entire truth."

Zapata, with a disquiet in his voice that seemed sincere, said he felt ashamed for Peru. This occurred because the state had not reached those regions isolated from the law and lacking institutions. The government was determined to act. That is why he was here. That is why an upright judge like Dr. Valcárcel would arrive soon. President Leguía himself wanted to cleanse the honor of Peru, putting an end to these atrocious abuses. He had said as much, in those very words. His Majesty's government would be able to confirm that the guilty would be punished and the indigenous protected starting now. He asked if the report to his government would be public. When Roger replied that at first the report would be for the internal use of the

British government, and undoubtedly would be sent to the Peruvian government so they could decide whether to publish it or not, the prefect sighed with relief: "Thank goodness," he exclaimed. "If all this is made public, it will do enormous harm to the image of our country in the world."

Roger was about to tell him that what would harm Peru more would not be the report but the fact that what motivated it took place on Peruvian soil. On the other hand, the prefect wanted to know if the Barbadians who had come to Iquitos—Bishop, Brown, and Lawrence—would agree to confirm to him their testimonies regarding Putumayo. Roger assured him that tomorrow first thing he would send them to the Prefecture.

Stirs, who had served as interpreter in this conversation, left the interview crestfallen. Roger had noted that the consul added many phrases—at times real commentaries—to what Roger said in English, and that these interventions always tended to weaken the harshness of facts relating to the exploitation and suffering of the Indians. All of this increased his distrust of the consul who, in spite of being here for several years and knowing very well what was going on, never had informed the Foreign Office about it. The reason was simple: Juan Tizón had disclosed that Stirs did business in Iquitos and for that reason also depended on Señor Julio C. Arana's company. No doubt his present concern was that the scandal might be prejudicial to him. The consul had a small soul and his values were subordinate to his greed.

In the days that followed, Roger tried to see Father Urrutia, but at the mission they told him the superior of the Augustinians was in Pebas, where the Yagua Indians lived—Roger had seen them on a stop the *Liberal* made there and been impressed by the tunics of spun fibers they used to cover their bodies—because he was going to open a school there.

And so in the days before he boarded the *Atahualpa*, which was still unloading in the port of Iquitos, Roger devoted himself to working on the report. Then, in the afternoons, he walked and, on a few occasions, went to the Cine Alhambra, on the Plaza de Armas in Iquito. It had existed for a few months, and silent films were shown there accompanied by an orchestra of three very out-of-tune musicians. The real spectacle for Roger was not the black-and-white figures on the screen but the fascination of the audience, Indians from the tribes and soldiers from the mountains in the local garrison who watched it all, amazed and disconcerted.

Another day he walked to Punchana along a trail that on his return had become a quagmire because of the rain. But the countryside was very beautiful. One afternoon he attempted to go to Quistococha by foot—he took Omarino and Arédomi with him—but an interminable downpour surprised them and they had to take shelter in the undergrowth. When the storm ended, the trail was so full of puddles and mud they had to hurry back to Iquitos.

The *Atahualpa* sailed for Manaus and Pará on December 6, 1910. Roger was in first class and Omarino, Arédomi, and the Barbadians in second class. When the ship, in the clear, hot morning, moved away from Iquitos and the people and houses on the banks grew smaller and smaller, Roger again felt in his bosom that feeling of freedom that comes with the disappearance of great danger. Not a physical danger, but a moral one. He had the feeling that if he had stayed longer in that terrible place, where so many people suffered so unjustly and cruelly, he too, for the simple fact of being white and European, would be contaminated and debased. He told himself that fortunately he would never set foot in these places again. The thought encouraged him and in part took him out of the despondency and lethargy that kept him from working with his old concentration and drive.

When, on December 10, the *Atahualpa* docked in the port of Manaus at dusk, Roger had already left behind his dejection and recovered his energy and capacity for work. The fourteen Barbadians were in the city. Most had decided not to return to Barbados but to accept contracts for work on the Madeira–Mamoré railroad, which offered good terms. The rest continued with him to Pará, where the boat docked on December 14. Here Roger found a ship going to Barbados and put the Barbadians and Omarino and Arédomi on board. He put the boys in Frederick Bishop's care, asking him to take them to the Reverend Frederick Smith in Bridgetown with instructions to matriculate them in the Jesuit school where, before they continued on to London, they would receive a basic education that would prepare them to face life in the capital of the British Empire.

Then he looked for a ship to take him to Europe. He found the SS *Ambrose* of the Booth Line. Since it would not leave until December 17, he used the free days to visit the places he frequented when he was British consul in Pará: bars, restaurants, the Botanical Garden, the immense, chaotic, variegated market in the port. He did not feel nostalgia for Pará, for his stay here had not been happy, but he acknowledged the joy that emanated from the people, the grace of the women and idle boys who strolled and displayed themselves on the embankments along the river. Once again he told himself the Brazilians had a healthy, happy relationship with their bodies, very different from the Peruvians, for example, who, like the English, always seemed uncomfortable with their physical being. But here they showed it off boldly, especially if they felt young and attractive.

On the 17th he set sail on the SS *Ambrose*, and as he traveled he decided that since this ship would reach the French port of Cherbourg at the end of December, he would disembark there and take the train to Paris to spend the New Year with Herbert Ward and Sarita, his wife. He would return to London on the first working day next year. It would be purifying to spend a few days with these friends, a cultured couple, in their beautiful studio filled with sculptures and African mementos, talking of beautiful, elevated things, art, books, theater, music, the best produced by those contradictory human beings also capable of the extreme wickedness that reigned on the rubber plantations of Julio C. Arana in Putumayo.

II

When the fat sheriff opened the door of his cell, came in, and without saying anything sat on a corner of the cot where he was lying, Roger was not surprised. Ever since the sheriff violated the rules and permitted him to take a shower, he had felt, without a word passing between them, a rapprochement with the jailer who, without realizing it, perhaps in spite of himself, had stopped hating him and holding him responsible for the death of his son in the trenches in France.

It was dusk, and the small cell was almost dark. Roger, from the cot, saw the very still shadow of the sheriff's wide, cylindrical silhouette. He heard him panting deeply, as if exhausted.

"He had flat feet and could have avoided active duty," he heard him say in a monotone, pierced by emotion. "At the first recruitment center, in Hastings, they rejected him when they examined his feet. But he didn't accept that and went to another center. He wanted to go to war. Whoever heard of anything so crazy?"

"He loved his country, he was a patriot," Roger said quietly. "You ought to be proud of your son, Sheriff."

"What good does it do that he was a hero if he's dead now," the jailer replied in a lugubrious voice. "He was all I had in the world. Now, it's as if I stopped living too. Sometimes I think I've turned into a ghost."

In the shadowy cell it seemed to him the sheriff sobbed. But perhaps it was a false impression. Roger thought of the fifty-three volunteers of the Irish Brigade who remained in Germany, in the small military camp of Zossen, where Captain Robert Monteith had trained them in the use of rifles, machine guns, tactics, and military maneuvers, trying to keep their morale high in spite of an uncertain situation. And the questions he had asked himself a thousand times tormented him again. What did they think when he disappeared without saying goodbye, along with Captain Monteith and Sergeant Bailey? That they were traitors? That after entangling them in a rash adventure they had gone to fight in Ireland, leaving them surrounded by barbed wire, in the hands of the Germans, and hated by the Irish prisoners in Limburg, who considered them turncoats and disloyal to their comrades who had died in the trenches of Flanders?

Once again he told himself that his life had been a permanent contradiction, a series of confusions and cruel complications, where by chance or because of his own clumsiness, the truth of his intentions and actions was always obscured, distorted, turned into a lie. Those fifty-three pure, idealistic patriots, who'd had the courage to confront more than two thousand of their comrades in the camp at Limburg and join the Irish Brigade to fight "beside but not inside" the German army for the independence of Ireland, would never know about the titanic struggle Roger had waged with the German military high command to keep them from being dispatched to Ireland in the *Aud* along with the twenty thousand rifles the Germans were sending to the Volunteers for the Holy Week Rising.

"I am responsible for those fifty-three members of the Brigade," Roger told Captain Rudolf Nadolny, in charge of Irish affairs for the General Staff in Berlin. "I exhorted them to desert the British army. Under English law, they are traitors. They will be hanged immediately if the Royal Navy captures them, which will happen, irremediably, if the Rising takes place without the support of a German military force. I can't send these compatriots to death and dishonor. They will not go to Ireland with the twenty thousand rifles."

It hadn't been easy. Captain Nadolny and the officers of the high command tried to force him to yield with blackmail. "Very well, we will communicate immediately to the leaders of the Irish Volunteers in Dublin and the United States that in view of Mr. Roger Casement's opposition to the Rising, the German government is suspending shipment of twenty thousand rifles and five million rounds."

It was necessary to discuss, negotiate, explain, always remaining calm. Roger was not opposed to the Rising, only to the Volunteers and the Citizen Army committing suicide, launching an attack against the British Empire without the Kaiser's submarines, Zeppelins, and assault troops to distract the British armed forces and prevent them from brutally crushing the rebels and setting back Irish independence for who knows how many years. The twenty thousand rifles were indispensable, of course. He would go to Ireland with the weapons and explain to Tom Clarke, Patrick Pearse, Joseph Plunkett, and the other leaders of the Volunteers the reasons why, in his judgment, the Rising ought to be postponed.

Finally he succeeded. The ship with the weapons, the

Aud, set sail, and Roger, Monteith, and Bailey also set out for Ireland in a submarine. But the fifty-three Brigade members remained in Zossen, not understanding anything, no doubt wondering why those liars went to Ireland to fight and left them behind after training them for an action denied to them now with no explanation at all.

"When the baby was born, his mother left and abandoned us both," the sheriff's voice said suddenly and Roger gave a start on the cot. "I never heard from her again. So I had to become mother and father for the boy. Her name was Hortense and she was half crazy."

The cell was now in total darkness. Roger could no longer see the jailer's silhouette. His voice sounded very close and seemed more like an animal lament than a human expression.

"In the early years almost all my salary went to a woman who nursed him and took care of him," the sheriff continued. "I spent all my free time with him. He was always an obedient, sweet child. Never one of those boys who run wild and steal and get drunk and drive their parents crazy. He was apprenticed to a tailor, who thought very highly of him. He might have had a career there if he hadn't got it into his head to enlist, in spite of his flat feet."

Roger didn't know what to say. He felt very sorry for the sheriff's suffering and would have liked to console him, but what words could alleviate the animal pain of this poor man? He would have liked to ask his name and the name of his dead son; in this way he would have felt closer to both of them, but he didn't dare interrupt him.

"I received two letters from him," the sheriff went on. "The first, during his training. He told me he liked life in camp and when the war was over, perhaps he would stay in the army. His second letter was very different. The censor had crossed out many paragraphs in black ink. He didn't complain, but there was a certain bitterness, even some fear, in what he wrote. I never heard from him again. Until a condolence letter came from the army, announcing his death. Saying he had died a hero in the battle of Loos. I never heard of that place. I looked for Loos on a map. It must be an insignificant village."

For the second time Roger heard that sob, similar to the screech of a bird. And he had the impression that the jailer's shadow trembled.

What would happen now to those fifty-three compatriots of his? Would the German high command respect its agreements and permit the small Irish Brigade to remain together and separate in the camp at Zossen? It wasn't certain. In his discussion with Captain Rudolf Nadolny in Berlin, Roger detected the contempt the German military had for a ridiculous contingent of some fifty men. How different their attitude had been at first when, letting themselves be persuaded by Roger's enthusiasm, they supported his initiative to bring together all the Irish prisoners in the Limburg camp, supposing that once he spoke to them, hundreds would enroll in the Irish Brigade. What a failure, and what a disappointment! The most painful of his life. A failure that made him look ridiculous and shattered his patriotic dreams. Where was his mistake? Captain Robert Monteith believed his error was to speak to the 2,200 prisoners together instead of in small groups. With twenty or thirty, a dialogue would have been possible, he could have responded to objections and clarified what they found confusing. But before a mass of men suffering from defeat and the humiliation of being prisoners, what could he expect? They understood only that Roger was asking them to ally themselves with yesterday's and today's enemies, which is why they reacted with so much belligerence. No doubt there were many ways to interpret their hostility. But no theory could erase the bitterness of finding himself insulted, called a traitor, yellow, a cockroach, a sell-out by compatriots for whom he had sacrificed his time, his honor, and his future. He thought of Herbert Ward's jokes when, mocking his nationalism, he exhorted him to return to reality and leave "the dream of the Celt" into which he had retreated.

On the eve of his departure from Germany on April 11, 1916, Roger wrote a letter to Imperial Chancellor Theobald von Bethmann-Hollweg, reminding him of the terms of the agreement signed by him and the German government regarding the Irish Brigade. The accord stated that Brigade members could only be sent to fight for Ireland and in no case used as a mere support force to the German army in other theaters of war. By the same token, it stipulated that if hostilities did not conclude with a victory for Germany, the soldiers of the Irish Brigade were to be sent to the United States or a neutral country that would take them, and under no circumstances to Great Britain, where they would be summarily executed. Would the Germans fulfill these agreements? Uncertainty had returned over and over again since his capture. What if Captain Rudolf Nadolny had dissolved the Irish Brigade as soon as he, Monteith, and Bailey left for Ireland and returned its members to the Limburg Camp? They would be insulted, discriminated against by the other Irish prisoners, and run the daily risk of being lynched.

"I would have liked them to return his remains to me." The grieving voice of the sheriff took him by surprise again. "To give him a religious burial, in Hastings where he was born, like me, my father, and my grandfather. They told me no. That given the circumstances of war, the return of remains was impossible. Do you understand what they mean by 'the circumstances of war'?"

Roger didn't answer because he realized the jailer wasn't talking to him but to himself through him.

"I know very well what it means," the sheriff continued. "That there's nothing left of my poor son. That a grenade or a mortar pulverized him. In that damn place Loos. Or they put him in a common grave with other dead soldiers. I'll never know where his grave is so I can bring him flowers and say a prayer for him once in a while."

"The important thing isn't his grave but his memory, Sheriff," said Roger. "That's what counts. All that matters to your son, where he is now, is knowing you remember him with so much love."

The sheriff's shadow had made a surprised movement when he heard Roger. Perhaps he had forgotten he was in the cell beside him.

"If I knew where his mother was, I'd have gone to see her, to give her the news, and the two of us could have cried for him together," said the sheriff. "I don't have any rancor toward Hortense for leaving me. I don't even know if she's still alive. She never bothered to ask about the son she abandoned. I told you before: she wasn't a bad woman, just half crazy."

Now Roger wondered once again, as he had been doing constantly, day and night, since the dawn of his arrival on the beach of Banna Strand, in Tralee Bay, when he had heard larks singing and had seen near the beach the first wild violets, why the hell there had been no Irish boat or pilot waiting for the freighter *Aud* that was carrying rifles, machine guns, and ammunition for the Volunteers, or for the submarine carrying him, Monteith, and Bailey. What had happened? He read with his own eyes the peremptory letter from John Devoy to Count Johann Heinrich von Bernstorff, who transmitted it to the German chancellery, advising that the uprising would take place between Good Friday and Easter Sunday, and therefore the rifles had to arrive without fail at Fenit Pier, in Tralee Bay, on April 20. A pilot would be waiting there experienced in navigating the area, and rowboats and other vessels with Volunteers to unload the weapons. These instructions were reconfirmed in the same urgent terms on April 5 by Joseph Plunkett to the German chargé d'affaires in Berne, who retransmitted the message to the chancellery and the high command in Berlin: the weapons had to reach Tralee Bay at nightfall on the 20th, not earlier or later. And that was the exact date when both the *Aud* and the U-19 submarine had reached the appointed place. What the devil had happened? Why was no one waiting for them? Why did the catastrophe occur that had buried him in prison and contributed to the failure of the uprising? Because according to the information his interrogators gave him, the *Aud* was caught by the Royal Navy in Irish waters long after the date agreed on for its landing—risking its safety, it had continued to wait for the Volunteers—which obliged the captain to sink his ship and send to the bottom of the ocean the twenty thousand rifles, ten machine guns, and five million rounds of ammunition that, perhaps, would have given another direction to the rebellion the English crushed with the ferocity that was to be expected.

In fact, Roger could imagine what had happened: nothing great or transcendental, one of those stupid trifles, slips, counter-orders, differences of opinion among the leaders of the High Council of the IRB, Tom Clarke, Sean McDermott, Patrick Pearse, Joseph Plunkett, and a few others. Some or perhaps all of them must have changed their minds about the best date for the *Aud* to reach Tralee Bay and sent the rectification to Berlin, not thinking the counter-order might be lost or arrive when the freighter and submarine were already out to sea and, due to the awful atmospheric conditions at the time, practically cut off from Germany. It must have been something like that. A minor confusion, an error in calculation, a piece of foolishness, and first-rate weapons were now at the bottom of the ocean instead of in the hands of the Volunteers killed during the week of street battles in Dublin.

He hadn't been wrong to think it was a mistake to stage an armed rebellion without a concurrent German action, but that didn't make him happy. He would have preferred to be wrong. And to have been there, with those lunatics, the hundred Volunteers who at dawn on April 24 captured the Post Office on Sackville Street, or with those who attempted to capture Dublin Castle, or with those who tried to blow up the Magazine Fort in the Phoenix Park. A thousand times better to die like them, with a gun in his hand—a heroic, noble, romantic death—and not face the indignity of the gallows, like a murderer or rapist. No matter how impossible and unreal the plan of the Volunteers, the Irish Republican Brotherhood, and the Irish citizen Army might have been, it must have been beautiful and thrilling—no doubt everyone there cried and felt their hearts pounding—to hear Patrick Pearse read the manifesto that proclaimed the Republic. Though only for an exceedingly brief parenthesis of seven days, "the dream of the Celt" became a reality: Ireland, emancipated from the British occupier, was an independent nation.

"He didn't like me doing this work." The sheriff's anguished voice startled him again. "It embarrassed him that people in the neighborhood, in the tailor's shop, knew his father was a prison employee. People suppose that because we rub elbows day and night with criminals, the guards become infected and turn into men outside the law too. Have you ever heard anything more unjust? As if somebody didn't have to do this job for the good of society. I gave him the example of Mr. John Ellis, the hangman. He's also a barber in his home town, Rochdale, and nobody there speaks ill of him. On the contrary, all the residents think very highly of him. They wait in line to be served by him in his barbershop. I'm sure my son wouldn't have let anyone speak ill of me in front of him. He not only had a good deal of respect for me. I know he loved me."

Again Roger heard the stifled sob and felt the jailer's trembling move the cot. Did it do the sheriff good to unburden himself in this way, or did it increase his pain? His monologue was a knife scraping a wound. He didn't know what attitude to take: speak to him? Try to comfort him? Listen to him in silence?

"He never failed to give me something for my birthday," the sheriff added. "He gave me all of his first salary at the tailor's shop. I should have insisted he keep the money. What boy today shows so much respect for his father?"

The sheriff sank back into silence and immobility. There weren't many things Roger had been able to learn about the Rising: the taking of the Post Office, the failed attacks on Dublin Castle and the Magazine Fort in the Phoenix Park. And the summary shootings of the principal leaders, among them his friend Sean McDermott, one of the first contemporary Irishmen to have written prose and poetry in Gaelic. How many more had been shot? Did they execute them in the dungeons of Kilmainham Gaol? Or were they taken to Richmond Barracks? Alice told him that James Connolly, the great trade-union organizer, so badly wounded he couldn't stand, had been placed before the firing squad in a wheelchair. Barbarians! The fragmented facts about the Rising that Roger had learned from his interrogators, from his lawyer, his sister Nina, and Alice Stopford Green, did not give him a clear idea of what had happened, only a sense of great disorder with blood, bombs, fires, and shooting. His interrogators kept referring to the news reaching London when there was still fighting in the streets of Dublin and the British army was suppressing the last rebel strongholds. Fleeting anecdotes, casual phrases, threads he tried to situate in context using his fantasy and intuition. From the questions asked by Thomson and Hall during their interrogations, he discovered that the English government suspected he had come from Germany to lead the insurrection. That is how history is written! He had come to try to stop the Rising, and was transformed into its leader as a result of British error. For some time the government had attributed to him an influence among the supporters of independence that was far from reality. Perhaps that explained the campaigns of vilification in the English press when he was in Berlin, accusing him of selling himself to the Kaiser, of being a mercenary in addition to a traitor, and at the present time, the base acts attributed to him by the London papers. A campaign to plunge into ignominy the supreme leader he never was or wanted to be! That was history, a branch of fable-writing attempting to be science.

"Once he had a fever and the doctor at the infirmary said he was going to die." The sheriff took up his monologue again. "But between Mrs. Cubert, the woman who nursed him, and me, we took care of him, kept him warm, and with love and patience saved his life. I spent many sleepless nights rubbing his whole body with camphorated alcohol. It did him good. It broke my heart to see him so small, shivering with cold. I hope he didn't suffer. I mean over there, in the trenches, in that place, Loos. I hope his death was quick and he didn't realize it. I hope God wasn't cruel enough to inflict a long agony on him, letting him bleed to death slowly or asphyxiate on mustard gas. He always attended Sunday services and fulfilled his Christian obligations."

"What was your son's name, Sheriff?" Roger asked.

He thought the jailer gave another start in the darkness, as if he had just discovered again that he was there.

"His name was Alex Stacey," he said at last. "Like my father. And like me."

"I'm glad to know it," said Roger. "When you know their names, you can imagine people better. Feel them, though you don't know them. Alex Stacey is a nice-sounding name. It gives the idea of a good person."

"Well-mannered and helpful," murmured the sheriff. "Perhaps a little timid. Especially with women. I had observed him since he was a boy. With men he felt comfortable, he got along with no difficulty. But with women he became intimidated. He didn't dare look them in the eye. And if they spoke to him, he began to stammer. That's why I'm sure Alex died a virgin."

The sheriff fell silent again and sank into his thoughts and total immobility. Poor boy! If what his father said was true, Alex Stacey died without having known the warmth of a woman. The warmth of a mother, a wife, a lover. Roger at least had known, though for a short time, the happiness of a beautiful, tender, delicate mother. He sighed. He hadn't thought about her for some time, which never had happened before. If an afterlife existed, if the souls of the dead observed from eternity the fleeting life of the living, he was sure that Anne Jephson had been watching over him all this time, following his footsteps, suffering over and distressed by his misfortunes in Germany, sharing his disappointments, setbacks, and the awful feeling of having been wrong—in his ingenuous idealism, in the romantic propensity Herbert Ward so often mocked—of having idealized the Kaiser and the Germans too much, of having believed they would make the Irish cause their own and become loyal and enthusiastic allies of the dream of independence.

Yes, it was certain his mother had shared, during those

five unspeakable days, his pain, vomiting, nausea, and cramps in the U-19 submarine that transported him, Monteith, and Bailey from the German port of Heligoland to the coast of Kerry. Never in his life had he felt so bad, physically and spiritually. His stomach could tolerate no food except for sips of hot coffee and small mouthfuls of bread. The captain of the U-19, Raimund Weisbach, had him take a swallow of brandy, but instead of stopping his nausea, it made him vomit bile. When the submarine navigated on the surface, at about twelve miles an hour, it moved the most and his seasickness was most devastating. When it submerged, it moved less but its speed diminished. Blankets and overcoats could not alleviate the cold that gnawed at his bones, nor the permanent feeling of claustrophobia that had been like an anticipation of what he would feel later, in Brixton Prison, in the Tower of London, or in Pentonville Prison.

Undoubtedly because of his nausea and horrible malaise during the trip in the U-19, he left in one of his pockets the train ticket from Berlin to the German port of Wilhelmshaven. The police who arrested him in McKenna's Fort discovered it when they searched him in the Tralee police station. The train ticket would be shown by the prosecutor at his trial as one of the proofs that he had come to Ireland from Germany, an enemy country. But even worse was that in another of his pockets, the police of the Royal Irish Constabulary found the paper with the secret code the German admiralty had given him so that in an emergency, he could communicate with the Kaiser's military commanders. How was it possible he hadn't destroyed so compromising a document before leaving the U-19 and jumping into the boat that would take them to the beach? It was a question that festered in his mind like an infected wound. And yet, Roger remembered clearly that before taking their leave of the captain and crew of the U-19 submarine, on the insistence of Captain Robert Monteith, he and Sergeant Daniel Bailey had searched their pockets one last time to destroy any compromising object or document regarding their identity and origin. How could he have been careless to the extreme of overlooking the train ticket and secret code? He recalled the smile of satisfaction with which the prosecutor displayed the code during the trial. What damage did that information in the hands of British intelligence do to Germany?

What explained that very grave distraction was undoubtedly his calamitous physical and psychological state, destroyed by seasickness, the deterioration of his health during his last months in Germany, and above all, the concerns and anguish that political events—from the failure of the Irish Brigade to his learning that the Volunteers and the IRB had decided the military rising would take place during Easter Week—caused in him, affecting his lucidity and mental equilibrium, making him lose his reflexes, his ability to concentrate, his serenity. Were these the first symptoms of madness? It had happened to him before, in the Congo and the Amazonian jungle, faced with the spectacle of the mutilations and countless other tortures and atrocities to which the indigenous people were subjected by the rubber barons. On three or four occasions he had felt that his strength was leaving him, that he was dominated by a feeling of impotence in the face of the excess of evil he saw around him, the circle of cruelty and ignominy, so extensive, so overwhelming it seemed chimerical to confront and try to destroy it. Someone who feels so profound a demoralization can commit oversights as serious as the ones he had committed. These excuses relieved him for an instant or two; then, he rejected them, and the feelings of guilt and remorse became worse.

"I've thought about taking my own life." Once again, the sheriff's voice caught him unawares. "Alex was my only reason for living. I have no other relatives. Or friends. Barely acquaintances. My life was my son. Why go on in this world without him?"

"I know that feeling, Sheriff," Roger said softly. "And yet, in spite of everything, life also has beautiful things. You'll find other reasons. You're still a young man."

"I'm forty-seven, though I look much older," the jailer answered. "If I haven't killed myself, it's because my religion forbids suicide. But doing it isn't impossible. If I can't overcome this sadness, this feeling of emptiness, that nothing matters now, I will. A man should live as long as he feels life is worth it. If not, not."

He spoke without drama, with calm certainty. Again he fell silent and became still. Roger tried to listen. It seemed that from somewhere outside came reminiscences of a song, perhaps a choir. But the sound was so soft and distant he couldn't decipher the words or the melody.

Why did the leaders of the Rising want to keep him from coming to Ireland? Why did they ask the German authorities that he remain in Berlin with the ridiculous title of "ambassador" from the Irish nationalist organizations? He had seen the letters, read and reread the sentences that concerned him. According to Captain Monteith, it was because the leaders of the Volunteers and the IRB knew Roger was opposed to a rebellion without German action to paralyze the British army and the Royal Navy. Why hadn't they said it to him directly? Why had they sent him their decision through the German authorities? They were suspicious, perhaps. Did they believe he was no longer trustworthy? Perhaps they had credited the stupid, irrational rumors circulated by the English government accusing him of being a British spy. He hadn't been at all concerned about the slander, had always supposed his friends and comrades would realize these were toxic operations by the British secret services to sow suspicion and division among the nationalists. Perhaps one, some of his comrades had let themselves be deceived by the colonizer's tricks. Well, now they must be convinced that Roger Casement was still a fighter loyal to the cause of Irish independence. Could those who doubted his loyalty have been some of the men shot in Kilmainham Gaol? What did the understanding of the dead matter to him now?

He sensed the jailer standing and moving toward the cell door. He heard his slow, listless steps, as if he were dragging his feet. When he reached the door, he heard him say: "What I've done is wrong. A violation of the rules. No one should say a word to you, least of all me, the sheriff. I came because I couldn't stand it any more. If I didn't talk to someone my head or my heart would have exploded."

"I'm glad you came, Sheriff," Roger said in an undertone. "In my situation, speaking to someone is a great relief. The only thing I regret is not being able to console you for the death of your son."

The jailer grunted something that might have been a

goodbye. He opened the cell door and left. From the outside he locked it again with the key. Once again the darkness was total. Roger lay down, closed his eyes, and tried to sleep, but he knew sleep wouldn't come tonight either, and the hours until dawn would be very slow, an interminable wait.

He thought of the jailer's words: "I'm sure Alex died a virgin." Poor boy. To reach nineteen or twenty without having known the pleasure, the feverish swoon, the suspension of what was around you, the sensation of instantaneous eternity that barely lasted as long as the ejaculation and yet, so intense, so profound that it excited all the fibers of your body and made even the last vestige of your soul participate and come to life. He might have died a virgin too if instead of leaving for Africa when he turned twenty, he had remained in Liverpool working for the Elder Dempster Line. His timidity with women had been the same as—perhaps worse than—that of the young man with flat feet, Alex Stacey. He remembered the jokes of his girl cousins, and especially of Gertrude, the beloved Gee, when they wanted to make him blush. They just had to talk about girls, to tell him, for example: "Have you seen how Dorothy looks at you?" "Do you realize that Malina always arranges to sit next to you at picnics?" "She likes you, cousin." "Do you like her too?" The discomfort these jests produced in him! He lost his confidence and began to stammer, to stutter, to talk nonsense, until Gee and her friends, overcome with laughter, calmed him down: "It was a joke, don't be like that."

Still, from the time he was very young he'd had a keen esthetic sense, known how to appreciate the beauty of bodies and faces, contemplating with delight and joy a harmonious silhouette, eyes that were lively and mischievous, a delicate waist, muscles that denoted the unconscious strength predatory animals exhibit in the wild. When did he become aware that the beauty that exalted him most, adding a flavor of uneasiness and alarm, the impression of committing a transgression, did not belong to girls but to boys? In Africa. Before he set foot on the African continent, his Puritan upbringing, the rigidly traditional and conservative customs of his paternal and maternal families, had repressed in embryo any hint of that kind of excitation, faithful to an environment in which the mere suspicion of sexual attraction between persons of the same sex was considered an abominable aberration, rightly condemned by law and religion as a crime and a sin without justification or extenuating circumstances. In Magherintemple, in Antrim, in the house of his great-uncle John, in Liverpool, in the house of his aunt and uncle and cousins, photography had been the pretext that allowed him to enjoy—only with his eyes and mind—those sleek, beautiful male bodies he felt attracted to, deceiving himself with the excuse that the attraction was only esthetic.

Africa, that horrible but beautiful continent with its enormous suffering, was also the land of freedom, where human beings could be mistreated in the most iniquitous way but, at the same time, show their passions, fantasies, desires, instincts, and dreams without the restraints and prejudices that stifled pleasure in Great Britain. He remembered an afternoon of stifling heat and high sun in Boma, when it wasn't even a village but a tiny settlement. Suffocating and feeling that his body was on fire, he had gone to swim in the stream on the outskirts that, shortly before rushing into the waters of the Congo River, formed small lagoons and murmuring falls among the rocks in a spot with very tall mango trees, coconut palms, baobabs, and giant ferns. Two young Bakongos were swimming there, naked as he was. Though they didn't speak English, they answered his greeting with smiles. They seemed to be swimming, but Roger soon realized they were fishing with their bare hands. Their excitement and laughter were due to the difficulty they had holding on to the slippery little fish that escaped between their fingers. One of the two boys was very beautiful. He had a long, blue-black, well-proportioned body, deep eyes with a lively light in them, and he moved in the water like a fish. With his movements, the muscles in his arms, back and thighs became prominent, gleaming with the drops of water clinging to his skin. On his dark face, with its geometric tattoos and flashing glances, his very white teeth stood out. When they finally caught a fish, with a great clamor, the other boy left the stream and went to the bank where, it seemed to Roger, he began to cut and clean the fish and prepare a fire. The one who had stayed in the water looked into his eyes and smiled. Roger, feeling a kind of fever, swam toward him, smiling as well. When he reached his side, he didn't know what to do. He felt shame, discomfort, and at the same time, unlimited joy.

"Too bad you don't understand me," he heard himself say softly. "I would have liked to take photographs of you. Talk with you. Become your friend."

And then he felt the boy impelling himself forward with his feet and arms, shortening the distance that separated them. Now he was so close they were almost touching. And then Roger felt someone else's hands searching out his belly, touching and caressing his sex, which had been erect for a while. In the darkness of his cell, he sighed with desire and anguish. Closing his eyes, he tried to revive that scene from so many years ago: the surprise, the indescribable excitement that nonetheless did not attenuate his misgivings and fear, and his body embracing the boy's whose stiff penis he could also feel rubbing against his legs and belly.

It was the first time Roger made love, if he could call it making love when he became excited and ejaculated in the water against the body of the boy who masturbated him and undoubtedly also ejaculated, though Roger didn't notice that. When he came out of the water and dressed, the two Bakongos invited him to a few mouthfuls of the fish they had smoked over a small fire on the edge of the pool the stream had formed.

What shame he felt afterward. All the rest of the day he was in a daze, sunk in remorse that mixed with sparks of joy, the awareness of having gone past the limits of a prison and achieved a freedom he had always desired in secret and never dared look for. Was he remorseful, did he intend to make amends? Yes, yes. He did. He promised himself, for the sake of his honor, the memory of his mother, his religion, that it would not be repeated, knowing very well he was lying to himself, and now that he had tasted the forbidden fruit, felt how his entire being was transformed into a dizzying blazing torch, he could not avoid its being repeated. That was the only, or in any case, one of the few times in which pleasure had not cost him money. Had the fact of paying his lovers of a few minutes or hours freed him very quickly from the pangs of conscience that at first hounded him after those adventures? Perhaps. As if, being converted into a commercial transaction—you give me your mouth and penis and I give you my tongue, my asshole, and several pounds—those rapid encounters in parks, dark corners, public bathrooms, stations, foul hotels, or in the middle of the street—*like dogs*, he thought—with men with whom he often could communicate only by gestures and looks because they did not speak his language, stripped those acts of all moral significance and turned them into a pure exchange, as neutral as buying ice cream or a pack of cigarettes. It was pleasure, not love. He had learned to enjoy but not to love or be loved. Occasionally in Africa, Brazil, Iquitos, London, Belfast, or Dublin, after a particularly intense encounter, some feeling had been added to the adventure and he had told himself: *I'm in love*. False: he never was. That didn't last. Not even with Eivind Adler Christensen, for whom he had developed affection, but not that of a lover, perhaps an older brother or father. Miserable wretch. In this area too his life had been a complete failure. Many lovers for a price—dozens, perhaps hundreds—and not a single loving relationship. Pure sex, hurried and animal.

For that reason, when he made a reckoning of his sexual and emotional life, Roger told himself it had been belated and austere, made up of sporadic, always hasty adventures, as transient, as lacking in consequences, as the one in the stream with waterfalls and pools in the outskirts of what was still an encampment half lost in a place on the Lower Congo called Boma.

He was seized by the profound sadness that had almost

always followed his furtive amorous encounters, generally outdoors, like the first one, with men and boys who were often foreigners whose names he did not know or forgot as soon as he learned them. They were ephemeral moments of pleasure, nothing that could compare to the stable relationship, lasting over months and years, in which added to the passion were understanding, complicity, friendship, dialogue, solidarity, the relationship between Herbert and Sarita Ward that he had always envied. It was another of the great voids, the great nostalgias, of his life.

He saw that there where the jamb of his cell door was supposed to be, a ray of light had appeared.

12

I'll leave my bones on that damn trip, Roger thought when Chancellor Sir Edward Grey told him that in view of the contradictory news coming from Peru, the only way for the British government to know what it could believe with regard to what was occurring there was for Casement to go back to Iquitos and see on the ground whether the Peruvian government had done something to end the iniquities in Putumayo or was using delaying tactics because it would not, or could not, confront Julio C. Arana.

Roger's health was going from bad to worse. Since his return from Iquitos, even during the few days at the end of the year that he spent in Paris with the Wards, he was again tormented by conjunctivitis and a return of malaria. And he was bothered again by hemorrhoids, though without the hemorrhages he'd had earlier. As soon as he returned to London, early in January 1911, he went to see doctors. The two specialists he consulted decided his condition was the result of the immense fatigue and nervous tension of his time in Amazonia. He needed rest, a very quiet vacation.

But he couldn't take one. Writing the report that the British government urgently required, and many meetings at the ministry when he had to inform them of what he had seen and heard in Amazonia, as well as visits to the Anti-Slavery Society, took up a great deal of time. He also had to meet with the English and Peruvian directors of the

Peruvian Amazon Company, who, during their first interview, after listening to his impressions of Putumayo for almost two hours, were left paralyzed. Their long faces, with partially opened mouths, looked at him in disbelief and horror, as if the floor had begun to open under their feet and the ceiling to fall in on their heads. They didn't know what to say. They took their leave without formulating a single question for him.

Julio C. Arana attended the second meeting of the board of directors of the Peruvian Amazon Company. It was the first and last time Roger saw him in person. He had heard so much about him, heard so many different people deify him as they tend to do with religious saints or political leaders (never with businessmen) or attribute horrendous cruelties and crimes to him—monumental cynicism, sadism, greed, avarice, disloyalty, swindles, and all kinds of knavery—that he sat observing him for a long while, like an entomologist with a mysterious insect that has not yet been classified.

It was said he understood English but never spoke it because of timidity or vanity. He had an interpreter beside him who translated everything into his ear in a very quiet voice. He was a fairly short man, dark, with mestizo features and an Asian trace in his slanted eyes, a very broad forehead, and thinning hair, carefully combed with a center part. He had a small mustache and goatee, recently combed, and he smelled of cologne. The legend of his mania regarding hygiene and attire must be true. He dressed impeccably, wearing a suit of fine wool that may have been cut on Savile Row. He didn't open his mouth while the other directors interrogated Roger with a thousand questions undoubtedly prepared for them by Arana's lawyers. They attempted to make him fall into contradictions and insinuated the mistakes, exaggerations, susceptibilities, and scruples of an urbane, civilized European who is disconcerted by the primitive world.

As he responded and added testimonies and precise facts that made what he had told them at the first meeting even worse, Roger did not stop glancing at Julio C. Arana. As still as an idol, he didn't move in his seat and didn't even blink. His expression was indecipherable. There was something inflexible in his hard, cold gaze. It reminded Roger of the eyes, empty of humanity, of the station chiefs on the rubber plantations in Putumayo, the eyes of men who had lost (if they ever had possessed it) the capacity to discriminate between good and evil, kindness and wickedness, the human and the inhuman.

This small, elegant, slightly plump man, then, was master of an empire the size of a European country, the hated, adulated master of the lives and property of tens of thousands of people, who in that miserably poor world of Amazonia had accumulated a fortune comparable to that of the great potentates of Europe. He had begun as a poor boy in the small forsaken village Rioja must have been, in the high Peruvian jungle, selling straw hats from door to door which his family had woven. Little by little, compensating for his lack of education—only a few years of primary instruction—with a superhuman capacity for work, a brilliant instinct for business, and an absolute lack of scruples, he climbed the social pyramid. From a traveling pedlar of hats in vast Amazonia, he became a financial backer of the wretched rubber workers who ventured at their own risk into the jungle, whom he supplied with machetes, carbines, fishing nets, knives, cans for the rubber, canned goods, yucca flour, and domestic utensils in exchange for part of the rubber they harvested and that he took care of selling in Iquitos and Manaus to export companies, until, with the money he had earned, he could move from supplier and agent to producer and exporter. At first he became partners with Colombian rubber planters who, less intelligent or diligent than he, or less lacking in morality, eventually sold their land, depositories, and indigenous laborers to him at a loss, and at times went to work for him. Distrustful, he installed his brothers and brothers-in-law in key positions in the enterprise, which, in spite of its vast size and having been registered on the London stock market since 1908, continued to function in practice like a family business. How great was his fortune? The legend undoubtedly exaggerated the reality. But in London, the Peruvian Amazon Company had this valuable building in the heart of the City, and Arana's mansion on Kensington Road was in no way inferior to the palaces of princes and bankers that surrounded it. His house in Geneva and his elegant summer house in Biarritz were furnished by fashionable decorators and displayed paintings and luxurious objects. But it was said that he led an austere life, didn't drink or gamble or have lovers, and dedicated all his free time to his wife. He had loved her since he was a boy—she was also from Rioja—but Eleonora Zumaeta said yes only after many years, when he was already wealthy and powerful and she was a schoolteacher in the small village where she had been born.

When the second meeting of the board of directors of

the Peruvian Amazon Company had ended, Julio C. Arana guaranteed through his interpreter that his company would do everything necessary to correct immediately any deficiency or malfunction on the rubber plantations of Putumayo, for it was the policy of his firm to always act within the law and altruistic morality of the British Empire. Arana took his leave of the consul with a nod, not offering his hand.

Writing the *Report on Putumayo* took Roger a month and a half. He began writing it in a room at the Foreign Office, assisted by a typist, but then he preferred to work in his Philbeach Gardens apartment, in Earls Court, next to the beautiful little church of St. Cuthbert and St. Matthias, where he sometimes went to listen to the magnificent organist. And since even there he was interrupted by politicians and members of humanitarian and anti-slavery organizations and people from the press, for the rumor that his *Report on Putumayo* would be as devastating as the one he had written about the Congo circulated throughout London and gave rise to conjectures and talk in the London gossip columns and rumor mills, he requested authorization from the Foreign Office to travel to Ireland. There, in a room in Buswells Hotel on Molesworth Street in Dublin, he completed his work early in March of 1911. Congratulations from his superiors and colleagues immediately poured in. Sir Edward Grey himself summoned him to his office to praise his *Report* and at the same time suggest a few minor corrections. The text was immediately sent to the government of the United States so that London and Washington could put pressure on President Augusto B. Leguía, demanding in the name of the world that he put an end to the slavery, torture, abductions, rapes, and annihilation of the indigenous communities, and take those incriminated to court.

Roger could not yet take the rest prescribed by his physicians, which he needed so much. He had to meet several times with committees from the government, parliament, and the Anti-Slavery Society which were studying the most practical way for public and private institutions to alleviate the situation of the Amazonian natives. At his suggestion, one of their first initiatives was to pay for the establishment of a religious mission in Putumayo, something that Arana's company had always prevented but now was pledged to facilitate.

Finally, in June 1911, he was able to leave for a vacation in Ireland. He was there when he received a personal letter from Sir Edward Grey. The chancellor informed him that on his recommendation, His Majesty George V had decided to knight him for exemplary service to the United Kingdom in the Congo and Amazonia.

While relatives and friends showered him with congratulations, Roger, who almost burst into laughter the first few times he heard himself called Sir Roger, was filled with doubts. How could he accept a title granted by a regime toward which, in the depths of his heart, he felt enmity, the same regime that had colonized his country? On the other hand, didn't he serve this king and this government as a diplomat? He had never been so aware of the hidden duplicity in which he had lived for years, working on one hand with discipline and efficiency in the service of the British Empire, and on the other devoted to the cause of the emancipation of Ireland and becoming increasingly drawn not to the moderates like John Redmond who aspired to Home Rule, but to the radicals like the IRB, secretly led by Tom Clarke, whose goal was independence through armed action. Consumed by these vacillations, he chose to thank Sir Edward Grey in a courteous letter for the honor he had conferred on him. The news spread throughout the press and helped to increase his prestige.

The demand made to the Peruvian government by Britain and the United States that the principal criminals cited in the *Report*—Fidel Velarde, Alfredo Montt, Augusto Jiménez, Armando Normand, José Inocente Fonseca, Abelardo Agüero, Elías Martinengui, and Aurelio Rodríguez—be arrested and tried seemed at first to bear fruit. The chargé d'affaires for the United Kingdom in Lima, Mr. Lucien Gerome, cabled the Foreign Office that the eleven principal employees of the Peruvian Amazon Company had been dismissed. Judge Carlos Valcárcel, sent from Lima, organized an expedition as soon as he arrived in Iquitos to investigate the rubber plantations in Putumayo, but he couldn't join it because he fell ill and had to travel to the United States for surgery. He put an energetic, respectable person at the head of the expedition: Rómulo Paredes, editor of the newspaper *El Oriente*, who traveled to Putumayo with a doctor, two interpreters, and an escort of nine soldiers. The commission visited all the rubber stations of the Peruvian Amazon Company and had just gone back to Iquitos, where a recuperated Judge Valcárcel had also returned. The Peruvian government had promised Mr. Gerome that as soon as it received the report from Paredes and Valcárcel, it would take action.

However, a short while later, Gerome again reported that Leguía's government was distressed to inform him that most of the criminals whose arrest it had ordered had fled to Brazil. The others perhaps were hiding in the jungle or had entered Colombian territory clandestinely. The United States and Great Britain attempted to have the Brazilian government extradite the fugitives to Peru to be brought to justice. But the chancellor of Brazil, the Baron de Río Branco, replied to both governments that there was no extradition treaty between Peru and Brazil and therefore those persons could not be returned without provoking a delicate problem in international law.

Days later, the British chargé d'affaires reported that in a private interview, the Peruvian minister of foreign relations had admitted, unofficially, that President Leguía was in an impossible situation. Due to its presence in Putumayo and the security forces it had to protect its installations, the company of Julio C. Arana was the only restraint that kept the Colombians, who had been reinforcing their border garrisons, from invading the region. The United States and Great Britain were asking for something absurd: closing or harassing the Peruvian Amazon Company meant handing to Colombia the immense territory it coveted, pure and simple. Neither Leguía nor any other Peruvian leader could do such a thing without committing suicide. And Peru lacked the resources to establish in the remote wilds of Putumayo a military garrison strong enough to protect national sovereignty. Lucien Gerome added that for all these reasons, it was not possible to expect the Peruvian government to do anything efficacious now except make statements and gestures lacking in substance.

This was the reason the Foreign Office decided, before His Majesty's government made his *Report on Putumayo* public and asked western nations for sanctions against Peru, that Roger Casement should return to the territory and confirm in Amazonia, with his own eyes, whether any reforms had been realized, a judicial process was in progress, and the legal action initiated by Dr. Valcárcel was genuine. Sir Edward Grey's insistence meant that Roger found himself obliged to agree, telling himself something that in the next few months he would have many occasions to repeat: *I'll leave my bones on that damned trip*.

He was preparing for his departure when Omarino and Arédomi arrived in London. In the five months they had spent in his care in Barbados, Father Smith had given them English lessons and notions of reading and writing, and had accustomed them to dressing in the western manner. But Roger found two young boys whom civilization, in spite of giving them enough to eat and not hitting or flogging them, had saddened and dulled. They always seemed fearful that the people around them, subjecting them to inexhaustible scrutiny, looking at them from head to toe, touching them, passing their hands over their skin as if they thought they were dirty, asking them questions they didn't understand and didn't know how to answer, would hurt them. Roger took them to the zoo, to have ice cream in Hyde Park, to visit his sister Nina, his cousin Gertrude, and for an evening with intellectuals and artists at the house of Alice Stopford Green. Everyone treated them with affection, but the curiosity with which they were examined, above all when they had to take off their shirts and show the scars on their backs and buttocks, disturbed them. At times, Roger discovered the boys' eyes filled with tears. He had planned to send them to be educated in Ireland, on the outskirts of Dublin, at St. Enda's bilingual school directed by Patrick Pearse, whom he knew well. He wrote to him about it, telling him the origin of both boys. Roger had given a talk at St. Enda's on Africa and financially supported Pearse's efforts, both in the Gaelic League and its publications and in this school, to promote the diffusion of the ancient Irish language. Pearse agreed to take them both, even offering a discount on the matriculation and room and board at St. Enda's. But when he received Pearse's answer, Roger had already decided to consent to what Omarino and Arédomi pleaded for every day: to return them to Amazonia. Both were profoundly unhappy in England, where they felt they had been turned into human anomalies, objects on display that surprised, amused, moved, and at times frightened people who would never treat them as equals but always as exotic outsiders.

On the trip back to Iquitos, Roger would think a great deal about this lesson reality had given him on how paradoxical and ungraspable the human soul was. Both boys had wanted to escape the Amazonian hell where they were mistreated and made to work like animals and given barely anything to eat. He had made efforts and spent a good amount of his scant funds to pay for their passages to Europe and support them for the past six months, thinking that in this way he was saving them, giving them access to a decent life. Yet here, though for different reasons, they were as far from happiness or, at least, a tolerable existence, as they had been in Putumayo. Though they weren't beaten and instead were treated with affection, they felt alienated, alone, and aware they would never form part of this world.

Shortly before Roger left for the Amazon, the Foreign Office, following his advice, appointed a new consul, George Michell, in Iquitos. It was a magnificent choice. Roger had met him in the Congo. Michell was persistent and worked enthusiastically in the campaign to denounce the crimes committed under the regime of Leopold II. With regard to colonization, he held the same position as Roger. In the event, he would not hesitate to confront Casa Arana. They had two long conversations and planned a close collaboration.

On August 16, 1911, Roger, Omarino, and Arédomi left Southampton on the *Magdalena*, bound for Barbados. They reached the island twelve days later. As soon as the ship began to cut through the silvery blue water of the Caribbean, Roger felt in his blood that his sex, asleep in these re cent months of diseases, preoccupations, and great physical and mental effort, was waking again and filling his mind with fantasies and desires. In his diary he summarized his state of mind with three words: "I burn again."

As soon as they disembarked, he went to thank Father Smith for what he had done for the two boys. He was moved to see how Omarino and Arédomi, so sparing in the display of their feelings in London, embraced and patted the cleric with great familiarity. Father Smith took them to visit the Ursuline convent. In that serene cloister with carob trees and the purple blossoms of bougainvillea, where noise from the street did not reach and time seemed suspended, Roger moved away from the others and sat down on a bench. He was observing a line of ants carrying a leaf in the air, like the men carrying the platform of the Virgin in processions in Brazil, when he remembered: today was his birthday. Forty-seven! He couldn't say he was an old man. Many men and women his age were in their prime physically and psychologically, with energy, desires, and projects. But he felt old, with the unpleasant feeling of having entered the final stage of his life. Once, in Africa, with Herbert Ward, they had imagined how their final years would be. The sculptor envisioned a Mediterranean old age, in Provence or Tuscany, in a house in the countryside. He would have a huge studio and many cats, dogs, ducks, and chickens, and on Sundays he would cook dense, spiced dishes like bouillabaisse for a long line of relatives. Roger, on the other hand, startled, declared: "I won't reach old age, I'm certain." It had been a presentiment. He vividly recalled that premonition and felt it again as true: he would never be an old man.

Father Smith agreed to put up Omarino and Arédomi for the week they would spend in Bridgetown. The day following his arrival, Roger went to a public bath he had frequented the last time he had been on the island. As he expected, he saw young, athletic, statuesque men, for here, just as in Brazil, people were not ashamed of their bodies. Men and women cultivated their bodies and displayed them without shame. A very young boy, an adolescent of fifteen or sixteen, disquieted him. He had the pallor frequent in mulattos, a smooth, gleaming skin, large, audacious green eyes, and from his tight swimsuit emerged hairless, limber thighs that caused the beginnings of vertigo in Roger. Experience had sharpened the intuition that allowed him to know very quickly, through signs imperceptible to anyone else—the hint of a smile, a light in the eyes, an inviting movement of the hand or body—whether a boy understood what he wanted and was willing to grant it or, at least, to negotiate it. With pain in his heart, he felt that this beautiful boy was completely indifferent to the furtive messages he was sending with his eyes. Still, he approached and talked with him for a moment. He was the son of a Barbadian clergyman and hoped to be an accountant. He was studying in a commercial academy and soon, during vacation, he would accompany his father to Jamaica. Roger invited him to have ice cream, but the boy refused.

Back at his hotel, seized with excitement, he wrote in his diary, in the vulgar, telegraphic language he used for the most intimate episodes. "Public bath. Clergyman's son. Very beautiful. Long, delicate penis that stiffened in my hands. I took him into my mouth. Happiness for two minutes." He masturbated and bathed again, soaping himself carefully as he tried to drive away the sadness and feeling of loneliness that tended to afflict him at times like this.

The next day, at noon, as he was having lunch on the terrace of a restaurant in the port of Bridgetown, he saw Andrés O'Donnell. He called to him. Arana's former overseer, the chief of the Entre Ríos station, recognized him immediately. He looked at him for a few seconds with distrust and some fright. But finally he shook his hand and agreed to sit down with him. He drank coffee and a glass of brandy while they talked. He admitted that Roger's passing through Putumayo had been like the curse of a Huitoto witch doctor for the rubber barons. As soon as he left, the rumor circulated that police and judges would soon arrive with arrest orders, and that all the chiefs, overseers, and foremen on the rubber plantations would have problems with the law. And, since Arana's company was English, they would be sent to England and tried there. For that reason many of them, like O'Donnell, had preferred to leave the area and head for Brazil, Colombia, or Ecuador. He had come here on the promise of a job on a sugar-cane plantation but didn't obtain it. Now he was trying to leave for the United States where, it seemed, there were opportunities on the railroads. Sitting on the terrace, with no boots, no pistol, and no whip, wearing old overalls and a frayed shirt, he was nothing more than a poor devil agonizing over his future.

"You don't know it, but you owe me your life, Señor Casement," he remarked with a bitter smile as he was saying goodbye. "Though undoubtedly you won't believe me."

"Tell me in any event," Roger urged.

"Armando Normand was convinced that if you left there alive, all of us plantation chiefs would go to prison. The best thing would be if you drowned in the river or were eaten by a puma or an alligator. You understand me. The same thing that happened to that French explorer, Eugène Robuchon, who began to make people nervous with all the questions he asked, and they made him disappear."

"Why didn't you kill me? It would have been very easy with all the practice you've had."

"I made them see the possible consequences," Andrés O'Donnell declared with a certain arrogance. "Víctor Macedo supported me. Since you were English, and Don

Julio's company too, they'd try us in England under English laws. And hang us."

"I'm not English, I'm Irish," Roger corrected him. "Things probably wouldn't have happened as you think. In any case, thanks very much. But it would be better if you left right away and didn't tell me where you were going. I'm obliged to report that I've seen you, and the English government will quickly issue an order for your arrest."

That afternoon, he returned to the public bath. He had better luck than the day before. A brawny, smiling, dark-skinned mulatto, whom he had seen lifting weights in the exercise room, smiled at him. Taking his arm, he led him to a small room where they sold drinks. As they drank pineapple and banana juice and he told him his name, Stanley Weeks, he moved very close to him until their legs touched. Then, with a little smile filled with mischief, he led him by the arm to a small dressing room, whose door he locked with a bolt as soon as they entered. They kissed, nibbled at ears and neck as they removed their trousers. Roger observed, choking with desire, Stanley's very black phallus and red, wet glans, growing thick before his eyes. "Two pounds if you suck it," Roger heard him say. "Then, I'll take you up the ass." He agreed, kneeling. Afterward, in his hotel room, he wrote in his diary: "Public bath. Stanley Weeks, athletic, young, 27. Enormous, very hard, 9 inches at least. Kisses, bites, penetration with a shout. Two pounds."

Roger, Omarino, and Arédomi left Barbados for Pará on September 5 on the *Boniface*, an uncomfortable, small, crowded ship that smelled bad and had dreadful food. But

Roger enjoyed the passage to Pará because of Dr. Herbert Spencer Dickey, a North American physician. He had worked for Arana's company in El Encanto and, in addition to corroborating the horrors that Roger already knew about, he recounted many anecdotes, some savage and others amusing, about his experiences in Putumayo. He turned out to be a man of adventurous spirit who had traveled half the world, sensitive, and well read. It was pleasant to watch night fall on the deck sitting beside him, smoking, drinking whiskey out of the bottle, and listening to his intelligent comments. Dr. Dickey approved the efforts made by Great Britain and the United States to remedy the atrocities in Amazonia, but he was a fatalist and a skeptic: things would not change there, not today or in the future.

"We carry wickedness in our souls, my friend," he said, half joking, half serious. "We won't be rid of it so easily. In the countries of Europe, and in mine, it is more disguised and reveals itself only when there's a war, a revolution, a riot. It needs pretexts to become public and collective. In Amazonia, on the other hand, it can reveal itself openly and perpetrate the worst monstrosities without the justifications of patriotism or religion. Only pure, hard greed. The evil that poisons us is everywhere that human beings are, its roots buried deep in our hearts."

But immediately after making these lugubrious statements, he would tell a joke or recount an anecdote that seemed to disprove them. Roger enjoyed talking to Dr. Dickey, even though, at the same time, it depressed him a little. The *Boniface* reached Pará on September 10 at noon. All the time he had been there as consul, he had felt frustrated and suffocated. Still, several days before arriving in the port he experienced waves of desire as he thought about the Praça do Palácio. He would go there at night to pick up one of the boys who strolled there looking for clients or adventures under the trees, wearing very tight trousers that showed off their ass and testicles.

He stayed at the Hotel do Comércio, feeling in his body the rebirth of the old fever that took possession of him when he undertook those walks on the Praça. He recalled—or was he inventing them?—some names from those encounters that generally ended in a nearby shabby hotel or, at times, in a dark corner on the grass in the park. He anticipated those rapid, unplanned meetings, feeling his heart racing. But tonight he was unlucky too, because Marco, Olympio, and Bebé (were those their names?) did not appear, and instead he was nearly assaulted by two ragged vagrants who were almost children. One tried to put his hand in his pocket, looking for a wallet he did not carry, while the other asked him for directions. He got rid of them by giving one a shove that sent him rolling on the ground. When they saw his decisive attitude, they ran away. He returned to the hotel in a fury. He calmed down by writing in his diary: "Praça do Palácio: a thick, very hard one. Breathless. Drops of blood on my underwear. A pleasurable pain."

The next morning he visited the English consul and some European and Brazilian acquaintances from his previous stay in Pará. His inquiries were useful. He located at least two fugitives from Putumayo. The consul and the local police chief assured him that José Inocente Fonseca and Alfredo Montt, after spending some time on a plantation on the banks of the Yavarí River, were now settled in

Manaus, where Casa Arana had found them work in the port as customs inspectors. Roger immediately telegraphed the Foreign Office to ask the Brazilian authorities for an arrest order for this pair of criminals. Three days later they responded that Petrópolis looked favorably on this request. It would immediately order the Manaus police to arrest Montt and Fonseca. They would not be extradited but tried in Brazil instead.

His second and third nights in Pará were more fruitful than the first. At nightfall on the second day, a barefoot boy selling flowers practically offered himself when Roger sounded him out, asking the price of a bouquet of roses he had in his hand. They went to a small cleared lot where, in the shadows, Roger heard the panting of couples. These street encounters, in precarious conditions always full of risk, infused him with contradictory feelings: excitement and disgust. The flower seller smelled of armpits, but his thick breath and hot body and the strength of his embrace heated him and led very quickly to a climax. When he walked into the Hotel do Comércio, he realized that his trousers were covered with soil and stains and the receptionist was looking at him in surprise. "I was attacked," he told him.

The next night, on the Praça do Palácio, he had another encounter, this time with a young man who asked him for money. He invited him for a stroll, and at a kiosk they had a glass of rum. João took him to a hut of cane and rushes in an impoverished district. As they undressed and made love in the dark on a fiber mat on the dirt floor, listening to dogs barking, Roger was sure that at any moment he would feel the edge of a knife on his head or the blow of a stick. He was prepared: at times like this he never carried much money or his watch or silver pen, just a few bills and coins so he could let himself be robbed and placate the thieves. But nothing happened to him. João accompanied him to the area near his hotel and said goodbye, biting his mouth with a great guffaw. The next day, Roger discovered that João or the flower seller had given him crabs. He had to go to a pharmacy to buy calomel, which was always disagreeable: the druggist—it was worse if she was a woman—would stare at him in a way that embarrassed him and, at times, gave him a complicit little smile that both disconcerted and enraged him.

The best but also the worst experience in the twelve days he was in Pará was his visit to the Da Mattas. They were the closest friends he had made during his stay in the city: Junio, a road engineer, and his wife, Irene, who painted watercolors. Young, good-looking, joyful, easy-going, they exhaled love of life. They had a charming little girl, María, with large laughing eyes. Roger had met them at a social gathering or at an official ceremony, because Junio worked for the Department of Public Works in the local government. They saw one another frequently, walked along the river, went to the movies and the theater. They welcomed their old friend with open arms. They took him to supper at a restaurant that served very spicy Bahian food, and little María, who was five years old, danced and sang for him, making amusing faces.

That night, lying awake for a long time in his bed at the Hotel do Comércio, Roger fell into one of the depressions that had accompanied him almost his entire life, especially after a day or series of sexual encounters on the street. It saddened him to know he would never have a home like the one the Da Mattas had, that his life would be more and more solitary as he grew older. He paid dearly for those minutes of mercenary pleasure. He would die without having tasted that warm intimacy, a wife with whom to discuss the day's events and plan the future—travels, vacations, dreams—or children to carry on his name and memory when he had left this world. His old age, if he ever had one, would be like that of stray animals. And just as miserable, for even though he had earned a decent salary as a diplomat, he had never been able to save because of the number of donations and support he gave to humanitarian associations that fought against slavery, for the survival of primitive peoples and cultures, and now, the organizations defending Gaelic and the traditions of Ireland.

But even more than all that, it embittered him to think he would die without having known true love, a shared love, like Junio's and Irene's, the silent complicity and intelligence one could guess at between them, the tenderness with which they held hands or exchanged smiles seeing little María's enthusiasm. As usual during these crises, he lay awake for many hours, and when he finally managed to sleep, he sensed the languid figure of his mother taking shape in the shadows of his room.

On September 22, Roger, Omarino, and Arédomi left Pará for Manaus on the steamboat *Hilda* of the Booth Line, an ugly, calamitous ship. The six days they spent sailing to Manaus were torture for Roger, because of the narrowness of his cabin, the pervasive filth, the execrable food, and the clouds of mosquitoes that attacked the passengers from dusk to dawn.

As soon as they disembarked in Manaus, Roger resumed the hunt for fugitives from Putumayo. Accompanied by the English consul, he went to see the governor, Señor Dos Reis, who confirmed that an order had come from the central government in Petrópolis to arrest Montt and Fonseca. And why hadn't the police detained them yet? The governor gave him an answer he thought either stupid or a simple pretext: they had been waiting for his arrival. Could they do it right now, before the two birds flew? They would do it today.

The consul and Roger, with the arrest order from Petrópolis, had to make two trips back and forth between the government and the police. Finally, the police chief sent two officers to detain Montt and Fonseca in the customs office in the port.

The next morning, the crestfallen English consul came to announce to Roger that the arrest attempt had had a grotesque, farcical outcome. He had just been informed by the chief of police, who begged a thousand pardons and promised to make amends. The two officers sent to arrest Montt and Fonseca knew them, and before taking them to the police station, they all went to have a few beers. They had become very drunk, and the criminals had fled. Since one couldn't discount the possibility that they had received money to allow their escape, the police in question were under arrest. If corruption were proven, they would be severely punished. "I'm sorry, Sir Roger," the consul said, "but even though I didn't say anything to you, I expected something like this. You were a diplomat in Brazil, and you know this kind of thing all too well. It's normal here."

Roger felt so ill that the vexation increased his physical indisposition. He stayed in bed most of the time with fever and muscular pains as he waited for the ship to Iquitos to sail. One afternoon, as he struggled against the feeling of impotence that overcame him, he fantasized in his diary: "Three lovers in one night, two sailors among them. They fucked me six times! I walked back to the hotel, my legs wide like a woman in labor." In the middle of his bad humor, the barbarity he had written made him laugh out loud. He, so well bred and polished in his vocabulary with other people, always felt, in the privacy of his diary, an irresistible need to write obscenities. For reasons he didn't understand, salacious language made him feel better.

The *Hilda* continued the journey on October 3, and after a rough voyage with torrential rains and an encounter with a small embankment, it reached Iquitos at dawn on October 6, 1911. Waiting for him at the port, hat in hand, was Mr. Stirs. His replacement, George Michell, along with his wife, would arrive soon. The consul was finding a house for them. This time Roger didn't stay at his residence but in the Hotel Amazonas, near the Plaza de Armas, while Stirs took Omarino and Arédomi with him temporarily. Both boys had decided to stay in the city and work as domestic servants instead of returning to Putumayo. Stirs promised to take care of finding them a family that wanted to employ them and would treat them well.

As Roger feared, given what had happened in Brazil, the news here wasn't encouraging either. Stirs didn't know how many of the long list of 237 Casa Arana managers presumed guilty, whom Dr. Valcárcel had ordered to be arrested after receiving Rómulo Paredes's report on his expedition to Putumayo, had actually been detained. He hadn't been able to find out because a strange silence reigned in Iquitos regarding the subject, as well as the whereabouts of Judge Valcárcel. He had been impossible to locate for several weeks. The general manager of the Peruvian Amazon Company, Pablo Zumaeta, who appeared on that list, seemed to be in hiding, but Stirs assured Roger his concealment was a farce because Arana's brother-in-law and his wife Petronila showed up at restaurants and local fiestas and no one bothered them.

Later, Roger would remember these eight weeks in Iquitos as a slow shipwreck, a gradual sinking into a sea of intrigues, false rumors, flagrant or intractable lies, contradictions, a world where no one told the truth because that made enemies and problems or, more frequently, because people lived inside a system in which it was practically impossible to distinguish falsehood from truth, reality from a swindle. Ever since his years in the Congo, he had known that desperate feeling of having fallen into quicksand, a muddy ground that swallowed him up and where his efforts served only to plunge him deeper into a viscous substance that would eventually engulf him. He had to get out right away!

The day after his arrival he went to visit the prefect of Iquitos. Again, there was a new one. Señor Adolfo Gamarra—heavy mustache, prominent belly, lit cigar, nervous clammy hands—received him in his office with embraces and congratulations: "Thanks to you," he said, opening his arms theatrically and clapping his hands, "a monstrous social injustice has been uncovered in the heart of Amazonia. The Peruvian government and people have acknowledged you, Señor Casement."

Immediately afterward he added that the report the Peruvian government had charged Judge Carlos A. Valcárcel with writing to satisfy the requirements of the English government was "formidable" and "devastating." It consisted of close to three thousand pages and confirmed all the accusations England had transmitted to President Augusto B. Leguía. But when Roger asked if he could have a copy of the report, the prefect replied that this was a state document and it lay outside his jurisdiction to authorize a foreigner to read it. The honorable consul ought to present a request in Lima to the supreme government, through official channels, and he undoubtedly would obtain permission. When Roger asked what he could do to have an interview with Judge Valcárcel, the prefect became very serious and recited in a single breath: "I have no idea where Dr. Valcárcel is. His mission has ended and I understand he's left the country."

Roger left the prefecture completely stunned. What was really going on? This individual had told him nothing but lies. That same afternoon he went to the offices of *El Oriente* to speak with its editor, Dr. Rómulo Paredes. He found a very dark-skinned man of about fifty in his shirtsleeves, covered with perspiration, irresolute, in the grip of panic. He was turning gray. As soon as Roger began to speak, he silenced him with a peremptory gesture that seemed to say: *Careful, walls have ears*. He took him by the arm and led him to a small bar on the corner called La Chipirona. He had him sit at an isolated table.

"I beg you to forgive me, Consul," he said, always looking around him with suspicion. "I can't and shouldn't tell you very much. I'm in a very compromised situation. If people were to see me with you it would represent a great risk to me."

He looked pale, his voice trembled, and he had begun to bite a nail. He ordered a glass of brandy and drank it down. He listened in silence to Roger's account of his interview with Prefect Gamarra.

"He's a supreme hypocrite," he said at last, emboldened by his drink. "Gamarra has a report of mine, corroborating all of Judge Valcárcel's accusations. I gave it to him in July. More than three months have passed and he hasn't sent it to Lima. Why do you think he's kept it so long? Because everybody knows that Prefect Adolfo Gamarra is, like half of Iquitos, also an employee of Arana's."

As for Judge Valcárcel, Dr. Paredes said he had left the country. He didn't know where he had gone but did know that if the judge had remained in Iquitos he would have been a corpse by now. He stood abruptly: "Which is what will probably happen to me as well at any moment, Consul." He wiped away perspiration as he spoke and Roger thought he was going to burst into tears. "Because I, unfortunately, can't leave. I have a wife and children and my only occupation is the paper."

He left without even saying goodbye. Roger went back to see the prefect, infuriated. Señor Gamarra admitted that, in fact, the report written by Dr. Paredes couldn't be sent to Lima "because of logistical problems, happily resolved." It would go out this week without fail, "and with a courier for greater security, for President Leguía himself is urgently demanding it."

It was all like this. Roger felt rocked in a lulling eddy,

going round and round in place, manipulated by tortuous, invisible forces. All the measures, promises, pieces of information fell apart and dissolved without the facts ever corresponding to the words. What was done and what was said were worlds apart. Words negated facts and facts gave the lie to words and it all functioned in a generalized fraud, a chronic divorce between saying and doing that everyone practiced.

During the week, he made multiple inquiries regarding Judge Valcárcel. Like Saldaña Roca, he inspired respect, affection, pity, and admiration in Roger. Everyone promised to help him, find out, take him the message, locate him, but he was sent from one place to another without anyone offering any serious explanation about the judge's situation. Finally, seven days after arriving in Iquitos, he managed to escape his maddening web thanks to an Englishman who lived in the city. Mr. F. J. Harding, manager of John Lilly & Company, was a tall, robust bachelor, almost bald, and one of the few businessmen in Iquitos who did not seem to dance to the tune of the Peruvian Amazon Company.

"No one is telling you or will tell you what has happened to Judge Valcárcel because they're afraid to find themselves involved in the imbroglio, Sir Roger." They were talking in Mr. Harding's small house near the embankment. On the walls were engravings of Scottish castles. They were having a coconut drink. "Arana's connections in Lima arranged for Judge Valcárcel to be dismissed, accused of lying and I don't know how many other falsehoods. The poor man, if he's alive, must bitterly regret the worst mistake of his life: accepting this assignment. He came to put his head in the lion's mouth and has paid dearly for it.

He was highly respected in Lima, it seems. Now they've dragged him through the mud and perhaps killed him. No one knows where he is. I hope he did leave. Talking about him in Iquitos has become taboo."

In fact, the story of the upright and fearless Dr. Carlos A. Valcárcel who came to Iquitos to investigate the "horrors of Putumayo" could not be sadder. Roger reconstructed it in the course of these weeks as if it were a puzzle. When he had the audacity to issue an arrest order against 237 people for alleged crimes, almost all of them connected to the Peruvian Amazon Company, a shudder ran through Amazonia, not only in the Peruvian Amazon but the Colombian and Brazilian as well. The machinery of Julio C. Arana's empire immediately denounced the blow and began a counter-offensive. The police could locate only nine of the 237 men incriminated. Of the nine, the only really important one was Aurelio Rodríguez, one of the section chiefs in Putumayo, responsible for a long criminal record of abductions, rapes, mutilations, kidnappings and murders. But the nine men arrested, including Rodríguez, presented a writ of *habeas corpus* in the Superior Court of Iquitos and the court granted them provisional freedom while it studied their documents.

"Unfortunately," the prefect said to Roger without blinking, putting on a deeply sorrowful face, "these bad citizens, taking advantage of their provisional freedom, fled. As you must know, it will be difficult to find them in the immensity of Amazonia if the Superior Court revalidates the arrest order."

The court was in no hurry to do so, for when Roger went to ask the judges when they would review the documents, they explained that this was done "following a strict first-come-first-served order of cases." A large number of cases were in line "ahead of the one that interests you." One of the court clerks permitted himself to add, in a mocking tone: "Here justice is sure but slow, and these procedures can last for many years, Consul."

Pablo Zumaeta, from his supposed hiding place, orchestrated the judicial offensive against Judge Valcárcel through figureheads, initiating multiple denunciations for prevarication, embezzlement, false witness, and various other crimes. One morning a Bora woman and her daughter, only a few years old, accompanied by an interpreter, came to the Iquitos police station to accuse Judge Valcárcel of "an attempt against the honor of a minor." The judge had to spend most of his time defending himself against slanderous fabrications, making statements, delivering and writing communications instead of devoting himself to the investigation that had brought him to the jungle. The entire world was falling down on him. The small hotel where he was staying, the Yurimaguas, evicted him. He did not find an inn or a pension in the city that would dare take him in. He had to rent a small room in Nanay, a district filled with garbage dumps and standing pools of foul water, where at night he heard rats running beneath his hammock and he stepped on cockroaches.

Roger learned all of this piece by piece, the details whispered here and there, while his admiration grew for the magistrate whose hand he would have liked to shake and whom he wanted to congratulate for his decency and courage. What had happened to him? The only thing he could find out with certainty, though the word "certainty" did not seem to have firm roots in the soil of Iquitos, was that when the order to dismiss him came from Lima, Carlos A. Valcárcel had already disappeared. From then on no one in the city could say where he was. Had they killed him? The story of the journalist Benjamín Saldaña Roca was being repeated. Hostility toward him had been so great he had no choice but to run. In a second interview, in the house of Mr. Stirs, Rómulo Paredes told him: "I myself advised Judge Valcárcel to move before they killed him, Sir Roger. He had already received a fair number of warnings."

What kind of warnings? Provocations in the restaurants and bars where Judge Valcárcel went to eat or have a beer. Suddenly a drunk would insult him and challenge him to a fight, displaying a knife. If the judge made an accusation to the police or at the Prefecture, they had him fill out interminable forms, recounting the facts in detail, and assured him "they would investigate his complaint."

Roger soon felt as Judge Valcárcel must have felt before he escaped Iquitos or was annihilated by one of the killers on Arana's payroll: deceived wherever he went, turned into the laughing stock of a community of puppets whose strings were moved by the Peruvian Amazon Company that all of Iquitos obeyed with base subservience.

He had proposed returning to Putumayo, though it was evident that if here in the city Arana's company had successfully mocked the sanctions and avoided the announced reforms, on the rubber plantations everything would be the same or worse than before as far as the indigenous were concerned. Rómulo Paredes, Consul Stirs, and Prefect Adolfo Gamarra urged him to give up that trip. "You won't get out alive, and your death will serve no purpose," the editor of *El Oriente* assured him. "Señor Casement, I'm sorry to tell you this, but you're the most hated man in Putumayo. Not even Saldaña Roca, or the gringo Hardenburg, or Judge Valcárcel are as despised as you. It was a miracle I came back alive from Putumayo. But that miracle won't be repeated if you go there to be crucified. Besides, do you know something? The most absurd thing will be that they'll have you killed with poisoned darts from the blowguns of the Boras and Huitotos you're defending. Don't go, don't be foolish. Don't commit suicide."

As soon as Prefect Gamarra learned of his preparations to travel to Putumayo, he came to see him at the Hotel Amazonas. He was very alarmed. He took him to have a beer at a bar where they played Brazilian music. It was the only time Roger thought the official spoke to him with sincerity.

"I beg you to reject this madness, Señor Casement," he said, looking him in the eye. "I have no way to guarantee your protection. I'm sorry to tell you that, but it's the truth. I don't want the burden of your corpse on my service record. It would be the end of my career. I tell you this with my heart in my hand. You won't reach Putumayo. I've arranged, with great effort, for no one to touch you here. It hasn't been easy, I swear. I've had to beg and threaten the men who give the orders. But my authority disappears beyond the city limits. Don't go to Putumayo. For your sake and for mine. For the sake of what you love best, don't ruin my future. I'm speaking to you as a friend, truly."

But what finally made him give up the trip was an unexpected, abrupt visitor in the middle of the night. He was already lying down and about to fall asleep when the reception clerk of the Hotel Amazonas knocked on his door. A gentleman was asking for him and said it was very urgent. He dressed, went downstairs, and saw Juan Tizón. He had lost track of him since his travels to Putumayo, when this high official in the Peruvian Amazon Company collaborated so loyally with the commission. He wasn't even a shadow of the self-confident man Roger recalled. He looked aged, exhausted, and above all demoralized.

They looked for a quiet place but it was impossible because the Iquitos night was filled with noise, drunkenness, gambling, and sex. They resigned themselves to sitting in the Pim Pam, a bar-nightclub where they had to get rid of two Brazilian mulattas who pestered them to dance. They ordered a couple of beers.

Always with the gentlemanly air and elegant manners that Roger remembered, Tizón spoke to him in a way that seemed absolutely sincere. "Nothing of what the company put forward has been done, in spite of the fact that after the request from President Leguía, we agreed to it at a meeting of the board of directors. When I presented my report, everyone, including Pablo Zumaeta and Arana's other brothers and brothers-in-law, agreed with me that radical improvements had to be made at the stations. To avoid problems with the law and for moral, Christian reasons. Sheer prattle. Nothing has been or will be done."

He told him that except for instructing its employees in Putumayo to take precautions and erase all traces of past abuses—make the corpses disappear, for example—the company had facilitated the flight of the most important of the men incriminated in the report London sent to the

Peruvian government. The system of harvesting rubber with a coerced indigenous labor force continued as before.

"It was enough for me to set foot in Iquitos to realize nothing had changed," Roger agreed. "And you, Don Juan?"

"I'm returning to Lima next week and don't think I'll be back here. My situation in the Peruvian Amazon Company became untenable. I preferred to leave before they could dismiss me. They'll buy back my shares, but at a miserable price. In Lima, I'll have to work at other things. I don't regret that in spite of having lost ten years of my life working for Arana. Even if I have to start at zero, I feel better. After what we saw in Putumayo, I felt dirty and guilty in the company. I consulted with my wife, and she supports me."

They spoke for close to an hour. Juan Tizón also insisted that Roger not go back to Putumayo for any reason: he wouldn't accomplish anything except their killing him and, perhaps, their becoming enraged in one of those excesses of cruelty he had already seen in his travels to the plantations.

Roger devoted himself to preparing a new report for the Foreign Office. He explained that no reforms at all had been made or the slightest punishment administered to the criminals of the Peruvian Amazon Company. There was no hope anything would be done in the future. The fault lay as much with the firm of Julio C. Arana as with the public administration and, perhaps, the entire country. In Iquitos, the Peruvian government was nothing more than Arana's agent. The power of his company was so great that all political, police, and judicial institutions worked actively to permit it to continue exploiting the indigenous at no risk, because all the officials either received money or feared reprisals from it.

As if wanting to prove him right, during this time the Superior Court in Iquitos suddenly halted the review the nine arrested men had requested. The stoppage was a masterpiece of cynicism: all judicial action was suspended until the 237 persons on the list drawn up by Judge Valcárcel could all be detained. With only a small group of prisoners, any investigation would be incomplete and illegal, the judges decreed. So the nine were definitively free and the case suspended until the police could bring all 237 suspects to trial, something, of course, that never would happen.

A few days later another event, even more grotesque, took place in Iquitos, putting Roger's capacity for astonishment to the test. As he was going from his hotel to Mr. Stirs's house, he saw people crowded into two locations that seemed to be state offices since their facades displayed the seal and flag of Peru. What was going on?

"Municipal elections," explained Mr. Stirs in his thin voice that was so disinterested it seemed impervious to emotion. "Very peculiar elections, because according to Peruvian election law, to have the right to vote you must own property and know how to read and write. This reduces the number of electors to a few hundred people. In reality, the elections are decided in the offices of Casa Arana. The names of the winners and the percentage of votes they receive."

It must have been true because that night, at a small rally on the Plaza de Armas, which Roger observed from a distance, bands played and brandy was distributed as they celebrated the election of Don Pablo Zumaeta as the new mayor of Iquitos! Julio C. Arana's brother-in-law emerged from his "hiding place" indemnified by the people of Iquitos—that's how he expressed it in his acceptance speech—for the slanders of the English–Colombian conspiracy, determined to continue fighting unyieldingly against the enemies of Peru and for the progress of Amazonia. After the distribution of alcoholic beverages, there was folk dancing with fireworks, guitars, and drums that lasted until dawn. Roger chose to withdraw to his hotel to escape being lynched.

George Michell and his wife finally arrived in Iquitos on a ship out of Manaus, on November 30, 1911. Roger was already packing for his departure. The arrival of the new British consul was preceded by frantic efforts by Mr. Stirs and Roger himself to find a house for the couple. "Great Britain has fallen into disgrace here because of you, Sir Roger," the outgoing consul told him. "Nobody wants to rent me a house for the Michells, even though I'm offering to pay a surcharge. Everyone's afraid of offending Arana, everyone refuses." Roger asked Rómulo Paredes for help, and the editor solved the problem for them. He rented the house and sublet it to the British consulate. It was an old, dirty house that had to be renovated against the clock and furnished somehow to receive its new tenants. Mrs. Michell was a cheerful, strong-willed woman whom Roger met for the first time at the foot of the gangplank, in the port, on the day of their arrival. She was not disheartened by the state of her new home or the town she had set foot in for the first time. She seemed immune to discouragement. Without delay, even before unpacking, she set about cleaning everything with energy and good humor.

Roger had a long conversation with his old friend and colleague, George Michell, in Mr. Stirs's small living room. He informed him in detail about the situation and didn't hide a single one of the difficulties he would face in his new position. Michell, a plump, lively man in his forties who manifested the same energy as his wife in all his gestures and movements, took notes in a small notebook, with brief pauses to ask for clarifications. Then, instead of appearing demoralized or complaining at the prospect of what awaited him in Iquitos, he only said, with a large smile: "Now I know what's at stake and I'm ready for the struggle."

During his last two weeks in Iquitos, the demon of sex once again took irresistible possession of Roger. During his previous stay he had been very prudent, but now, in spite of knowing the hostility so many people connected to the rubber business felt toward him, and the kinds of trap they could lay for him, he didn't hesitate to go out at night to stroll on the embankment along the river, where there were always women and men looking for clients. This was how he met Alcibíades Ruiz, if that was his name. He took him to the Hotel Amazonas. The night porter had no objection after Roger gave him a tip. Alcibíades agreed to pose for him, assuming the postures of classic statues that he indicated. After some bargaining he agreed to undress. Alcibíades was a mestizo, white and Indian, a *cholo*, and Roger noted in his diary that this racial mix produced a man of great physical beauty, even greater than that of the *caboclos* of Brazil, in whom indigenous gentleness and sweetness mixed with the coarse virility of the descendants of Spaniards. Alcibíades and he kissed and touched but did not make love that day or the next, when Alcibíades returned to the hotel. It was morning and Roger was able to photograph him naked, in various poses. When he left, Roger wrote in his diary: "Alcibíades Ruiz. *Cholo*. Dancer's movements. Thin and long, when it got hard it curved like a bow. Entered me like hand in glove."

During this time, Rómulo Paredes was attacked on the street. When he left the print shop of his newspaper, three nasty-looking individuals stinking of alcohol assaulted him. According to what he told Roger, whom he came to see in his hotel immediately after the episode, they would have beaten him to death if he hadn't been armed, and he frightened his three aggressors when he fired in the air. He had a suitcase with him. Don Rómulo was so shaken by what had happened he wouldn't go out for a drink as Roger suggested. His resentment and indignation toward the Peruvian Amazon Company knew no limits: "I was always Casa Arana's loyal collaborator and satisfied them in everything they wished," he complained.

They had sat on two corners of the bed and spoke in semi-darkness, because the flame of the gas lamp barely lit a corner of the room. "When I was a judge and when I started *El Oriente*, I never opposed their requests, even though they often were repugnant to my conscience. But I'm a realistic man, Consul, I know which battles can't be won. This commission, going to Putumayo on assignment from Judge Valcárcel, I never wanted to take it on. From the beginning I knew I'd get involved in trouble. They obliged me to. Pablo Zumaeta in person demanded it. I made this trip only because I was following his orders. My report, before I turned it in to the prefect, I gave it to Señor Zumaeta to read. He returned it without comment. Doesn't that mean he accepted it? Only then did I give it to the prefect. And now it turns out they've declared war on me and want to kill me. This attack is a warning for me to get out of Iquitos. And go where? I have a wife, five children, and two serving girls, Señor Casement. Have you ever seen anything like the ingratitude of these people? I suggest you leave right away too. Your life is in danger, Sir Roger. Until now nothing's happened to you, because they think if they kill an Englishman, especially a diplomat, there'll be an international incident. But don't trust that. Those scruples can disappear in any drunken brawl. Take my advice and leave, my friend."

"I'm not an Englishman, I'm Irish," Roger corrected him gently.

Rómulo Paredes handed him the suitcase he had brought with him. "Here are all the documents I compiled in Putumayo, on which I based my work. I was right not to give them to Prefect Adolfo Gamarra. They would have met the same fate as my report: eaten by moths in the Prefecture of Iquitos. Take them, I know you'll put them to good use. But I'm sorry to load you down with another piece of luggage."

Roger left four days later, after saying goodbye to Omarino and Arédomi. Mr. Stirs had placed them in a carpentry shop in Nanay where, in addition to working as domestics for the owner, a Bolivian, they would be his apprentices. In the port, where Stirs and Michell came to say goodbye, Roger learned that the volume of rubber exported in the past two months had surpassed the previous year's record. What better proof that nothing had changed, that the Huitotos, Boras, Andoques, and the rest of the indigenous groups in Putumayo were still being squeezed without mercy?

For the five days of the voyage to Manaus, he barely left his cabin. He felt demoralized, sick, and disgusted with himself. He barely ate and went on deck only when the heat in the narrow room became unbearable. As they sailed down the Amazon and the riverbed widened and the banks were lost from view, he thought he would never return to this jungle. And about the paradox—he had often thought the same thing in Africa, navigating on the Congo River—that this majestic landscape with its flocks of pink herons and screeching parrots that sometimes flew overhead, and the wake of small fish following the ship, leaping and doing tricks as if to attract the passengers' attention, harbored in the interior of these jungles vertiginous suffering caused by the greed of the avid, cruel men he had known in Putumayo. He thought of the motionless face of Julio C. Arana at the meeting of the board of directors of the Peruvian Amazon Company in London. He swore again that he would fight until the last drop of energy in his body to see him punished, this small, well-groomed man who had set in motion and was the principal beneficiary of the machinery that crushed human beings with impunity to satisfy his hunger for riches. Who would dare say now that Julio C. Arana didn't know what was going on in Putumayo? He had put on a show to deceive everyone—the Peruvian government, the British above all—in order to continue extracting rubber from jungles as mistreated as the indigenous peoples who inhabited them.

In Manaus, where he arrived in the middle of December, he felt better. While he waited for a ship that would leave for Pará and Barbados, he could work in his hotel room, adding comments and details to his report. He spent one afternoon with the English consul, who confirmed that in spite of his demands, the Brazilian authorities had done nothing effective to capture Montt and Agüero or the other fugitives. It was rumored everywhere that several of Julio C. Arana's managers in Putumayo now worked for the Madeira–Mamoré railroad that was under construction.

For the week he stayed in Manaus, Roger led a spartan life, not going out at night in search of adventures. He would take walks along the riverbanks and streets of the city, and when he wasn't working, he spent many hours reading the books on the ancient history of Ireland recommended to him by Alice Stopford Green. A passion for his country's affairs would help rid his mind of images of Putumayo and the intrigues, lies, and abuses of the widespread political corruption he had seen in Iquitos. But it wasn't easy to concentrate on Irish affairs, for he constantly thought he had not finished his assignment and would have to bring it to its conclusion in London.

On December 17 he set sail for Pará, where he finally found a communication from the Foreign Office. They had received his telegrams sent from Iquitos and were aware that in spite of the Peruvian government's promises, nothing real had been done against the excesses in Putumayo except for permitting the escape of those accused.

On Christmas Eve, he left for Barbados on the *Denis*, a comfortable ship carrying barely a handful of passengers. It was a calm crossing to Bridgetown. There, the Foreign

Office had reserved passage for him on the SS *Terence*, bound for New York. The English authorities had decided to take energetic action against the British company responsible for events in Putumayo and wanted the United States to join their effort and protest together to the government of Peru for its unwillingness to respond to public opinion.

In the capital of Barbados, as he waited for the ship to sail, Roger's life was as chaste as it had been in Manaus: not one visit to the public bath, not one nocturnal escapade. He had re-entered one of those periods of sexual abstinence that sometimes lasted many months. At times his mind became filled with religious concerns. In Bridgetown he visited Father Smith every day. He had long conversations with him about the New Testament, which he usually carried with him on his journeys. He reread it from time to time, alternating this reading with the Irish poets, above all Yeats, some of whose poems he had memorized. He attended a Mass at the convent of the Ursulines and, as had happened to him before, felt the desire to take communion. He told Father Smith and he, smiling, reminded him he wasn't a Catholic but a member of the Anglican Church. If he wanted to convert, he offered to help him take the first steps. Roger was tempted but changed his mind thinking about the weaknesses and sins he would have to confess to this good friend, Father Smith.

On December 31 he left on the SS *Terence* for New York, and immediately upon arriving, without time even to admire the skyscrapers, he took the train to Washington D.C. The British ambassador, James Bryce, surprised him by announcing that the President of the United States,

William Howard Taft, had agreed to see him. He and his advisers wanted to hear from the mouth of Sir Roger, who personally knew what was going on in Putumayo and was a man trusted by the British government, the situation on the rubber plantations, and whether the campaign being waged in the United States and Great Britain by various churches, humanitarian organizations, and liberal journalists and publications was true or sheer demagoguery and exaggeration, as the rubber enterprises and the Peruvian government insisted.

Staying in the residence of Ambassador Bryce, treated like royalty and hearing himself called Sir Roger wherever he went, he visited a barber shop and had his hair and beard trimmed and his nails manicured. And he renewed his wardrobe in the elegant shops of Washington D.C. Often during this time he thought about the contradictions in his life. Less than two weeks before he had been a poor devil threatened with death in a run-down hotel in Iquitos, and now, an Irishman who dreamed about the independence of Ireland, he was the embodiment of an official sent by the British Crown to persuade the president of the United States to help the Empire demand that the Peruvian government respond forcefully to the ignominy of Amazonia. Wasn't life an absurdity, a dramatic representation that suddenly turned into farce?

The three days he spent in Washington D.C. were dizzying: daily working sessions with officials from the State Department and a long personal interview with the secretary for foreign relations. On the third day he was received at the White House by President Taft in the company of several advisers and the secretary of state. For an instant, before beginning his exposition on Putumayo, Roger had a hallucination: he wasn't there as a diplomatic representative of the British Crown but as a special envoy of the recently constituted Republic of Ireland. He had been sent by his provisional government to defend the reasons that had led the immense majority of the Irish, in a plebiscite, to break their connections to Great Britain and proclaim independence. The new Ireland wanted to maintain relations of friendship and cooperation with the United States, with whom they shared a devotion to democracy and where a large community of people of Irish background lived.

Roger fulfilled his obligations impeccably. The meeting was supposed to last half an hour but was three times as long, for President Taft, who listened with great attention to his report on the situation of the indigenous in Putumayo, asked many thoughtful questions and solicited his opinion regarding the best way to oblige the Peruvian government to put an end to the crimes on the rubber plantations. Roger's suggestion that the United States open a consulate in Iquitos, which would work together with the British to denounce the abuses, was well received by the president. And in fact, a few weeks later, the United States sent a career diplomat, Stuart J. Fuller, to Iquitos as consul.

More than the words he heard, the surprise and indignation with which President Taft and his colleagues listened to his report convinced Roger that from now on the United States would collaborate in a decisive way with England in denouncing the situation of the Amazonian Indians.

In London, even though his physical condition was constantly weakened by fatigue and his old ailments, he dedicated himself body and soul to completing his new report for the Foreign Office, demonstrating that the Peruvian authorities had not carried out the promised reforms and the Peruvian Amazon Company had boycotted every initiative, making life impossible for Judge Valcárcel and keeping in the Prefecture the report by Rómulo Paredes, whom they had attempted to kill for having described impartially what he had witnessed during the four months (from March 15 to July 15) he spent on Arana's rubber plantations. Roger began to translate into English a selection of the testimonies, interviews, and various documents the editor of *El Oriente* gave him in Iquitos. This material considerably enriched his own report.

He did this at night, because his days were filled with meetings at the Foreign Office where everyone from the chancellor to multiple commissions requested reports, advice, and suggestions regarding the ideas for taking action that the British government was considering. The atrocities a British company was committing in Amazonia had been the object of a vigorous campaign initiated by the Anti-Slavery Society and *Truth*, and this was supported now by the liberal press and many religious and humanitarian organizations.

Roger insisted that the *Report on Putumayo* be published immediately. He had lost all hope that the silent diplomacy the British government attempted with President Leguía would have an effect. In spite of resistance from several sectors in the administration, Sir Edward Grey finally agreed and the cabinet approved its publication as a blue book. Roger spent many nights awake, smoking constantly and drinking countless cups of coffee, revising the final copy word by word.

The day the definitive text at last went to the printer, he felt so ill that, fearing something might happen if he were alone, he took refuge in the house of his friend Alice Stopford Green. "You look like a skeleton," the historian said, taking him by the arm and leading him to the living room. Roger was shuffling his feet and, in a daze, felt that at any moment he would lose consciousness. Almost immediately he fell asleep or fainted. When he opened his eyes, he saw sitting beside him, together and smiling, his sister Nina and Alice.

"We thought you would never wake up," he heard one of them say.

He had slept close to twenty-four hours. Alice called the family doctor, whose diagnosis was exhaustion. They should let him sleep. He didn't recall having slept. When he tried to stand his legs folded and he let himself fall back onto the sofa. *The Congo didn't kill me but the Amazon will*, he thought.

After having some light refreshment, he was able to stand, and a car took him to his Philbeach Gardens apartment. He took a long bath that helped clear his mind. But he felt so weak he had to lie down again.

The Foreign Office obliged him to take a ten-day vacation. He resisted leaving London before the appearance of his report, but he finally agreed to go. Accompanied by Nina, who requested leave from the school where she taught, he spent a week in Cornwall. His fatigue was so great he could barely concentrate on reading. His mind scattered in dissolute images. Thanks to a quiet life and healthy diet, he began recuperating his strength. He could take long walks in the countryside, enjoying some mild days. There could be nothing more different from the pleasant, civilized landscape of Cornwall than Amazonia, and yet, in spite of the well-being and serenity he felt here, seeing the routine of the farmers, the beatific cows grazing, the horses neighing in the stables, with no threat of wild animals, snakes, or mosquitoes, one day he found himself thinking this populated, civilized nature, revealing centuries of agricultural labor in the service of humanity, had lost its state of being part of the natural world—its soul, pantheists would say—compared to the savage, agitated, indomitable, untamed territory of Amazonia, where everything seemed to be birthing or dying, an unstable, risky, shifting world where a man felt torn out of the present and thrown into the most distant past, in communication with his ancestors, returned to the dawn of human history. And he discovered in surprise that he recalled it all with nostalgia, in spite of the horrors it hid.

His report on Putumayo was published in July 1912. From the first day it produced an upheaval that, with London as its center, advanced in concentric waves through all of Europe, the United States, and many other parts of the world, especially Colombia, Brazil, and Peru. *The Times* dedicated several pages to it, and an editorial that praised Roger Casement to the skies, saying that once again he had demonstrated exceptional gifts as a "great humanitarian," and at the same time demanded immediate actions against this British company and its shareholders who benefitted financially from an industry that practiced slavery and torture and was exterminating indigenous peoples.

But the praise that moved Roger most was the article written by Edmund D. Morel, his friend and ally in the campaign against Leopold II, King of the Belgians, in the *Daily News*. Commenting on the report, he said of Roger that he "had never seen as much magnetism in a human being as in him." Always allergic to public display, Roger did not enjoy in any way this new wave of popularity. Rather, he felt uncomfortable and sought to avoid it. But it was difficult because the uproar caused by the document meant that dozens of English, European, and North American publications wanted to interview him. He received invitations to give lectures at academic institutions, political clubs, religious and charitable centers. A special service on the subject was held in Westminster Abbey, and Canon Herbert Henson gave a sermon harshly attacking the stockholders in the Peruvian Amazon Company for reaping profits from the practice of slavery, murder, and mutilation.

The chargé d'affaires for Great Britain in Peru, Des Graz, reported on the stir caused in Lima by the accusations in Roger's report. The Peruvian government, fearing an economic boycott by western countries, announced the immediate implementation of reforms and the dispatch of military and police forces to Putumayo. But Des Graz added that the announcement probably wouldn't be effective this time either, since there were governmental sectors that viewed the actions cited in the report as a conspiracy of the British Empire to favor Colombian claims in Putumayo.

The atmosphere of interest in and solidarity with the indigenous peoples of Amazonia awakened in the public by the report meant that the project of opening a Catholic mission in Putumayo received a great deal of economic support. The Anglican Church had some objections but eventually let itself be convinced by Roger's arguments after countless meetings, appointments, letters, and dialogues: in a country where the Catholic Church was so deeply rooted, a Protestant mission would awaken suspicions and the Peruvian Amazon Company would be sure to slander it, presenting it as the spearhead of the Crown's colonizing appetites.

In Ireland and England, Roger had meetings with Jesuits and Franciscans, two orders he had always liked. Ever since he had been in the Congo, he had read about the past efforts of the Society of Jesus in Paraguay and Brazil to organize the Indians, catechize them, and gather them into communities where, while they maintained their traditions of working in common, they practiced an elementary Christianity, which had raised their standards of living and freed them from exploitation and extermination. For that reason, Portugal destroyed the Jesuit missions and plotted until they convinced Spain and the Vatican that the Society of Jesus had become a state within the state and constituted a danger to papal authority and Spanish imperial sovereignty. Nonetheless, the Jesuits did not receive the project of an Amazonian mission with much warmth. On the other hand, the Franciscans adopted it enthusiastically.

This was how Roger became familiar with the efforts of the Franciscan worker-priests in the poorest neighborhoods of Dublin. They labored in factories and workshops and experienced the same difficulties and privations as the workers. Conversing with them, seeing the devotion with which they carried out their ministry as they shared the fate of the disinherited, Roger thought no one was better prepared than these religious men for the challenge of establishing missions in La Chorrera and El Encanto.

Alice Stopford Green, with whom Roger went in a state of euphoria to celebrate the departure for the Peruvian Amazon of the first four Irish Franciscans, predicted: "Are you sure you still belong to the Anglican Church, Roger? Though you may not realize it, you're on a one-way road to a papist conversion."

Among the habitual participants in Alice's evenings in the abundant library of her house on Grosvenor Road were Irish nationalists: Anglicans, Presbyterians, and Catholics. Roger had never noticed frictions or disputes. After Alice's observation, he often asked himself during this time if his approach to Catholicism was strictly a spiritual and religious disposition or a political one, a way of committing himself even more closely to the nationalist option, since the immense majority of the supporters of independence in Ireland were Catholic.

In order to somehow escape the pursuit of which he was the object as author of the *Report on Putumayo*, he asked the ministry for a few days more of leave and went to spend them in Germany. Berlin made an extraordinary impression on him. German society, under the Kaiser, seemed a model of modernity, economic development, order, and efficiency. Though brief, this visit helped to make concrete a vague idea he had been turning over in his mind for some time, and from then on it became one of the main points of his political action. To win its freedom, Ireland could not count on the understanding, much less the benevolence, of the British Empire. It was being demonstrated at this time. The mere possibility that the British parliament would again discuss the draft of a law to grant Ireland Home Rule, which Roger and his radical friends considered an insufficient formal concession, had provoked a jingoistic, enraged response not only among conservatives but also in large liberal and progressive sectors, including labor unions and artisans' guilds. In Ireland, the prospect of the island having administrative autonomy and its own parliament mobilized and inflamed the unionists of Ulster. There were meetings, an army of Volunteers was being formed, public collections were made to buy weapons, and tens of thousands of people signed a covenant in which Irishmen of the North proclaimed they would not accept Home Rule if it were approved and would defend Ireland's remaining in the Empire with their weapons and their lives. Under these circumstances, Roger thought, the supporters of independence ought to seek solidarity with Germany. The enemy of my enemy is my friend, and Germany was England's most notable rival. In the event of war, the military defeat of Great Britain would open a unique possibility for Irish emancipation. At this time, Roger often repeated to himself the old nationalist saying: "England's difficulty is Ireland's opportunity."

But as he reached these political conclusions that he shared only with nationalist friends on his trips to Ireland, or in London at Alice Stopford Green's house, it was England that showed affection and admiration for what he had done. Thinking about this made him feel ill.

In all this time, in spite of the desperate efforts of the Peruvian Amazon Company to avoid it, each day it was more obvious that the fate of Julio C. Arana's enterprise was threatened. Its loss of prestige was accentuated by the scandal produced when Horace Thorogood, a reporter for the *Morning Leader* who went to the firm's main offices in the City to try to interview the board of directors, received from one of them, Abel Larco, a brother-in-law of Arana, an envelope filled with money. The reporter asked what it meant. Larco replied that the company was always generous to its friends. The reporter, indignant, returned the intended bribe, denounced what had happened in his paper, and the Peruvian Amazon Company had to make a public apology, saying it was a misunderstanding and those responsible for the bribery attempt would be dismissed.

The stocks of Julio C. Arana's enterprise began to fall on the London market. And though this was due in part to competition from new exports of rubber from British colonies in Asia—Singapore, Malaya, and Ceylon—planted there with shoots taken out of Amazonia in an audacious smuggling operation by the English scientist and adventurer Henry Alexander Wickham, the key fact in the collapse of the Peruvian Amazon company was the bad image it acquired in both public opinion and the financial media because of the publication of Roger's *Report on Putumayo*. Lloyd's cut off its credit. Throughout Europe and the United States, a good number of banks followed this example. The boycott promoted by the Anti-Slavery Society and other organizations deprived the company of many clients and associates.

The coup de grâce for Julio C. Arana's empire was given by the establishment in the House of Commons, on March 14, 1912, of a special committee to investigate the responsibility of the Peruvian Amazon Company in the Putumayo atrocities. Made up of fifteen members and presided over by a prestigious parliamentarian, Charles Roberts, it met over fifteen months. During thirty-six sessions, twenty-seven witnesses were questioned in public hearings filled with reporters, politicians, and members of lay and religious societies, among them the Anti-Slavery Society and its president, the missionary John Harris. Newspapers and magazines reported in detail on the meetings, and abundant articles, caricatures, gossip, and jokes commented on them.

The most anticipated witness, whose presence attracted a larger audience, was Sir Roger Casement. He appeared before the commission on November 13 and December 11 of 1912. He described precisely and soberly what he had seen with his own eyes on the rubber plantations: the pillory, the great instrument of torture in all the camps, the backs with the scars of floggings, the whips and Winchester rifles carried by the station overseers and the "boys" or "rationals" responsible for maintaining order and attacking the tribes in the *correrías*, and the regimen of slavery, over-exploitation, and starvation to which the indigenous were subjected. Then he summarized the testimonies of the Barbadians, whose veracity, he pointed out, was guaranteed by the fact that almost all of them had acknowledged their own responsibility for torture and murder. At the request of the committee members, he also explained the prevailing Machiavellian system: section chiefs received not salaries but commissions on the rubber harvested, which induced them to demand more and more of the harvesters in order to increase their own earnings.

In his second appearance, Roger put on a show. Before

the surprised gaze of the parliamentarians, he began taking out of a large bag, held by two ushers, objects he had acquired in the stores of the Peruvian Amazon Company in Putumayo. He demonstrated how the Indian laborers were swindled: to keep them forever in debt, the company sold them articles for work or home, or decorative trinkets on credit, at prices several times higher than in London. He showed an old one-barrel shotgun whose price in La Chorrera was forty-five shillings. To pay this amount a Huitoto or Bora would have had to work for two years, assuming that they were paid what a street sweeper earned in Iquitos. He showed them shirts of unbleached linen, coarse twill trousers, necklaces of colored beads, little boxes of powder, belts of pita fiber, toy tops, oil lamps, hats of untreated straw, ointments for bites, calling out the prices these objects might fetch in England. The eyes of the parliamentarians opened in indignation and astonishment. It was even worse when Sir Roger set out before Charles Roberts and the other members of the committee dozens of photographs he had taken himself in El Encanto, La Chorrera, and other stations in Putumayo: there were backs and buttocks with "the mark of Arana" in the form of scars and sores, the bitten and pecked-at corpses rotting in the undergrowth, the incredible emaciation of men, women, and children who in spite of their skeletal thinness carried on their heads great sausages of solidified rubber, the parasite-swollen bellies of newborns about to die. The photographs were an unassailable testimony to the condition of beings living almost without food and mistreated by greedy men whose only goal in life was to extract more rubber even if to do that entire villages had to be consumed.

An emotional aspect of the sessions was the questioning of the British directors of the Peruvian Amazon Company, when the Irishman Swift McNeill, the veteran parliamentarian for South Donegal, stood out for his pugnacity and subtlety. He proved beyond the shadow of a doubt that outstanding businessmen like Henry M. Read and John Russell Gubbins, stars of London society and aristocrats or independently wealthy men like Sir John Lister-Kaye and Baron de Sousa-Deiro, were totally uninformed about what went on in Julio C. Arana's company, whose board meetings they attended and whose proceedings they signed, collecting huge sums of money. Not even when *Truth* began publishing the denunciations made by Benjamín Saldaña Roca and Walter Hardenburg did they bother to find out how much truth lay in those accusations. They were content with the releases Abel Larco or Julio C. Arana himself gave them, which consisted of accusing the accusers of being blackmailers resentful at not having received from the company the money they attempted to extort by means of threats. No one bothered to verify on site if the enterprise to which they gave the prestige of their names was committing those crimes. Even worse, not one of them had taken the trouble to examine the papers, accounts, reports, and correspondence of a company whose files showed signs of those villainies. Because, as incredible as it might seem, until the scandal broke, Julio C. Arana, Abel Larco, and the other hierarchs felt so secure they did not hide traces of the outrages in their books: for example, not paying salaries to the indigenous laborers and spending enormous quantities of money to buy whips, revolvers, and rifles.

A moment of heightened drama took place when Julio C. Arana appeared to make a statement before the committee. His first appearance had to be postponed because his wife, Eleonora, who was in Geneva, suffered a nervous breakdown because of the tension in the life of her family, which after having climbed to the highest position, now saw its situation quickly disintegrating. Arana entered the House of Commons dressed with his usual elegance, and as pale as the malaria victims in Amazonia. He appeared surrounded by aides and advisers, but in the hearing room he was permitted to have only his lawyer with him. At first he seemed serene and arrogant. As questions from Charles Roberts and the elderly Swift McNeill kept cornering him, he began falling into contradictions and making mistakes, which his translator went out of his way to moderate. He provoked laughter among members of the public when, in response to a question from the head of the committee—why were there so many Winchester rifles on the Putumayo stations, for the *correrías* or attacks on the tribes in order to take people away to the rubber plantations?—he said: "No, Señor, to defend themselves against the tigers that abound in the region." He tried to deny everything but suddenly acknowledged that yes, it was true, he once had heard that an indigenous woman was burned alive. Except that was a long time ago. Abuses, if they had been committed, were always a thing of the past.

The greatest confusion for the rubber king occurred when he tried to disqualify the testimony of Walter Hardenburg, accusing the North American of having falsified a bill of exchange in Manaus. Swift McNeill interrupted to ask if he would dare call Hardenburg a counterfeiter to his face—it was believed he was living in Canada.

"Yes," replied Arana.

"Do it then," responded McNeill. "Here he is."

The arrival of Hardenburg caused a commotion in the hearing room. Advised by his attorney, Arana retracted his statement and said he wasn't accusing Hardenburg but "someone" of having cashed a bill in a Manaus bank that turned out to be counterfeit. Hardenburg demonstrated that it had been a trap to discredit him set by Arana's company, using an individual with a criminal record named Julio Muriedas, who at present was in prison in Pará for fraud.

Arana collapsed following this episode. He gave only hesitant, confused answers to all the questions, betraying his uneasiness and especially the lack of veracity that was the most obvious feature of his testimony.

As the parliamentary committee was in the middle of its work, a new catastrophe crushed the entrepreneur. Judge Swinfen Eady, of the High Court of Justice, at the request of a group of stockholders, decreed an immediate halt to the business of the Peruvian Amazon Company. The judge stated that the company obtained benefits "from collecting rubber in the most awful manner imaginable" and that "if Mr. Arana did not know what was occurring, his responsibility was even more serious, since he, more than anyone, had the absolute obligation to know what went on in his domain."

The final report of the parliamentary committee was no less lapidary. It concluded: "Mr. Julio C. Arana, like his associates, had knowledge of and therefore is the principal party responsible for the atrocities perpetrated by his agents and employees in Putumayo."

When the committee made its report public, sealing the final discredit of Julio C. Arana and ruining the empire that had made a rich and powerful man of this humble resident of Rioja, Roger had already begun to forget Amazonia and Putumayo. Irish issues had become his principal concern. After a short vacation, the Foreign Office proposed that he return to Brazil as the consul general in Rio de Janeiro, and at first he agreed. But his departure kept being postponed, and even though he gave the ministry and himself various pretexts for this, the truth was that in his heart he had already decided he would not serve the British Crown again as a diplomat or in any other capacity. He wanted to make up for lost time, pour his intelligence and energy into fighting for what would be from now on the exclusive goal of his life: the emancipation of Ireland.

For that reason he followed from a distance, without too much interest, the final incarnations of the Peruvian Amazon Company and its owner. It had been made clear at the committee sessions during the confession of the general manager, Henry Lex Gielgud, that the enterprise of Julio C. Arana did not possess any title of ownership to the lands of Putumayo and that it exploited them only "by right of occupation," which increased the mistrust of the banks and other creditors. They immediately pressured its owner, demanding he satisfy all outstanding payments and commitments (his debts amounted to more than £250,000 in City institutions alone). Threats of seizure and judicial auction of his goods rained down on him. Publicly protesting that, to save his honor, he would pay every last cent, Arana put up for sale his elegant London house on Kensington Road, his mansion in Biarritz, and his house in Geneva. But the money received from these sales was not sufficient to appease his creditors, who obtained judicial orders to freeze his savings and bank accounts in England. At the same time his personal fortune was disintegrating, the decline in his business continued to be unstoppable. The fall in the price of Amazonian rubber because of competition from Asia was parallel to the decision of many European and North American importers not to buy Peruvian rubber again until it was proved by an independent international commission that slave labor, torture, and attacks on the tribes had stopped, salaries were paid to the indigenous harvesters of latex, and the labor laws in effect in England and the United States were respected on the rubber stations.

There was no opportunity even to attempt to meet these demands. The flight of the principal overseers and chiefs of the stations in Putumayo, afraid of being imprisoned, threw the entire region into a state of absolute anarchy. Many Indians—entire communities—also took advantage of the situation to escape, which meant that the extraction of rubber was reduced to a minimum and soon ceased altogether. The fugitives left after pillaging stores and offices and taking everything valuable, principally weapons and foodstuffs. Then it was learned that the company, frightened at the possibility that those runaway killers might become prosecution witnesses in possible future trials, gave them large sums to facilitate their escape and buy their silence.

Roger followed the decay of Iquitos through letters

from his friend George Michell, the British consul, who told him about the closing of hotels, restaurants, and shops where articles imported from Paris and New York had once been sold, how the champagne that previously had been uncorked with so much generosity disappeared as if by magic along with whiskey, cognac, port, and wine. In the taverns and brothels there was now only the brandy that scratched your throat and poisonous drinks of suspicious provenance, supposed aphrodisiacs that often, instead of inflaming sexual desire, had the effect of dynamite blasts in the stomachs of the unwary.

Just as in Manaus, the collapse of Casa Arana and rubber produced a general crisis in Iquitos as fast-moving as the prosperity the city had enjoyed for fifteen years. The first to emigrate were the foreigners—merchants, explorers, traffickers, tavern owners, professional people, technicians, prostitutes, pimps, and madams—who returned to their own countries and went in search of places more auspicious than this one, which was sinking into ruin and isolation. Prostitution did not disappear, but it changed agents. Brazilian prostitutes vanished, along with those who said they were "French" and in reality were usually Poles, Flemings, Turks, or Italians, and were replaced by *cholas* and Indians, many of them girls and adolescents who had worked as domestics and lost their jobs because their employers had left in pursuit of more favorable winds or because, with the economic crisis, they could no longer dress or feed them. The British consul, in one of his letters, gave a pathetic description of little fifteen-year-old emaciated Indian girls strolling along the embankment in Iquitos, painted like clowns, looking for clients. Newspapers and magazines disappeared, even the weekly bulletin that announced the departure and arrival of ships, because river transport, once so intense, decreased until it almost stopped. The event that sealed the isolation of Iquitos, its break from the wider world with which it had such intense commerce for some fifteen years, was the decision of the Booth Line to gradually reduce traffic on its freight and passenger lines. When the movement of ships stopped completely, the umbilical cord that joined Iquitos to the world was cut. The capital of Loreto made a journey back in time. In a few years it again became a remote, forgotten town in the heart of the Amazonian plain.

One day in Dublin, Roger, who had gone to see a doctor about his arthritic pain, was crossing the damp grass on St. Stephen's Green when he saw a Franciscan waving to him. It was one of the four worker-priests who had gone to Putumayo to establish a mission. They sat on a bench to talk, near the pond with ducks and swans. The missionaries' experience had been very hard. The hostility they encountered in Iquitos from the authorities, who obeyed the orders of Arana's company, did not drive them away—they had the help of the Augustinian fathers—and neither did the attacks of malaria or the insect bites that, during the first months in Putumayo, put their spirit of sacrifice to the test. In spite of the obstacles and mishaps, they managed to settle in the outskirts of El Encanto, in a hut similar to the ones the Huitotos built in their camps. Their relations with the indigenous, after a beginning when the Indians were sullen and suspicious, had been good, even cordial. The four Franciscans began to learn Huitoto and Bora and built a crude outdoor church with a roof of palm leaves over the altar. But suddenly the general flight of people of all kinds took place. Managers and employees, artisans and guards, Indian domestics and laborers were leaving as if they had been expelled by some malignant force or an epidemic of panic. When they were alone, the life of the Franciscans became more difficult every day. One of them, Father McKey, contracted beriberi. Then, after long discussions, they too chose to leave the place that seemed to be the victim of a divine curse.

The return of the Franciscans was a Homeric journey and a *via crucis*. With the radical decrease in rubber exports and the disorder and depopulation of the stations, the only means of transport out of Putumayo, which were the ships of the Peruvian Amazon Company, especially the *Liberal*, were halted overnight, with no prior warning. That meant the missionaries were cut off from the world, stranded in an abandoned place, with one of their number gravely ill. When Father McKey died, his companions buried him on a knoll and put an inscription on his grave in four languages: Gaelic, English, Huitoto, and Spanish. Then they left, having made no preparations. Some Indians helped them to sail down the Putumayo in a pirogue until it met with the Yavarí. On the long trip the lightweight boat capsized several times and they had to swim to shore. They lost the few possessions they had. On the Yavarí, after a long wait, a boat agreed to carry them to Manaus on condition they not occupy cabins. They slept on deck, and with the rains, the oldest of the three missionaries, Father O'Nety, came down with pneumonia. Finally in Manaus two weeks later, they found a Franciscan convent that took them in. There Father O'Nety died in spite of his companions' care. He was buried in the convent cemetery. The two survivors, after recovering from their disastrous vicissitudes, were repatriated to Ireland. Now they had taken up again their labor among the industrial workers of Dublin.

Roger remained sitting for a long time under the leafy trees on St. Stephen's Green. He tried to imagine what all that immense region of Putumayo would be like with the disappearance of the stations, the flight of the natives, the employees, guards, and killers of Julio C. Arana's company. Closing his eyes, he fantasized. Fecund nature would cover all the open spaces and clearings with bushes, lianas, underbrush, brambles, and when the forest was reborn, the animals would return to make their lairs. The place would be filled with the songs of birds, the whistles and grunts and shrieks of parrots, monkeys, serpents, capybara, curassows, and jaguars. With the rains and mudslides, in a few years there would be no trace of those camps where human greed and cruelty had caused so much suffering, so many mutilations and deaths. The wood in the buildings would rot in the rain and the houses would collapse, their wood devoured by termites. All kinds of creatures would make burrows and refuges in the debris. In a not very distant future, every trace of humans would have been erased by the jungle.

Ireland

13

He woke, caught between alarm and surprise. Because in the confusion of his nights, on this one the thought of his friend—ex-friend now—Herbert Ward had kept him frightened and tense as he dreamed. But it was not in Africa, where they had met when both were working for the expedition of Sir Henry Morton Stanley, or afterward, in Paris, where Roger had gone to visit Herbert and Sarita several times, but on the streets of Dublin, precisely in the midst of the uproar, the barricades, the shots, the cannon fire, and the great collective sacrifice of Easter Week. Herbert Ward in the middle of the insurgent Irish, the Irish Volunteers and the Irish Citizen Army, fighting for the independence of Ireland! How could the human mind, given over to sleep, construct such absurd fantasies?

He recalled that a few days earlier the British cabinet had met without reaching any decision regarding the petition for clemency. His lawyer, George Gavan Duffy, had told him. What was going on? Why this new delay? Gavan Duffy thought it was a good sign: there was dissension among the ministers, who had not achieved the required unanimity. There was hope, then. But waiting meant dying many times each day, each hour, each minute.

Thinking of Herbert Ward saddened him. They would never be friends again. The death of the Wards' son Charles, so young, so handsome, so healthy, on the Neuve

Chapelle front in January 1916, had opened a chasm between them that nothing could close. Herbert was the only real friend he had made in Africa. From the first moment he had seen in this man, somewhat older than himself, who had an outstanding personality and had traveled half the world—New Zealand, Australia, San Francisco, Borneo—and was more cultured than all the Europeans around them, including Stanley, someone with whom he had learned a good number of things and with whom he shared concerns and longings. Unlike the other Europeans recruited by Stanley for this expedition in the service of Leopold II, who aspired only to obtaining money and power in Africa, Herbert loved the adventure for its own sake. He was a man of action but had a passion for art, and he approached the Africans with respectful curiosity. He investigated their beliefs, their customs and religious objects, their apparel and adornments, which interested him from an esthetic and artistic, as well as an intellectual and spiritual point of view. Herbert sketched and made small sculptures with African motifs. In their long conversations at nightfall, when they put up the tents, prepared the food, and got ready to rest after the marches and labors of the day, he confided to Roger that one day he would leave all these tasks to devote himself only to being a sculptor and leading an artist's life in Paris, "the art capital of the world." His love for Africa never left him. On the contrary, distance and the passage of time had increased it. He recalled the Wards' London house, 53 Chester Square, filled with African objects. And, above all, his studio in Paris, its walls covered by spears, javelins, arrows, shields, masks, paddles, and knives in all shapes and sizes. Among the stuffed heads of animals on the floor and the animal skins covering leather armchairs, they had spent entire nights recalling their travels through Africa. Frances, the Wards' young daughter whom they called Cricket, sometimes dressed in native tunics, necklaces, and adornments, and performed a Bakongo dance that her parents accompanied with clapping and monotonous singing.

Herbert was one of the few people to whom Roger confided his disenchantment with Stanley, Leopold II, and the idea that brought him to Africa: that the Empire and colonization would open to Africans the way to modernization and progress. Herbert agreed completely with him, when they confirmed that the real reason for the presence of Europeans in Africa was not to help the Africans out of paganism and barbarism, but to exploit them with a greed that acknowledged no limits to abuse and cruelty.

But Herbert Ward never took very seriously the progressive conversion of Roger to the nationalist ideology. He tended to mock him, in the affectionate manner typical of him, warning him against tinsel patriotism—flags, anthems, uniforms—which, he would say, always represented, sooner or later, a regression to provincialism, mean-spiritedness, and the distortion of universal values. And yet, this citizen of the world, as Herbert liked to call himself, when faced with the inordinate violence of the world war, had reacted like so many millions of Europeans and had also taken refuge in patriotism. The letter in which he broke off his friendship with Roger was filled with the patriotic sentiment he had once mocked, the love for the flag and his native land that once had seemed primitive and contemptible to him. Imagining Herbert Ward, that

Parisian Englishman, involved with the men of Arthur Griffith's Sinn Fein, James Connolly's Irish Citizen Army, Patrick Pearse's Volunteers, fighting in the streets of Dublin for the independence of Ireland, was sheer nonsense. And yet, as he waited for dawn, lying on the narrow cot in his cell, Roger told himself that after all, there was something rational in the depths of that irrationality, for in his dream he had tried to reconcile two things he loved and longed for: his friend and his country.

Early in the morning, the sheriff came to announce a visitor. Roger felt his heart racing when he went into the visitors' room and saw Alice Stopford Green sitting on the single small bench in the narrow room. When she saw him the historian stood and walked forward, smiling, to embrace him.

"Alice, Alice dear," Roger said. "How wonderful to see you. I thought we wouldn't see each other again. At least in this world."

"It wasn't easy to obtain this second permit," Alice said. "But, as you see, my obstinacy finally convinced them. You don't know how many doors I knocked on."

His old friend, who usually dressed with studied elegance, and had done so on her previous visit, now wore a rumpled dress, a kerchief tied carelessly around her head, some gray strands peeking out. On her feet were muddied shoes. Not only her attire had become impoverished. Her expression denoted weariness and discouragement. What had happened to her during this time to account for the change? Had Scotland Yard harassed her again? She denied that, shrugging, as if that old episode had no importance. Alice didn't touch on the petition for clemency and its postponement until the next Council of Ministers. Roger supposed nothing was known yet about this and didn't mention it either. Instead he told her about the absurd dream he'd had, imagining Herbert Ward mixing with Irish rebels in the middle of the skirmishes and battles of Holy Week in the center of Dublin.

"Gradually more news about how things happened is getting out," Alice said, and Roger noted that his friend's voice became sad and enraged at the same time. And he also noticed that, when they heard them talking about the Irish insurrection, the sheriff and guard, standing near them with their backs turned, became rigid and no doubt listened more carefully. He was afraid the sheriff would warn them it was prohibited to speak about this subject, but he didn't.

"Then have you learned something else, Alice?" he asked, lowering his voice until it became a murmur.

He saw that the historian turned slightly pale as she nodded. She was silent for a long while before answering, as if wondering if she ought to perturb her friend by bringing up a subject that was painful to him, or as if she had so many things to say about it, she didn't know where to begin. Finally she chose to answer that though she had heard and still was hearing many versions of what had been experienced in Dublin and some other cities in Ireland the week of the Rising—contradictory things, facts mixed with fantasies, myths, realities and exaggerations and inventions, which occurred when an event aroused an entire people—she gave a good deal of credit to the testimony above all of Austin, a nephew of hers, a Capuchin monk recently arrived in London. He was a fountain of first-hand information, for he was there, in Dublin, in the middle of the fighting, as a nurse and spiritual attendant, going from the General Post Office, the general headquarters from which Patrick Pearse and James Connolly directed the uprising, to the trenches on St. Stephen's Green, where Countess Constance Markievicz commanded the action, with a buccaneer's large pistol and her impeccable Volunteer's uniform, to the barricades constructed in the Jacob's Biscuit Factory and places in Boland's Mill occupied by the rebels under Éamon de Valera, before the English troops surrounded them. The testimony of Brother Austin, Alice thought, probably came closest to that unreachable truth only future historians would completely reveal.

There was another long silence Roger didn't dare to interrupt. It was only a few days since he had seen her, but Alice seemed to have aged ten years. She had wrinkles on her forehead and neck, and her hands were covered with spots. Her clear eyes were no longer shining. He noted her sadness but was sure Alice would not cry in front of him. Could it be that clemency had been denied and she didn't have the courage to tell him?

"Do you know what my nephew remembers most, Roger?" Alice added. "It isn't the shooting, the bombs, the wounded, the blood, the flames of the fires, the smoke that didn't let them breathe, but the confusion. The immense, enormous confusion that reigned all week in the revolutionaries' positions."

"Confusion?" Roger repeated, very quietly. Closing his eyes, he tried to see, hear, and feel it.

"The immense, enormous confusion," Alice repeated, with emphasis. "They were prepared to be killed, and at the same time, they experienced moments of euphoria. Incredible moments. Of pride. Of freedom. Even though none of them, not the leaders and not the militants, ever knew exactly what they were doing or what they wanted to do. That's what Austin says."

"Did they know at least why the weapons they were expecting hadn't arrived?" Roger murmured when he saw that Alice had again fallen into a long silence.

"They didn't know anything about anything. Among themselves they said the most fantastic things. No one could disprove them because nobody knew what the real situation was. Extraordinary rumors circulated that everybody believed because they needed to believe there was a way out of the desperate situation they found themselves in. That a German army was approaching Dublin, for example, and companies, battalions had landed at different points on the island and were advancing toward the capital. That in the interior, in Cork, Galway, Wexford, Meath, Tralee, everywhere, including Ulster, the Volunteers and the Citizen Army had risen up by the thousands, occupying barracks and police stations and advancing from every direction toward Dublin with reinforcements for the besieged fighters. They fought half dead from thirst and hunger, almost without ammunition, and had all their hopes pinned on unreality."

"I knew that would happen," said Roger. "I didn't arrive in time to stop the madness. Now, once again, Irish freedom is farther away than ever."

"Eoin MacNeill tried to stop them when he found out," said Alice. "The military command of the IRB kept him in the dark about the plans for the Rising because he was opposed to an armed action if there was no German support. When he learned that the military command of the Volunteers, the IRB, and the Irish Citizen Army had called on people for military maneuvers on Easter Sunday, he gave a counter-order prohibiting that march and forbidding the Volunteers to go out to the streets if they didn't receive instructions signed by him. This sowed a good deal of confusion. Hundreds, thousands of Volunteers stayed home. Many tried to communicate with Pearse, Connolly, Clarke, but couldn't. Afterward, those who obeyed MacNeill's counter-order had to fold their arms while those who disobeyed it got themselves killed. For that reason, many Sinn Fein and Volunteers now hate MacNeill and consider him a traitor."

Again she fell silent, and Roger became distracted. Eoin MacNeill a traitor! How stupid! He imagined the founder of the Gaelic League, the editor of the *Gaelic Journal*, one of the founders of the Irish Volunteers, who had dedicated his life to fighting for the survival of the Irish language and culture, accused of betraying his brothers and sisters for wanting to prevent a romantic uprising doomed to failure. In the prison where they had sent him he must be the object of abuse, perhaps that icy contempt Irish patriots used to punish the tepid and the cowardly. How bad that gentle, cultured university professor must feel, filled with love for the language, customs, and traditions of his country, torturing himself, wondering, *Did I do the wrong thing when I gave the counter-order? I wanted only to save lives, but have I contributed instead to the failure of the rebellion by sowing disorder and division among the revolutionaries?* He identified with Eoin MacNeill. They resembled each other in the contradictory positions that history and circumstances had placed them in. What would have happened if, instead of being detained in Tralee, he had managed to speak with Pearse, Clarke, and the other leaders of the military command? Would he have convinced them? Probably not. And now, perhaps, they'd also call him a traitor.

"I'm doing something I shouldn't do, darling," said Alice, forcing a smile. "Giving you only the bad news, the pessimistic view."

"Can there be any other after what has happened?"

"Yes, there is," the historian declared in a resolute voice, blushing. "I was also against this rising, in these circumstances. And yet . . ."

"And yet what, Alice?"

"For a few hours, a few days, an entire week, Ireland was a free country, darling," she said, and it seemed to Roger that Alice trembled with emotion. "An independent, sovereign republic, with a president and a provisional government. Austin hadn't arrived yet when Patrick Pearse came out of the Post Office and read the Proclamation of the Irish Republic and the creation of the constitutional government of the Republic of Ireland, signed by the seven. There weren't many people there, it seems. Those who were and heard him must have felt something very special, don't you agree, darling? I was opposed, as I've told you. But when I read that text I began to cry aloud, in a way I've never cried before. 'In the name of God and of the dead generations from which she receives her old tradition of nationhood, Ireland, through us, summons her children to her flag and strikes for her freedom . . .' You see, I've memorized it. And I've regretted with all my strength not having been there with them. You understand, don't you?"

Roger closed his eyes. He saw the scene, clear and vibrant. Outside the General Post Office, under an overcast sky that threatened rain, before a hundred or two hundred people armed with shotguns, revolvers, knives, pikes, cudgels, most of them men but also a good number of women in kerchiefs, rose the slender, graceful, sickly figure of Patrick Pearse, with his thirty-six years and his steely gaze, filled with a Nietzschean "will to power" that had always allowed him, especially from the time he was seventeen, joined the Gaelic League, and soon became its indisputable leader, to rise above every misfortune, sickness, repression, internal struggle, and give material form to his life's mystic dream—the armed uprising of the Irish against the oppressor, the martyrdom of the saints that would redeem an entire people—reading, in the messianic voice that the emotion of the moment magnified, the carefully chosen words that brought to a close centuries of occupation and servitude and initiated a new era in the history of Ireland. He listened to the religious, sacred silence that Pearse's words must have created in that corner of the center of Dublin, still intact because the shooting hadn't begun yet, and he saw the faces of the Volunteers who looked out from the windows of the Post Office and nearby buildings on Sackville Street taken by the rebels, to contemplate the simple, solemn ceremony. He listened to the clamor, the applause, the long-lives, the hurrahs with which, when the reading of the seven names that signed the Proclamation had concluded, the words of Patrick Pearse were rewarded by the people on the street, at the windows, on the roofs, and the brevity and intensity of the moment when

Pearse himself and the other leaders ended the celebration, explaining there was no time to lose. They had to return to their posts, fulfill their obligations, prepare to fight. He felt his eyes grow wet. He too had begun to tremble. In order not to cry, he said hurriedly: "It must have been very moving, of course."

"It's a symbol and history is made of symbols," Alice Stopford Green agreed. "It doesn't matter that they shot Pearse, Connolly, Clarke, Plunkett, and the rest of the signers of the Proclamation of the Republic. On the contrary. Those shootings have baptized this symbol with blood, giving it a halo of heroism and martyrdom."

"Exactly what Pearse and Plunkett wanted," said Roger. "You're right, Alice. I would have liked to be there with them too."

Just as she was inspired by the action outside the Post Office, Alice was moved that so many members of the rebel women's organization, Cumann na mBan, had taken part in the uprising. The Capuchin monk had seen that with his own eyes. In all the rebel centers women were charged by the leaders to cook for the combatants, but then, as skirmishes broke out, the importance of the action opened the fan of responsibilities for the militants of Cumann na mBan, whom the shooting, bombs, and fires tore out of improvised kitchens and turned into nurses. They bandaged the wounded and helped surgeons remove bullets, suture wounds, and amputate limbs threatened with gangrene. But perhaps the most important role of those women—adolescents, adults, those approaching old age—had been as couriers when, because of the increasing isolation of the rebel barricades and posts, it was indispensable to turn to the cooks and nurses and send them on their bicycles and, when those became scarce, on foot, to fetch and carry messages, oral or written reports (with instructions to destroy, burn, or eat those papers if they were wounded or captured). Brother Austin assured Alice that for the six days of the rebellion, in the midst of bombings and gunfire, explosions that demolished roofs, walls, and balconies and transformed the center of Dublin into an archipelago of fires and mountains of scorched, blood-stained rubble, he never stopped seeing those angels in skirts, going and coming, grasping the handlebars like Amazons on their mounts and pedaling furiously, serene, heroic, intrepid, defying the bullets, carrying the messages and reports that broke the quarantine that the British army tried to impose strategically on the rebels, isolating them before crushing them.

"When they could no longer serve as couriers because troops were occupying the streets and traffic was impossible, many took the revolvers and rifles of their husbands, fathers, and brothers and fought as well," said Alice. "Along with them, Constance Markievicz showed that not all women belong to the weaker sex. Many fought as she did and died or were wounded with their weapons in their hands."

"Do you know how many?"

Alice shook her head. "There are no official figures. Those that are mentioned are pure fantasy. But one thing is certain. They fought. The British soldiers who detained them and dragged them to the barracks at Richmond and to Kilmainham Prison know it. They wanted to subject them to courts martial and shoot them too. I know from a very good source: a minister. The British cabinet was terrified, and with reason, to think that if they began shooting women, all of Ireland would be up in arms this time. Prime Minister Asquith himself telegraphed the military chief in Dublin, Sir John Maxwell, categorically forbidding him to shoot a single woman. That's how Constance Markievicz's life was saved. A court martial condemned her to death but the sentence has been commuted to life imprisonment due to pressure from the government."

But it hadn't all been enthusiasm, solidarity, and heroism in the civilian population of Dublin during the week of fighting. The Capuchin monk witnessed looting in the shops and stores on Sackville Street and other centrally located streets, committed by vagrants, petty criminals, or simply the poor from marginal neighborhoods, which put the leaders of the IRB, the Volunteers, and the Citizen Army in a difficult position, since they had not foreseen this delinquent deviation in the rebellion. In some cases the rebels tried to stop the sacking of hotels, even firing shots in the air to frighten away the looters devastating the Gresham Hotel, but in others they left them alone, confused by how these humble, hungry people, in whose interests they thought they were fighting, confronted them in a fury to be allowed to rob the elegant stores in the city.

Not only thieves confronted the rebels on the streets of Dublin. So did many mothers, wives, sisters, and daughters of the police and soldiers the insurgents had attacked, wounded, or killed during the Rising, sometimes large groups of fearless women agitated by grief, desperation, and rage. In some cases these women even attacked rebel outposts, insulting, stoning, and spitting at the combatants, cursing them and calling them murderers. That had been the most difficult trial for those who believed they had justice, goodness, and truth on their side: discovering that those confronting them were not the enemy dogs of Empire, the soldiers of the army of occupation, but humble Irish women blinded by suffering, who did not see in them the liberators of their country but the murderers of their loved ones, Irishmen like themselves whose only crime was being poor and taking up the trade of soldier or policeman, the way the poor of this world have always earned their living.

"Nothing is black and white, darling," Alice remarked. "Not even in so just a cause. Here too those confused grays appear that cloud everything."

Roger agreed. What his friend had just said applied to him. No matter how cautious one was in planning actions with the greatest lucidity, life, more complex than any calculation, made schemes explode and replaced them with uncertain, contradictory situations. Wasn't he a living example of those ambiguities? His interrogators, Reginald Hall and Basil Thomson, believed he came from Germany to lead a rising whose leaders hid it from him until the last moment because they knew he thought it could not succeed. Could you ask for greater incongruities?

Would demoralization now spread among the nationalists? Their best cadres were dead, shot, or in prison. Rebuilding the independence movement would take years. The Germans, whom so many of the Irish, like him, trusted, had turned their backs. Years of sacrifice and perseverance dedicated to Ireland, irremediably lost. And he, here in an English prison, waiting for the outcome of a petition for clemency that probably would be turned down. Wouldn't it have been better to die there, with the poets and mystics, shooting and being shot at? His death would have had a rounded meaning instead of an equivocal ending on the gallows, like a common criminal. Poets and mystics. That's what they were and that's how they had acted, choosing as the focus of the rebellion not a barracks or Dublin Castle, the citadel of colonial power, but a civilian building, the Post Office, recently renovated. Chosen by civilized citizens, not politicians or soldiers. They wanted to win over the population before defeating the English soldiers. Hadn't Joseph Plunkett told him so clearly in their discussions in Berlin? A rebellion of poets and mystics longing for martyrdom to shake the sleeping masses who believed, as John Redmond did, in the pacific way and the good will of the Empire to achieve the freedom of Ireland. Were they ingenuous or clairvoyant?

He sighed, and Alice patted his arm affectionately. "It's sad and exciting to talk about this, isn't it, darling Roger?"

"Yes, Alice. Sad and exciting. At times I feel enraged at what they did. Other times, I envy them with all my soul, and my admiration for them has no limits."

"The truth is, all I do is think about this. And about how much I need you, Roger," said Alice, taking him by the arm. "Your ideas, your lucidity, would help me to see the light in the midst of so much darkness. Do you know something? Not now, but some time soon, something good will come out of everything that's happened. There are already signs."

Roger agreed without understanding completely what the historian meant.

"For the present, the followers of John Redmond are losing more strength every day throughout Ireland," she added. "We, who were in the minority, now have the majority of the Irish people on our side. You may think it's a lie, but I swear to you it isn't. The shootings, the courts martial, the deportations are doing us a great service."

Roger noticed that the sheriff, always with his back to them, moved as if he were going to turn and order them to be quiet. But again he didn't do it. Alice seemed optimistic now. According to her, perhaps Pearse and Plunkett were not so misguided. Because every day in Ireland, in the streets, churches, neighborhood associations, and guilds, spontaneous demonstrations of sympathy for the martyrs, those who had been shot or sentenced to long prison terms, were multiplying, along with shows of hostility toward the police and soldiers of the British army. They were the object of insults and taunts from passers-by, to the extent that the military government ordered police and soldiers to always patrol in groups, and when they weren't on duty to dress in civilian clothes, because the people's hostility was demoralizing to the forces of law and order.

According to Alice, the most notable change was in the Catholic Church. The hierarchy and most of the clergy always were closer to the pacifist and gradualist theses, more in favor of Home Rule for Ireland and John Redmond and his followers in the Irish Parliamentary Party than the separatist radicalism of Sinn Fein, the Gaelic League, the IRB, and the Volunteers. But since the Rising, this had changed. Perhaps the religious conduct of the insurgents during the week of fighting had an influence on this. The testimonies of priests, among them Brother Austin, present at the barricades, buildings, and places transformed into rebel centers, were conclusive: they had celebrated Masses, offered confession and communion, and many combatants had asked for their blessing before beginning to fire. In all the strongholds the insurgents respected the leaders' categorical prohibition against consuming even a drop of alcohol. In the periods of calm, the rebels kneeled and prayed the rosary aloud. Not one of those executed, including James Connolly, who had proclaimed himself a socialist and was known as an atheist, had failed to request the assistance of a priest before facing the firing squad. In a wheelchair, still bleeding from the bullet wounds he had received in battle, Connolly was shot after kissing a crucifix handed to him by the chaplain of Kilmainham Prison. Since May, Masses of thanksgiving and homages to the martyrs of Holy Week proliferated throughout Ireland. There was not a Sunday when the priests in their sermons at Mass did not exhort the faithful to pray for the souls of the patriots executed and buried in secret by the British army. Sir John Maxwell had made a formal protest to the Catholic hierarchy, and instead of giving him explanations, Bishop O'Dwyer justified his priests, accusing the general of being "a military dictator" and acting in an anti-Christian manner with the executions and above all his refusal to return the bodies of those shot to their families. That the military government, sheltered by the suppression of guarantees under martial law, would have buried the patriots in secret to avoid their graves becoming centers of republican pilgrimage caused indignation even among sectors that until now had not seen themselves in sympathy with the radicals.

"In short, the papists gain more ground every day and we Anglican nationalists are shrinking like *La Peau de chagrin*, that novel by Balzac. All that's missing is for you and me to convert to Catholicism too, Roger," Alice joked.

"I already practically have," replied Roger. "And not for political reasons."

"I never would. Don't forget, my father was a clergyman in the Church of Ireland," the historian said. "Your converting doesn't surprise me, I've seen it coming for some time. Do you remember how we joked with you at the gatherings in my house?"

"Those unforgettable gatherings," Roger said with a sigh. "I'm going to tell you something. Now, with so much free time to think, on many days I've added it up: where and when was I happiest? At the Tuesday gatherings, in your house on Grosvenor Road, dear Alice. I never told you, but I would leave those meetings in a state of grace. Exalted and happy. Reconciled with life. Thinking: 'What a shame I didn't study, didn't go to university.' Listening to you and your friends, I felt as distant from culture as the natives of Africa or Amazonia."

"Something similar happened to me and them with you, Roger. We envied your travels, your adventures, your having lived so many different lives in those places. I once heard Yeats say: 'Roger Casement is the most universal Irishman I've known. A real citizen of the world.' I don't think I ever told you that."

They recalled a discussion about symbols, years earlier in Paris, with Herbert Ward. He had shown them the recent casting of one of his sculptures he was very pleased with: an African sorcerer. In fact, it was a beautiful piece that, in spite of its realistic character, showed everything secret and mysterious in the man, his face covered with cuts, armed with a broom and a skull, conscious of the powers conferred upon him by the divinities of the forest, streams, and animals in whom the men and women of the tribe trusted blindly to save them from spells, diseases, fears, and to put them in touch with the afterlife.

"We all carry inside us one of these ancestors," said Herbert, pointing at the bronze sorcerer who, with half-closed eyes, seemed enraptured in one of those dreams into which infusions of herbs plunged him. "The proof? The symbols we pay homage to with reverential respect. Coats of arms, flags, crosses."

Roger and Alice disagreed, claiming that symbols should not be seen as anachronisms from the irrational era of humanity. On the contrary, a flag, for example, was the symbol of a community that felt solidarity and shared beliefs, convictions, customs, respecting individual differences and discrepancies that did not destroy but strengthened the common denominator. Both confessed that seeing an Irish republican flag waving in the wind always moved them. How Herbert and Sarita had mocked them for that statement.

Alice, when she learned that while Pearse read the Proclamation of the Republic, a good number of Irish republican flags had been raised on the roofs of the Post Office and Liberty Hall, and then saw the photos of buildings occupied by the rebels in Dublin, like the Hotel Metropole and the Imperial, with flags at the windows and parapets that blew in the wind, had felt a lump in her throat. That must have caused endless joy in those who experienced it.

Later she also learned that in the weeks before the insurrection, while the Volunteers were preparing homemade bombs, sticks of dynamite, grenades, pikes, and bayonets, the members of Cumann na mBan, the women's auxiliary, were gathering medicines, bandages, disinfectants, and sewing the tricolor flags that erupted on the morning of Monday, April 24, on the roofs of central Dublin. The house of the Plunketts in Kimmage had been the most active workshop for weapons and flags for the uprising.

"It was a historic event," Alice declared. "We abuse words. Politicians especially apply the word 'historic' to any piece of foolishness. But those republican flags in the sky of old Dublin were historic. It will always be remembered with great fervor. A historic event. It has gone around the world, darling. In the United States many papers published it on the front page. Wouldn't you have liked to see it?"

Yes, he would have liked to see that too. According to Alice, more and more people on the island were defying the prohibition and placing republican flags on the facades of their houses, even in Belfast and Londonderry, pro-British citadels.

On the other hand, in spite of the war on the Continent, with disturbing news every day—military actions produced dizzying numbers of victims and the outcome was still uncertain—in England many people were prepared to help those deported from Ireland by the military authorities. Hundreds of men and women considered subversive had been expelled and were now scattered throughout England, ordered to settle in remote localities and, in the great majority of cases, without resources to survive. Alice, who belonged to humanitarian associations that were sending them money, foodstuffs, and clothing, told Roger they had no difficulty collecting funds and help from the general public. In this too the participation of the Catholic Church had been important.

Among the deportees were dozens of women. Many of them—Alice had spoken personally with some—in the midst of their solidarity, held a certain rancor toward the commanders of the rebellion who had made it difficult for women to collaborate with the insurgents. And yet almost all of the commanders, willingly or not, eventually admired the women in the strongholds and made use of them. The only one who flatly refused to admit women into Boland's Mill and all the neighboring territory controlled by his companies was Éamon de Valera. His arguments irritated the militants of Cumann na mBan because they were conservative: a woman's place was in the home and not on the barricade, and her natural tools were the distaff, pots and pans, flowers, needle and thread, not the pistol or the rifle. And her presence could distract the combatants who, to protect her, would neglect their obligations. The tall, thin professor of mathematics, leader of the Irish Volunteers, with whom Roger had often spoken and maintained an abundant correspondence, was condemned to death by one of those secret, hasty courts martial that tried the leaders of the Rising. But he was saved at the last minute. At the moment when, having confessed and taken communion, he waited with complete serenity, a rosary between his fingers, to be taken to the back wall of Kilmainham Gaol where the shootings took place, the court decided to commute the death sentence to life imprisonment. According to rumors, the companies under the command of Éamon de Valera, in spite of his complete lack of military training, acted with great efficiency and discipline, inflicting a good number of losses on the enemy. They were the last to surrender. But the rumors also said the tension and sacrifices of those days had been so harsh that at one moment his subordinates in the station where his command post operated thought he was losing his mind because of his erratic behavior. His was not the only case. In the rain of lead and fire, without sleep, food, or water, some had gone mad or suffered nervous breakdowns at the barricades.

Roger had become distracted, recalling the elongated silhouette of Éamon de Valera, his solemn, ceremonious speech. He noticed that Alice was referring now to a horse, with feeling and tears in her eyes. The historian had a great love for animals, but why did this one affect her in so special a way? Gradually he understood that her nephew had told her the story. It dealt with the horse of one of the British lancers who, on the first day of the insurrection, charged the Post Office and were driven back, losing three men. The horse was shot several times and collapsed in front of a barricade, badly wounded. It neighed in terror and piercing pain. It managed at times to stand, but weakened by loss of blood, fell again after attempting to walk a few steps. Behind the barricade an argument broke out between those who wanted to kill it so it wouldn't suffer any more and those who opposed this, thinking it would recover. Finally, they shot it. It took two rifle rounds to put an end to its agony.

"It wasn't the only animal that died on the streets," said Alice, distressed. "Many died, horses, dogs, cats, innocent victims of human brutality. Many nights I have nightmares about them. Poor things. We humans are worse than animals, aren't we, Roger?"

"Not always, darling. I assure you some are as ferocious as we are. I'm thinking about snakes, for example, whose venom kills you slowly, as you gasp for breath. And the candirú fish of the Amazon that enters your body through the anus and causes hemorrhages. In short . . ."

"Let's talk about something else," said Alice. "Enough of war, battles, the wounded, and the dead."

But a moment later she told Roger it was amazing how support for Sinn Fein and the IRB was growing among the hundreds of Irish deported and brought to English prisons. Even moderates and independents, and known pacifists, were affiliating with these radical organizations. And a great number of petitions were appearing all over Ireland asking for amnesty for the condemned. In the United States too, in all the cities where there were Irish communities, protest demonstrations continued against the excesses of the repression following the Rising. John Devoy had done fantastic work and succeeded in having the best of North American society, from artists and entrepreneurs to politicians, professors, and journalists, sign the petitions for amnesty. The House of Representatives approved a motion, written in very severe terms, condemning the summary death sentences for adversaries who had surrendered their weapons. In spite of the defeat, things had not gotten worse with the Rising. In terms of international support, the situation had never been better for the nationalists.

"The visit has run over time," the sheriff interrupted. "You have to say goodbye now."

"I'll get another permit, I'll come to see you before . . ." Alice said and then fell silent, standing up. She had turned very pale.

"Of course, Alice dear," Roger agreed, embracing her. "I hope you do. You don't know how good it is for me to see you. How it calms me and fills me with peace."

But it didn't happen this time. He went back to his cell with a tumult of images in his mind, all related to the Holy Week rebellion, as if the memories and testimonies of his friend had taken him out of Pentonville Prison and thrown him into the midst of the street fighting, into the din of battle. He felt an immense nostalgia for Dublin, its buildings and red-brick houses, the tiny gardens protected by wooden fences, the noisy streetcars, the misshapen neighborhoods of precarious dwellings and impoverished, barefoot people surrounding islands of affluence and modernity. How did all that look after artillery fire, incendiary bombs, collapsed buildings? He thought of the Abbey Theatre, the Olympia, the warm, fetid bars smelling of beer, the conversations throwing off sparks. Would Dublin be again what it once was?

The sheriff didn't offer to take him to the showers and he didn't ask him to. The jailer looked so dejected, his expression so detached and absent, he didn't want to bother him. It made him unhappy to see the man suffering in this way, saddened he could do nothing to lift his spirits. Violating regulations, the sheriff had come twice to his cell to talk at night, and each time Roger had agonized at not being able to give Mr. Stacey the serenity he was searching for. The second time, like the first, he had spoken only of his son Alex and his death in combat against the Germans in Loos, the unknown place in France he referred to as if it were a cursed spot. Once, after a long silence, the jailer confessed to Roger how bitter the memory was of the time he whipped Alex, still a little boy, for stealing a pastry from the bakery on the corner. "It was wrong and should have been punished," said Mr. Stacey, "but not so harshly. Whipping a young boy like that was unpardonable cruelty." Roger tried to reassure him, reminding him that he and his siblings, including his sister, were sometimes hit by Captain Casement, his father, and they had never stopped loving him. But was Mr. Stacey listening to him? He remained silent, ruminating on his pain, his respiration deep and agitated.

When the jailer closed the cell door, Roger lay down on his cot. He sighed, restless. The conversation with Alice had not done him good. Now he felt sadness at not having been there in his Volunteer uniform, Mauser in hand, taking part in the Rising, not caring that this armed action would end in a slaughter. Perhaps Patrick Pearse, Joseph Plunkett, and the others were right. It wasn't a question of winning but of resisting as much as possible. Of sacrificing oneself, like the Christian martyrs of heroic times. Their blood was the seed that germinated, did away with pagan idols and replaced them with Christ the Redeemer. The blood shed by the Volunteers would also bear fruit, it would open the eyes of the blind and win freedom for Ireland. How many companions and friends from Sinn Fein, the Volunteers, the Citizen Army, the IRB had been at the barricades, knowing it was a suicidal battle? No doubt hundreds, thousands, Patrick Pearse the first among them. He always believed martyrdom was the principal weapon of a just struggle. Didn't that form part of the Irish character, the Celtic inheritance? The Catholic ability to accept suffering was already in Cuchulain, in the mythic heroes of Éireann and their great feats, and by the same token, in the serene heroism of the saints his friend Alice had studied with so much love and knowledge: an infinite capacity for great gestures. An impractical spirit of the Irish, perhaps, but compensated for by immoderate generosity in embracing the most daring dreams of justice, equality, and happiness. Even when defeat was inevitable. No matter how rash the plan of Pearse, Tom Clarke, Plunkett, and the others, in those six days of unequal combat the spirit of the Irish people had come into view for the world to admire: indomitable in spite of so many centuries of servitude, idealistic, fearless, ready for anything in a just cause. How different from the attitude of those compatriots who were prisoners in the Limburg camp, blind and deaf to his exhortations. Theirs was the other face of Ireland: the face of the submissive, those who, because of centuries of colonization, had lost the valiant spark that brought so many women and men to the barricades of Dublin. Had he made another mistake in his life? What would have happened if the German weapons on the *Aud* had reached the hands of the Volunteers on the night of April 20 in Tralee Bay? He imagined hundreds of patriots on bicycles, in automobiles and carts, on mules and donkeys, spreading out under the stars and distributing weapons and ammunition throughout the territory of Ireland. Would the twenty thousand rifles, ten machine guns, and five million rounds of ammunition in the hands of the insurgents have changed things? At least the battles would have lasted longer, the rebels would have defended themselves better and inflicted more losses on the enemy. Happily he noted he was yawning. Sleep would erase those images and calm his disquiet. He thought he was sinking.

He had a pleasant dream. His mother appeared and disappeared, smiling, beautiful, and graceful in her wide straw hat, a ribbon hanging from it that floated in the breeze. A coquettish flowered parasol protected the whiteness of her cheeks from the sun. Anne Jephson's eyes were fixed on him and Roger's were fixed on her and nothing and no one seemed capable of interrupting their silent, tender communication. But suddenly Captain Roger Casement appeared in the grove wearing his resplendent Light Dragoons uniform. He looked at Anne Jephson with eyes that showed an obscene greed. So much vulgarity offended and frightened Roger. He didn't know what to do. He didn't have the strength to prevent what would happen or to start running and rid himself of that horrible presentiment. With tears in his eyes, trembling with terror and indignation, he saw the captain lift up his mother. He heard her give a scream of surprise and then a forced, complaisant little laugh. Trembling with disgust and jealousy, he saw her kick in the air, showing her slim ankles, while his father ran, carrying her among the trees. They were becoming lost from sight in the grove and their laughter tapered off until it disappeared. Now he heard the wind sighing and the warbling of the birds. He didn't cry. The world was cruel and unjust, and rather than suffering like this, it would be better to die.

The dream went on for a long while, but when he woke, still in darkness, minutes or hours later, Roger no longer remembered its outcome. Not knowing the time disturbed him again. At times he forgot, but the slightest uneasiness, doubt, or worry made the piercing distress of not knowing what moment of the day or night he was in produce ice in his heart, the feeling of having been expelled from time, of living in a limbo where before, now, afterward did not exist.

A little more than three months had passed since his capture, and he felt as if he had spent years behind bars, in an isolation in which day by day, hour by hour, he was losing his humanity. He didn't tell Alice, but if he once had been encouraged by the hope the British government would accept the petition for clemency and commute the death penalty to imprisonment, he had lost it now. In the climate of rage and desire for vengeance in which the Easter Rising had placed the Crown, in particular the military, England needed an exemplary punishment for the traitors who saw in Germany, the enemy against whom the Empire was fighting in the fields of Flanders, Ireland's ally in her struggle for emancipation. The strange thing was that the cabinet had put off the decision for so long. What were they waiting for? Did they want to prolong his agony, making him pay for his ingratitude toward the country that decorated him and knighted him and which he had repaid by conspiring with its adversary? No, in politics feelings didn't matter, only interest and profit. The government must be coldly evaluating the advantages and damages his execution would bring. Would it serve as a warning? Would the government's relations with the Irish people worsen? The campaign to discredit him claimed no one would cry over this human disgrace, this degenerate that decent society would be rid of thanks to the gallows. It was stupid to have left those diaries for anyone to find when he went to the United States. A piece of negligence that the Empire would make very good use of and that for a long time would cloud the truth of his life, his political conduct, and even his death.

He fell back to sleep. This time, instead of a dream, he had a nightmare he hardly remembered the next morning. In it there appeared a little bird, a canary with a clear voice martyrized by the bars of the cage in which it was enclosed. This could be seen in the desperation with which it beat its small golden wings unceasingly, as if with this movement the bars would widen and let it leave. Its eyes moved constantly in their sockets, pleading for commiseration. Roger, a boy in short pants, told his mother that cages shouldn't exist, or zoos, and animals always ought to live in freedom. At the same time, something secret was happening, a danger was approaching, something invisible that his sensibility detected, something insidious, treacherous, already there and prepared to strike. He was perspiring, trembling like a small sheet of paper.

He woke, so agitated he could barely breathe. He was choking. His heart was pounding so hard it perhaps was the beginning of a heart attack. Should he call the guard on duty? He stopped immediately. What could be better than dying here, on his cot, a natural death that would free him from the gallows? Moments later his heart calmed down and he could breathe again normally.

Would Father Carey come today? He wanted to see him and have a long conversation about subjects and concerns that had a great deal to do with the soul, religion, and God, and very little to do with politics. And immediately, as he became more tranquil and began to forget his recent nightmare, he recalled his last meeting with the prison chaplain and the moment of sudden tension that filled him with anxiety. They were talking about his conversion to Catholicism. Father Carey told him once again he shouldn't talk about "conversion," for having been baptized as a child, he had never left the Church. The act would be a reactualization of his status as a Catholic, something that didn't need any formal step. In any case—and at that moment, Roger noticed that Father Carey hesitated, searching carefully for words to avoid offending him—His Eminence Cardinal Bourne had thought that if it seemed suitable to Roger, he could sign a document, a private text between him and the Church, expressing his will to return, a reaffirmation of his status as a Catholic and at the same time a testimony of renunciation and repentance for old errors and faults.

Father Carey could not hide how uncomfortable he felt.

There was silence. Then, Roger said softly: "I won't sign any document, Father Carey. My reincorporation into the Catholic Church should be something intimate, with you as the only witness."

"That's how it will be."

Another tense silence followed.

"Was Cardinal Bourne referring to what I suppose?" Roger asked. "I mean, the campaign against me, the accusations concerning my private life. Is that what I should atone for in a document in order to be readmitted to the Catholic Church?"

Father Carey's breathing had become more rapid. Again he searched for words before responding.

"Cardinal Bourne is a good and generous man, with a compassionate spirit," he finally stated. "But don't forget, Roger, you have on your shoulders the responsibility to watch over the good name of the Church in a country where Catholics are a minority and there are still those who foment great phobias concerning us."

"Tell me frankly, Father Carey: has Cardinal Bourne made it a condition of my being readmitted to the Catholic Church that I sign a document repenting of the vile, vicious things I'm accused of in the press?"

"It isn't a condition, merely a suggestion," said the cleric. "You can accept it or not and that won't change anything. You were baptized. You're a Catholic and will go on being one. Let's not talk about this matter any further."

And in fact, they spoke no more about it. But the thought of that dialogue returned periodically and led him to wonder whether his desire to return to the Church of his mother was pure or stained by the circumstances of his situation. Wasn't it an act decided for political reasons? To show his solidarity with the Irish Catholics in favor of independence and his hostility to the minority, most of them Protestant, who wanted to continue as part of the Empire? In the eyes of God, what validity would a conversion have that at bottom obeyed nothing spiritual but his longing to feel sheltered by a community, to be part of a great tribe? God would see in that kind of conversion the gesticulations of a shipwrecked man.

"What matters now, Roger, is not Cardinal Bourne, or me, or the Catholics in England, or the ones in Ireland," said Father Carey. "What matters now is you. Your reencounter with God. There's the strength, the truth, the peace you deserve after an intense life filled with the many trials you've had to face."

"Yes, yes, Father Carey," Roger agreed eagerly. "I know. Exactly. I try to make myself heard, to reach Him. At some times, very few, it seems I have. Then I finally feel a little peace, that incredible calm. Like certain nights in Africa, with a full moon, the sky filled with stars, not a drop of wind moving the trees, the murmur of the insects. Everything so beautiful, so tranquil, I would always think: 'God exists. How, seeing what I see, could I even imagine He doesn't?' But at other times, most of the time, I don't see Him, He doesn't answer, He doesn't listen to me. In my life, most of the time, I've felt very alone. Nowadays it happens very frequently. But God's solitude is much worse. Then, I tell myself: 'God doesn't listen to me and won't listen to me. I'm going to die as alone as I've lived.' It's something that torments me day and night, Father."

"He is there, Roger. He listens to you. He knows what you feel, that you need Him. He will not fail. If there's something I can guarantee, that I'm absolutely sure of, it's that God will not fail you."

In the dark, stretched out on his cot, Roger thought Father Carey had imposed on himself a task as heroic as, or even more heroic than, that of the rebels at the barricades: bringing consolation and peace to desperate, destroyed creatures who were going to spend many years in a cell or were preparing themselves for the gallows. A terrible, potentially dehumanizing work that on many days must have driven Father Carey, above all at the beginning of his ministry, to despair. But he knew how to hide it. He always stayed calm and at every moment transmitted that feeling of comprehension and solidarity that did Roger so much good. Once they had talked about the Rising.

"What would you have done, Father Carey, if you had been in Dublin during those days?"

"Go to lend spiritual aid to whoever needed it, as so many priests did." He added that it wasn't necessary to agree with the rebels' idea that the freedom of Ireland would be achieved only with weapons to offer them spiritual support. Of course it wasn't what Father Carey believed; he had always urged a visceral rejection of violence. But he would have gone to hear confessions, give communion, pray for whoever asked him to, help the nurses and doctors. That is what a good number of male and female religious had done, and the hierarchy had supported them. Shepherds had to be where the flock was, didn't they?

All of that was true, but it was also true there was never enough room for the idea of God in the limited space of human reason. It had to be squeezed in with a shoehorn because it never fit completely. Roger and Herbert Ward had often spoken about this. "In matters concerning God, you have to believe, not reason," Herbert would say. "If you reason, God vanishes like a mouthful of smoke."

Roger had spent his life believing and doubting. Not even now, at the door of death, was he capable of believing in God with the resolute faith of his mother, his father, or his brothers and sister. How lucky those people were for whom the existence of the Supreme Being had never been a problem but a certainty, thanks to which the world was ordered and everything had an explanation and a reason for being. People who believed in that way would undoubtedly achieve a resignation in the face of death never known by those, like him, who had lived playing hide and seek with God. Roger recalled that he had once written a poem with that title: "Hide and Seek with God." But Herbert Ward assured him it was very bad, and he threw it away. Too bad. He would have liked to reread and correct it now.

Dawn was beginning to break. A small ray of light appeared between the bars on the high window. Soon they'd come to let him take away the bucket of urine and excrement and bring him breakfast.

He thought the first meal of the day arrived later than usual. The sun was already high in the sky and a cold, golden light illuminated his cell. He spent a long time reading and rereading the maxims of Thomas à Kempis regarding the mistrust of knowledge that makes human beings arrogant, and the waste of time it is to "ponder dark, mysterious things," ignorance of which we would not be reproached for at the Final Judgment, when he heard the large key turn in the lock and the cell door open.

"Good morning," said the guard, leaving the dark roll and cup of coffee on the floor. Or would it be tea today? For inexplicable reasons, breakfast frequently changed from tea to coffee or coffee to tea.

"Good morning," said Roger, standing and going to pick up the bucket. "Are you later today than usual or am I mistaken?"

Faithful to the order of silence, the guard didn't answer and it seemed he avoided looking him in the eye. He moved away from the door to let him pass, and Roger went out to the long, soot-filled passageway, carrying the bucket. The guard walked two paces behind him. He felt his spirits rise with the summer sun reflecting on the thick walls and stone floor, producing gleams that seemed like sparks. He thought about the parks of London, the Serpentine, the tall plane trees, poplars, and chestnut trees of Hyde Park, and how beautiful it would be to walk there right now, anonymous among the sportsmen riding horses or bicycles and the families with children who, taking advantage of the good weather, had come to spend the day outdoors.

In the deserted bathroom—they must have given instructions that his time for cleaning up would be different from the other prisoners'—he emptied and scrubbed the bucket. Then he sat on the toilet without success—constipation had been a lifelong problem—and, finally, removing the blue prison smock, he vigorously washed and scrubbed his body and face. He dried himself with the partially damp towel hanging from a screw eye. He returned slowly to his cell with the clean bucket, enjoying the sun that came into the passageway from the barred windows high on the wall and the noises—unintelligible voices, horns, steps, motors, squeaks—that gave him the impression of having re-entered time and disappeared as soon as the guard locked the cell door with a key.

The drink could be tea or coffee. He didn't care how tasteless it was, since the liquid, as it went down in his chest toward his stomach, did him good and relieved the acidity that always troubled him in the morning. He kept the roll in case he became hungry later.

Lying on his cot, he resumed reading *The Imitation of Christ*. At times he thought it childishly ingenuous, but then, when he turned the page, he encountered a thought that disturbed him and led him to close the book. He began to meditate. The monk said it was useful for a man to suffer sorrows and adversities from time to time because that reminded him of his condition: he was "exiled on this earth" and should not place any hope in the things of this world, only in those of the hereafter. It was true. The German monk in his convent at Agnetenberg, five hundred years earlier, had hit the nail on the head, expressed a truth that Roger had experienced first-hand. Or, to be specific, ever since his mother's death when he was a boy plunged him into an orphanhood he could never escape. That was the word that best described what he had always felt himself to be in Scotland, England, Africa, Brazil, Iquitos, Putumayo: an exile. For a good part of his life, he had boasted of his status as a citizen of the world, which, according to Alice, Yeats admired in him: someone who isn't from anywhere because he's from everywhere. For a long time he had told himself that this privilege granted him a freedom unknown to those who lived anchored in a single place. But Thomas à Kempis was right. He had never felt he was from anywhere because that was the human condition: exile in this vale of tears, a transient destiny until, with death and the hereafter, men and women would return to the fold, their nutritive source, where they would live for all eternity.

On the other hand, Thomas à Kempis's prescription for resisting temptation was naïve. Had that pious man, there in his solitary convent, ever been tempted? If he had, it couldn't have been so easy for him to resist and defeat the "devil who never sleeps and is always on the prowl hunting for someone to devour." Thomas à Kempis said no one was so perfect that he never felt temptation, and it was impossible for a Christian to see himself absolved from "concupiscence," the root of all the others.

He had been weak and succumbed to concupiscence many times. Not as many as he had written in his pocket diaries and notebooks, even though writing what he hadn't experienced, what he only had wanted to experience, was undoubtedly also a way—cowardly and timid—to have the experience and therefore surrender to temptation. Was he paying for that in spite of not really having enjoyed it except in the uncertain, ungraspable way fantasies were experienced? Would he have to pay for everything he hadn't done, had only desired and written about? God would know how to differentiate and surely would punish those rhetorical errors less severely than the sins he had really committed.

In any event, writing what he hadn't experienced, in order to pretend he had, already carried an implicit punishment: the sensation of failure and frustration in which the lying games in his diaries always ended (as did the real experiences, for that matter). But now those irresponsible games had placed in the hands of the enemy a formidable weapon to vilify his name and memory.

Yet it wasn't easy to know which temptations Thomas à Kempis was referring to. They could come so disguised, so deceptive, that they were confused with benign things, with esthetic enthusiasms. Roger recalled, in those distant years of his adolescence, that his first feelings for well-formed bodies, virile muscles, the harmonious slimness of adolescents, did not seem a malicious, concupiscent emotion but a manifestation of sensibility and esthetic enthusiasm. This is what he had believed for a long time. And this same artistic vocation was what had induced him to learn how to take photographs in order to capture those beautiful bodies on pieces of cardboard. At some moment he realized, when he was already living in Africa, that his admiration was not healthy or, rather, it was not only healthy but healthy and unhealthy at the same time, for those harmonious, sweating, muscular bodies, without a drop of oil, in which he could perceive the material sensuality of felines, produced in him, along with ecstasy and admiration, avidity, desire, a mad longing to caress them. This was how temptations became part of his life, revolutionized it, filled it with secrets, anguish, fear, but also with startling moments of pleasure. And remorse and bitterness, of course. At the supreme moment, would God do the arithmetic? Would He pardon him? Punish him? He felt curious, not terrified. As if it didn't concern him but was an intellectual exercise or conundrum.

And at that moment, he heard with surprise the heavy key entering the lock again. When the door of his cell opened, a sudden blaze of light came in, the strong sun that suddenly seemed to set August mornings in London on fire. Blinded, he was aware that three people had entered the cell. He couldn't make out their faces. He stood. When the door closed he saw that the person closest to him, almost touching him, was the governor of Pentonville Prison, whom he had seen only a few times. He was an older man, thin and wrinkled, dressed in a dark suit. His expression was grave. Behind him was the sheriff, as white as a sheet, and a guard who looked at the floor. It seemed to Roger that the silence lasted for centuries.

Finally, looking into his eyes, the governor spoke, at

first with a hesitant voice that became firmer as his statement proceeded: "I am fulfilling my duty to communicate to you that this morning, August 2, 1916, the Council of Ministers of the government of His Majesty the King has met, studied the petition for clemency presented by your lawyers, and rejected it in a unanimous vote of the ministers present. Consequently, the sentence of the court that tried and condemned you for high treason will be carried out tomorrow, August 3, 1916, in the courtyard of Pentonville Prison, at nine o'clock in the morning. According to established custom, for his execution the criminal does not have to wear the prison uniform and may put on the civilian clothes taken from him when he entered the prison, which will be returned to him. Similarly, I am obliged to communicate to you that the chaplains, the Catholic priest Father Carey and Father MacCarroll of the same faith, will be available to lend you spiritual assistance if you so desire. They will be the only persons with whom you may communicate. If you wish to leave letters for family members with your final arrangements, the establishment will provide writing materials. If you have some other request to make, you may do so now."

"At what time will I be able to see the chaplains?" Roger asked, and he thought his voice was hoarse and icy.

The governor turned to the sheriff, they exchanged a few whispered phrases, and the sheriff responded: "They'll come early in the afternoon."

"Thank you."

After a moment's hesitation, the three men left the cell and Roger listened to how the guard inserted the key in the lock.

14

Roger Casement initiated the period in his life when he would be most deeply immersed in the problems of Ireland by traveling to the Canary Islands in January 1913. As the ship sailed into the Atlantic, a great weight lifted. He was detaching himself from images of Iquitos, Putumayo, the rubber plantations, Manaus, the Barbadians, Julio C. Arana, the intrigues of the Foreign Office, and he retrieved a capability he could now focus on his country's affairs. He had already done what he could for the natives of Amazonia. Arana, one of their worst persecutors, would not raise his head again: a ruined man who had lost his good name, it was not impossible he would end his days in prison. Now he had to concern himself with other natives, the ones from Ireland. They too needed to free themselves from the Aranas exploiting them, though with weapons more refined and hypocritical than those of the Peruvian, Colombian, and Brazilian rubber barons.

But in spite of the liberation he felt on leaving London, both during the crossing and the month he stayed in Las Palmas, he was bothered by deteriorating health. The pains of arthritis in his hip and back occurred at any time of the day and night. Analgesics did not have the effect they'd once had. He had to spend hours lying in bed in his hotel or in a cold sweat in an armchair on the terrace. He moved with difficulty, always with a cane, and he could no longer take long excursions through the countryside or along the foothills as he had on earlier trips, for fear that in the middle of the walk the pain would paralyze him. His best memories of those weeks in early 1913 were the hours he spent submerged in Ireland's past, thanks to his reading of a book by Alice Stopford Green, *The Old Irish World*, in which history, mythology, legend, and traditions were combined to portray a society of adventure and fantasy, conflicts and creativity, in which a struggling, generous people grew in the face of a difficult nature, and celebrated courage and inventiveness with their songs, their dances, their hazardous games, their rites and customs: an entire patrimony that the English occupation came to shatter and attempt to annihilate, without complete success.

On the third day he was in the city of Las Palmas he went out, after supper, to walk around the port, a district filled with taverns, bars, and small hotels connected to brothels. In Santa Catalina Park, near Las Canteras beach, after examining his surroundings, he approached two young men with the air of sailors to ask for a light. He spoke with them for a moment. His imperfect Spanish, mixed with Portuguese, provoked hilarity in the boys. He suggested going for a drink, but one of them had a date, and so he was with Miguel, the younger one, a dark boy with curly hair just out of adolescence. They went to a narrow, smoky bar called Almirante Colón, Admiral Columbus, where an older woman was singing accompanied by a guitar player. After the second drink, Roger, sheltered by the semi-darkness of the place, extended a hand and rested it on Miguel's leg. The boy smiled, agreeing. Emboldened, Roger moved his hand toward his fly. He felt the boy's sex and a wave of desire ran through him from head to toe. For many months—*how many?* he thought, *three, six?*—he had been a man without sex, desires, or fantasies. It seemed to him that with his excitement, youth and love of life returned to his veins. "Can we go to a hotel?" he asked. Miguel smiled, not agreeing or refusing, but he didn't make the slightest effort to get up. Instead, he asked for another glass of the strong, spicy wine they had been served. When the woman finished singing, Roger asked for the bill. He paid and they left. "Can we go to a hotel?" he eagerly asked again in the street. The boy seemed undecided, or perhaps he delayed answering in order to make him beg and increase the fee he'd obtain for his services. Then Roger felt what seemed the slash of a knife in his hip that made him hunch over and lean against the railing of a window. This time the pain didn't come gradually, as it had on other occasions, but all at once, and more intense than usual. Like the slash of a knife, yes. He had to sit on the ground, doubled over. Frightened, Miguel hurried away, not asking what had happened or saying goodbye. Roger stayed there a long time, hunched over, eyes closed, waiting for the red-hot blade mortifying his back to lessen. When he could stand, he had to walk several blocks, very slowly, dragging his feet, until he found a car that would take him to the hotel. Only at dawn did the pain ease, allowing him to sleep. In his sleep, agitated and filled with nightmares, he suffered and felt pleasure at the edge of a precipice he was constantly in danger of falling into.

The next morning, as he had breakfast, he opened his diary and, writing slowly in a tiny hand, made love to Miguel several times, first in the darkness of Santa Catalina

Park hearing the murmur of the sea, and then in the foul room of a small hotel where they heard the howl of the ships' sirens. The dark boy rode him, mocking him, "You're an old man, that's what you are, a very old old man," and slapping him on the buttocks, which made him moan, perhaps in pain, perhaps with pleasure.

He did not attempt another sexual adventure for the rest of the month he spent in the Canaries, or during his trip to South Africa and the weeks he was in Cape Town and Durban with his brother Tom and sister-in-law Katje, paralyzed by the fear of experiencing again, because of his arthritis, a situation as ridiculous as the one that frustrated his encounter with the Canarian sailor in the Santa Catalina park. From time to time, as he had done so often in Africa and Brazil, he made love alone, scribbling on the pages of his diary, in a nervous, hurried hand, synthetic phrases, sometimes as unrefined as those lovers of a few minutes or hours whom he then had to gratify. These simulacra plunged him into a depressing stupor, and so he tried to space them, for nothing made him so conscious of his solitude and clandestine situation, which, he knew very well, would be with him until his death.

The enthusiasm he felt for Alice Stopford Green's book about old Ireland made him ask his friend for more reading material on the subject. The package of books and pamphlets Alice sent him arrived when he was about to sail on the *Grantully Castle* for South Africa, on February 6, 1913. He read day and night during the crossing and continued reading in South Africa, so that in spite of the distance, during those weeks he again felt very close to Ireland, the one of today, yesterday, and the remote one, a past he seemed to be making his own with the texts Alice selected for him. In the course of the voyage the pains in his back and hip diminished.

The encounter with Tom, after so many years, was difficult. Contrary to what Roger had thought when he decided to visit him, hoping the trip would bring him closer to his older brother and create between them an emotional connection that in fact had never existed, it confirmed instead that they were strangers. Except for the blood kinship, the two had nothing in common. All these years they had written to each other, generally when Tom and his first wife, Blanche Baharry, an Australian, had financial problems and wanted Roger to help them. He had never failed to do so, except when the loans his brother and sister-in-law asked for were too large for his budget. Tom's second marriage was to a South African, Katje Ackerman, and they had started a tourist business that wasn't going well. His brother looked older than he was and had turned into a prototypical South African, rustic, browned by the sun and life outdoors, with informal, somewhat coarse manners, and even the way he spoke English sounded much more South African than Irish. He wasn't interested in what was going on in Ireland, Great Britain, or Europe. His obsessive subject was the financial problems he faced in the lodge he had opened with Katje in Durban. They thought the beauty of the place would attract tourists and hunters, but not many came and the maintenance costs were higher than they had calculated. They'd had many hopes for this project and were afraid that if the situation continued, they would have to sell the lodge at a loss. Even though his sister-in-law was more amusing and interesting than his brother—she had a liking for the arts as well as a sense of humor—Roger eventually regretted having made the long journey only to visit the couple.

In mid-April he began the return to London. By then he felt more energetic and, thanks to the South African climate, the arthritis pains had eased. Now his attention was focused on the Foreign Office. He could not go on postponing the decision or requesting more unpaid leave. Either he would take up the consulate in Rio de Janeiro again, as his superiors had requested, or give up diplomacy. The idea of returning to Rio, a city he never liked, for in spite of the physical beauty of its surroundings, he'd always felt it was hostile to him, became intolerable. But that wasn't all. He did not want to live duplicitously again, work as a diplomat in the service of an empire he condemned emotionally and in principle. During the entire voyage back to England he made calculations: he had scant savings, but by living a frugal life—it was easy for him—and with the pension he would receive for the years he had accumulated as a functionary, he would manage. When he reached London, his decision was made. The first thing he did was go to the Foreign Office with his resignation, explaining that he was retiring from the service for reasons of health.

He remained in London for only a few days, arranging his retirement from the Foreign Office and preparing to travel to Ireland. He did this happily, but also with some anticipatory nostalgia, as if he were leaving England forever. He saw Alice a few times and his sister Nina, from whom, in order not to worry her, he hid Tom's financial losses. He tried to see Edmund D. Morel, who, curiously, had not answered any of the letters he had written in the past three months. But his old friend, the Bulldog, could not receive him, claiming trips and obligations that clearly were excuses. What could have happened to this companion in struggles whom he admired and loved so much? Why had he turned cold? What gossip or intrigue had estranged him? A short while afterward, Herbert Ward told him in Paris that Morel, having learned of the harshness with which Roger criticized England and the Empire with regard to Ireland, avoided seeing him in order not to have to tell him of his opposition to those kinds of political attitude.

"The thing is that even though you don't realize it, you've turned into an extremist," Herbert said, half in jest, half seriously.

In Dublin, Roger rented a small old house at 55 Lower Baggot Street. It had a minuscule garden with geraniums and hydrangeas that he trimmed and watered early in the morning. It was a quiet district of shopkeepers, artisans, and cheap stores where on Sundays families would go to Mass, the women dressed as if for a party and the men in their dark suits and caps, their shoes polished. In the corner pub that had cobwebs and a barmaid who was a dwarf, Roger would drink dark beer with the neighborhood greengrocer, tailor, and shoemaker, discuss the news of the day, and sing old songs. The fame he had achieved in England for his campaigns against the crimes in the Congo and Amazonia had spread to Ireland, and in spite of his desire to lead a simple, anonymous life, since his arrival in Dublin he found himself pursued by a great variety of people—politicians, intellectuals, journalists, and members of cultural clubs and centers—to give talks, write articles, and attend social gatherings. He even had to pose for a well-known painter, Sarah Purser. In her portrait of him, Roger appeared rejuvenated, with an air of certainty and triumph; he didn't recognize himself.

Once again he resumed his studies of old Irish. His teacher, Mrs. Temple, with a cane, spectacles, and a little veiled hat, came three times a week to give him Gaelic lessons and make assignments that she would correct afterward with a red pencil and rate with generally low grades. Why did he have so much difficulty learning the language of the Celts with whom he so wanted to identify? He had a facility for languages, had learned French, Portuguese, at least three African languages, and could make himself understood in Spanish and Italian. Why did the vernacular language to which he felt so connected elude him in this way? Each time he learned something with great effort, in a few days, sometimes in a few hours, he would forget it. From then on, without saying anything to anyone, least of all in political discussions when, out of principle, he maintained the opposite, he began to wonder whether the dream of people like Professor Eoin MacNeill and the poet and pedagogue Patrick Pearse was realistic, whether it wasn't chimerical to believe they could revive the language persecuted and made clandestine by the colonizer, turned into the language of a minority, almost extinguished, and transform it back into the mother tongue of the Irish. Was it possible that in the Ireland of the future English would recede and, thanks to the schools, the newspapers, the sermons of parish priests, and politicians' speeches, be replaced by the language of the Celts? In public Roger said yes, it was not only possible but necessary if Ireland was to recover its authentic personality. It would be a long process, taking several generations, but inevitable because only when Gaelic was again the national language would Ireland be free. Still, in the solitude of his study on Lower Baggot Street, when he faced the Gaelic composition exercises Mrs. Temple had left him, he told himself it was a useless effort. Reality had advanced too far in one direction to turn back. English had become the way to communicate, speak, be, and feel for an immense majority of the Irish, and trying to renounce it was a political whim whose only result would be a Babelic confusion that would culturally transform his beloved Ireland into an archeological curiosity, isolated from the rest of the world. Was it worth it?

In May and June of 1913 his quiet life of study was brusquely interrupted when, as the result of a conversation with a journalist from the *Irish Independent*, who spoke to him of the poverty and primitivism of the fishermen of Connemara, he decided on an impulse to travel to that region in the west of Galway where, he had heard, a more traditional Ireland was still intact and the people kept old Irish alive. Instead of a historical relic, in Connemara Roger encountered a spectacular contrast between the beauty of the sculpted mountains, the slopes swept by clouds, and virgin bogs at whose edges the dwarf horses native to the region loitered, and people who lived in ghastly poverty, without schools and without doctors, in total destitution. To make matters worse, some cases of typhus had just appeared. The epidemic could spread and cause havoc. The man of action in Roger, at times dormant but never dead, immediately went to work. He wrote an article in the *Irish Independent*, "The Irish Putumayo," and created an assistance fund to which he was the first donor and subscriber. At the same time, he pursued public action with the Anglican, Presbyterian, and Catholic Churches and various welfare associations, and urged physicians and nurses to go to the villages of Connemara as volunteers to support the scant official public health efforts. The campaign was successful. Many donations came in from Ireland and England. Roger made three trips to the region bringing medicines, clothing, and foodstuffs for the affected families. Moreover, he created a committee to provide Connemara with health dispensaries and construct elementary schools. Because of the campaign, in those two months he had exhausting meetings with clergymen, politicians, authorities, intellectuals, and journalists. He was surprised at the consideration with which he was treated, even by those who disagreed with his nationalist positions.

In July he returned to London to see his doctors, who had to inform the Foreign Office whether the reasons of health he claimed for giving up diplomacy were correct. Even though he didn't feel bad in spite of his intense activity in Connemara, he thought the examination would be a mere formality. But the physicians' report was more serious than he had expected: the arthritis in his spinal column, iliac joints, and knees had worsened. It could be relieved with rigorous treatment and a very quiet life, but it couldn't be cured. And he should not ignore the fact that if it progressed, it might leave him crippled. The Foreign Office accepted his resignation and in view of his condition, granted him a decent pension.

Before returning to Ireland, he decided to go to Paris, accepting an invitation from Herbert and Sarita Ward. He was happy to see them again and share the warm atmosphere of the African enclave of their house in Paris. All of it seemed like an emanation from the large studio, where Herbert showed him a new collection of his sculptures of Africa's men and women and some of its fauna. They were vigorous pieces in bronze and wood from the last three years, which he would exhibit in the fall in Paris. While Herbert showed them to him, recounting anecdotes, showing him sketches and small models of each one, abundant images returned to Roger's memory of the time when he and Herbert worked for the Stanley and Sanford expeditions. He had learned a great deal listening to Herbert describe his adventures in half the world, the picturesque people he met on his Australian wanderings, his vast reading. His intelligence was just as sharp, his spirit just as jovial and optimistic. His wife, Sarita, a North American heiress, was his spiritual twin, an adventurer as well, and something of a bohemian. They got along wonderfully. They traveled on foot through France and Italy. They had brought up their children with the same cosmopolitan, restless, curious spirit. Now the two boys were at boarding school in England, but they spent all their vacations in Paris. The little girl, Cricket, lived with them.

The Wards took him for supper to a restaurant in the Tour Eiffel where they could see the bridges over the Seine and the neighborhoods of Paris, and to the Comédie Française to see Molière's *Le Malade imaginaire*. But not everything was friendship, understanding, and affection in the days he spent with the couple. He and Herbert had disagreed about many things but their friendship had never cooled; on the contrary, disagreements vivified it. This time was different. One night they argued so sharply that Sarita had to intervene, obliging them to change the subject.

Herbert had always had a tolerant, somewhat amused attitude toward Roger's nationalism. But that night he accused his friend of embracing the nationalist idea in a way that was too exalted, not very rational, almost fanatical. "If the majority of the Irish want to separate from Great Britain, well and good," he said. "I don't think Ireland will gain very much by having a flag, a coat of arms, and a president of the republic. Or that her economic and social problems will be solved because of it. In my opinion, it would better to adopt the Home Rule advocated by John Redmond and his followers. They're Irish too, aren't they? And the great majority compared to those like you who want secession. Well, the truth is, none of it concerns me very much. But, on the other hand, I am concerned to see how intolerant you've become. Before, you gave reasons, Roger. Now you only shout with hatred against a country that's yours too, the country of your parents and brothers and sister. A country you've served so honorably all these years and that has recognized this, isn't that so? It has knighted you, given you the most important decorations in the kingdom. Doesn't that mean anything to you?"

"Should I become a colonialist in gratitude?" Roger interrupted. "Should I accept for Ireland what you and I rejected for the Congo?"

"Between the Congo and Ireland there's an astronomical distance, it seems to me. Or on the peninsulas of Connemara are the English chopping off the hands of the natives and destroying their backs with whippings?"

"The methods of colonization in Europe are more refined, Herbert, but no less cruel."

During his last days in Paris, Roger avoided touching again on the subject of Ireland. He didn't want his friendship with Herbert damaged. He told himself sadly that in the future, when he found himself increasingly involved in the political struggle, no doubt the distances between himself and Herbert would keep growing until, perhaps, they destroyed their friendship, one of the closest he'd had in his life. *Am I turning into a fanatic?* he would ask himself from then on, at times with alarm.

When he returned to Dublin at the end of the summer, he could not resume his study of Gaelic. The political situation had become agitated, and from the first moment he found himself drawn to take part in it. The Home Rule proposal which would have given Ireland a parliament and ample administrative and economic freedom, supported by John Redmond's Irish Parliamentary Party, had been approved in the House of Commons in November 1912. But the House of Lords rejected it two months later. In January 1913, in Ulster, a unionist citadel dominated by the local Anglophile and Protestant majority, the enemies of Home Rule led by Sir Edward Carson unleashed a virulent campaign. They formed the Ulster Volunteer Force, with more than forty thousand members enrolled. It was a political organization and a military force, prepared, if Home Rule was approved, to combat it with weapons. Redmond's Irish Parliamentary Party continued fighting for Home Rule. The second reading of the bill was approved in the House of Commons and again defeated in the House of Lords. On September 23 the Unionist Council approved reconstituting itself as the Provisional Government of Ulster, that is, separating from the rest of Ireland if Home Rule was passed.

Roger began writing in the nationalist press, now using his full name, criticizing the Ulster unionists. He denounced the abuses by the Protestant majority of the Catholic minority in the province, firing Catholic workers from factories and discriminating against the town councils of Catholic districts in budgets and jurisdictions. "When I see what is occurring in Ulster," he stated in one article, "I no longer feel Protestant." In all of them he deplored the fact that the attitude of the ultras divided the Irish into enemy bands, something with tragic consequences for the future. In another article he censured the Anglican clergy for protecting abuses against the Catholic community with their silence.

In spite of the fact that in his political conversations he appeared skeptical about the idea that Home Rule would free Ireland of her dependence, in his articles he allowed a glimmer of hope: if the law were approved without changes that would distort it, and Ireland had a parliament, elected her officials, and administered her revenues, she would be on the threshold of sovereignty. If that brought peace, what did it matter if her defense and diplomacy continued in the hands of the British Crown?

During this time he became closer friends with two Irishmen who had devoted their lives to the defense, study, and diffusion of the language of the Celts: Professor Eoin MacNeill and Patrick Pearse. Roger came to feel a great affinity for the radical, intransigent crusader for Gaelic and independence that Pearse was. He had joined the Gaelic League in his adolescence and dedicated himself to literature, journalism, and teaching. He had founded and directed two bilingual schools, St. Enda's for boys and St. Ita's for girls, the first institutions committed to recovering Gaelic as the national language. In addition to writing poems and drama, in pamphlets and articles he maintained his thesis that if the Celtic language were not regained, independence would be useless because Ireland would continue to be a colonial possession culturally. His intolerance in this area was absolute; in his youth he had even gone so far as to call Yeats—whom he would later admire without reservation—a "traitor" for writing in English. He was shy, a bachelor with a robust, imposing physique, a tireless worker with a small defect in one eye, and an exalted, charismatic speaker. When it wasn't a question of Gaelic or the emancipation, and he was with people he knew well, Patrick Pearse became a man crackling with humor and congeniality, talkative and extroverted, who sometimes surprised his friends by disguising himself as an old beggar woman who begged for alms in the center of Dublin, or a brassy young lady who immodestly strolled through the doors of taverns. But his life was characterized by monkish sobriety. He lived with his mother and brothers, didn't drink or smoke, and had no known love affairs. His best friend was his inseparable brother Willie, a sculptor and art teacher at St. Enda's. On the entrance wall of the school, surrounded by the tree-covered hills of Rathfarnham, Pearse had engraved a sentence the Irish sagas attributed to Cuchulain: "I care not though I were to live but one day and one night, if only my fame and deeds live after me." People said he was celibate. He practiced his Catholic faith with military discipline, to the extreme of fasting often and wearing a hair shirt. During this time, when he was so involved in the hectic activity, intrigues, and incitements of political life, Roger often told himself that perhaps the invincible affection Patrick Pearse inspired was due to his being one of the very few politicians he knew whom politics had not deprived of his sense of humor, and because his civic action was totally principled and disinterested: he cared about ideas and scorned power. But he was made uneasy by Pearse's obsession with conceiving of Irish patriots as the contemporary version of the early martyrs: "Just as the blood of the martyrs was the seed of Christianity, that of the patriots will be the seed of our liberty," he wrote in an essay. A beautiful phrase, Roger thought. But wasn't there something ominous in it?

For him, politics aroused contradictory feelings. On one hand, it made him live with unrecognizable intensity—at last he had thrown himself body and soul into Ireland!—but he was irritated by the sense of time wasted in interminable discussions that preceded and at times impeded agreements and action, by the intrigue, vanity, and meanness mixed with the ideals and ideas in daily tasks. He had heard and read that politics, like everything else connected to power, at times brought to light the best in a human being—idealism, heroism, sacrifice, generosity—but also the worst, cruelty, envy, resentment, pride. He confirmed that this was true. He lacked political ambitions, power did not tempt him. Perhaps for that reason, in addition to the prestige he carried along with him as a great international fighter against the abuse of indigenous peoples in Africa and South America, he had no enemies in the nationalist movement. That, at least, is what he believed, for everyone showed him respect. In the autumn of 1913, he mounted a platform to test his wings as a political orator.

At the end of August he had moved to the Ulster of his childhood and youth in an attempt to organize the Irish Protestants opposed to the pro-British extremism of Carson and his followers who, in their campaign against Home Rule, trained their military force in full view of the authorities. Roger helped to form a committee that called for a demonstration at Ballymoney Town Hall. It was agreed that he would be one of the speakers along with Alice Stopford Green, Captain Jack White, Alex Wilson, and John Dinsmore, a young activist. He gave the first public speech of his life on the rainy late afternoon of October 24, 1913, in a meeting room in Ballymoney Town Hall, before five hundred people. The night before, he was very nervous and wrote out his speech and memorized it. He had the feeling that when he went up on the platform he would be taking an irreversible step, that from now on there would be no turning back from the path he had started out on. In the future his life would be devoted to a task that, under the circumstances, would perhaps make him run as many risks as those he faced in the African and South American jungles. His speech, dedicated entirely to denying that the division of the Irish was both religious and political (nationalist Catholics and unionist Protestants) and calling for "unity in the diversity of creeds and ideals of all Irish men and women," was applauded enthusiastically. After the event, Alice Stopford Green, as she embraced him, whispered in his ear: "Let me play prophet. I see a great political future for you."

For the next eight months, Roger felt he did nothing else but go up on and come down from platforms, delivering speeches. He read them only at first, then he improvised, following a small outline. He traveled all over Ireland, attended meetings, encounters, discussions, round tables, some public, some secret, arguing, alleging, proposing, refuting, for hours and hours, often giving up meals and sleep. This total devotion to political action sometimes enthused him and sometimes produced in him a profound dejection. In dispirited moments the pains in his hip and back bothered him again.

During those months at the end of 1913 and the beginning of 1914, political tension continued to increase in Ireland. The division between the unionists of Ulster and the Home Rulers and those favoring independence became so exacerbated it seemed the prelude to civil war. In November 1913, in response to the formation of Carson's Ulster Volunteers, the Irish Citizen Army was established, whose principal organizer, James Connolly, was a union head and labor leader. This was a military group, and its public reason for being was to defend workers against the aggression of employers and authorities. Its first commander, Captain Jack White, had served with distinction in the British army before turning to Irish nationalism. In the founding ceremony a statement of support from Roger was read, for at the time his political friends had sent him to London to collect financial aid for the nationalist movement.

The Irish Volunteers emerged at almost the same time as the Irish Citizen Army through an initiative of Professor Eoin MacNeill, whom Roger supported. From the beginning the organization counted on the support of the clandestine Irish Republican Brotherhood, a militia which demanded Irish independence and was directed, from the innocent tobacco shop that served as his cover, by Tom Clarke, a legendary figure in nationalist circles. He had spent fifteen years in British prisons accused of terrorist activities with dynamite. Then he went into exile in the United States. From there he was sent by the leaders of the Clan na Gael to Dublin to establish a clandestine network, using his genius for organization. He had succeeded. At the age of fifty-two, he was healthy, tireless, and strict. His true identity had not been detected by British espionage. The two organizations would work in close, though not always easy, collaboration, and many adherents would be loyal to both at the same time. The Volunteers were also joined by members of the Gaelic League, militants from Sinn Fein, taking its first steps under the leadership of Arthur Griffith, affiliates of the Ancient Order of Hibernians, and thousands of independents.

Roger worked with Professor MacNeill and Patrick Pearse in writing the founding manifesto of the Volunteers and thrilled among the mass of those attending the first public meeting of the organization on November 25, 1913, at the Rotunda in Dublin. From the beginning, just as MacNeill and Roger proposed, the Volunteers was a military movement, dedicated to recruiting, training, and arming its members, who were divided into squads, companies, and regiments all over Ireland to be ready for any outbreak of fighting, something that, given the intemperate political situation, seemed imminent.

Roger committed himself to working tirelessly for the

Volunteers. In this way he became acquainted and established close friendships with its principal leaders, among whom were poets and writers like Thomas MacDonagh, who wrote plays and taught at the university, and the young Joseph Plunkett, disabled and suffering from lung disease who, in spite of his physical limitations, exhibited extraordinary energy: he was as Catholic as Pearse, a reader of the mystics, and one of the founders of the Abbey Theatre. Roger's activities in favor of the Volunteers occupied his days and nights between November 1913 and July 1914. He spoke every day at its meetings in the large cities, Dublin, Belfast, Cork, Derry, Galway, and Limerick, or in tiny villages and hamlets, before hundreds or barely handfuls of people. His speeches began calmly ("I'm a Protestant from Ulster who defends the sovereignty and liberation of Ireland from the English colonial yoke . . ."), but as he went on he became more impassioned and tended to conclude in epic transports. He almost always set off thunderous applause in the audience.

At the same time he collaborated in strategic planning for the Volunteers. He was one of the leaders most determined to equip the movement for the struggle for sovereignty that, he was convinced, would pass inevitably from the political plane to military action. To arm themselves they needed money, and it was crucial to persuade Irish lovers of freedom to be generous to the Volunteers.

This was how the idea of sending Roger to the United States was born. The Irish communities there had financial resources and could increase their assistance through a campaign to win over public opinion. Who better to promote it than a celebrated Irishman? The Volunteers decided to consult John Devoy, the leader of the powerful Clan na Gael which united the large Irish nationalist community in North America. Devoy, born in Kill in County Kildare, had been a covert activist since he was a young man and, accused of terrorism, was sentenced to fifteen years in prison but served only five. He had been in the Foreign Legion, in Algeria. In the United States he founded a newspaper, the *Gaelic American*, in 1903, and formed close ties to the North American establishment. As a consequence, the Clan na Gael had political influence.

While John Devoy studied the proposal, Roger was still dedicated to promoting the Irish Volunteers and their militarization. He became a good friend of Colonel Maurice Moore, inspector general of the Volunteers, whom he accompanied on his tours around the island to see how training was carried out and if the weapons caches were secure. At the request of Colonel Moore, he joined the general staff of the organization.

He was sent to London several times. A clandestine committee operated there, presided over by Alice Stopford Green who, in addition to collecting money, arranged in England and several European countries for the secret purchase of rifles, revolvers, grenades, machine guns, and ammunition, which she brought secretly into Ireland. At these London meetings with Alice and her friends, Roger observed that a war in Europe had stopped being a mere possibility and become a reality in progress: all the politicians and intellectuals who frequented the historian's evenings at Grosvenor Road believed Germany had already reached the same conclusion, and they didn't wonder whether there would be a war but when it would break out.

Roger had moved to Malahide, on the coast north of Dublin, though because of his political travels he spent few nights at home. Soon after he settled there, the Volunteers warned him the Royal Irish Constabulary had opened a file on him and that he was being followed by the secret police. One more reason for him to leave for the United States: he would be more useful there to the nationalist movement than if he remained in Ireland and was put behind bars. John Devoy indicated that the leaders of the Clan na Gael approved his coming. Everyone believed his presence would accelerate the collection of donations.

He agreed but delayed his departure for a project that intrigued him: a great celebration on April 23, 1914, of the nine hundredth anniversary of the Battle of Clontarf, when the Irish under Brian Boru defeated the Vikings. MacNeill and Pearse supported him, but the other leaders saw in this initiative a waste of time: why squander energy on an operation of historical archeology when the important thing was the present? There was no time for distractions. The project didn't materialize, and neither did another initiative of Roger's, a campaign to collect signatures asking that Ireland participate in the Olympic Games with its own team of athletes.

As he prepared for the journey, he continued speaking at meetings, almost always with MacNeill and Pearse, and sometimes Thomas MacDonagh, in Cork, Galway, Kilkenny. On St. Patrick's Day he stood on the platform in Limerick, addressing the largest public meeting he had ever seen in his life. The situation worsened day by day. The Ulster unionists, armed to the teeth, openly held marches and military maneuvers until the British government had to take action, sending more soldiers and sailors to the north of Ireland. Then the Curragh Mutiny took place, an episode that would have a significant effect on Roger's political ideas. At the height of the mobilization of British soldiers and sailors to put a stop to a possible armed action by the ultras of Ulster, General Sir Arthur Paget, commander-in-chief of Ireland, informed the English government that a good number of British officers at the Curragh military camp had told him that if he ordered them to attack Sir Edward Carson's Ulster Volunteers, they would ask to resign their commissions. The English government gave in to the blackmail and none of the officers was sanctioned.

This event shored up Roger's conviction: Home Rule would never be a reality because in spite of all its promises, the English government, whether conservative or liberal, would never accept it. John Redmond and those Irish who believed in Home Rule would be frustrated time and time again. This was not the solution for Ireland. Independence was, pure and simple, and that would never be granted willingly. It would have to be seized through political and military action, at the cost of great sacrifices and great heroism, just as Pearse and Plunkett wanted. That was how all the free peoples in the world had obtained their emancipation.

In April 1914, the German journalist Oskar Schweriner arrived in Ireland. He wanted to write some articles on the poor of Connemara. Since Roger had been so active helping the villagers during the typhus epidemic, Schweriner sought him out. They traveled there together and visited the fishing villages and the schools and dispensaries that were beginning to operate. Then Roger translated Schweriner's articles for the *Irish Independent*. In conversations with the German reporter, who supported the nationalist cause, Roger reaffirmed the idea he'd had on his trip to Berlin, to connect Ireland's struggle for emancipation to Germany if an armed conflict broke out between her and Great Britain. With this powerful ally, there would be more possibilities of obtaining from England what Ireland with her limited means—a pygmy against a giant—would never achieve. Among the Volunteers the idea was well received: it wasn't novel, but the imminence of war gave it new currency.

Under these circumstances, it was learned that the Ulster Volunteers had succeeded in secretly bringing into Ulster, through the port of Larne, 216 tons of weapons. Added to the ones they already had, this shipment gave the unionist militias a power far superior to that of the nationalist Volunteers. Roger had to accelerate his departure for the United States.

He did, but first he had to accompany Eoin MacNeill to London to meet with John Redmond, the leader of the Irish Parliamentary Party. In spite of all the reversals, Redmond was still convinced that Home Rule would eventually be approved. He defended the good faith of the liberal British government. A stout, dynamic man, he spoke very quickly, machine-gunning his words. The absolute self-confidence he displayed helped increase the antipathy he inspired in Roger. Why was he so popular in Ireland? His position that Home Rule ought to be obtained in cooperation and friendship with England enjoyed the support of the majority of the Irish. But Roger was certain this popular confidence would begin to disappear as public opinion saw that Home Rule was an illusion used by the imperial government to keep the Irish deceived, demobilizing and dividing them.

What irritated Roger most at the meeting was Redmond's statement that if war broke out with Germany, the Irish ought to fight alongside England as a matter of principle and strategy: in this way they would gain the confidence of the English government and English public opinion, which would guarantee Home Rule in the future. Redmond demanded that twenty-five representatives of his party be on the executive committee of the Volunteers, something the Volunteers were resigned to accepting in order to maintain unity. But not even this concession changed Redmond's opinion of Roger Casement, whom he accused periodically of being a "radical revolutionary." In spite of this, during his final weeks in Ireland, Roger wrote two friendly letters to Redmond, exhorting him to act so that the Irish could remain united in spite of their eventual differences. He assured him that if Home Rule became a reality, he would be the first to support it. But if the English government, because of its vulnerability to the Ulster extremists, could not impose Home Rule, the nationalists ought to have an alternative strategy.

Roger was speaking at a meeting of the Volunteers in Cushendun on June 28, 1914, when the news came that a Serbian terrorist had assassinated Archduke Franz Ferdinand of Austria in Sarajevo. At that moment no one there attributed much importance to an episode that, a few weeks later, would be the pretext that unleashed the First World War. Roger's last speech in Ireland was given in

Carn on June 30. By now he was hoarse from speaking so much.

Seven days later he sailed, clandestinely, from the port of Glasgow on the ship *Cassandra*—the name was a symbol of what the future held for him—bound for Montreal. He traveled in second class, under an assumed name. He had also altered his clothing, generally elegant and now extremely modest, and his face, changing the way he combed his hair and cutting his beard. After so much time, he spent some tranquil days on board. During the crossing, he told himself in surprise that the agitation of recent months had the virtue of calming his arthritic pains. He practically had not suffered from them again, and when they did return they were more bearable than before. On the train from Montreal to New York, he prepared the report he would make to John Devoy and the other leaders of the Clan na Gael regarding the state of things in Ireland and the need of the Volunteers for financial assistance to buy weapons, for considering how the political situation was evolving, violence could break out at any moment. Then too, the war would open an exceptional opportunity for Irish supporters of independence.

When he reached New York on July 18, he stayed at the Belmont, a modest hotel frequented by Irishmen. That same day, walking along a street in the burning heat of the New York summer, his encounter occurred with the Norwegian, Eivind Adler Christensen. A casual encounter? That's what he believed then. Not for an instant did he suspect it could have been planned by the British espionage services who had been following him for months. He was certain his precautions to leave Glasgow in secret had been sufficient. And he had no suspicion at the time of the cataclysm this young man of twenty-four would cause in his life: his physical appearance was not at all that of the helpless vagrant half dead of hunger he claimed to be. In spite of his shabby clothing, Roger thought he was the most beautiful, attractive man he had ever seen. As he watched him eating the sandwich and sipping the drink he had invited him to have, he was confused, ashamed, because his heart had begun to pound and he felt an excitement in his blood he had not experienced for some time. He, always so careful in his gestures, so rigid an observer of good manners, was on the point several times that afternoon and evening of violating good form and following the inducements assaulting him to caress those muscular arms with their golden down or to grasp Eivind's narrow waist.

When he learned that the young man had no place to sleep, he invited him to his hotel. He took a small room for him on the same floor as his. In spite of the accumulated fatigue of his long journey, that night Roger didn't close his eyes. He savored and suffered imagining the athletic body of his new friend immobilized by sleep, his blond hair tousled and that delicate face, with its very light blue eyes, resting on his arm, sleeping perhaps with lips open, showing his white, even teeth.

Having met Eivind Adler Christensen was so powerful an experience that the next day, at his first appointment with John Devoy, with whom he had important matters to discuss, that face and figure returned to his memory, distancing him for moments at a time from the small office where they talked, overwhelmed by the heat.

The old, experienced revolutionary, whose life resembled an adventure novel, made a strong impression on Roger. He carried his seventy-two years with vigor and transmitted an infectious energy in his gestures, movements, and way of speaking. Taking notes in a small notebook with a pencil whose point he periodically wet in his mouth, he listened to Roger's report on the Volunteers without interrupting, but when he stopped he asked innumerable questions, requesting details. Roger marveled that John Devoy was so extensively informed about what went on in Ireland, including matters supposedly kept absolutely secret.

He was not a cordial man. He had been hardened by his years in prison, by clandestinity and struggle, but he inspired confidence, the sense that he was frank, honest, and held granite-like convictions. In that talk and those they would have for the rest of the time he remained in the United States, Roger saw that he and Devoy coincided point by point in their opinions on Ireland. Devoy, too, believed it was too late for Home Rule, that now the only objective of Irish patriots was emancipation, and that armed actions would be an indispensable complement to negotiations. The English government would agree to negotiate only when military operations created a situation so difficult that granting independence would be a lesser evil for London. In this imminent war, approaching Germany was vital for the nationalists: her logistical and political support would give the independence movement greater efficacy. Devoy told him that in the Irish community in the United States, there was no unanimity in this matter. John Redmond's theses also had partisans here, even though the leadership of the Clan na Gael agreed with Devoy and Roger.

In the days that followed, Devoy introduced him to most of the organization's leaders in New York, as well as John Quinn and William Bourke Cockran, two influential North American lawyers who lent assistance to the Irish cause. Both had relationships with high circles in the executive branch and the US Congress.

Roger noted the good impression he made on the Irish communities when, at John Devoy's request, he began to speak at meetings and gatherings to collect funds. He was known for his campaigns in defense of the indigenous peoples of Africa and Amazonia, and his rational, emotive oratory reached everyone in the audience. At the end of the meetings where he spoke, in New York, Philadelphia, and other east-coast cities, contributions increased. The leaders of the Clan na Gael joked with him that at this rate they'd become capitalists. The Ancient Order of Hibernians invited him to be the main speaker at the largest meeting in the United States that Roger took part in.

In Philadelphia he met another of the great nationalist leaders in exile, Joseph McGarrity, a close collaborator of John Devoy's in the Clan na Gael. In fact, Roger was in his house when they heard the news of the successful unloading of fifteen hundred rifles and ten thousand rounds of ammunition for the Volunteers at Howth. The news provoked immense joy among the leaders and was celebrated with a toast. A short while later he learned that after the unloading, there was a serious incident at Bachelor's Walk between Irishmen and British soldiers of the King's Own Scottish Borderers Regiment, with three dead and more than forty wounded. Was the war beginning then?

In almost all his travels around the United States, at meetings of the Clan na Gael, and public events, Roger appeared accompanied by Eivind Adler Christensen. He introduced him as his assistant and confidant. He had bought him more presentable clothing and had brought him up to date on the Irish problem, about which the young Norwegian said he was totally ignorant. He was uncultured but not a fool, he learned quickly and proved very discreet at Roger's meetings with John Devoy and other members of the organization. If the presence of Christensen aroused their misgivings, they kept it to themselves, for they never asked Roger intrusive questions about his companion.

When Great Britain declared war on Germany on August 4, 1914, the closest circle of leaders of the Clan na Gael had already decided that Roger would leave for Germany. He would go as a representative of the supporters of independence to establish a strategic alliance in which the Kaiser's government would lend political and military assistance to the Volunteers. In return they would campaign against the enlistment of Irishmen in the British army, which the Ulster unionists as well as the followers of John Redmond defended. This project was discussed with a small number of leaders of the Volunteers, including Patrick Pearse and Eoin MacNeill, who approved it without reservation. The German embassy in Washington, to which the Clan na Gael had links, collaborated in the plans. The German military attaché, Captain Franz von Papen, came to New York and met twice with Roger. He expressed enthusiasm at the rapprochement among the Clan na Gael, the Irish IRB, and the German government. After consulting Berlin, he informed them that Roger Casement would be welcomed in Germany.

Roger expected the war, like almost everyone else, and as soon as the threat became a reality, he threw himself into action with the enormous energy he was capable of. His position in favor of the Reich was charged with an anti-British virulence that surprised his colleagues in the Clan na Gael, even though many of them were also wagering on a German victory. He had a violent argument with John Quinn, who had invited him to spend a few days at his luxurious residence, for affirming that this war was a plot caused by England's resentment and envy as a country in decadence faced with a vigorous power at the height of its industrial and economic development and with a growing population. Germany represented the future because it carried no colonial ballast, while England, the very incarnation of an imperial past, was condemned to extinction.

In August, September, and October of 1914, Roger, as during his best times, worked day and night, writing articles and letters, giving talks and speeches in which, with maniacal insistence, he accused England of being the cause of this European catastrophe and urged the Irish not to give in to the siren songs of John Redmond, campaigning for them to enlist. Meanwhile the Liberal government approved Home Rule in parliament but postponed putting it into effect until the war was over. The division within the Volunteers was inevitable. The organization had grown at an extraordinary rate, and Redmond and the Irish Parliamentary Party were in the large majority. More than 150,000 Volunteers followed him, while barely eleven thousand remained with Eoin MacNeill and Patrick Pearse.

None of this lessened the pro-German fervor of Roger Casement who, at every meeting in the United States, presented the Kaiser's Germany as the victim in this war and the best defender of western civilization. "It isn't love of Germany that speaks through your mouth but hatred of England," John Quinn said during their argument.

In September 1914, Roger published a small book in Philadelphia: *Ireland, Germany, and Freedom of the Seas: A Possible Outcome of the War of 1914*, a collection of his essays and articles favorable to Germany. The book would later be published in Berlin with the title *The Crime Against Europe*. His pronouncements in favor of Germany impressed the accredited diplomats of the Reich in the United States. The German ambassador in Washington, Count Johann von Bernstorff, traveled to New York to meet privately with him and the trio of leaders of the Clan na Gael, John Devoy, Joseph McGarrity, and John Keating. Captain Franz von Papen was also present. It was Roger, as agreed upon by his companions, who expounded the nationalists' request to the German diplomat: fifty thousand rifles and ammunition, which could be unloaded in secret at various Irish ports by Volunteers. They would be used in an anti-colonialist military uprising that would immobilize significant English military forces, which ought to be taken advantage of by the Kaiser's naval and military forces to unleash an offensive against the military garrisons on the English coast. To broaden pro-German feeling in Irish public opinion, it was indispensable for the German government to issue a statement guaranteeing that, in the event of victory, it would support the Irish desire for liberation from the colonial yoke. By the same token, the German government had to commit to giving special treatment to Irish soldiers who might be taken prisoner, separating them from the English and giving them the opportunity to join an Irish Brigade that would fight "alongside, but not inside" the German army against the common enemy. Roger would organize the brigade.

Count von Bernstorff, with his robust appearance, monocle, and chest covered with medals, listened attentively. Captain von Papen took notes. The ambassador had to consult Berlin, of course, but he added that the proposal seemed reasonable to him. And, in effect, a few days later, at a second meeting, he informed them that the German government was prepared to hold talks on the matter in Berlin, with Roger as the representative of the Irish nationalists. He gave them a letter asking the authorities to offer every assistance to Sir Roger during his stay in Germany.

He immediately began to prepare for his trip. He saw that Devoy, McGarrity, and Keating were surprised when he told them he would travel to Germany with his assistant, Eivind Adler Christensen. Since it had been planned, for reasons of security, that he would travel by ship from New York to Christiania, the Norwegian's help as a translator in his own country would be useful, and in Berlin as well, for Eivind also spoke German. He did not request additional funds for his assistant. The amount the Clan na Gael gave him for travel and housing—$3,000—would be enough for both of them.

If his New York comrades saw something strange in his determination to be accompanied to Berlin by the young Viking who remained mute at their meetings, they said nothing about it. They agreed without comment. Roger wouldn't have been able to take the trip without Eivind. With him a tide of youth, of hope, and—the word made him blush—of love had entered his life. It hadn't happened to him before. He'd had sporadic street adventures with people whose names, if they were their names and not mere nicknames, he forgot almost immediately, or with the phantoms his imagination, desires, and solitude invented on the pages of his diaries. But with the "beautiful Viking," as he called him when they were alone, he had the sensation during these weeks and months that, beyond pleasure, he had at last established a loving relationship that could endure and take him out of the solitude his sexual preference had condemned him to. He didn't talk about these things with Eivind. He wasn't ingenuous and often told himself the most probable thing, even the certain thing, was that the Norwegian was with him out of self-interest, because with Roger he ate twice a day, had a roof over his head, slept in a decent bed, had clothes and the security that, as he had confessed, he hadn't enjoyed for a long time. But in the end Roger discarded all precautions in his daily exchanges with the boy, who was attentive and affectionate with him, seemed to live to attend to him, handed him articles of clothing, was willing to take care of every errand. He always behaved respectfully toward him, even at the most intimate moments, maintaining distance, not allowing himself any abuse of confidence, any vulgarity.

They bought second-class passage on the *Oskar II* from New York to Christiania, which sailed in mid-October. Roger, who carried papers with the name James Landy, changed his appearance, cutting his hair close to the scalp and whitening his tanned complexion with creams. The ship was intercepted by the British navy on the high seas and escorted to Stornoway, in the Hebrides, where it was subjected to a rigorous search. But Roger's true identity was not detected. The couple reached Christiania safe and sound at nightfall on October 28. Roger had never felt better. If anyone had asked, he would have responded that in spite of all the problems, he was a happy man.

And yet, at the very hour and minute when he believed he had caught the will-o'-the-wisp—happiness—the most bitter period in his life was beginning, a failure, he would think afterward, that would cloud everything good and noble in his past. The day they arrived in the capital of Norway, Eivind told him he had been kidnapped for a few hours by strangers and taken to the British consulate, where he was interrogated about his mysterious companion. Roger naïvely believed him, and thought this episode offered a providential opportunity to demonstrate the artful deceptions and murderous intentions of the British authorities. In reality, as he would find out later, Eivind had gone to the consulate offering to sell him out. This matter only served to obsess Roger and make him waste weeks and months in useless measures and preparations that, in the end, brought no benefit to the Irish cause and undoubtedly were the butt of jokes in the Foreign Office and British Intelligence, where they must have viewed him as a pathetic novice conspirator.

When did his disillusionment begin with the Germany that, perhaps simply because of his rejection of England, he had begun to admire and call a model of efficiency, discipline, culture, and modernity? Not during his first weeks in Berlin. On the fairly bizarre trip from Christiania to the German capital, accompanied by Richard Meyer, who would be his intermediary to the Kaiser's Ministry of Foreign Relations, he was still filled with illusions, convinced Germany would win the war and her victory would be decisive for the emancipation of Ireland. His first impressions of the cold, rainy, fogbound city that Berlin was that autumn were good. Both the under-secretary of state for foreign relations, Arthur Zimmermann, and Count Georg von Wedel, chief of the British section at the chancellery, received him with amiability and were enthusiastic about his plans for a brigade composed of Irish prisoners. Both were advocates of the German government making a statement in favor of Irish independence. And in effect, on November 20, 1914, the Reich did just that, perhaps not in terms as explicit as Roger had hoped for, but clear enough to justify the position of those like him who defended an alliance of Irish nationalists with Germany. Still, by that date, in spite of his enthusiasm for the statement—undoubtedly one of his successes—and the fact that the secretary of state for foreign relations finally told him the military high command had ordered Irish prisoners of war to be placed in a single camp where he could visit them, Roger began to sense that reality would not yield to his plans but instead would do everything to make them fail.

The first hint that things were taking unexpected paths came when he learned, from the only letter from Alice Stopford Green he received in eighteen months—a letter that took a transatlantic parabolic detour to reach him, making a stop in New York, where the envelope, name, and address were changed—that the British press had reported his presence in Berlin. This had instigated an intense polemic between the nationalists who favored and those who opposed his decision to side with Germany in the war. Alice objected to it: she told him so in categorical terms. She added that many firm advocates of independence agreed with her. At most, said Alice, she could accept Irish neutrality in the European war but not making common cause with Germany. Tens of thousands of Irishmen were fighting for Great Britain: how would these compatriots feel knowing that noted Irish nationalists identified with the enemy firing cannon at them and gassing them in the trenches of Belgium?

Alice's letter had the effect of a lightning bolt. That the person he most admired, the one he thought agreed with him politically more than any other, should condemn what he was doing, and tell him so in those terms, left him stunned. Things probably were seen differently from London, without the perspective of distance. But even though he told himself every justification, something remained in his consciousness, disturbing him: his political mentor, friend, and teacher disagreed with him for the first time and thought that instead of helping he was harming the Irish cause. From then on, a question echoed in his mind with the sound of an evil omen: *What if Alice is right and I've made a mistake?*

During that same month of November, the German authorities had him travel to the front, in Charleville, to talk with military leaders about the Irish Brigade. Roger told himself that if he was successful and a military unit was formed that would fight beside German forces for the independence of Ireland, perhaps the scruples of many of his comrades, like Alice, would disappear. They would accept that sentimentality was a hindrance in politics, that Ireland's enemy was England and the enemies of her enemies were Ireland's friends. The trip, though brief, left him with a good impression. The high-ranking German officers fighting in Belgium were certain of victory. They all applauded the idea of an Irish Brigade. He didn't see very much of the war itself: troops on the roads, hospitals in the villages, lines of prisoners guarded by armed soldiers, distant cannon fire. When he returned to Berlin, good news was waiting for him. Acceding to his request, the Vatican had agreed to send two priests to the camp where the Irish prisoners were being assembled: an Augustinian, Father O'Gorman, and a Dominican, Father Thomas Crotty. O'Gorman would stay for two months and Crotty for as long as necessary.

And if Roger had not met Father Thomas Crotty? He probably would not have survived the terrible winter of 1914–15, when all of Germany, especially Berlin, was pounded by snow storms that made roads and streets impassable, gales that uprooted bushes and shattered windows, and temperatures fifteen and twenty degrees below zero that, because of the war, often had to be endured without light or heat. Physical ailments again assailed him brutally: the pains in his hip and iliac bone made him shrink into his seat, unable to stand. On many days he thought he would be permanently crippled here in Germany. Hemorrhoids bothered him again. Going to the bathroom became a torment. His body felt weakened and fatigued, as if twenty years had suddenly fallen on him.

During this period his lifesaver was Father Thomas

Crotty. *Saints exist, they're not myths*, he would say to himself. What else was Father Crotty? He never complained, he adapted to the worst situations with a smile on his lips, symptom of his good humor and vital optimism, his personal conviction that there were enough good things in life to make it worth living.

He was a fairly short man with thinning gray hair and a round, red face in which his light eyes seemed to sparkle. He came from a very poor peasant family in Galway, and sometimes, when he was happier than usual, he would sing Gaelic lullabies he had heard his mother sing when he was a boy. When he learned that Roger had spent twenty years in Africa and close to a year in Amazonia, he told him that ever since he was in the seminary, he had dreamed of working as a missionary in a remote country, but the Dominican order decided on another destiny for him. In the camp he became friends with all the prisoners because he treated all of them with the same consideration, not caring about their ideas and beliefs. Since he saw from the beginning that only a tiny minority would be persuaded by Roger's ideas, he kept rigorously impartial, never speaking for or against the Irish Brigade. "Everyone here is suffering, and they are God's children and for that reason our brothers, isn't that so?" he said to Roger. In his long conversations with Father Crotty, politics rarely was mentioned. They talked a great deal about Ireland, her past, her heroes, saints, and martyrs, but in the mouth of Father Crotty, the Irish who appeared most often were those long-suffering, anonymous laborers who worked from sunrise to sundown to earn a crust of bread, and those who had been obliged to emigrate to America, South Africa, and

Australia in order not to die of hunger.

It was Roger who led Father Crotty to speak about religion. The Dominican was very discreet in this as well, no doubt thinking that Roger, as an Anglican, preferred to avoid an area of conflict. But when Roger spoke of his spiritual perplexity and confessed that recently he had been feeling more and more attracted by Catholicism, the religion of his mother, Father Crotty gladly agreed to discuss the subject. Patiently he dealt with his curiosity, his doubts and questions. Once Roger dared to ask him point blank: "Do you think that what I'm doing is the right thing or am I mistaken, Father Crotty?"

The priest became very serious: "I don't know, Roger. I wouldn't want to lie. I simply don't know."

Roger didn't know now either, after the first days of December 1914, when, following a walk through the Limburg camp with the German generals De Graaf and Exner, he finally spoke to the hundreds of Irish prisoners. No, reality did not respect his predictions. *How naïve and foolish I was*, he would tell himself, his mouth suddenly filled with the taste of ashes, remembering the bewildered faces, the mistrust, the hostility of the prisoners when he explained, with all the fire of his love for Ireland, the reason for the Irish Brigade, the mission it would carry out, the gratitude of their motherland for the sacrifice. He recalled the sporadic hurrahs for John Redmond that interrupted him, the disapproving, even threatening noises, the silence that followed his words. Most humiliating of all was that when his speech was over, the German guards surrounded him and accompanied him out of the camp, because even though they hadn't understood his words, the attitudes of most of the prisoners let them surmise that this could end in aggression against the speaker.

And that was exactly what happened the second time Roger went to Limburg to speak to them, on January 5, 1915. On this occasion, the prisoners were not content to make angry faces and show their disgust with gestures and looks. They whistled and insulted him. "How much did Germany pay you?" was the most frequent shout. He had to stop speaking because the shouts were deafening. He had become the target of a rain of pebbles, spit, and various projectiles. The German soldiers hurried him away.

He never recovered from that experience. The memory, like a cancer, would unceasingly eat away at him inside.

"Should I give this up, in view of the general rejection, Father Crotty?"

"You should do what you believe is best for Ireland, Roger. Your ideals are pure. Unpopularity is not always a good indication for deciding the justice of a cause."

From then on he would live in a wrenching duplicity, pretending to the German authorities that the Irish Brigade was moving forward. True, there were few members so far, but that would change when the prisoners overcame their initial distrust and understood the advantage for Ireland, and consequently for themselves, of friendship and collaboration with Germany. In his heart he knew very well that what he was saying wasn't true, there would never be mass support for the Brigade, and it would never be more than a small, symbolic group.

If this was true, why continue? Why not go into reverse? Because that would have been the equivalent of suicide, and Roger did not want to commit suicide. Not yet. Not that way, at any rate. And therefore, with ice in his heart, in the first months of 1915, as he continued wasting time on the communications between Eivind and Consul Findlay, he negotiated an agreement with the authorities of the Reich on the Irish Brigade. He demanded certain conditions and his interlocutors, Arthur Zimmermann, Count Georg von Wedel, and Count Rudolf Nadolny, listened to him very seriously, writing in their notebooks. At the next meeting they informed him the German government accepted his demands: the Brigade would have its own uniforms and Irish officers; it would choose the battlefields where it would take part in the action; the costs would be returned to the German government by the republican government of Ireland as soon as it was constituted. He knew as well as they that all this was a pantomime, because the Irish Brigade in early 1915 did not even have the volunteers to form a company: it had barely recruited forty men, and it was unlikely that all of them would persevere in their commitment. He often asked himself: *How long will the farce go on?* In his letters to Eoin MacNeill and John Devoy he felt obliged to assure them that, even though slowly, the Irish Brigade was becoming a reality. Little by little, the number of volunteers was increasing. It was imperative for them to send him Irish officers to train the Brigade and head the future sections and companies. They promised they would, but they failed too: the only officer who arrived was Captain Robert Monteith. Though it's true the unbreakable Monteith by himself was worth an entire battalion.

The first indications Roger had of what would come were at the end of winter, when the first green buds began to appear on the trees along Unter den Linden. The undersecretary of state for foreign relations, at one of their periodic meetings, told him the German high command did not have confidence in his assistant Eivind Adler Christensen. There were signs he might be an informant for British Intelligence. Roger ought to distance himself from him immediately.

The warning took him by surprise and initially he discounted it. He asked for proof. They replied that the German intelligence services would not have made such a statement if they didn't have powerful reasons to do so. At this time Eivind wanted to go to Norway for a few days to visit his family, and Roger encouraged him to leave. He gave him money and saw him off at the station. He never saw him again. From then on, another reason for distress was added to the earlier ones: could it be possible the Viking god was a spy? He searched through his memory trying to find in these recent months, when they had lived together, some action, attitude, contradiction, stray word that would betray him. He found nothing. He tried to find calm by telling himself this lie was a maneuver by prejudiced and puritanical Teutonic aristocrats who, suspecting his relations with the Norwegian were not innocent, wanted them to separate, using any ruse, even slander. But doubt returned and kept him awake at night. When he learned that Eivind Adler Christensen had decided to go back to the United States from Norway, without returning to Germany, he was glad.

On April 20, 1915, young Joseph Plunkett arrived in Berlin as a delegate from the Volunteers and the IRB, after incredible travels through half of Europe to escape the nets of British Intelligence. How had he made that kind of effort in his physical state? He couldn't have been more than twenty-seven but was emaciated, partially crippled by polio, and suffering from a case of tuberculosis that was devouring him and at times gave his face the look of a skull. The son of a prosperous aristocrat, Count George Noble Plunkett, director of the National Museum in Dublin, Joseph, who spoke English with an aristocratic accent, dressed haphazardly in baggy trousers, a frock coat that was too big for him, and a hat pulled down to his eyebrows. But it was enough to hear him speak, and to talk with him a while, to discover that behind the clownish appearance, the ruined body in its carnival attire, was a superior intelligence, more penetrating than most, an enormous literary culture, and an ardent spirit with a vocation for struggle and sacrifice for the Irish cause that moved Roger greatly when he conversed with him in Dublin. He wrote mystical poetry, was, like Patrick Pearse, a devout believer, and had a thorough knowledge of the Spanish mystics, especially St. Teresa of Ávila and St. John of the Cross, whose verses he would recite from memory in Spanish. Like Patrick Pearse, within the Volunteers he had always aligned himself with the radicals, and this brought him closer to Roger. Listening to them, Roger often told himself that Pearse and Plunkett seemed to be searching for martyrdom, convinced that only by showing the extravagant heroism and contempt for death of those titanic heroes who marked Irish history, from Cuchulain and Finn MacCool and Owen Roe to Wolfe Tone and Robert Emmet, and sacrificing themselves like the Christian martyrs of early times, would they persuade the majority that the only way to achieve freedom was to pick up weapons and wage war. From the immolation of the children of Éireann a free country would be born without colonizers or exploiters, where law, Christianity, and justice would reign. The somewhat mad romanticism of Joseph Plunkett and Patrick Pearse had frightened Roger at times in Ireland. But during these weeks in Berlin, listening to the young poet and revolutionary on pleasant days when spring filled the gardens with flowers and trees in the parks were recovering their green, Roger felt touched, longing to believe everything the newcomer was telling him.

He brought inspiring news from Ireland. The division in the Volunteers because of the European war had served to clarify matters, according to him. True, a large majority still followed the theses of John Redmond about remaining loyal to the Empire and enlisting in the British army, but the minority loyal to the Volunteers counted on many thousands of people resolved to fight, a real army, united, compact, lucid about its objectives, resolved to die for Ireland. And now there was close cooperation between the Volunteers, the IRB, as well as the Irish Citizen Army, formed by Marxists and trade unionists like Jim Larkin and James Connolly, and the Sinn Fein of Arthur Griffith. Even Sean O'Casey, who had ferociously attacked the Volunteers, calling them "bourgeois, daddy's spoiled little boys," seemed to favor the collaboration. The Provisional Committee, led by Tom Clarke, Patrick Pearse, and Thomas MacDonagh, among others, prepared for insurrection day and night. Circumstances were favorable. The European war created a unique opportunity. It was imperative for Germany to help them with the shipment of some fifty thousand rifles and a simultaneous action by their army on British territory, attacking the Irish ports militarized by the Royal Navy. The combined action would perhaps decide the German victory. Ireland would finally be independent and free.

Roger agreed: this had been his concept for a long time and the reason he came to Berlin. He insisted again that the Provisional Committee should establish that offensive action by the German navy and army was a *sine qua non* for the Rising. Without that invasion, the rebellion would fail, for the logistical force was too unequal.

"But Sir Roger," Plunkett interrupted, "you are forgetting a factor that prevails over military weaponry and the number of soldiers: mysticism. We have it. The English don't."

They spoke in a half-empty tavern. Roger had beer and Joseph a soft drink. They smoked. Plunkett told him that Larkfield Manor, his house in the neighborhood of Kimmage, in Dublin, had been turned into a forge and an arsenal where grenades, bombs, bayonets, and pikes were made and flags were sewn. He said all this with exalted gestures, in a state of trance. He told him too that the Provisional Committee had decided to hide from Eoin MacNeill the agreement about the Rising. Roger was surprised. How could that kind of secret be kept from someone who had been the founder of the Volunteers and was still its president?

"We all respect him and no one doubts Professor MacNeill's patriotism and honesty," Plunkett explained. "But he's soft. He believes in persuasion and peaceful means. He'll be informed when it's too late to stop the Rising. Then, as no one doubts, he'll join us at the barricades."

Roger worked day and night with Joseph preparing a thirty-two-page plan with details of the Rising. They both presented it to the chancellery and the admiralty. The plan maintained that the British armed forces in Ireland were dispersed in reduced garrisons and could easily be overcome. The German diplomats, functionaries and military men listened, impressed, to this malformed young man dressed like a clown who, when he spoke, was transformed, explaining with mathematical precision and great intellectual coherence the advantages of a German invasion to coincide with the nationalist revolution. Those, in particular, who spoke English listened to him intrigued by the assurance, fierceness, and lofty rhetoric with which he expressed himself. But even those who didn't understand and had to wait for the interpreter to translate his words looked with astonishment at the zeal and frenetic gesticulation of this damaged emissary of the Irish nationalists.

They listened to him, took notes on what Joseph and Roger asked of them, but their replies did not commit them to anything. Not the invasion nor the shipment of fifty thousand rifles and the necessary ammunition. All of that would be studied within the war's global strategy. The Reich agreed with the aspirations of the Irish people and intended to support their legitimate desires: they went no further than that.

Joseph Plunkett spent almost two months in Germany, living with a frugality comparable to that of Roger himself, until June 20, when he left for the Swiss border, on his way back to Ireland via Italy and Spain. The young poet paid no particular attention to the small number of adherents the Irish Brigade had attracted. Otherwise, he did not show the least sympathy for it. The reason? "To serve in the Brigade, the prisoners have to break their oath of loyalty to the British army," he told Roger. "I was always opposed to our people enlisting in the ranks of the occupier. But once they did, a vow made before God cannot be broken without sinning and losing one's honor."

Father Crotty heard this conversation and kept silent. He was like that, a sphinx, for the entire afternoon the three spent together, listening to the poet who monopolized the conversation. Afterward, the Dominican remarked to Roger: "This boy is out of the ordinary, no doubt about it. Because of his intelligence and devotion to a cause. His Christianity is that of the Christians who died in Roman circuses, devoured by wild beasts. But also of the Crusaders who reconquered Jerusalem by killing all the ungodly Jews and Muslims they encountered, including women and children. The same burning zeal, the same glorification of blood and war. I confess, Roger, that people like him, even though they may be the ones who make history, fill me with more fear than admiration."

A recurrent subject in the conversations between Roger and Joseph at this time was the possibility the insurrection might occur without the German army invading England at the same time or, at least, bombarding the ports on Irish territory protected by the Royal Navy. Even in that case Plunkett advocated going ahead with the insurrectionist plans: the European war had created an opportunity that should not be squandered. Roger thought it would be suicide. No matter how heroic and intrepid they were, the revolutionaries would be crushed by the machinery of the Empire. It would use the opportunity to carry out an implacable purge. The liberation of Ireland would be delayed another fifty years.

"Am I to understand that if the revolution breaks out with no intervention by Germany, you will not be with us, Sir Roger?"

"Of course I'll be with you. But knowing it will be a useless sacrifice."

Young Plunkett looked him in the eye for a long time, and Roger seemed to detect a feeling of pity in his gaze.

"Permit me to speak to you frankly, Sir Roger," he murmured at last, with the gravity of someone who knows he possesses an irrefutable truth. "There is something you haven't understood, it seems to me. This isn't a question of winning. Of course we're going to lose this battle. It's a question of enduring. Of resisting. For days, weeks. And dying in such a way that our death and our blood will increase the patriotism of the Irish until it becomes an irresistible force. It's a question of a hundred revolutionaries being born for each one of us who dies. Isn't that what happened with Christianity?"

He didn't know how to answer. The weeks that followed Plunkett's departure were very intense for Roger. He continued asking that Germany free those Irish prisoners who deserved it for reasons of health, age, intellectual and professional status, and good behavior. This gesture would make a good impression in Ireland. The German authorities had been reluctant but now began to give in. They drew up lists and discussed names. Finally, the military high command agreed to free a hundred professionals, teachers, students, and businessmen with respectable credentials. There were many hours and days of discussions, a tug of war that left Roger exhausted. On the other hand, he agonized over the idea that the Volunteers, following the ideas of Pearse and Plunkett, would unleash an insurrection before Germany had decided to attack England, and pressed the chancellery and admiralty to give him an answer regarding the fifty thousand rifles. Their responses were vague, until one day, at a meeting in the Ministry of Foreign Relations, Count Blücher said something that disheartened him: "Sir Roger, you don't have an accurate idea of proportions. Examine a map objectively and you will see how little Ireland represents in geopolitical terms. No matter how much sympathy the Reich may have for your cause, other countries and regions are more important to German interests."

"Does this mean we won't receive the weapons, Count? Germany flatly rejects an invasion?"

"Both things are still under study. If it were up to me, I'd reject the invasion, of course, in the near future. But the specialists will decide. You'll have a definitive answer any time now."

Roger wrote a long letter to John Devoy and Joseph McGarrity, giving them his reasons for opposing an uprising. He urged them to use their influence with the Volunteers and the IRB to dissuade them from acting precipitately. At the same time, he assured them he was still making every effort to obtain the weapons. But his conclusion was dramatic: "I have failed. I'm useless here. Let me return to the United States."

During this time his ailments flared up. Nothing had any effect on his arthritis pains. Constant colds with high fevers frequently obliged him to stay in bed. He had lost weight and suffered from insomnia. To make matters worse, in this condition he learned that the *New York World* had published an article, surely filtered through British counter-espionage, according to which Sir Roger Casement was in Berlin receiving large sums of money from the Reich to foment a rebellion in Ireland. He sent a letter of protest—"I work for Ireland, not Germany"—that wasn't published. His friends in New York dissuaded him from the idea of a lawsuit: he would lose and the Clan na Gael was not prepared to waste money on judicial litigation.

In May 1915, the German authorities acceded to an insistent demand of Roger's: that the volunteers in the Irish Brigade be separated from the other prisoners in Limburg. On May 20, the fifty Brigade members, harassed by their companions, were transferred to the small camp in Zossen, near Berlin. They celebrated the occasion with a Mass officiated by Father Crotty, and there were toasts and Irish songs in an atmosphere of camaraderie that helped to raise Roger's spirits. He announced to Brigade members that within a few days they would receive the uniforms he had designed himself, and a handful of Irish officers would arrive soon to direct their training. They, who constituted the first company of the Irish Brigade, would pass into history as the pioneers of a great exploit.

Immediately after this meeting, he wrote another letter to Joseph McGarrity, telling him about the opening of the Zossen camp and apologizing for the catastrophic tone of his previous letter. He had written it in a moment of discouragement but now felt less pessimistic. The arrival of Joseph Plunkett and the camp at Zossen were a stimulus. He would continue working for the Irish Brigade. Though small, it was an important symbol in the big picture of the European war.

Early in the summer of 1915, he left for Munich. He stayed in the Basler Hof, a modest but pleasant hotel. The Bavarian capital depressed him less than Berlin, though here he led an even more solitary life than in the capital. His health continued to deteriorate, and pains and chills obliged him to stay in his room. His monkish life consisted of intense intellectual work. He drank many cups of coffee and constantly drew on black tobacco cigarettes that filled his room with smoke. He wrote endless letters to his contacts in the chancellery and the admiralty and maintained a daily spiritual and religious correspondence with Father Crotty. He reread the priest's letters and guarded them like a treasure. One day he attempted to pray. He hadn't for a long time, at least not in this way, concentrating, trying to open to God his heart, his doubts, his anguish, his fear of having been wrong, asking for mercy and guidance in his future conduct. At the same time he wrote short essays about the errors an independent Ireland ought to avoid, using the experience of other nations, in order not to fall into corruption, exploitation, the astronomical distances that everywhere separated the poor and the rich, the powerful and the weak. But at times he became discouraged: what was he going to do with these texts? It made no sense to distract his friends in Ireland with essays about the future when they found themselves submerged in an overwhelming present.

When the summer was over, feeling somewhat better, he traveled to the camp at Zossen. The men in the Brigade had received the uniforms he had designed, and all of them looked good with the Irish insignia on their visors. The camp seemed well ordered and functioning. But inactivity and confinement were undermining the morale of the fifty Brigade members in spite of Father Crotty's efforts to raise their spirits. He organized athletic competitions, meetings, classes and debates on a variety of subjects. Roger thought it a good time to flash before them the incentive of action.

He gathered them in a circle and explained a possible strategy that would get them out of Zossen and give them back their freedom. If at this moment it was impossible for them to fight in Ireland, why not do it under other skies where the same battle for which the Brigade was created was being fought? The world war had spread to the Middle East. Germany and Turkey were fighting to expel the British from their Egyptian colony. Why couldn't they participate in the struggle against colonization and for the independence of Egypt? Since the Brigade was still small, it would have to join another unit of the army, but they would do it preserving their Irish identity.

The proposal had been discussed by Roger with the German authorities and accepted. Devoy and McGarrity agreed. Turkey would take the Brigade into its army, under the conditions Roger described. There was a long discussion. In the end, thirty-seven members declared they were prepared to fight in Egypt. The rest needed to think about it. But what concerned all the Brigade members now was something more urgent: the prisoners at Limburg had threatened to denounce them to the English authorities so their families in Ireland would stop receiving combatant pensions from the British army. If this happened, their parents, wives, and children would starve to death. What was Roger going to do about that?

It was obvious the British government would impose this kind of reprisal and it hadn't even occurred to him. Seeing the anxious faces of the Brigade members, he managed only to assure them that their families would never be unprotected. If they stopped receiving the pensions, patriotic organizations would help them. That same day he wrote to the Clan na Gael asking that a fund be established to compensate the families of Brigade members who were victims of this reprisal. But Roger had no illusions: the way things were going, the money that came into the coffers of the Volunteers, the IRB, and the Clan na Gael was for buying weapons, the first priority. In anguish he told himself that because of him, fifty humble Irish families would go hungry and perhaps be ravaged by tuberculosis next winter. Father Crotty tried to calm him, but this time his words brought him no tranquility. A new subject for concern had been added to those tormenting him, and his health suffered another relapse. Not only his physical but his mental health as well, as had happened during his most difficult times in the Congo and Amazonia. He felt himself losing his mental equilibrium. At times his head seemed like an erupting volcano. Would he lose his mind?

He returned to Munich and from there continued sending messages to the United States and Ireland regarding financial support for the families of the Brigade members. Since his letters, in order to mislead British Intelligence, passed through several countries where envelopes and addresses were changed, replies took one or two months to arrive. His anxiety was at its height when Robert Monteith finally appeared to take military command of the Brigade. The officer brought not only his impetuous optimism, decency, and adventurous spirit, but also a formal promise that the families of Brigade members, if they were the object of reprisals, would receive immediate assistance from the Irish revolutionaries.

Captain Monteith, who traveled to see Roger as soon as he arrived in Germany, was disconcerted to find him so ill. He admired him, treated him with enormous respect, and told him no one in the Irish movement suspected he was in so precarious a state. Roger forbade him to tell anyone about his health and traveled with him back to Berlin. He introduced Monteith at the chancellery and the admiralty. The young officer was burning with impatience to begin work and displayed an unshakeable optimism regarding the future of the Brigade which Roger, deep inside, had lost. During the six months he remained in Germany, Robert Monteith was, like Father Crotty, a blessing for Roger. Both kept him from sinking into a discouragement that perhaps might have pushed him to madness. The cleric and the soldier were very different and yet, Roger told himself many times, they were incarnations of two prototypes of Irishmen: the saint and the warrior. Alternating with them, he recalled some conversations with Patrick Pearse, when he combined the altar with arms and stated that the result of the fusion of these two traditions, martyrs and mystics and heroes and warriors, would be the spiritual and physical strength to break the chains that bound Ireland.

They were different but there were in both a natural integrity, generosity, and devotion to the ideal, which, seeing that Father Crotty and Captain Monteith did not waste time in changes of mood and periods of demoralization, as he did, often made Roger ashamed of his doubts and fluctuations. Both men had laid out a path and followed it without deviation, without being intimidated by obstacles, convinced that in the end victory awaited them: of God over evil and of Ireland over her oppressors. *Learn from them, Roger, be like them*, he repeated to himself, like a short, fervent prayer.

Robert Monteith was a man very close to Tom Clarke, for whom he also professed a religious devotion. He spoke of his tobacco shop—his clandestine general headquarters—at the corner of Great Britain Street and Sackville Street as a "sacred place." According to the captain, the old fox, survivor of many English prisons, was the one who directed from the shadows all the revolutionary strategy. Wasn't he deserving of admiration? From his small shop on a poor street in the center of Dublin, this veteran whose body was small, thin, spare, worn by suffering and the years, who had devoted his life to fighting for Ireland, spending fifteen years in prison because of it, had managed to lead the IRB, a secret military and political organization that reached every corner of the country, and not be captured by the British police. Roger asked if the organization was really as successful as he said. The captain's enthusiasm was overflowing: "We have companies, sections, platoons with their officers, weapons depots, messengers, codes, slogans," he affirmed, gesturing euphorically. "I doubt there's an army in Europe more efficient and motivated than ours, Sir Roger. I'm not exaggerating in the least."

According to Monteith, preparations had reached their high point. German weapons were all that was missing for the insurrection to break out.

Monteith began working immediately, instructing and organizing the fifty recruits at Zossen. He went frequently to the Limburg camp to try to overcome resistance to the Brigade among the other prisoners. He persuaded a few, but the immense majority continued to show him complete hostility. Nothing could demoralize him. His letters to Roger, who had returned to Munich, swelled with enthusiasm and gave him encouraging news about the tiny Brigade.

The next time they saw each other in Berlin, a few weeks later, they had supper alone in a small restaurant in Charlottenburg filled with Romanian refugees. Captain Monteith, arming himself with valor and choosing his words very carefully in order not to offend him, said suddenly: "Sir Roger, don't think of me as meddling or insolent. But you cannot go on in this condition. You're too important to Ireland, to our struggle. For the sake of the ideals you have done so much for, I beg you to consult a physician. You have a nervous ailment. It's not uncommon. Responsibility and worries take their toll. It was inevitable that this would happen. You need help."

Roger stammered a few evasive words and changed the subject. But the captain's recommendation alarmed him. Was his mental state so evident that this officer, always so respectful and discreet, had found the courage to tell him something like this? He heeded what he said. After some inquiries, he decided to visit Dr. Oppenheim, who lived outside the city among the trees and streams of Grunewald. He was an elderly man who inspired confidence, for he seemed experienced and reliable. They had two long sessions in which Roger told him about his condition, his problems, insomnia, and fears. He had to submit to mnemotechnical tests and very detailed questions. Finally, Dr. Oppenheim assured him he needed to go to a sanatorium and receive treatment. If he didn't, his mental state would continue the process of destabilization that had already begun. The doctor called Munich himself and arranged an appointment for him with a colleague and disciple, Dr. Rudolf von Hoesslin.

Roger did not become a patient in Dr. von Hoesslin's clinic but saw him several times a week for several months. The treatment did him good. "I'm not surprised, with the things you have seen in the Congo and the Amazon and what you are doing now, that you suffer from these problems," the psychiatrist said. "What's noteworthy is that you're not a raving madman and haven't committed suicide."

He was still a young man, passionate about music, a vegetarian, and a pacifist. He was opposed to this war and all wars and dreamed that one day universal brotherhood—"a Kantian peace," he called it—would be established all over the world, borders would disappear, and men would acknowledge one another as brothers. Roger would leave his sessions with Dr. von Hoesslin calmed and encouraged. But he wasn't sure he was getting better. He'd always had this sense of well-being when he chanced to meet a healthy, good, idealistic person.

He made several trips to Zossen where, as was to be expected, Robert Monteith had won over all the recruits in the Brigade. Thanks to his intense efforts, there were ten more volunteers. The marches and training were going wonderfully. But Brigade members continued to be treated like prisoners by German soldiers and officers, and at times mistreated. Captain Monteith took steps at the admiralty so that the volunteers would have a margin of freedom, as Roger had been promised, be allowed to go into town and have a beer in a tavern from time to time. Weren't they allies? Why were they still treated as enemies? So far these efforts had not produced the slightest result.

Roger lodged a protest. He had a violent scene with General Schneider, commander of the garrison in Zossen, who told him he could not give more freedom to men who lacked discipline, had a propensity for fighting, and even committed robberies in the camp. According to Monteith, the accusations were false. The only incidents were the result of German sentries insulting Brigade members.

Roger's final months in Germany were filled with constant arguments and moments of great tension with the authorities. The sense of having been deceived only grew until he left Berlin. The Reich had no interest in the liberation of Ireland. It never took seriously the idea of a joint action with the Irish revolutionaries. The chancellery and the admiralty had made use of his naïveté and good faith, making him believe things they had no intention of doing. The project of the Irish Brigade fighting with the Turkish army against the English in Egypt, studied in every detail, was frustrated when it seemed about to be realized, with absolutely no explanation. Zimmermann, von Wedel, Nadolny, and all the officials who took part in the planning suddenly became shifty and evasive. They refused to receive him on trivial pretexts. When he did succeed in speaking to them, they were always extremely busy, could grant him only a few minutes; the matter of Egypt was not their responsibility. Roger became resigned: his dream of the Brigade as a small symbolic force in the Irish struggle against colonialism had gone up in smoke.

Then, with the same ardor he had brought to his admiration of Germany, he began to feel toward that country a dislike that was turning into hatred, similar to, or perhaps greater than, the hatred England inspired in him. He said as much in a letter to the lawyer John Quinn, after telling him about the mistreatment he was receiving from the authorities. "And so it is, my friend, that I have come to hate the Germans so much that, rather than die here, I prefer a British gallows."

His state of irritation and physical indisposition obliged him to return to Munich. Dr. von Hoesslin insisted he become a patient in a rest home in Bavaria, using a categorical argument: "You're on the brink of a crisis from which you will never recover unless you rest and forget about everything else. The alternative is that you will lose your reason or suffer a psychic break that will incapacitate you for the rest of your days."

Roger obeyed. For some days his life entered a period of so much peace he felt disembodied. Pills made him sleep ten and twelve hours a day. Then he would take long walks, on the cold mornings of a winter that refused to leave, through a nearby wood of maple and ash trees. He was denied tobacco and alcohol and ate frugal vegetarian meals. He had no desire to read or write. He would spend hours with his mind blank, feeling like a ghost.

Robert Monteith violently pulled him out of this lethargy one sunny morning early in March 1916. Because of the importance of the matter, the captain had obtained leave from the German government to come to see him. Still under the influence of what had happened, he spoke in a rush: "An escort came to take me out of the camp at Zossen and to Berlin, to the admiralty. A large group of officers, including two generals, was waiting for me. This is what they told me: 'The Irish Provisional Committee has decided the uprising will take place on April 23.' In other words, in a month and a half."

Roger leaped out of bed. His fatigue seemed to disappear all at once and his heart turned into a drum beating furiously. He couldn't speak.

"They're asking for rifles, riflemen, artillerymen, machine guns, ammunition," Monteith continued, agitated by emotion. "They want the ship escorted by a submarine. The weapons ought to reach Fenit on Tralee Bay, in County Kerry, on Easter Sunday at about midnight."

"Then they aren't going to wait for German armed action," Roger said at last. He thought of a catastrophe, of rivers of blood dyeing the water of the Liffey.

"The message also has instructions for you, Sir Roger," Monteith added. "You should remain in Germany as ambassador of the new Republic of Ireland."

Roger let himself fall back on the bed, crushed. His comrades hadn't told him of their plans before informing the German government. And they had ordered him to stay here while they had themselves killed in one of those acts of defiance that Patrick Pearse and Joseph Plunkett liked so much. Did they mistrust him? There was no other explanation. Since they were aware of his opposition to a unilateral uprising, they thought he would be a hindrance in Ireland and preferred him to remain here with his arms folded, holding the bizarre position of ambassador of a republic this rebellion and this bloodbath would make more remote and improbable.

Monteith waited, in silence.

"We're going to Berlin immediately, Captain," said Roger, sitting up again. "I'll dress, pack my bag, and we'll leave on the first train."

They did. Roger managed to write a few hurried lines of thanks to Dr. Rudolf von Hoesslin. His mind churned endlessly on the long trip, with small intervals for exchanging ideas with Monteith. When he reached Berlin, his line of conduct was clear. His personal problems had moved into the background. The priority now was to pour his energy and intelligence into obtaining what his comrades had requested: rifles, ammunition, and German officers who could organize military actions efficiently. Second, he would leave for Ireland with the cargo of weapons. There he would try to persuade his friends to wait; with a little more time the European war might create situations more favorable to the insurrection. Third, he had to keep the fifty-three members of the Irish Brigade from leaving for Ireland. The British government would unceremoniously execute them as traitors if they were captured by the Royal Navy. Monteith had complete freedom to decide what he wanted to do. Knowing him, it was certain he would go to die with his comrades for the cause to which he had consecrated his life.

In Berlin they stayed in the Eden Hotel. The next morning they began negotiations with the authorities. The meetings took place in the shabby, ugly building of the admiralty. Captain Nadolny received them at the door and led them to a room where there were always people from the chancellery and military men. New faces were mixed with those of old acquaintances. From the start they were told categorically that the German government refused to send officers to advise the revolutionaries.

On the other hand, they agreed to the weapons and ammunition. For hours and days they did calculations and studies of the most reliable way for them to reach the designated place on the date indicated. Finally, they decided the shipment would go in the *Aud*, an English ship that had been seized, reconditioned, and painted, and would fly a Norwegian flag. Neither Roger nor Monteith nor any Brigade member would travel on the *Aud*. This issue caused arguments, but the German government did not give in: the presence of Irishmen on board would compromise the subterfuge of passing the ship off as Norwegian, and if the deception was discovered, the Reich would be in a delicate situation in terms of international opinion. Then Roger and Monteith insisted on traveling to Ireland at the same time as the weapons. There were hours of proposals and counter-proposals, when Roger tried to convince them that if he went there he could persuade his friends to wait until the war was more favorable to the German side, so that the Rising could be combined with a parallel action by the German navy and infantry. Finally the admiralty agreed that Casement and Monteith would travel to Ireland in a submarine and take along a Brigade member to represent his comrades.

Roger's refusal to let the Irish Brigade travel to join the insurrection instigated serious clashes with the Germans. But he didn't want Brigade members summarily executed without even having the opportunity to die fighting. That wasn't a responsibility he would take on.

On April 7, the high command informed Roger that the submarine they would travel on was ready. Captain Monteith chose Sergeant Bailey to represent the Brigade. They gave him false papers bearing the name Julian Beverly. The high command confirmed to Roger that even though the revolutionaries had asked for fifty thousand rifles, only twenty thousand, with ten machine guns and five million rounds of ammunition, would arrive north of Inishtooskert Island in Tralee Bay on the day indicated, after ten at night: a pilot with a rowboat or launch, identified by two green lights, should wait for the ship.

Between April 7 and the day of departure, Roger did not close his eyes. He wrote a short will asking that if he died, all his correspondence and papers ought to be given to Edmund D. Morel, "an exceptionally just and noble person," so that with the documents he might compose a "memoir to save my reputation after my passing."

Even though Monteith, like Roger, intuited that the Rising would be crushed by the British army, he burned with impatience to leave. They had a private conversation for a couple of hours on the day one of the German officers, Captain Boehm, gave them the poison they had asked him for in the event of their capture. He told them it was Amazonian curare. The effect would be instant. "Curare is an old friend of mine," Roger said, smiling. "In Putumayo, in fact, I saw Indians who paralyzed birds in flight with darts dipped in this poison."

Roger and Monteith went for a beer in a nearby *Kneipe*. "I imagine it hurts you as much as it does me to leave without saying goodbye or giving explanations to Brigade members," said Roger.

"I'll always have it on my conscience," Monteith agreed. "But it's the correct decision. The Rising is too important for us to run the risk of its being infiltrated."

"Do you think I have any chance of stopping it?"

The officer shook his head. "I don't think so, Sir Roger. But you're very respected there and perhaps your words will have an effect. In any case, you have to understand what is happening in Ireland. We've been preparing for this for years. What do I mean, years? Centuries, I should say. How much longer will we go on being a captive nation? And in the twentieth century. Besides, there's no doubt that thanks to the war, this is the moment when England is weaker than Ireland."

"Aren't you afraid of death?"

Monteith shrugged. "I've seen it up close many times. In South Africa, during the Boer War, it was very close. We're all afraid of death, I imagine. But there are deaths and then there are deaths, Sir Roger. To die fighting for your homeland is a death as honorable as dying for your family or your faith. Don't you agree?"

"Yes, I do," Roger said. "I hope if it comes to it, we die like that and not by swallowing this Amazonian potion that must be indigestible."

On the eve of their departure, Roger went to Zossen for a few hours to say goodbye to Father Crotty. He didn't go into the camp. He sent for the Dominican, and they took a long walk through a wood of firs and birches beginning to turn green. Father Crotty was distraught as he listened to Roger's confidences, not interrupting him once. When he finished speaking, the priest crossed himself. He was silent for a long time.

"To go to Ireland thinking the Rising is doomed to failure is a form of suicide," he said, as if thinking aloud.

"I'm going with the intention of stopping it, Father. I'll talk to Tom Clarke, Joseph Plunkett, Patrick Pearse, all the leaders. I'll make them see the reasons why this sacrifice seems useless to me. Instead of accelerating independence, it will delay it. And . . ." He felt his throat closing and he stopped speaking.

"What is it, Roger? We're friends, and I'm here to help you. You can trust me."

"I have a vision I can't get out of my head, Father Crotty. Those idealists and patriots who are going to be mangled, leaving their families destroyed and indigent, subject to terrible reprisals, at least are conscious of what they are doing. But do you know who I think about all the time?"

He told him that in 1910 he had gone to give a talk at the Hermitage, the place in Rathfarnham, in the outskirts of Dublin, where St. Enda's, Patrick Pearse's bilingual school, was located. After speaking to the students, he gave them an object he had brought from his trip through Amazonia—a Huitoto blowgun—as a prize for the best composition in Gaelic by a final-year student. He had been enormously moved by these dozens of young men exulting in the idea of Ireland, the militant love with which they recalled its history, its heroes, its saints, its culture, the state of religious ecstasy in which they sang the ancient Celtic songs. And, too, the profoundly Catholic spirit that reigned in the school along with their fervent patriotism: Pearse had succeeded in having both things fuse and become one in those young people, as they had in him and his brother and sister, Willie and Margaret, who also taught at St. Enda's.

"All those young men will be killed, they're going to be cannon fodder, Father Crotty. With rifles and revolvers they won't even know how to fire. Hundreds, thousands of innocents like them facing cannon, machine guns, the officers and soldiers of the most powerful army in the world. And they'll achieve nothing. Isn't it terrible?"

"Of course it's terrible, Roger," the cleric agreed. "But perhaps it's not accurate to say they'll achieve nothing." He paused again for a long time and then began to speak slowly, distressed and moved. "Ireland is a profoundly Christian country, as you know. Perhaps because of its particular situation as an occupied country, it was more receptive than others to Christ's message. Or because we had enormously persuasive missionaries and apostles like St. Patrick, the faith took deeper root there than in other places. Ours is a religion above all for those who suffer. The humiliated, the hungry, the defeated. That faith has prevented us from disintegrating as a country in spite of the force crushing us. In our religion martyrdom is central. To sacrifice oneself, immolate oneself. Didn't Christ do that? He became flesh and subjected himself to the most awful cruelty. Betrayal, torture, death on the cross. Didn't it do any good, Roger?"

Roger thought of those young men convinced the struggle for liberty was both mystic and civic. "I understand what you mean, Father Crotty. I know that people like Pearse, Plunkett, even Tom Clarke, who's thought of as realistic and practical, are aware the Rising is a sacrifice.

And they're certain that their being killed will create a symbol that will move all the energies of the Irish. I understand their will to sacrifice. But do they have the right to bring in people who lack their experience and lucidity, young people who don't know they're going to the slaughter only to set an example?"

"I don't admire what they're doing, Roger, I've already told you that," Father Crotty murmured. "Martyrdom is something a Christian resigns himself to, not an end he seeks out. But hasn't history perhaps made humanity progress in this way, with gestures and sacrifices? In any case, the person who concerns me now is you. If you're captured, you won't have the chance to fight. You'll be tried for high treason."

"I became involved in this, Father Crotty, and my obligation is to be consistent and follow through to the end. I'll never be able to thank you for everything you've done for me. Can I ask for your blessing?"

He kneeled, Father Crotty blessed him, and they said goodbye with an embrace.

15

When Fathers Carey and MacCarroll entered his cell, Roger had already received the paper, pen, and ink he had asked for, and with a steady hand and no hesitation he had written two brief letters in succession, one to his cousin Gertrude and another open letter to his friends. The letters were very similar. To Gee, along with some deeply felt phrases telling her how much he had loved her and the good memories he had of her, he said: "Tomorrow, St. Stephen's Day, I'll have the death I've looked for. I hope God forgives my errors and accepts my prayers." The letter to his friends showed the same tragic fortitude: "My final message for everyone is a *sursum corda*. I wish the best to those who will take my life and those who have tried to save it. All of you are now my brothers."

John Ellis, the hangman, always dressed in dark colors and accompanied by his assistant, a young man who introduced himself as Robert Baxter and seemed nervous and frightened, came to take his measurements—height, weight, and neck size—in order, he explained without constraint, to determine the height of the gallows and the thickness of the rope. As he measured him with a yardstick and wrote in a notebook, he told him that in addition to this job, he continued to practice his profession as a barber in Rochdale, where his clients tried to draw out the secrets of his work, but with respect to that subject, he was a sphinx. Roger was glad when they left.

A short while later, a guard brought the last delivery of letters and telegrams already reviewed by the censors. They were from people he didn't know: they wished him luck or insulted him and called him traitor. He barely looked through them, but a long telegram caught his attention. It was from the rubber king Julio C. Arana. It was dated in Manaus and written in a Spanish even Roger could tell was filled with mistakes. He exhorted him "to be just by confessing his guilt, known only by Divine Justice, to a human court, with regard to his behavior in Putumayo." He accused him of having "invented facts and influenced the Barbadians to confirm irresponsible acts that never happened" with the sole purpose of "obtaining titles and a fortune." It ended this way: "I forgive you, but it is necessary for you to be just and declare now in a total and truthful way the real facts that nobody knows better than you." Roger thought: *His lawyers didn't write this telegram: he did.*

He felt calm. The fear that in the previous days and weeks would produce sudden shudders and send chills down his spine had completely disappeared. He was certain he would go to his death with the same serenity as Patrick Pearse, Tom Clarke, Joseph Plunkett, James Connolly, and all the valiant men who had sacrificed themselves in Dublin during that week in April so Ireland would be free. He felt detached from problems and distress and ready to make his peace with God.

Father Carey and Father MacCarroll were very serious when they came in and shook his hand with affection. He had seen Father MacCarroll three or four times but had not spoken much to him. He was a Scot and had a small tic of the nose that gave his expression a comic slant. On the other hand, with Father Carey he felt fully confident. He returned the copy of *The Imitation of Christ* by Thomas à Kempis. "I don't know what to do with it, please give it to someone. It's the only book they've allowed me to read in Pentonville Prison. I don't regret it. It has been good company. If you ever communicate with Father Crotty, tell him he was right. Thomas à Kempis was, as he told me, a saintly man, simple and filled with wisdom."

Father MacCarroll told him the sheriff was taking care of his civilian clothes and would bring them in soon. In the prison storeroom they had become wrinkled and dirty, and Mr. Stacey himself was having them cleaned and pressed.

"He's a good man," said Roger. "He lost his only son in the war and he too has been half dead with grief."

After a pause, he asked them to concentrate now on his conversion to Catholicism.

"Reincorporation, not conversion," Father Carey reminded him again. "You were always a Catholic, Roger, by the decision of your mother you loved so much and whom you'll soon see again."

The narrow cell seemed even more cramped with three people in it. They barely had room to kneel. For twenty or thirty minutes they prayed, at first silently and then aloud, Our Fathers and Hail Marys, the clerics at the beginning of the prayer and Roger at the end.

Then Father MacCarroll withdrew so that Father Carey could hear Roger's confession. The priest sat on the edge of the bed and Roger remained on his knees at the beginning of his long, very long enumeration of his real or presumed sins. When he first burst into tears in spite of the efforts he made to contain them, Father Carey had him sit beside him. This was how the final rite proceeded, in which, as he spoke, explained, remembered, asked, Roger felt that in effect he was coming closer and closer to his mother. For moments he had the fleeting impression that Anne Jephson's slim silhouette appeared and disappeared on the red brick wall of the prison.

He cried often, as he didn't recall ever having cried, no longer trying to hold back his tears, because with them he felt unburdened of tension and bitterness and it seemed to him not only his spirit but also his body became much lighter. Father Carey, silent and unmoving, let him speak. At times he asked a question, made an observation, a brief, calming comment. After telling him his penance and giving him absolution, he embraced him: "Welcome again to what was always your home, Roger."

A very short while later the cell door opened again and Father MacCarroll came in, followed by the sheriff. Mr. Stacey carried his dark suit and white shirt and collar, his tie and his vest, and Father MacCarroll had his high shoes and socks. It was the clothing Roger had worn on the day the court at the Old Bailey had condemned him to death by hanging. The articles were immaculately cleaned and pressed, and his shoes had just been blackened and polished.

"I'm very grateful for your kindness, Sheriff."

Mr. Stacey nodded. His face, as usual, was chubby and sad. But now he avoided looking him in the eye.

"Could I shower before putting on these clothes, Sheriff? It would be a shame to dirty them with this disgusting body of mine."

Mr. Stacey agreed, this time with a complicit little half-smile. Then, he left the cell.

Squeezing together, the three men managed to sit on the cot. They sat there, at times silent, at times praying, at times conversing. Roger spoke to them of his childhood, his early years in Dublin, in Jersey, of the vacations he and his brothers and sister had spent with his maternal uncles in Scotland. Father MacCarroll was happy to hear Roger say the Scottish vacations had been for him as a boy an experience of paradise, that is, of purity and joy. In a low voice he softly sang some of the children's songs his mother and uncles had taught him, and also recalled how the great deeds of the Light Dragoons in India, which Captain Roger Casement recounted to him and his siblings when he was in a good mood, made him dream.

Then he let them speak, asking them to tell him how they became priests. Had they entered the seminary led by a vocation or forced by circumstances, hunger, poverty, the desire to receive an education, as was the case with so many Irish clerics? Father MacCarroll had been orphaned when very young. He was taken in by aged relatives, who enrolled him in a parish school where the priest, who was fond of him, convinced him the Church was his vocation.

"What could I do but believe him?" Father MacCarroll reflected. "The truth is, I entered the seminary without much conviction. The call from God came afterward, during my later years of study. I became very interested in theology. I would have liked to devote myself to studying and teaching. But as we know, man proposes and God disposes."

Father Carey's case had been very different. His family,

well-to-do merchants in Limerick, were Catholic in name more than in deed, so he did not grow up in a religious environment. In spite of this he had heard the call very young and could even point out the event that perhaps had been decisive: a eucharistic congress, when he was thirteen or fourteen years old, where he heard a missionary priest, Father Aloysius, recount the work carried out in the jungles of Mexico and Guatemala by the male and female religious with whom he had spent twenty years of his life. "He was so good a speaker he overwhelmed me," said Father Carey. "It's his fault I'm still doing this. I never saw him again or heard anything about him. But I've always remembered his voice, his fervor, his rhetoric, his long beard. And his name: Father Aloysius."

When the cell door was opened and his usual frugal supper brought in—broth, salad, and bread—Roger realized they had spent several hours talking. The afternoon was dying and night beginning, though some sun still shone through the bars on the small window. He refused the supper and kept only the bottle of water.

And then he recalled that on one of his first expeditions in Africa, in the first year of his stay on the Dark Continent, he had spent a few days in the small village of a tribe whose name he had forgotten (the Bangui, perhaps?). With the help of an interpreter he talked with several villagers. In this way he learned that the community elders, when they felt they were going to die, made a small bundle of their few possessions, and discreetly, without saying goodbye to anyone, trying to pass unnoticed, went into the jungle. They looked for a tranquil place, a small beach on the shore of a lake or river, the shade of a large tree, a rocky knoll. There they lay down to wait for death without disturbing anyone. A wise, elegant way to depart.

Fathers Carey and MacCarroll wanted to spend the night with him, but Roger refused. He assured them he was fine, calmer than he had been in the last three months. He preferred to be alone and rest. It was true. When the clerics saw the serenity he displayed, they agreed to go.

When they had gone, Roger spent a long time looking at the clothes the sheriff had left him. For a strange reason, he had been certain he would bring him the clothing he had on when he was captured that desolate dawn of April 21 in the circular fortification the Celts called McKenna's Fort, consisting of eroded stones overlaid with dead leaves, bracken, and damp, and surrounded by trees where birds sang. Barely three months and they seemed like centuries. What could have happened to those clothes? Had they been archived too, along with his file? The suit Mr. Stacey pressed for him, the one he would die in within a few hours, had been bought for him by the lawyer, Gavan Duffy, so he would appear presentable before the court that tried him. In order not to wrinkle it, he laid it flat under the thin mattress on the cot. And he lay down, thinking a long night of insomnia awaited him.

Astonishingly, he fell asleep quickly. He must have slept for many hours because, when he opened his eyes with a small start, though the cell was dark, he could see dawn beginning to break in the small barred rectangle of the window. He recalled having dreamed about his mother. Her face was sorrowful and he, a child, consoled her by saying, "Don't be sad, we'll see each other again soon." He felt calm, without fear, wanting it to be over once and for all.

Not long afterward, or perhaps it was but he hadn't realized how much time had gone by, the door opened and from the threshold the sheriff—his face tired and his eyes bloodshot, as if he hadn't closed them all night—said: "If you want to shower, it should be now."

Roger nodded. When they were walking toward the bathroom along the long corridor of blackened bricks, Mr. Stacey asked if he had been able to get some rest. When Roger said he had slept a few hours, the sheriff murmured: "I'm happy for you." Then, as Roger was anticipating how pleasant it would be to feel the stream of cool water on his body, Mr. Stacey told him that many people, priests and ministers among them, had spent all night at the entrance to the prison, praying and holding crucifixes and signs opposing the death penalty. Roger felt strange, as if he were no longer himself, as if someone else were replacing him. He stood for some time under the cold water. He soaped carefully and rinsed, rubbing his body with both hands. When he returned to the cell, Father Carey and Father MacCarroll were there again. They told him the number of people crowded at the doors to Pentonville, praying and waving placards, had grown a great deal since the previous night. Many were parishioners brought by Father Edward Murnane from the small Holy Trinity Church which was attended by Irish families in the district. But there was also a group cheering the execution of the "traitor." The news left Roger indifferent. The clerics waited outside his cell while he dressed. He was surprised at how much weight he had lost. The clothes and shoes swam on him.

Escorted by the two priests and followed by the sheriff and an armed guard, he went to the chapel of Pentonville

Prison. He hadn't been there before. It was small and dark, but there was something welcoming and peaceful in this space with the oval ceiling. Father Carey celebrated Mass and Father MacCarroll was the acolyte. Roger was moved as he followed the ritual, though he didn't know whether it was because of the circumstances or because he would take communion for the first and last time. "It will be my first communion and my viaticum," he thought. Afterward he attempted to say something to Fathers Carey and MacCarroll but couldn't find the words and remained silent, trying to pray.

When he returned to his cell, breakfast had been left next to his bed, but he didn't want to eat anything. He asked the time, and now they finally told him: 8.40 a.m. *I have twenty minutes*, he thought. At almost the same time the governor of the prison arrived, along with the sheriff and three men in civilian clothes, one of them undoubtedly the doctor who would confirm his death, another a functionary of the Crown, and the hangman with his young assistant. Mr. Ellis, a rather short, powerful man, also wore dark clothes, like the others, but the sleeves of his jacket were rolled up in order for him to work more comfortably. He carried a rope coiled around his arm. In his well-bred, hoarse voice he asked him to put his hands behind his back because he had to tie them. As he bound his hands, Mr. Ellis asked a question that seemed absurd: "Am I hurting you?" He shook his head no.

Father Carey and Father MacCarroll had begun to say litanies aloud. They continued saying them as they accompanied him, one on each side, on the long walk through areas of the prison he was not familiar with: stairways, halls, a small courtyard, all of them deserted. Roger barely noticed the places he was leaving behind. He prayed and responded to the litanies and felt happy that his step was firm and no sob or tear escaped him. At times he closed his eyes and begged God for mercy, but what appeared in his mind was the face of Anne Jephson.

At last they came out on an open site flooded with sun. A squad of armed guards was waiting for them. They surrounded a square wooden framework that had a small staircase with eight or ten steps. The governor read a few phrases, no doubt the sentence, which Roger paid no attention to. Then he asked whether Roger wanted to say anything. Again he shook his head, but very quietly he whispered: "Ireland." He turned to the priests and both embraced him. Father Carey gave him the blessing.

Then Mr. Ellis approached and asked him to stoop so he could put on the blindfold, since Roger was too tall for him. He bent down, and as the hangman put on the blindfold that submerged him in darkness, he thought Mr. Ellis's fingers were less firm now, less in control than when he had tied his hands. Taking him by the arm, the hangman helped him climb the steps to the platform, slowly so he wouldn't stumble.

He listened to some movements, the priests' prayers, and finally, again, a whisper from Mr. Ellis asking him to lower his head and bend down a little, please, sir. He did, and then he felt him place the rope around his neck. He could still hear Mr. Ellis's last whisper: "If you hold your breath, it will be faster, sir." He obeyed.

Epilogue

> I say that Roger Casement
> Did what he had to do.
> He died upon the gallows,
> But that is nothing new.
>
> W. B. Yeats

The story of Roger Casement shoots up, dies out, and is reborn after his death like those fireworks that after soaring and exploding in the night in a rain of stars and thunder, die away, are still, and moments later are resuscitated in a trumpet fanfare that fills the sky with fires.

According to the physician present at the execution, Dr. Percy Mander, it was carried out "without the slightest hindrance," and the death of the offender was instantaneous. Before authorizing his burial, the doctor, following the orders of the British authorities, who wanted some scientific certainty regarding the "perverse tendencies" of the man they had executed, proceeded, after putting on rubber gloves, to explore his anus and the beginning of his bowel. He confirmed that "to the naked eye" the anus showed a clear dilation, as did "the lower portion of the intestine, as far as my fingers could reach." The doctor concluded that his exploration confirmed "the practices to which the executed man apparently was devoted."

After being subjected to this handling, the remains of

Roger Casement were buried without a stone, cross, or initials, next to the equally anonymous grave of Dr. Crippen, a celebrated murderer who had been tried some time earlier. The pile of shapeless dirt that was his grave was adjacent to the Roman Way, the trail along which, at the beginning of the first millennium of our era, the Roman legions entered the remote corner of Europe that would later be England in order to civilize it.

Then the story of Roger Casement seemed to vanish. The measures taken by the lawyer George Gavan Duffy with regard to the British authorities, in the name of Roger's siblings, to have his remains handed over to his family for Christian burial in Ireland, were denied then and each time his relatives made similar attempts, for another half century. For a long time, except for a small number of people—among them the hangman, John Ellis, who in the memoir he wrote shortly before committing suicide said that "He appeared to me the bravest man it fell to my unhappy lot to execute"—no one spoke of him. He disappeared from public attention, in Britain and in Ireland.

It took a long time for him to be admitted to the pantheon of the heroes of Irish independence. The secretive campaign launched by British Intelligence to slander him, using fragments of his secret diaries, was successful. It hasn't completely dissipated even now: a gloomy aureole of homosexuality and pedophilia surrounded his image throughout all of the twentieth century. His figure discomfited his country because Ireland, until not many years ago, officially maintained an extremely harsh morality in which the mere suspicion of being a "sexual deviant" sank a person into ignominy and expelled him from public consideration. For much of the twentieth century the name, accomplishments, and travails of Roger Casement were confined to political essays, newspaper articles, and biographies by historians, many of them English.

With the revolution in customs, principally in the area of sexuality, in Ireland Casement gradually, though always with reluctance and prudery, began to be accepted for what he was: one of the great anti-colonial fighters and defenders of human rights and indigenous cultures of his time, and a sacrificed combatant for the emancipation of Ireland. Slowly his compatriots became resigned to accepting that a hero and martyr is not an abstract prototype or a model of perfection but a human being made of contradictions and contrasts, weakness and greatness, since a man, as José Enrique Rodó wrote, "is many men," which means that angels and demons combine inextricably in his personality.

The controversy regarding the so-called *Black Diaries* did not end and probably never will. Did they really exist and did Roger Casement write them in his own hand, with all their noxious obscenities, or were they falsified by the British secret services to execute their former diplomat both morally and politically in order to create an exemplary warning and dissuade potential traitors? For dozens of years the British government refused to authorize independent historians and graphologists to examine the diaries, declaring them a state secret, which added fuel to the suspicions and arguments in favor of falsification. When, a relatively few years ago, the prohibition was lifted and investigators could examine them and subject the texts to scientific tests, the controversy did not end. Probably it will go on for a long time. Which isn't a bad thing. It's not a bad thing that a climate of uncertainty hovers over Roger Casement as proof that it is impossible to know definitively a human being, a totality that always slips through the theoretical and rational nets that try to capture it. My own impression—that of a novelist, obviously—is that Roger Casement wrote the famous diaries but did not live them, at least not integrally, that there is in them a good deal of exaggeration and fiction, that he wrote certain things because he would have liked to live them but couldn't.

In 1965, Harold Wilson's government finally permitted Casement's bones to be repatriated. They arrived in Ireland in a military plane and received public homage on February 23 of that year. For four days they lay in state in the Garrison Church of the Saved Heart like those of a hero. A gathering estimated at several hundred thousand people passed by to pay their respects. There was a military escort to the pro-cathedral and military honors were paid him in front of the historic Post Office building, general headquarters of the Easter Rising of 1916, before his casket was carried to Glasnevin cemetery, where he was buried on a rainy, gray morning. To deliver the speech of tribute, Éamon de Valera, the first president of Ireland, an outstanding combatant in the 1916 uprising, and a friend of Roger Casement's, got up from his death bed and said the moving words usually spoken to say farewell to great men.

Neither in the Congo nor in Amazonia is there any trace left of the man who did so much to denounce the great crimes committed in those lands in the days of the rush for rubber. In Ireland, scattered throughout the island, some memories of him remain. On the heights of Glenshesk in Antrim, in the glen which goes down to the small inlet of Murlough, not far from the family house of Magherintemple, Sinn Fein put up a monument to him which the radical unionists of Northern Ireland destroyed. The pieces have remained there, dispersed on the ground. In Ballyheigue, in County Kerry, on a small square facing the sea, stands the figure of Roger Casement sculpted by Oisín Kelly. In the Kerry County Museum in Tralee is the camera Roger took on his trip to Amazonia in 1911, and if you ask, you can also see the overcoat of rough wool he wore on the German U-19 submarine that brought him to Ireland. A private collector, Sean Quinlan, has in his cottage in Ballyduff, not far from the outlet of the Shannon into the Atlantic, a rowboat that (he states emphatically) is the same one that carried Roger, Captain Monteith, and Sergeant Bailey to Banna Strand. In the Roger Casement School in Tralee, the office of the director has on display the ceramic plate from which Casement ate, in the public bar of the Seven Stars, when he went to the Court of Appeals in London where his case was decided. In McKenna's Fort there is a small monument—a black stone column—recording in Gaelic, English, and German that he was captured there by the Royal Irish Constabulary on April 21, 1916. And on Banna Strand, the beach where he landed, stands a small obelisk where the face of Roger Casement appears next to the face of Captain Robert Monteith. On the morning I went there, it was covered with the white droppings of the screeching gulls that flew around overhead, and everywhere one could see the wild violets that moved him so much that dawn when he returned to Ireland to be captured, tried, and hanged.

Madrid, April 19, 2010

Acknowledgments

It would not have been possible to write this novel without the collaboration, conscious or unconscious, of many people who helped me on my journeys through the Congo and Amazonia and in Ireland, the United States, Belgium, Peru, Germany and Spain, sent me books and articles, facilitated my access to archives and libraries, gave me testimonies, advice, and above all, their encouragement and friendship when I felt myself weakening in the face of the difficulties of the project I had in hand. Among them, I want in particular to thank Verónica Ramírez Muro for her invaluable help during my visit to Ireland and in the preparation of the manuscript. I alone am responsible for the deficiencies of this book, but without these people, its eventual successes would have been impossible. Many thanks to:

In the Congo: Colonel Gaspar Barrabino, Ibrahima Coly, Ambassador Félix Costales Artieda, Ambassador Miguel Fernández Palacios, Raffaella Gentilini, Asuka Imai, Chance Kayijuka, Placide-Clement Mananga, Pablo Marco, Father Barumi Minavi, Javier Sancho Más, Karl Steinecker, R. Tharcisse Synga Ngundu de Minova, Juan Carlos Tomasi, Xisco Villalonga, Emile Zola, and the *poètes du renouveau* of Lwemba.

In Belgium: David van Reybrouck.

In Amazonia: Alberto Chirif, Father Joaquín García

Sánchez, and Roger Rumrill.

In Ireland: Christopher Brooke, Anne and Patrick Casement, Hugh Casement, Tom Desmond, Jeff Dudgeon, Sean Joseph, Ciara Kerrigan, Jit Ming, Angus Mitchell, Griffin Murray, Helen O'Carroll, Séamas O'Siochain, Donal J. O'Sullivan, Sean Quinlan, Orla Sweeney, and the staff of the National Library of Ireland and the National Photographic Archive.

In Peru: Rosario de Bedoya, Nancy Herrera, Gabriel Meseth, Lucía Muñoz-Nájar, Hugo Neira, Juan Ossio, Fernando Carvallo, and the staff of the Biblioteca Nacional.

In New York: Bob Dumont and the staff of the New York Public Library.

In London: John Hemming, Hugh Thomas, Jorge Orlando Melo, and the staff of the British Library.

In Spain: Fiorella Battistini, Javier Reverte, Nadine Tchamlesso, Pepe Verdes, Anteon Yeregui, and Muskilda Zancada.

Héctor Abad Faciolince, Ovidio Lagos, and Edmundo Murray.